SHERRYL WOODS

The Summer Garden

MIRA®

MIRA®

Recycling programs
for this product may
not exist in your area.

ISBN-13: 978-0-7783-1309-0

THE SUMMER GARDEN

For questions and comments about the quality of this book please contact us
at Customer_eCare@Harlequin.ca.

www.Harlequin.com

Printed in U.S.A.

Dear Friends,

Whenever I begin a new series, I always wonder if readers will fall in love with the characters as I have. You have definitely embraced the O'Briens as the complicated, boisterous, loving family I was envisioning as I wrote that first book, *The Inn at Eagle Point.*

Now, as I finish *The Summer Garden,* which will wrap up this series, I wanted to be sure it's a worthy finale. What better than a dual love story, plus the birth of a baby? Even as the series ends, there will be so many new beginnings. And isn't that the cycle of life?

I hope you'll enjoy watching Nell find her own well-deserved happy ending, even as Luke, the youngest of her grandchildren, finds his love with a most unlikely woman.

And for each of you, I wish you strong family ties and the joy of laughter.

All best,

Sherryl

1

Maddening Moira was still in his head!

Luke O'Brien had been home from Ireland for a month now. He'd been obsessing over his plans for the pub he wanted to open in Chesapeake Shores, worrying about the likely uproar with his family. He'd gone out a few times with the sophisticated, delectable Kristen Lewis, picking up where they'd left off during a brief rendezvous in Ireland. Truth be told, it was a matter of convenience for both of them, not a meeting of the hearts, but until recently it had been an excellent distraction, if only because it had complications galore that appealed to Luke's desire for a taste of rebellion.

But then along came Moira Malone with the sharp tongue and wry wit.

"I'll not be taken in by smooth talk and a wink," she'd told Luke, firmly putting him in his place. "I've been around such men all my life."

They'd met on the O'Brien family's holiday excursion to Ireland a few months ago. She was the granddaughter of his own grandmother's old flame, Dillon O'Malley. She was beautiful, but impossible. In fact, it was entirely likely that she was the most frustrating female he'd ever had the pleasure of meeting, in part because she'd been mostly immune to his charm. She'd complicated his life in an entirely different way. She'd unexpectedly engaged his heart.

After staying on in Ireland for several weeks after the rest of the family had returned to Chesapeake Shores, Luke had eventually come home, ready to move on with his life. Ready to finally get serious about life, according to his impatient father, who'd vocally protested the wasting of his college education.

He had a degree in history, for heaven's sakes! Had anyone seriously thought he'd use that? He certainly hadn't. He'd chosen history because he enjoyed the subject as much as any other and he'd needed to get the college off his back by declaring a major.

Now, though, the clock was ticking, and the tightly knit O'Briens were all watching and waiting to see what he—the youngest of family matriarch Nell's grandchildren—planned to make of himself. He doubted that opening an Irish pub on Shore Road was what anyone in the family would have guessed his calling to be.

Restless after going over his plans for the thousandth time, hoping to be so sure of himself, so confident of his path that no one would even attempt to talk him out of it, he wandered over to his brother's office.

Matthew was currently proving himself to be almost as talented and innovative an architect as their world-renowned uncle Mick. Like most of Luke's family, Matthew had discovered his passion early on. Luke had envied everyone in his family, not only for knowing what they wanted, but also for succeeding at it, sometimes phenomenally well. He had daunting examples to follow.

When Luke arrived, Matthew was so absorbed in the blueprints on his desk he never even glanced up, which gave Luke more pacing time to get his thoughts in order. He intended to try out his idea first on the most receptive audience he was likely to find.

Eventually, Matthew looked up, spotted him and blinked. "How long have you been here?"

"Long enough," Luke said. "How many towns and villages have you designed today?"

"Only the one," Matthew replied, grinning. "I think the plans for this community in Florida are just about set to go to the developer for final approval. He's very anxious to break ground, judging by the frequency of his calls for updates on my progress."

Luke had seen his share of architectural renderings over the years, but he had to admit that he lacked the vision to translate them into brick-and-mortar towns. Still, he peered over his brother's shoulder, prepared to feign the proper enthusiasm. What he saw, though, as he leafed through the pages, left him dumbstruck.

"You designed this? From scratch? A whole community, from houses to Main Street to schools, a library and even a church? You just looked over a few acres of vacant land and imagined all this?"

Matthew's grin spread as he nodded. "Pretty awesome, if I do say so myself."

"I guess all that time you spent playing with Lego as a kid wasn't wasted, after all. Has Uncle Mick seen it?"

"Of course. He's in here pestering me every other

day. I gather when he isn't calling me, the developer's calling Uncle Mick to nudge things along."

"And?"

"Uncle Mick says it's as good as anything he's ever done," Matthew said, looking pleased.

"Which means it's a thousand times better," Luke concluded. "He's not going to say so on your first big job and risk your having a swelled head and demanding a bigger salary."

Matthew shrugged off the compliment. "Things can always be better. Uncle Mick has even talked to me about things he would have done differently if he had Chesapeake Shores to design over again."

Luke regarded him with surprise. "Really? Like what?"

"He admits that Uncle Thomas was right about wanting the community to be built in an environmentally friendly way. He says he wouldn't have given him such a tough time about it."

Luke laughed. "No, he'd just give him a tough time on general principle, the same as he does with Dad."

"More than likely," Matthew agreed. "So what brings you by here at the end of the day?"

"I was hoping you'd have time for a drink."

"Sure. Mind if Laila tags along? I was going to meet her for dinner in an hour. You can join us."

"That'll work. There are some things I'd like to run by her, anyway."

His brother regarded him suspiciously. "Just what do you and my wife have to talk about?"

"Maybe we're conspiring to throw a surprise party for your birthday," Luke teased, knowing how much his brother abhorred the whole concept of surprise parties, even though he'd determinedly pulled off his own almost-surprise wedding in Ireland, keeping Laila mostly in the dark until his Christmas Eve proposal.

"My birthday was just a couple of months ago, and neither of you is that much of a long-range planner," Matthew retorted. "Try again."

"How about I explain it over drinks?" Luke countered.

"Fine. Brady's okay?"

"Actually, I have someplace else in mind. I need to stop by Dad's office first. Why don't I meet you on Shore Road in front of Panini Bistro in twenty minutes?"

"Suits me," Matthew said. "I'll call Laila and let her know. If I get there first, I'll grab a table."

"Actually, don't do that," Luke said. "Wait for me in front, okay? Tell Laila to grab a table, though, if she gets there before we're back."

"Back?" Matthew gave him an odd look. "Curiouser and curiouser."

"Trust me, okay?"

"Always," Matthew said at once. "See you in a few minutes."

Luke gave him a wave, then headed for his father's office. He was hoping to find his father gone for the day and perhaps only his sister still there. Susie might give him grief over his request, but she was less likely to pull rank and demand answers.

Even better, he found the real estate management company run by his father to be closed for the day. Using the key he had for the occasions when he helped out showing properties, he went in, plucked a key off the board for the properties they owned or managed and closed back up.

He beat Matthew to their appointed meeting spot by mere seconds.

"Where to now, o secretive one?" Matthew inquired.

"Not far," Luke said, heading down the block to a large empty space that had been occupied by a French restaurant that had gone belly-up, unable to survive during the slower winter months. Personally, he thought it had failed because of the god-awful uncomfortable chairs that had made the customers squirm through the torturous minutes it took to eat their overpriced food, but what did he know?

He led the way inside and flipped on lights, then turned to his older brother. "What do you think?"

Matthew looked blank. "Of what? It's an empty space."

Luke held his gaze. "Think you could help me turn it into a warm and welcoming Irish pub?"

The words were no sooner out of his mouth than he heard a hoot from the doorway and turned to see his uncle Mick standing there.

"I come to check on why lights are blazing in an empty property and find you making plans to open a pub?" Mick said, his expression incredulous.

Luke sighed. He hadn't wanted such a tough audience right from the outset, but maybe it was for the best. Mick had a good business head and a real understanding of what this town needed. He wondered if Mick would see the value of a gathering spot in the heart of town, a warm and welcoming place in the Irish tradition.

"That's what I'm thinking," Luke confirmed, looking Mick directly in the eye. "What's your opinion?"

Mick's gaze narrowed. "What makes you think you can do this? You never worked as a bartender, as far as I know. Never worked in a restaurant, either."

"Not entirely true," Luke said. "When I stayed on in Ireland, I worked for a time at McDonough's, the pub where we spent so much time while we were there. I also traveled all over the country visiting every pub I could find, from those in cities to those in small villages. I asked a million questions, took copious notes and cooked my share of fish 'n' chips. I even bought an antique bar in a place that was closing. It's being shipped over here for arrival in a month's time."

Matthew's expression was now as stunned as his uncle's. "I thought you stayed in Ireland after the family and Kristen left because you developed some misguided crush on the impossible Moira."

"That's what I wanted everyone to think," he admitted, and it had been partly true. "I wasn't ready to have all of you shoot down this idea of mine. I was still formulating it, testing it out in my heart and my head to see if it felt right." He leveled a look into his brother's eyes, pleading with him to understand and back him in this. "It does."

"But a pub?" Matthew said, his concern evident. "Why?"

"In a weird way, it was something Mack said a while back," Luke explained, referring to his sister Susie's husband. "I was giving him some advice and he made an offhand comment that maybe I should consider being a shrink like Will. He was actually being sarcastic, but the idea stuck."

"And that led you to this pub idea?" Mick said. "What kind of sense does that make?"

"Everyone knows people pour out their troubles to bartenders," Luke explained. "I like listening, not in any official capacity, the way Will does, but just being a sounding board. When we were in Ireland, I saw that kind of thing happening in every pub we went to, and it all kind of fell into place. Pubs create their own kind of community, not just for drinking but for food and friendship, for music and laughter. At least when they're done right. I'd like to be at the center of something like that."

"Well, I'll be," Matthew said.

Luke studied his brother's face to see if shock was edging toward approval. "So, do you think I'm insane?" he prodded.

"A little," Matthew said. "But I can also see it working. How about you, Uncle Mick? Look around. Imagine that antique bar across the back wall with a big mirror that will bring in the view of the bay, at least during the day. Maybe not as dark as the usual Irish pub, but one suited to a seaside town. Laila and I saw one like that in Howth with a view of the marina."

He glanced toward Luke. "You mentioned music. Does that mean you'd like a small area for a band?"

"Absolutely," Luke confirmed. "Nothing too large or fancy, just an area where musicians can set up. I'm hoping to book some authentic Irish groups from time to time. Bands, singers, whatever I can find."

"Got it," Matthew said, jotting notes on the pad that was ever-present in his pocket. "Uncle Mick, what do you think?"

Mick shook his head and began to pace. Only after

he'd been at it a few minutes did Luke realize he was mentally measuring. When he halted in front of Luke, he looked him in the eye. "You have a business plan? Times get tough around here in winter. You have to be able to weather that."

"I think the music will keep the locals coming in and maybe draw people from around the region. My figures seem sound enough to me, but I was hoping Laila could take a look at them," he said. "Math was never my strongest suit. I'm hoping she'll have time to take over that end of things for me, keep the finances on track and yank my chain when I'm tempted to bust the budget for one thing or another, as she does for Jess."

"Ah, so that's why she's waiting for us now at Panini Bistro," Matthew said. "We should probably get over there. Uncle Mick, care to come along?"

"Try to keep me away," Mick said at once. "I'll just walk to the corner, which is where I was headed when I spotted you two, and get Megan. She should be closing up her gallery about now."

On his way to get his wife, Luke surmised, Mick had apparently crossed paths with Luke's cousin Connor, who was meeting his wife, Heather, at her quilt shop and invited them along, because Connor and Heather accompanied Connor's parents to the restaurant.

By the time they were actually seated at Panini Bistro, they needed just about every vacant seat in the tiny restaurant. Naturally, it was Mick who seized the moment to announce Luke's news, which caused a noisy eruption of input from everyone in the room, until Mick finally slapped a hand on the table to get their attention. Then he turned to Luke.

"What do you plan to call this bar of yours?"

Luke grinned. "O'Brien's, of course. If I have a good Irish name, why would I call it anything else?"

A grin spread across his uncle's face. "And we're the first to know about this idea of yours?"

"You are," Luke confirmed, then realized what he'd done.

Yet again, Mick O'Brien had managed to trump one of his brothers, getting the hottest family news first. In a family as competitive as theirs, Luke's father would never hear the end of it.

"I don't suppose you'd let me be the one to tell Dad?" Luke pleaded. "Out of respect."

Mick was clearly torn, but when Megan poked him in the ribs with an elbow, he nodded with obvious reluctance. "Only fair, I suppose."

"Thank you," Luke said, then glanced around. "So, I have your support for this? Laila, you'll look over the budget, and, Connor, you'll check all the legalities?" As those two nodded readily, he glanced around. "And you all think it's a good idea?"

"I think it's a fine idea," Mick said to more enthusiastic choruses of agreement from the others. "And if it's something you're passionate about, only a fool would stand in your way."

Luke had a hunch that if his father didn't grant him unqualified support, his uncle would be more than happy to repeat the exact same message to him. Hopefully, it wouldn't come to that. The last thing Luke wanted was to launch another family feud.

Moira glanced at the snapshot she'd taken a few weeks ago of Luke O'Brien. It was one of her better pictures, she thought. It had captured him laughing, the sea in the background, his black hair tousled by the wind, his blue eyes sparkling with mirth. Just looking at it made her heart catch.

When Luke had turned up at her grandfather's house along with the rest of his boisterous family for a Christmas season celebration, she'd been in one of her increasingly dark moods, ready to snap at anyone who crossed her path. Her grandfather and her mum were used to her mood swings and her rebellions. They openly worried about her and her lack of direction, which only made her more miserable.

Amazingly, she hadn't scared Luke off with her tart tongue. He'd stuck to her that night like glue, teased her until she'd even managed a smile or two. And when they'd all gathered for his brother's impromptu wedding to Laila just days later, Luke had even coaxed her onto the dance floor, crooning in her ear as if he were settling a nervous filly until she finally relaxed in his arms. And fell just a little bit in love with him.

Truthfully, she'd fallen for his whole family. They were so different from her own. For all the evidence that they argued and battled wits, the O'Briens were also openly affectionate with one another. There was none of the bitterness that emanated from her own mum, or the nonstop worry she saw in her grandfather's eyes. Brothers, sisters and cousins, along with their spouses, actually seemed to love one another, while Moira could honestly say there were days when she wished her own self-absorbed, thoughtless brothers would vanish in a puff of smoke.

"Moira, the fellow at the table in the corner has been trying to catch your eye for a while now," Peter Mc-

Donough said. "Seems he's ready for another Guinness."

Moira snapped herself back to the moment, then quickly returned the picture of Luke to her pocket. She took the drink and crossed the pub.

"Kevin, is it?" she said to the man, who was apparently a regular, while she was new to this particular pub, if not to waiting tables. "Sorry for the delay."

He gave her a friendly smile. "You looked distracted. Was it someone special in the picture you were studying so intently?"

Was Luke someone special? she wondered. Well, the answer to that was obvious. Of course he was! He was a charming rogue, the kind of man her dad had been, if her mother's bitter stories were to be believed. She'd understood for the first time how her mother could have been taken in by such a man. In just a few short weeks she'd started imagining herself with Luke forever.

"A friend," she said now, knowing that she and Luke were at least that much.

The time they'd spent together had been amazing. They saw eye-to-eye on so many things, were both struggling to figure out their places in the world. Together, they'd shared laughter and a passion that had been entirely new to her. At twenty-two, she'd thought she'd been in love a time or two, but now she knew better. What she'd felt with Luke had been different. She'd looked beyond immediate gratification to a future. She only wished she could be sure he'd done the same.

His emails since he'd returned home to Chesapeake Shores had been thoroughly unsatisfying. They'd told her only that she'd crossed his mind, but little else about what he was doing or, more important, feeling. They'd made her cautious in her own responses, not wanting to reveal too much about how desperately she missed him. It seemed impossible that someone could mean so much to her after so little time. Perhaps those days and nights they'd spent together had been nothing more than a wonderful but temporary fantasy come true.

The one practical result being with Luke had accomplished was to motivate her to finally leave the small village where she'd grown up to come to Dublin. For the moment she was staying with her grandfather, but if this job continued the way it had begun, with more than decent tips at the end of the day, she'd soon have enough to find a small place of her own or with a girlfriend. Finally, she'd be doing something she enjoyed without her mum gazing at her in disappointment because she wasn't continuing her education or aiming higher.

What Kiera Malone had never understood was that Moira enjoyed talking to people, making them smile, being surrounded by their laughter. The only activity more satisfying to her was photography, but she hadn't a clue how to turn that into a career. For now, she was happy enough taking pictures just for her own pleasure, giving them to friends when she'd captured them at a moment when their personality was evident in the shot.

Back at the bar, she drew the picture of Luke from her pocket once more and smiled. She'd done exactly that in this shot of Luke at his carefree, charming best.

"What's that?" Peter asked, glancing over her shoulder, then recognizing Luke from the time he'd spent in the pub asking questions and filling in behind the bar. "Ah, you've caught the essence of Luke, that's for sure." His expression turned thoughtful. "Have you taken others?"

"Sure. Why?"

"Could you do the same thing in here, perhaps snap some pictures of the regulars? We could frame them and hang them on the walls."

She regarded him with astonishment. "Seriously?" It was the first time anyone had even hinted that she was good enough at photography to do more than take snapshots for her own enjoyment.

"You've been coming around here with your grandfather for years. Have you ever known me not to be serious when it comes to this business?" he asked. "I think it will add something special to the place." He shrugged. "Who knows? It might also bring you a few customers who'd like you to take pictures for their family events."

Moira hesitated. Was she really good enough for that? Was that even something she wanted? She heard Luke's voice in her head, encouraging her to take chances, to reach for things she found truly satisfying.

"I'll do it," she told Peter, feeling a faint stirring of excitement. "No charge for you, of course. We'll just see how they turn out."

"If you take them, I'll pay for them," her boss insisted. "You'll have to be setting your rates now, won't you?" He grinned. "And then you can give me a generous first-time customer discount."

She laughed. "Deal."

A day that had started out in a very dreary way had taken a definite turn for the better. And to think it was her snapshot of Luke that had made that happen. Even from such a long distance, it seemed he was her good-luck charm. If only he were a little closer, Moira thought, she could thank him in person. At least tonight she could send him an email with something exciting to report from her own life, something that might engage him in the sort of exchange they'd had so often during his visit.

Jeff O'Brien regarded his younger son with dismay. "A pub? Are you serious?"

"I am," Luke said, keeping his gaze level and not backing down under Jeff's blatant skepticism.

"But why? You have a college degree. Why not put it to good use? You could teach history at the high school."

"Me? In a classroom? I'd lose my freaking mind," Luke replied.

Jeff smiled at the adamant response. "Sorry. I don't know what I was thinking. Even as the words were coming out of my mouth, I realized it was a bad fit. You played hooky every chance you got, didn't you? How many times was your mother hauled out of her classroom or I was called in from work to bail you out of a jam with the principal? I doubt you'd be any happier at the front of the room. You were never fond of routines and predictability."

"Exactly," Luke said, then leaned forward earnestly. "I know this isn't anything we ever talked about, Dad, but the minute the pieces started falling into place, it felt right. I don't know if it was being in Ireland and really connecting with my Irish roots, or what Mack said about my being a good listener, or maybe both together, but for the first time I thought, this is something I can do, something I can be really excited about."

Jeff heard that excitement in his son's voice and, though he had a thousand reservations, he didn't want to be the one to put a damper on his enthusiasm. Still, he couldn't help expressing caution.

"Businesses come and go in this town," he warned. "And the start-up costs money. Where will you find it?"

Luke hesitated, then admitted, "I was thinking I could sell the waterfront land on Beach Lane that you've been holding for me."

Jeff regarded him with dismay. "Not an option," he said flatly. "That land is worth a fortune and I held on to it so you could build a home of your own one day, not as an investment for you to sell on a whim."

"It's not a whim, Dad. I've needed a goal and finally I have one."

"You'll regret selling it," Jeff predicted. "Find another way."

"I don't want to start off mired down with loans," Luke told him. "Please, Dad, just think about it. You've always said the land was to be mine. Doesn't that suggest I should be able to do with it whatever I want to do?"

"First, tell me how you plan to weather the slow winters. Have you even considered that?"

"Of course. I've even discussed it with Laila and she agrees that it's a solid plan."

Jeff stilled at that. "You've told your sister-in-law about all this?"

Luke winced, his expression immediately guilty. "I did. I wanted her financial input. How could I come to you without knowing my plan was solid?"

Jeff accepted the logic of that, but he wasn't entirely pacified. "Then I assume Matthew knows as well?"

"And Uncle Mick and Connor," Luke admitted. "I'm sorry, Dad. I didn't intend for them to find out before I spoke to you, but you know how it is around this town. Uncle Mick has big eyes and even bigger ears. He saw Matthew and me on Shore Road the other night, then dragged Connor, Megan and Heather along to dinner with us. The next thing I knew, they were all in on it. I made them promise to keep quiet until I could speak to you myself."

Jeff tried not to let his annoyance show. After all, it was true that his older brother saw everything and stuck his nose where it didn't belong more often than not.

"And Mick approves?" he asked.

Luke nodded. "He does, but his opinion doesn't matter more than yours, Dad. He was just there and you weren't. I'm coming to you now."

"But you've already decided to move forward, haven't you? Other than getting me to let you sell that land, this is little more than a courtesy call." Jeff hated that he was unable to hide his bitterness more effectively. It had always been this way between him and Mick, a rivalry that never ended, no matter their mother's attempts to keep peace. It shouldn't be that way between brothers—and thank God he'd avoided it happening with *his* sons—but he, Thomas and Mick could spar over the color of the sky.

Luke looked chagrined. "It's not like that, Dad. Not at all. My mind has been made up for a few weeks now, since Ireland, in fact. I just wanted to get all the pieces together before I shared them with anyone. I never meant to slight you or suggest that your opinion doesn't matter. You do know I respect you, right?"

Jeff fought off feelings that had less to do with Luke

than they did with Mick, and nodded. "Of course, son. And though I have some concerns, I'll support you in this. Whatever you need, I'm behind you. Though I want you to think long and hard before you decide to sell land that you'll never be able to replace."

"I promise to look for other options first," Luke said, then gave him a sly look. "Does your backing include giving me a break on the rent for the property on Shore Road? I'm thinking a deal is in order. It's been sitting empty for a few months now. Better to have a reliable tenant in there at a bargain price than to have prime property vacant when the summer season kicks off."

Jeff let go of the last of his annoyance. "With clever thinking like that, you'll do just fine, son. I'll look over the numbers and get back to you."

Looking relieved, Luke nodded. "Thank you." He hesitated, then asked, "And we're okay?"

Jeff hated that his son even had to ask. "Of course we're okay. I'm always on your side, Luke." Now it was his turn to hesitate. "Who's going to do the cooking in this pub of yours? Last time I checked, your skill in the kitchen ran to frying eggs into charcoal."

"I learned a few Irish pub recipes before I left Ireland," Luke admitted. "And I'm counting on Gram to coach me through the rest. The customers won't starve."

Jeff regarded him with surprise. "You're going to take cooking lessons from Ma?"

"Actually, I haven't mentioned that to her just yet," Luke said. "I'm hoping to get a few minutes with her on Sunday to see how she'd feel about it."

"She'll be ecstatic," Jeff predicted, knowing how much Nell wanted someone in the family to step in and learn all the traditional dishes. "That experiment with getting the grandchildren to take over the cooking for Sunday dinners went sadly awry. Only Kevin made anything edible. Thank the Lord, Ma abandoned it before we all died of ptomaine poisoning."

Luke grinned. "I'm hoping her reputation in town as a terrific cook will carry the day. Thankfully, no one ever had to eat anything made by those O'Brien culinary pretenders."

Jeff laughed. "Yes, thank goodness for that."

As he sent Luke on his way, Jeff said a little prayer for the success of his son's dream. He knew that Luke had struggled as the youngest in a large family of overachievers. Now that Luke had finally found a vision for himself—even one that Jeff wouldn't necessarily have chosen for him—Jeff wanted nothing more than for his son to achieve the happiness his brother, sister and cousins had found, both personally and professionally.

And, truth be told, he wouldn't mind having a nearby place where he could indulge in a bit of Guinness from time to time, along with the nostalgia he often felt for Ireland. The taste he'd had of it with the family at Christmas had only whetted his appetite for more.

2

By the weekend, word of Luke's plan had spread through the entire family. He'd taken his share of ribbing about his lack of culinary skills, but in general everyone had been as supportive as he could have hoped for. The only person Luke hadn't spoken to yet was his grandmother.

He sought Nell out after the regular Sunday family dinner at his uncle Mick's. She was in the kitchen, which everyone conceded was her domain, whether in her son's house, where she was today, or in her own cottage up the road.

She didn't seem the least bit surprised to find her grandson hovering there after the dishes had been washed and put away. She simply poured them each a cup of tea, then pointed to a chair.

"I understand you have big plans," Nell said, a twinkle in her bright blue eyes. She might be in her eighties, but she had the lively curiosity and stamina of someone much younger. "I want to hear all about them." She regarded him with amusement. "I especially want to hear these plans you have to steal all my favorite recipes."

Luke laughed. "Not steal them," he insisted. "I'm hoping you'll give them to me willingly, and teach me to make them while you're at it. Otherwise, I'll have to hire you as my cook."

"I'm a little too old to be embarking on a career as a chef," she said. "But I'll be happy to give you all the lessons you'd like." She gave him a wink. "And perhaps come in to supervise from time to time just to be sure you're not messing them up and ruining the family reputation."

"Really, Gram? You're the best!" It was even more than he'd hoped for.

"Really," she confirmed. "Now, tell me everything."

Luke described how the idea for the pub had come to him, all the research he'd done before coming home from Ireland, how excited he was to get started so it could be open before the official start of the summer season in Chesapeake Shores.

"I'd like it ready by late April to give me a month to work out the kinks before it gets busy in town," he said. "But Matthew thinks I'm being overly optimistic since it's already the end of March. Apparently he likes to take his time drawing up plans."

"And what does Mick say?"

"He says anything can be done, at a cost."

She laughed. "Yes, that would be Mick's way, but I imagine he'll find some way to do the job *and* give you a bargain price. He seems especially enthusiastic about this plan of yours. I think he likes the idea of having a little taste of Ireland close by."

"Or perhaps he just likes knowing that my father isn't wildly enthusiastic about the idea. Dad's supportive, but he can't hide his doubts."

"It's Jeff's duty to express caution," Nell reminded him. "No father wants to see his son make a costly mistake." She studied him intently. "Do you have your financing?"

"That's the big sticking point with Dad," he admitted. "I want to sell the lot he's been holding for me on Beach Lane next to the homes Susie and Matthew have built on theirs. Dad's really upset about that."

"He thinks it's shortsighted, no doubt," she guessed.

"Exactly."

His grandmother nodded. "I have to agree with him, Luke," she said, her tone gently chiding. "Not only is that land quite valuable, but it's your legacy. I think you'll want a home of your own by the bay one of these days when you have a family. And at the rate waterfront land is selling around here, you won't find such a beautiful, pristine spot again."

"That's pretty much what Dad said."

"You should probably listen to him."

"A family's a long way down the road," Luke protested. "I can't even think that far ahead. I have to focus all my attention on the pub for now. I think it's going to be the key to my future."

"Still, it doesn't do to make a decision you'll likely live to regret," she said. "You may only be twenty-four, but there will come a day when the right person will come along and you'll want to settle down." She gave him a knowing look. "I thought perhaps you'd already found her."

Luke gave her a startled look. "Kristen? Heavens, no!"

"I was thinking of Moira, but the fact that you didn't mention her first is telling. Weren't the two of you quite close while you were in Ireland?" She gave him a penetrating look. "Or was Moira just another one of your flings?"

Luke knew he needed to tread carefully. Moira was the granddaughter of a man who was important to his grandmother. He didn't want her getting the wrong idea. Moira hadn't been a fling, not like so many others. She'd mattered, perhaps a little too much.

"Moira's special," he admitted. "Had the timing been different…" He shrugged. "I don't know. Maybe she could have been the one."

Nell regarded him with undisguised amusement. "Falling in love doesn't necessarily adhere to the timetable we'd choose," she suggested. "Are you in touch with her?"

"We're exchanging emails," he said. And she was in his head all the time, he acknowledged to himself, distracting him when he needed to stay focused. He didn't think his grandmother needed to hear that. She'd make too much of it. "Once I have this business up and running successfully, maybe then I'll pursue something with Moira."

"And you expect her to be sitting there waiting patiently?" Nell asked incredulously. "Do you seriously think that's her way? Given her temperament, you'll be lucky if she even takes your call."

Luke couldn't deny the truth of that. "I'll have to take the chance," he said stubbornly, convinced that it was his only choice.

"That's the second foolish thing I've heard from you today," she chastised him.

Luke winced. "Moira's not really the issue for now,"

he protested, desperate to get off the uncomfortable topic and back on track. "It's the pub. Do you approve?"

"A hundred percent," she said at once. "Which is why you'll take the money for it from me, rather than selling that land."

Luke couldn't have been more stunned if she'd offered to sprinkle him with Irish fairy dust. "Absolutely not," he said at once. "I didn't come to you for money."

"I know you didn't," she soothed. "But hear me out. I've told none of the others this, but your grandfather left me in charge of trusts for all of you. The money's been growing since each of you was born. Mick's children had their own trusts set up by him, so they won't receive these until I'm gone. Neither will Susie or Matthew. But I think you should have yours now. It's not huge, mind you, but it should provide just the capital you need to get started."

"Gram, no," he protested again. "I won't risk your money."

"It's not mine," she corrected. "It's yours. You'll just be getting it while I'm still here to see you put it to good use. Use it well, and it will give me great joy."

Luke didn't know what to say. A part of him thought he should turn it down. Another part was relieved to have the financial issue settled in a way that would keep his father off his back about selling that land.

He studied Nell closely. "Are you sure?"

She smiled at his obvious concern. "Is this your dream?"

He nodded. "It is."

"And you believe in it?"

"I really do."

"Then we'll go to see Lawrence Riley in the morning," she told him without hesitation. "It should be easy enough to make the arrangements to transfer the money into your name."

Luke lifted her out of her chair and spun her around, aware that she was like a feather in his arms.

"Stop that," she said, laughing. "You'll make me dizzy, and I've enough of that just standing up, thanks to this blood pressure medicine the doctor insists I take."

Luke set her gently on her feet, then regarded her with concern. "Blood pressure medicine? Since when? I've never known you to take more than the occasional aspirin, Gram."

"It's nothing to worry about," she insisted. "And you're not to go blabbing to everyone, or our deal is off. Is that understood?"

Luke nodded reluctantly. "You'd tell me if it was anything serious, wouldn't you?"

He held her gaze as he asked, and she looked him straight in the eye as she said, "Of course," but Luke didn't believe her. It was the first time he could ever recall that his grandmother had lied to him. It scared him to death.

It was her day off and Moira had taken a dust cloth, vacuum and pail of water from the kitchen and gone to work in her grandfather's house in Dublin. Just that morning she'd turned over to Peter all the pictures she'd taken at the pub and was awaiting his word about whether they were good enough to be hung. In the meantime, she'd needed a distraction.

She'd already scrubbed the house from top to bottom. She was in the kitchen polishing the silver when her grandfather came home for dinner. He regarded her with curiosity.

"I thought you came to stay with me because you wanted to try life in Dublin on for size, not to be my housemaid," Dillon O'Malley said to her.

"I was bored," she retorted, not ready to admit she was a nervous wreck because of the photos she'd given to Peter. If she was a failure at that after getting her hopes up, she didn't want anyone knowing about it. "Don't make too big a deal of this. It's not likely to happen again."

Her grandfather, never one to get to the point too quickly when there was a roundabout way to get there, poured himself a glass of Irish whiskey, looked to her and asked, "Would you like one, too?"

"No, thank you," she said, wrinkling her nose. "You can rot your insides, if you've a mind to, but I'll take more care of mine."

"I didn't get to be this age by mistreating my insides," Dillon retorted, amusement in his eyes. "Now, have a seat and let's chat a bit."

Normally, Moira would have taken the request as the perfect excuse to claim other plans and hightail it away, but tonight she had no desire to meet her friends for an evening of the same old conversation about the lousy men in their lives. The man in her life wasn't lousy, for one thing, she thought, then sighed. *If* he was even in her life. She'd been a little muddy on that point since Luke had left.

So, at loose ends and restless, she sat as her grandfather had asked. He studied her with a knowing expression.

"This boredom you're experiencing wouldn't have

anything to do with a young man who's gone back to America now, would it?"

She regarded him with astonishment, startled that this man she barely knew could read her so easily when her own mum seemed completely oblivious to what was going on in her head.

"You think this is about Luke?" she asked.

He smiled. "Is there another young man who was taking up most of your time from the new year until just recently? I'm fairly certain I have him to thank for your moving to Dublin. Am I wrong?"

Moira sighed. "No. It's Luke." The pictures, for all her excitement about them, were secondary.

"You miss him," her grandfather concluded. "I saw the way of things before he left. Did you speak of the future?"

She shook her head, oddly humiliated by the admission. "That makes me a total ninny, doesn't it? I shouldn't be pinning so much on a man who's said nothing about tomorrow, much less the future."

He laughed. "You're hardly a ninny. Speaking about feelings, especially when a relationship is new and not fully tested, doesn't come easily. For what it's worth, I saw the same sparks in his eyes that I saw in yours."

She wanted so desperately to believe him, but even she knew that sparks didn't always lead to something more. From everything she'd heard, her mum had been totally gaga over her dad and vice versa, but their marriage had lasted only until her mum came home from the hospital with her, their third child, and apparently her dad's breaking point. She'd seen him once or twice over the years, but there was no bond, just some shared DNA.

"Have you spoken to Luke since he left?" her grandfather asked.

"Just once. He called to let me know he'd arrived."

Dillon frowned. "And nothing since?"

"Emails, of course, but it's not the same as hearing his voice, if you know what I mean."

"I do," he admitted. "Nell's been sending letters and postcards from Chesapeake Shores, but it's an unsatisfying substitute. After a week or two of that, I started calling simply to hear the sound of her voice."

Moira was surprised that he understood so well. "I imagine her letters are full of news about the family," she suggested tentatively.

Her grandfather smiled. "She's mentioned Luke a few times, if that's what you're asking. It seems he's totally absorbed in this plan of his to open a pub." He regarded her curiously. "You knew about that?"

"We talked about it. It's the reason we traveled, so he could do some research."

"Has he been keeping you up-to-date on his progress?"

"He mentions it but, to be honest, he doesn't say much about anything. He sounds busy and distracted." She regarded her grandfather worriedly. "Do you think I was nothing more than a passing fancy, then?" she asked, unable to keep a note of fear out of her voice. Normally, it would have taken torture for her to admit to even a hint of insecurity, but she sensed that her grandfather wouldn't judge her. She could let down her guard with him in ways she never had with anyone else. "Will I just fade in his memory as time passes?"

Luke was the first man ever to fight through that wall she'd built around herself, the one meant to keep everyone out. He'd done it with patience, persistence and kindness, teasing her unmercifully until she'd no longer been able to maintain the angry, rebellious facade that she'd worn like a defensive cloak for most of her life. To find out it had all meant nothing would be heartbreaking.

"I don't think that's the kind of man he is," her grandfather said, his expression filled with compassion. "And if he says he's busy, I'm sure that's the truth. Men tend to get absorbed in their work to the exclusion of all else, especially when they're at the beginning of something. I imagine he has quite a lot at stake, not just financially, but emotionally as well. Men feel a need to prove themselves, especially in a family like his with so many high achievers."

Moira felt reassured by the explanation. She'd been telling herself much the same thing, but wasn't sure if she was only deluding herself. In most cases, she would have written off a man who treated her in such a cavalier way, but her stubborn, captivated heart wasn't yet ready to give up on Luke.

Her grandfather gave her a commiserating look. "I have a thought about how we can find out."

"What?" she inquired suspiciously. "I'm not going to ring him up and demand to know where we stand. That would be too pitiful. Why would I want someone who doesn't want me, anyway?"

"A strong and proper stance to take," Dillon agreed. "Add in the distance between you, and it will guarantee that you never learn the truth of things."

She heard something in his words that stirred the faintest hint of excitement. "What are you suggesting?"

"As you know, I'm leaving in two weeks to spend

some time with Nell in Chesapeake Shores, to experience her world firsthand. I was thinking it's a long trip for a man my age to take alone, especially when there's a lovely young woman who might like to go along."

Moira stared at him incredulously. "You want me to go with you to America?" Her mind raced ahead at the thought, imagining Luke's welcome, the way he'd draw her into a warm embrace. It would be her fantasy come true!

"Unless you've other, more important plans," her grandfather said, his eyes twinkling. "I know you've just started work at the pub. And, of course, you could stay and finally take those courses you never finished because you said school was a waste of your time. If you'd prefer that, I'd back you a hundred percent, of course."

"I *was* wasting my time at school," she said at once. The thought of abandoning her job at the pub was more worrisome, especially with the possibility of getting some additional real work as a photographer on the horizon. Still, how could she resist this chance to see Luke, to find out where they stood?

"I'll go with you," she said decisively.

"Then it's settled," he said, smiling at her.

"But it's not because of Luke," she declared quite firmly. "It's the chance to travel with you."

"Of course it is," her grandfather agreed soberly.

But even Moira couldn't miss the disbelieving sparkle in his eyes. Nor could she deny that yet again he understood her better than anyone else ever had.

Breaking the news to Peter was harder than Moira had expected it to be, especially when his first words to her were about the photographs she'd dropped off the day before.

"They're amazing, Moira. You've a real gift for this. I've already taken them in to be framed. They should be back and ready to hang by next week. I imagine you'll have people ringing you up to shoot their weddings and their babies in no time at all. In fact, I showed them to Tara O'Rourke just yesterday. Her daughter's getting married in a month, and she's eager to hire you for the wedding pictures. And I've word of a baby shower, too, if you're interested."

She stared at him in amazement, basking in the warm glow of finally accomplishing something of which she could be proud, something even her mum couldn't deny was a success. "Are you serious?"

He laughed at her shock. "I'm already preparing myself to lose you as a waitress in here. You won't have time for this."

"But I'm an amateur," she protested, still afraid that Peter had it all wrong. Tara O'Rourke was probably just looking to keep expenses low with a first-time photographer. The same was probably true for whoever was planning that baby shower.

"You may be an amateur now, but you have an ear for listening and figuring out who people are and getting them to relax enough so you can capture it on film," Peter said confidently. "You'll make a career of this, if it's what you want."

She thought about that. Was it what she wanted? She couldn't deny being intrigued by the possibility. How long had she waited for some hint about what her niche in life was meant to be? But why now, of all times? She couldn't give up this chance to go to America, to see Luke again. And it was only for a month's time.

She explained her plans to Peter. "I'm sorry. All of this came up just yesterday. I had no idea my grand-father would want me along on this trip. It's the opportunity of a lifetime for someone like me, who's never set foot outside of Ireland."

"And, of course, Luke wouldn't happen to be part of the draw, would he?" Peter asked slyly.

"He'll be there, yes, if that's all you're asking."

"And you'll be leaving when exactly?"

"In a week. Back a month after that, so photographing the wedding's not possible," she said with genuine regret. Was she making a mistake turning down such an opportunity when there were no guarantees about what she'd find when she arrived in Chesapeake Shores?

She shook off her doubts. There was only this one chance to test the waters with Luke. If Peter was right, there would be more opportunities for photography.

"I'd have to know the date of the baby shower. I might be back for that," she told him. The thought of having actual jobs lined up for her return was astonishing. What an amazing, exciting prospect!

Peter nodded. "I'll check on that and confirm it if the date works. I imagine I'll be needing a calendar to book all your jobs for your return," he said. "I'll be your official agent—how's that?"

She grinned at his enthusiasm. "You'd do that?"

"I discovered you, didn't I? I can't let you lose business before you've even begun."

"You won't go crazy, though, right? Just a few jobs,

till we know for sure if I'm any good at this. You could be biased, or half-blind, for all I know."

Peter laughed. "I'm neither, Moira. Just a smart businessman, who likes to think he's able to spot talent when he sees it. Go and have your adventure, then hurry back. Leave the rest to me."

"Can I finish out this week?" she asked. "I'll need some spending money for the trip."

"Of course you can. In fact, I think Kevin's in need of another pint and the couple in the corner are looking a bit bemused by the menu. You might stop and explain it to them."

"Will do," she said eagerly. She turned away with Kevin's Guinness, then whirled back so quickly she almost spilled it. "Thank you, Peter."

"For the work? It's nothing."

"For the inspiration," she corrected, thinking of his faith in her photography. Encouragement had been rare in her life. She felt the glow of it all the way through. "I'm excited about going, but now I'm almost as excited by the prospect of coming home."

Luke was exhausted by the end of the day. Between meetings with potential suppliers, hours in the kitchen with Gram, who'd turned out to be an exacting taskmaster, and pitching in on some of the actual construction work, he came home ready to fall directly into bed.

He forced himself to take a couple of minutes to switch on the computer, check his emails to see if there was one from Moira, then send a reply. One of these days, he vowed to take the time to sit down and call her. Judging from her increasingly terse responses, she was feeling left out and abandoned. He could hardly blame her, when the most he managed was a two-sentence capsule of his day. He knew her well enough to understand that in her mind that could easily be construed as a lack of interest. As Gram had hinted, Moira wasn't the kind of woman to put up with neglect for long.

Tonight he managed to keep his eyes open long enough to add a line pleading with her for understanding. "I want to tell you about all of this one of these days, but right now I hardly have two minutes to myself all day long. Hopefully, this will be enough to let you know that I'm thinking about you. Be patient with me. Luke."

He'd barely hit the send button and signed off when his cell phone rang. Without even looking at the caller ID, he knew it was Kristen. She'd grown even more impatient with him lately than Moira had. He debated letting the call go to voice mail, but knew it would only buy him one evening of peace. She'd call again tomorrow and the day after that. She might not be the love of his life, but she didn't deserve to be ignored any more than Moira did.

"Hey, Kristen," he said, injecting a note of forced cheer into his voice. "How are you?"

"Lonely," she said at once. "What are you doing?"

"I just got home and I'm about to fall into bed," he told her.

"Why not come to my place and fall into my bed?"

A few months ago, he would have eagerly taken her up on the offer. Right after he'd finished college and was at loose ends, their casual, no-strings understanding was exactly what he'd wanted in his life. Kristen had seemingly been content with it as well. He'd only grown dissatisfied after the trip to Ireland when their few days together after the family had left had felt awkward and vaguely unsatisfying, as if he were doing something wrong, rather than something mutually agreed to. That reaction had been magnified because he'd already sensed that he could have real feelings for someone else, for Moira.

Once Kristen had left Dublin and he'd stayed on, spending more and more time with Moira, he'd known that he'd have to end things with Kristen as soon as he returned to Chesapeake Shores. So far, though, he'd done nothing about the situation beyond avoiding her when he could. Yet another bit of cowardly behavior that wasn't fair to anyone.

"Luke, have you fallen asleep with me on the line?" she asked, a mix of amusement and impatience in her voice.

"Just about, I'm afraid," he said. "Not tonight, Kristen. I'm wiped out."

"You've been wiped out a lot lately."

"You know I've been totally consumed with turning this pub into a reality. It's going to be a real crunch to pull it off on time. I'm not going to have a lot of free time for a while."

"And then?" she asked pointedly.

He sighed. "And then we'll see, I guess. Look, Kristen, we've never been exclusive. I can't ask you to sit around and wait for my schedule to lighten up. That's not fair to you."

"Why do I get the feeling that this brush-off has less to do with your demanding schedule than it does with that woman you met in Ireland, the one everyone but you has mentioned. Moira, is it?"

He closed his eyes. He should have guessed someone in the family would have filled her in. Because of Kristen's past history with Mack and her blatant attempt to win him back despite his marriage to Susie, none of the O'Briens approved of Luke's relationship with her. They'd be all too eager to let her know he'd found someone else and dent what they considered to be her massively self-absorbed ego.

"It's not really about Moira or anyone else," he insisted, trying to cushion this with a half truth. "It's about my priorities right now. Opening this pub is my first chance to prove myself. I have to stay focused and get this right. There's no time for distractions."

"I suppose I should be flattered that a few hours in my bed would be too great a distraction for you," she commented wryly. "Okay, I get it, but I'll keep in touch, Luke. Eventually, you'll realize what you're sacrificing and want me back."

He realized that she had the confidence to believe every word she was saying. "Take care of yourself," he said, rather than arguing with her.

"See you soon," she replied, clearly undaunted.

Yes, he thought wearily, she probably would. Kristen was not the sort of woman to take rejection seriously, much less accept that it was irreversible. More's the pity.

3

"Have I made a mistake in inviting Moira to come along?" Dillon asked Nell when he called to let her know about his change of plans.

Nell laughed. "Absolutely not. I think it's delightfully devious. I think I'll keep it to myself so Luke is caught completely by surprise."

Dillon hesitated, then asked worriedly, "You don't think he's put her out of his head, do you? I don't want her to get there and be humiliated."

"I doubt that's likely," Nell reassured him, totally understanding his concern for his granddaughter's feelings. "I brought up her name just the other day and, though he said he had no time for a serious relationship right now, my impression is that he's still quite taken with her. He seems to regret the timing, but not his feelings for her. She made quite an impression from the moment he set eyes on her. We both saw that. I'm sure we can trust what we observed."

"And that other woman—the one who visited him here in Dublin right after the rest of the family left?"

"Kristen Lewis," she said, unable to keep the disdain

out of her voice. That was one who'd cause nothing but
trouble. Nell believed that her grandson was far smarter
than that. "Let's just say that Moira is far better suited
for Luke than Kristen could ever be. There's something
undeniably special between them. Your granddaughter
presents a challenge, just the kind Luke needs, whether
he knows it or not. She won't be easy."

Dillon chuckled. "No, our Moira definitely won't be
easy. Her mother and I could give written testimonials
to that." He fell silent for a moment, then said, "You
mentioned timing, Nell. Do you think the timing is
right for this visit, for us to be pushing them together?
Luke was a bit unsettled about his future when he was
here. I know he has plans for a pub now, but is it only
a pipe dream?"

"Oh, no, as I've told you in my letters, he's perfectly
serious about it," Nell replied. "All of that wandering
that he and Moira did—it had a purpose, after all. He's
even been coming over here every morning to learn
how to cook some of the traditional Irish dishes."

She laughed, thinking about how hard Luke had
struggled to pay attention to careful measurements. He
didn't have the temperament or patience for it, but, God
bless him, he was trying. "It's taken more than one attempt," she admitted, "but he mastered Irish stew yesterday."

Dillon chuckled. "Does he have an aptitude for cooking?"

Nell sighed. "Let's just say I expect to spend more
than a few of my days over there supervising unless
he breaks down and hires an experienced cook, which
would be my recommendation."

"Perhaps Moira can pitch in and help. I've discovered that she's not bad in the kitchen when she takes the time to cook a meal."

"That would definitely be a blessing," Nell agreed. "Do you think she'd be willing?"

"I think she'll do anything to spend time with Luke." He hesitated. "Nell, I truly hope I'm not setting her up to have her heart broken."

"That's not up to either of us," Nell responded decisively. "We're just getting them to the playing field. They'll decide how the game goes. Luke's a good man, Dillon."

"I know that. Even when the two of them were wandering about the countryside, I knew she was in safe hands."

Nell laughed delightedly. "Oh, I can't wait for you both to get here and to see how this plays out. For too many years, Mick's gotten all the credit in the family for matchmaking. I want to prove that I'm just as clever at it."

"And here I thought it was my arrival you'd be looking forward to," Dillon chided.

"Now, *that,* my dear old friend," she said, "goes without saying."

"I'll see you very soon, Nell. It's only been a few months, and I already miss you even more than I did the first time you left me all those years ago. At our age we don't have time to waste like this."

She knew exactly what he was saying, especially since the little wake-up call she'd gotten when she'd seen her doctor. In fact, she was thinking more and more about how she wanted to spend whatever time she did have left on this earth, and it wasn't alone.

* * *

Moira debated emailing Luke to tell him about her plans to come to Chesapeake Shores with her grandfather, but she hadn't heard from him for three straight days. Even making allowances for how busy he was, she found that disconcerting. And annoying.

Perhaps this trip was a mistake, after all. She finally had a chance to start a real business of her own. From the moment Peter had hung her pictures, there had been even more inquiries from the customers. She'd managed one session with a baby that had gone extraordinarily well, and had spread the word about her talent even more.

With regret she'd had to turn down Tara O'Rourke's wedding and the baby shower, because both were being held while she was to be away. After saying no, she waged an internal debate over the decision. If Luke couldn't even send a bloody email—which he hadn't for several days now—how much time would he have for her once she'd arrived?

Still stewing over Luke's silence, she left the pub on her break and walked the few blocks to her grandfather's tobacco shop.

"Don't you look as if you just lost your best friend," he said, studying her worriedly. "Shouldn't you be getting excited about this trip we're taking in a few days?"

"I've been reconsidering, to be honest," she said.

"Now why on earth would you do that? The plans are all made."

She explained about the photography gigs she was sacrificing.

"Is that the real reason, then?" her grandfather asked. "Or does it have something to do with Luke? Has he been neglecting you? It's only a few weeks until his pub opens. It's to be expected that he has a lot on his mind."

"Of course you'd defend him," she said irritably.

Her grandfather's gaze narrowed. "And why would I do that when you're my family and it's your feelings that count?"

"Because he's Nell's precious grandson," she said, though she knew better. As he'd said, his first loyalty would always be to her. She might not have known that over the years when he and her mother had been estranged, but he'd proved it time and again recently. She sighed. "I'm sorry. I know better."

"I hope you do," he chided. "I just don't want to see you get in your own way by stirring up problems when there are none. Have you told Luke you're coming to Chesapeake Shores?"

She shook her head. "I thought it might be best to surprise him."

"I agree, and I say we need to stick with that plan, unless you've decided he no longer matters quite so much to you."

The problem, of course, was that he mattered too much. "What if we get there and he has no interest in spending time with me?" she asked, then held up a hand. "And before you ask, that's not the same as having no time to spend with me."

"I believe I know the difference," he said, his expression amused.

"Well, what do I do then? Leave?"

"And give the man the satisfaction of having run you off on your very first trip to America?" he asked incredulously. "That's surely not the Moira I know."

She laughed. "No, it's surely not," she said. "I'm

letting myself be defeated before I even know whether there's to be a fight." She sobered and looked into her grandfather's eyes. "Does love make all of us just a little crazy?"

"You wouldn't be the first to lose sight of who you truly are," he admitted. "But I'll be right there to remind you. I doubt you'll stay lost for long. Keep in mind the woman that Luke chose to spend all that time with during his stay in Ireland. She captured his fancy. I feel certain she'll do so again."

Moira wished she were as confident of that. She was already in her twenties, but she swore that sometimes she felt as if she were no more than an unsophisticated sixteen-year-old country girl. That had never been more true than when she'd gotten a glimpse of the older woman who'd flown over to Ireland to be with Luke for a few days right after the family had left.

Luke had readily explained who Kristen was, explained how they'd come to be together and dismissed any notion that she meant anything to him. Moira had accepted his explanation because it was what she'd wanted to believe. What if things had changed now that he was back on Kristen's turf? That was something else she had to worry about as she counted down the days till her flight.

At this rate she was going to be a complete basket case before she landed on American soil.

Luke was up to his elbows in flour, and making a real mess of things in Gram's kitchen when his brother walked in. Matthew, blast him, burst out laughing.

"Oh, how I wish I had a camera right now," Matthew said. "This is a picture that needs to hang above the bar at O'Brien's once the doors open." His expression brightened. "Aha, look what I have." He pulled his cell phone from his pocket and snapped away.

"Bite me," Luke said.

"Watch your tongue, young man," Gram said, then turned to Matthew. "And if you don't intend to be helpful, you can leave."

Matthew regarded her with shock. "You'd kick me out? You've never thrown me out of your house before, no matter how badly I misbehaved."

"You're all grown up now and should know better than to tease your brother," she scolded.

"But giving Luke grief makes my life so much more enjoyable," Matthew said.

"Let him stay," Luke said as he tried to work the dough into the proper consistency for the scones his grandmother claimed were a necessity if he was to offer afternoon tea. He scowled at her now. "Are you absolutely certain I need to bake scones?"

"Afternoon tea is a ritual that will appeal to a lot of the women in town," she replied. "You want to draw the largest possible customer base, don't you? And everyone in Chesapeake Shores knows I make the best scones. They sell out at every bake sale and church bazaar. Yours need to reflect my teaching so you don't embarrass me."

He sighed and kept kneading, then glanced at his brother, who still hadn't wiped the amused expression off his face as he busily emailed the pictures to the family grapevine. "Why are you here, aside from a desire to torment me?"

"I wanted to let you know that the shipping company called. The bar will be here day after tomorrow."

Luke stilled. "Will we be ready to install it?"

Matthew shook his head. "I'm trying to stall them for at least another couple of days. If the piece is as old as you say, we don't want it getting damaged while we're still under construction."

"What did they say?"

"They'll try to work with us, but they say it's huge and they'll need to send it when they have the right truck available." He gave Luke a concerned look. "Did you actually measure it?"

Luke stilled. "Not exactly."

"You either did or you didn't," Matthew said impatiently. "Listening to this guy talk, I got the impression of really, really big. That's not a size that's going to fit across the back of the room."

"It'll fit," Luke said grimly. "It has to."

"I'd feel better if you had the measurements to back that up."

"Then I'll drive to the port in Baltimore and get them," Luke said grimly, heading for the sink to wash his sticky, flour-coated hands.

Gram gestured for him to return to the task at hand, then turned a pointed look on his brother. "Or Matthew could call this man back and ask him to take the measurements," she said, then added, "Since you're so worried about it, shouldn't you have asked when you had him on the phone?"

Matthew leaned down and pressed a kiss to her cheek. "You always took Luke's side over mine. It's because he's the youngest, isn't it? You love him best."

Gram rolled her eyes. "Nonsense, and I am *not* taking anyone's side. I'm just trying to get these scones made so they're edible. Right now your brother is trying to pound that dough into submission."

Luke sighed. "I think baking may be beyond me, Gram."

"*Nothing* is beyond you," she insisted. "Start over."

Luke stared at her. "You want me to start from scratch?"

"Only way I know to learn," she said blithely. "Matthew, if you intend to stick around, put on an apron and get busy. It wouldn't hurt you to learn how to make something. You never know when Luke will need backup in the kitchen. In this family we pull together in a crisis, no matter what kind it is."

"But that's why he has you," Matthew protested, already heading for the door. "Love you, Gram. Good luck with those scones, Luke. I'll go make that call."

Luke wished he had the nerve to go after his brother, but he was the one who'd asked for these cooking lessons. Gram clearly intended to see that he was a master Irish chef before she was through with him. He gave her a plaintive look now.

"Isn't there some way to salvage this dough?" he asked.

She shook her head. "It'll be too tough. Bake up a few and compare them. You'll see what I mean." She picked up a catalog that had come in the mail and fanned herself.

Luke regarded her worriedly. "Are you okay?"

"Just a little warm," she said, her breath hitching slightly, as if she couldn't quite catch it. "It's sitting in here with the oven on. I should have opened the windows first."

"I'll do it," Luke said at once, then took another look

at her flushed cheeks. "Are you sure that's all it is, Gram? You seem a little short of breath."

She gave him a defiant look. "Don't be ridiculous. Now get back to work. I don't have all day to spend on this. I have preparations of my own to make. There will be a crowd here in a few days to welcome Dillon to town. I want to get most of the food done early, so I'll be able to relax and enjoy the party."

"You know everyone would be happy to pitch in and help," he protested. "Don't wear yourself out."

"We both know there's not another soul in this family who cooks as well as I do," she countered. "And I won't have Jess asking Gail at the inn to cater a meal for us, not on Dillon's first night in town." She gave him a wry look. "And though you're improving, you're not up to the task yet, either."

Luke smiled at her. "You're really looking forward to his visit, aren't you?"

This time he had the feeling that the blush in her cheeks had nothing to do with being overheated. "I am," she admitted. She hesitated, then said, "Can I tell you a secret?"

"Of course."

"I'm going to do everything in my power to convince him to stay right here," she said, defiant sparks in her eyes. "I imagine Mick will have a thing or two to say about that, but it's my decision. And Dillon's, of course."

Luke knew his own surprise was nothing compared to the tizzy Uncle Mick would have over this news. He tried to tread carefully. "Have you and Dillon already discussed it? I thought the plan was for you both to travel back and forth."

"Plans sometimes have to change," she said, her voice turning sad. "I think Christmas was probably my last visit to Ireland."

Once again Luke had the sense that there was much more to the story that she wasn't telling him. "Gram, what's going on?"

After only the faintest flicker of despondency on her face, something so brief he couldn't even be sure he'd seen it, her expression brightened. "Not a thing," she said. "I'm just being realistic. It's a long way to go at my age."

"Are you sure Dillon will want to pack up and leave the life he's always known?"

"I'm certain of only one thing," she said, giving him a pointed look. "The only way to know a thing like that is to ask, and I intend to do just that. It's advice you might consider taking to heart."

Though the obvious inference would have been to assume she was talking about the call she'd advised him to make to determine the measurements of the bar, Luke knew better. It was her subtle way of reminding him not to wait too long to ask Moira to be a part of his life.

What bothered him wasn't that she'd made the suggestion, but the urgency he sensed behind it and behind her own plan to invite Dillon to stay. Something was wrong, and he knew in his gut he needed to find out what it was. What he didn't know was how he was going to pull that off without offending his grandmother's independent spirit.

Everyone in the family credited Jo O'Brien with being the most practical, sensible O'Brien aside from

Nell. Luke was still in awe of how well his mother had handled Susie's ovarian cancer and kept everyone else from falling apart. He concluded that she was his best bet to get to the bottom of what was going on with his grandmother.

She was easy enough to track down. After school, where she was both a teacher and a women's track coach, she was usually at practice with her team. Luke found her standing at the edge of the track with a stopwatch in one hand and a whistle in the other. With her hair caught up in a messy ponytail and dressed in jeans and a hoodie on the cool early May afternoon, she looked little older than her students.

"Hey, Mom!" he called out as he joined her.

Barely taking her eyes off the track for more than a split second, she gave him a smile. "What brings you by? I thought you were swamped getting the pub ready to open."

"I am, but I need to talk to you. Can you spare a couple of minutes? If not now, could you drop by the pub when you're finished here?"

She must have heard something in his voice, because she blew her whistle to get the attention of the girls. "That's it, ladies. It was a good practice. Take your showers and head on home. I'll see you tomorrow."

When they were finally on their way, she gestured toward the bleachers, then followed Luke over. "What's up?"

"I'm worried about Gram," he blurted. "Something's going on with her, and I don't think she's told anyone about it."

His mother regarded him with surprise. "Are you

sure? She's seemed fine to me when I've seen her the past few Sundays."

"She can put on a good show for a couple of hours," he said. "I've been spending more time with her lately. She's said a couple of things. When I called her on one of them, she told me I wasn't to blab."

"And yet here you are," Jo said. "Since I know you wouldn't break your word lightly, what exactly has happened?"

He told her about the casual mention of blood pressure medicine, then today's incident, when Nell had seemed overheated and short of breath. "It doesn't sound like much when I say it, but that's not all. She was talking about wanting Dillon to stay on here, about not being able to make another trip to Ireland herself. She sounded—I don't know—resigned or something."

To his relief—yet in a way his regret—his mother didn't laugh off his concerns. "That doesn't sound like Nell," she conceded. "You're right about that. When we got back from Ireland, all she could talk about was the next trip over there."

"Will you speak to her? Maybe she'll open up to you."

"Nell's not going to open up to anyone unless she wants them to know what's going on. It's not her way. I will keep closer tabs on her and, if I sense that it's necessary, I'll get your father, Mick and Thomas to look into it."

"Do you really want to get them all worked up, especially Mick? You know how he is. He'll haul her off to Johns Hopkins to be checked out whether she wants to go or not."

His mother laughed. "He would, wouldn't he? Well,

let's hope it doesn't come to that. She has a lot going on right now. I'm sure she's overly tired with all this planning for Dillon's visit. I'll go by this afternoon and offer to help." When Luke started to protest, she held up a hand. "I know she won't let me near her kitchen, but she might let me dust and vacuum for her."

Luke nodded. "I should have thought of that. The kitchen could use a good scrubbing, too. I offered to do it before I left this morning, but she told me she had her own ways of doing things."

"She didn't get to this age by not being independent and stubborn, like the rest of the O'Briens," Jo said.

"Ain't that the truth," Luke responded.

She squeezed his hand. "It's a good trait some of the time. Thanks for telling me about this. It's good she has you around so much right now. I know she's enjoying these lessons. Last Sunday at Mick's, your progress— or lack thereof—was all she could talk about while we were in the kitchen cleaning up."

Luke rolled his eyes. "Today might have tested her limits," he said, explaining about the mess he'd made of two batches of scones. "If she offers you one, I'd advise against taking it unless it comes with an affidavit that it's one she baked."

Jo laughed. "Trust me, if yours were that awful, they're in the trash by now or she's fed them to the birds."

"Poor robins," Luke said with a shake of his head.

"You'll get the knack of it. I believe in you. So does Nell. I can hardly wait to see how the pub is coming along."

"Stop by anytime," he said, though he'd been discouraging visitors. He wanted the family to be wowed by the finished product.

"I'll wait," she said. "I know you want to knock all our socks off on opening night. Have you set the date?"

"Tentatively," he confessed. "I'd like to open before Dillon goes home again. He made a lot of introductions for me in Ireland. I'd like him to see how much they helped."

"Oh, he'll love that," she said, then gave him a sly look. "Shouldn't you be inviting Moira over for the grand opening as well? She played a role in this, too, didn't she?"

The thought had occurred to Luke more than once, but he'd vetoed it. As much as he'd like to have Moira here to share the big opening, a part of him was afraid she might make too much of the invitation. He didn't want to send any more mixed signals than he already had.

No, when he invited Moira to come to Chesapeake Shores, it would be because he was ready for more than a date to a party, albeit the most important party of his life.

4

"Chesapeake Shores is a long way to go chasing after a man," Kiera said when she learned of Moira's trip. "You'll only be disappointed."

Moira regarded her mother with annoyance. "Thank you for the support. Are you sure it's not that you're jealous that Grandfather is taking me and not you?"

She saw that she'd hit the mark by the tightening of her mother's lips. Surprisingly, Moira felt bad about it, which proved just how much her attitude toward her mum had changed now that she'd finally put some distance between them. "I'm sorry. I shouldn't have accused you of such a thing."

Kiera sighed. "It's never wrong to speak the truth," she said, sounding weary. "I suppose I am a wee bit jealous that you have this chance and I don't." She held Moira's gaze. "But my concern for you is genuine. I don't want you to go over there with high expectations about what will happen when you and Luke are reunited. Men like Luke move on at a whim."

"The way Dad did?" Moira said, understanding with

unexpected clarity exactly where the concern came from—her mother's own experience.

"Yes, as your father did," Kiera said, her usual bitterness giving way to what almost sounded like sorrow.

Moira hesitated then asked the question she'd never dared to utter before. "Was it me? Was I too much for him?"

Kiera looked startled. "Is that what you think?" she asked in dismay. "That your father left because of you?"

"It's what I've always believed," Moira admitted. The timing of his departure could hardly allow for any other conclusion.

"Oh, my darling girl, it had nothing to do with you," Kiera said at once. "It was all of it—the pressure of me wanting more and more for our children, a job he hated, needing to come home at night rather than spending his time and money in a pub. He wasn't meant to be a family man. He liked things easy. In truth, the only surprise wasn't that he left, but that it took him so long."

Moira felt an odd sense of relief at that, but then thought about what her mum had actually revealed. She couldn't help wondering if the same mind-set applied to Luke. It was hardly the first time such a thought had crossed her mind.

"Does Luke remind you of Dad?" she asked. "Is that really why you're so worried about my going over there?"

To her dismay, her mother nodded. "I see some similarities, yes. And hearing that's he's opening a pub?" She shook her head. "It brings back too many memories of the pull such places had for your father."

"Was Dad a drinker, then?" Moira asked.

Her mother nodded. "He had a problem. I didn't

see it when we met, because all our friends liked to have a pint or two and enjoy the music on a Friday or Saturday night. It was only later, after we were married, that he spent more and more time with his mates and came home reeling. I can't tell you how often we argued about it. Ask your brothers. They're old enough to remember some of it, I'm sure, though we've never spoken of it."

"And isn't that our way?" Moira said with a touch of bitterness. "To never speak of the things that matter? How many years did it take before you even acknowledged we had grandparents living in Dublin? It was only when your mother became ill and Grandfather came looking for you that we discovered we had family."

Kiera sighed heavily. "You're right again," she conceded. "I'm sorry."

Moira found herself apologizing as well. "But Luke's not like Dad in that way—a drinker, I mean," she said earnestly. "I know he's not. In all that time we spent together and in so many different pubs, he rarely had anything to drink. He was totally focused on his research. It wasn't about the drinking, not at all."

"He wouldn't be the first man to open a pub so he'd have a ready excuse for being around alcohol," Kiera said.

Though Moira understood that it was Kiera's own experiences that had shaped her opinion, Moira still found it worrisome. She believed her defense of Luke and seized on Peter McDonough to prove it. "I've never seen Peter lift even a pint of ale during the course of an evening," she said. "How long has he owned that pub? Twenty years? Even longer?"

"Peter's a paragon, he is," Kiera said wryly. "Your grandfather has told me that often enough."

Moira couldn't hide her shock at the innuendo. "Grandfather has been encouraging something between you and Peter? For how long?"

"Since I was in my teens," Kiera admitted. "He was cited as the epitome of respectability, which I stupidly ignored in my pursuit of rebellion. Now that my marriage is over, his name is dropped into the conversation every chance your grandfather can find. Didn't you notice how many times it was suggested we drop in at McDonough's over the holidays?"

Moira tried to imagine a romance between her mother and Peter. Surprisingly, she could see it, though she wasn't sure she could explain just why. Maybe it had to do with Peter's easygoing nature, his willingness to meet people as they were and enjoy their company. Had he spent more time than usual hovering over the family when they'd made those holiday stops? Had the extra attention been about more than respect for her grandfather? As Luke had done with Moira, Peter had certainly been able to ignore Kiera's stubborn testiness and find ways to coax her into laughter. He'd even gotten her onto the dance floor a time or two, fighting off her reluctance with teasing determination.

"Peter's been very kind to me," she said, testing to see her mother's reaction.

Kiera frowned. "In what way?"

Moira explained about the photos. "Maybe you could come by while I'm at work tonight and see them for yourself."

"Peter says they're good?" Kiera asked.

Moira nodded. "And the proof seems to be that

people have been showing an interest in hiring me. I've already had one job, and more are lined up for my return from this trip with Grandfather. Enough that I might not have to wait tables for too much longer."

"Then why on earth would you pick now to leave town?" Kiera asked, looking more animated and approving than usual. "Shouldn't you stay right here and make the most of this opportunity? You've been talking about photography for years. I thought nothing would ever come of it."

"I honestly didn't know how to make anything happen," Moira said. "But Peter did. And he says this trip won't harm anything. He'll keep track of any potential bookings for me. Please, Mum, come by and take a look."

"Of course I will," she said.

Moira nodded. It would give her the chance to see if there were any sparks there between her mum and Peter, sparks that could be fanned a bit.

Kiera gave her a knowing look. "Don't be getting any ideas," she warned. "This is about looking at your pictures and only that."

"I understand," Moira replied dutifully.

"I don't need you joining your grandfather in meddling in my life."

"I wouldn't dream of it," Moira said.

But the truth was, she thought maybe her mum was protesting just a little too much. Surely, after all these years of being a struggling single mother, Kiera wasn't totally immune to the possibility of love.

Dillon had had his share of surprises through the years, but none had startled him more than the invitation by his granddaughter to join her and his daughter at McDonough's pub on the evening before their departure for Chesapeake Shores.

"What's this about?" he asked Moira when she called. "Usually it takes all my persuasive skills to get your mum to set foot inside that place."

"There's the lure of seeing some of my photos on the walls," Moira told him. "I'd like you to see them, too. I know you've been too busy to stop in since Peter hung them up."

He heard the hint of nervousness in her voice and knew these pictures meant more to her than she wanted him to know. "Peter's told me about them, you know. He thinks you've a real gift."

"He's told you that?" she asked, sounding pleased.

"And he wouldn't lie to an old friend," Dillon reassured her. "Nor would he say anything to you if he didn't have faith in your work. I'll be looking forward to seeing them for myself. I only wish you'd expressed an interest in this a long time ago. I would have encouraged you."

"Things happen when they're meant to," she replied. "Isn't that what you've told me about you and Nell reuniting after all these years?"

"True enough."

She fell uncharacteristically silent, which encouraged him to ask, "Was there something else on your mind?"

"Is it true that you've been matchmaking between my mum and Peter?"

Dillon chuckled. "Ah, she told you that, did she? It's true. I always thought they were well suited. Of course, that was the kiss of death back when they were young.

If I said there was a pot of gold to the north, your mum would head south just to spite me."

Moira laughed. "And you think she's changed?"

"No, which is why I'll be keeping my mouth firmly shut tonight," he said. "If there's any matchmaking to be done, I'll leave it to you."

"I can see it, too," she confessed. "That they'd be good together. Wouldn't it be lovely if something came of it after all this time?"

"It would," Dillon agreed. "Your mother deserves to find some happiness. She wasn't always bitter and sad the way she's been since your dad took off."

"I know. I see glimpses of it from time to time. Do you suppose she and I can make peace?" she asked, her tone plaintive.

"She and I have," he said. "So there's always hope. We'll see if tonight can give us a start on that."

In fact, he vowed to do his part to give things a push in that direction. He had a feeling that if Moira was to find her own happiness—with Luke or someone else— she needed to believe she was worthy of love. Circumstances and Kiera's own bitterness had done their part to rob her of that self-confidence. It was past time to fix that, too. For a man his age, it seemed he still had a lot to accomplish.

Peter refused to let Moira wait on a single table while her mother and grandfather were in the pub.

"Enjoy your family," he said. "Bask in their admiration."

She would have, but she was too nervous. As Dillon and Kiera circled the room, pausing in front of the photos, Moira waited behind the bar, polishing mugs despite Peter's best efforts to get her to stop hiding out. She couldn't help noticing that Peter seemed almost as anxious about their reactions as she was.

"Well?" he prodded, when they finally headed back toward the bar. "Is she as amazing as I think?"

"I'm stunned," Kiera said, a smile on her face. "Moira, they're truly remarkable."

Moira flushed at the praise. "Do you mean that?"

"I wouldn't say it if I didn't," her mother insisted, then glanced briefly at Peter. "Thank you for encouraging her." She looked away almost the instant the words were out of her mouth.

"It's been my pleasure," Peter said, his gaze on Kiera steady, despite her doing her best to avoid it. "I would have done the same for anyone, but it's meant more that it was your daughter I was helping."

The color in her mother's cheeks heightened at his words. So, Moira thought, her mum wasn't immune to him, after all.

She slipped out from behind the bar and tucked her arm through her grandfather's, then steered him away from the others to stand in front of one of the photos. "You haven't said much."

"You've left me speechless," he admitted. "I feel as if I know those people, not as I always have, but as if I've had a glimpse inside them. This is more than a hobby, Moira. You've a talent you should be nurturing."

Tears stung her eyes. "You have no idea what it means to me to have you say that. I'm almost starting to believe I could make a go of this."

"Then it's something you truly want?"

She nodded. "I've never allowed myself to believe it could happen. I was always the screwup, the rebellious one, not suited for anything I was learning in school. I talked a bit to Jess O'Brien about that feeling when she was here. She said she'd felt much the same way till she opened her inn." She met his gaze. "I think, in some ways, it's the same with Luke and his pub."

"I think it is," her grandfather agreed. "If you can understand that and give him the room to mature and grow, I think he'll do the same for you. You'll build your future together, one with room for both your gifts."

Moira looked around the pub at the photos on the walls, noted the way people were admiring them and felt a warm glow of satisfaction, but something else as well. This faint possibility of a career—this hope she was feeling—it was here, in Dublin, while Luke was across the ocean.

As if he'd read her mind, her grandfather smiled at her. "There are people to photograph in America, too," he said quietly. "If this is what you were meant to do and Luke is the man you're meant to be with, you'll find a way. Believe in that."

Moira nodded, wanted to believe, but over the years there'd been very little reason to have faith in herself. Suddenly the trip that she'd agreed to with one goal was about so much more.

Luke was standing amid wood shavings, drawing in the scent of paint and wondering if he'd been out of his mind to think he could create an Irish pub in barely more than a month. He'd trusted it to his brother and his uncle, but right at the moment all he could detect was chaos. Only the handsome sign that was meant to go above the door out front—*O'Brien's* written in the almost traditional raised gold letters against a dark green background—was ready.

The massive bar, the one he'd salvaged from a town in the countryside miles from Dublin, would be delivered tomorrow, assuming he dared to put it into place in this construction zone. It might be better off being left in the alley behind the building. Matthew was still grumbling about the tight fit it was going to be. There'd be barely inches to spare once it was in place across the back of the room. If Luke gained even a few ounces, he'd be squeezing past to make his way to the office in back. Thank goodness the doorway to the kitchen was off to the side. Otherwise, a waiter with a tray would be tempting fate each time he came and went.

For the past three weeks, he'd been in here every minute, working alongside his uncle's crew, testing the limits of his own skills with a hammer and paintbrush. Even his father had pitched in once or twice, though that help usually came with another well-meant cautionary lecture Luke didn't especially want to hear.

He was on the phone in the tiny space he'd set aside for an office when he looked up and saw Kristen making her way through the bar. In her spike heels, designer suit and flashing gold-and-diamond jewelry, she looked as out of place in here as he felt at those fancy Baltimore parties she'd dragged him to from time to time.

"You shouldn't be wandering around in here without a hard hat," he told her, not entirely glad to see her. She'd made her opinion of "this little project of yours" well-known. She hadn't been delighted about it. She thought running a bar was beneath him. It was one of the few heated arguments they'd ever had. Usually they discussed nothing else worth fighting about. In Luke's opinion, the handwriting was on the wall about their future...or lack thereof. Hadn't he made that clear the last time they'd spoken?

"Since you're spending all your time here these days, I thought you could show me around," she said, then took in the room, her expression dubious. "There's not much to see, is there?"

"It's coming along," he said defensively. "I can show you the plans if you'd like to take a look."

"I'd rather you take me to Brady's for dinner," she said.

He shook his head before the words were out of her mouth. "I can't. Sorry. I have to go to Gram's tonight. Dillon's arriving from Ireland, and she expects the family to drop by."

Kristen looked skeptical. "Will all of you even fit in that little cottage of hers?"

"We'll fit well enough," Luke told her.

She watched him intently, obviously waiting for an invitation he had no intention of extending. Eventually, she sighed.

"Still not welcome on O'Brien turf," she said wryly. "Is that ever likely to change?"

"I don't know," he told her candidly. "You did try to break up my sister's marriage. Susie can hold a grudge with the best of them, and I can promise you there's no one in the family who's unlikely to take her side."

She frowned at his observation. "Then what are we doing, Luke?"

"What we've always been doing," he replied candidly. "Enjoying each other's company when it suits both of us."

"What if that's not enough anymore?"

He'd been wondering the same thing, though for slightly different reasons, he suspected. "We talked about this the other night. It's time for you to move on. You don't want more from me, Kristen. You know you don't."

She held his gaze, then sighed. "I thought I might."

"Only because you knew it wasn't in the cards," he said with certainty. "Find someone you can fall in love with, someone who won't have all these obstacles to overcome."

"You're the only interesting game in town," she said, her expression surprisingly sad.

He laughed at that. "You know that's not true. It was just easier not to look because I was right there. And I think you thought it might make my brother-in-law a little crazy to know we were hooking up. It's always had more to do with your feelings for Mack than it has with me."

"You're wrong about that! It had nothing to do with Mack," she said, bristling even though they both knew the truth. She stood a little straighter, her pride obviously kicking in. "Okay, then. It's time to move on." She gave him a wickedly bold look. "Let me know if you change your mind. I'll see if I can still fit you into my schedule."

"I don't think I'll count on that," he said with total sincerity. "I imagine someone will snap you up the second they know you're available. You just have to get out there and mingle. I could—"

"If you offer to fix me up with someone, I'll have to kill you now," she said.

Luke laughed. "Okay, then, no matchmaking. I'm probably no good at it, anyway."

She stepped closer, leaned in and kissed his cheek. Then she shifted to capture his mouth in a move that normally aroused a sizzle in his bloodstream. Today, though, he seemed to be immune, and she obviously felt it. She sighed as she stepped away.

"Take care, Luke. It's been fun."

"It has been," he agreed, relieved to have it officially over, relieved they were parting with no scenes or recriminations. To his mind, that meant it had never amounted to much to either of them in the first place. This was good.

What he couldn't explain—or didn't want to—was why he seemed to have this great big empty hole in his heart. He had a hunch it had more to do with the woman across the ocean than it did with the one who'd just left his arms.

Moira was so excited about being in a country far, far away from her familiar little corner of Ireland that she couldn't quite decide where to look first. Baltimore's traffic was no more chaotic than Dublin's, though it seemed so as they raced along on what seemed to her to be the wrong side of the road. She'd been delighted to know that Mick O'Brien would be escorting Nell to the airport to pick them up. She was sure all the commotion wouldn't faze such a man in the least. She found Mick and his larger-than-life personality fascinating, albeit slightly intimidating.

Riding in the front with Mick while her grandfather rode in back with Nell, Moira had a million questions, but found she didn't need to utter a one of them. Mick

The Summer Garden71

provided a running commentary as they drove south, eventually making their way onto narrower roads and then to the community of Chesapeake Shores itself. Her first view of the bay, seen at the end of Main Street in a charming downtown, immediately captured her fancy and reminded her of villages back home.

"It's like home," she exclaimed with delight. "Yet it has a unique look of its own, brighter and a bit more modern and up-to-date." She turned to him with amazement. "And you created this, the whole town, from nothing?"

"I did," Mick confirmed.

"And is it Matthew that I remember is following in your footsteps?"

"One of these days he'll be even better than I am," Mick confided, "but don't tell him I said that."

She took in everything—Bree O'Brien's Flowers on Main with its buckets of brilliant bouquets on the sidewalk, the quaint bookstore she learned belonged to Shanna O'Brien, Mick's daughter-in-law, a boutique called Seaside Gifts and, at the end of the block, a store with a hodgepodge of things for every vacationer called Ethel's Emporium. They all faced a town green brightened with beds of red tulips and a few stray leftover daffodils from earlier in the spring.

"Where are Megan's art gallery and Heather's quilt shop?" she asked Mick as she gazed eagerly out the window.

"Just around the corner on Shore Road," he told her. "You can come into town tomorrow for the complete tour. For now, though, I'm sure your grandfather would like to get to Ma's so he can rest a bit before everyone descends for drinks and dinner a bit later. If you're not in need of rest, I'll take you for a walk along the bay, if you'd like. You'll begin to get your bearings."

"That would be perfect," she said with delight. "I'm far too excited to sleep."

Though she wanted desperately to ask if Luke would be at tonight's gathering, she held back. She'd heard tales about Mick's meddling. It was probably best if he remained in the dark about her real reasons for making this trip. Not that there was much question that he'd already have his suspicions.

As he turned off the road into a narrow driveway, she couldn't seem to suppress her delighted gasp of pleasure. It was like coming upon a doll's cottage by the edge of the sea. The yard was filled with flowers just beginning to bud. A white picket fence with climbing roses tumbling over it surrounded the yard and created a colorful backdrop against the bay just beyond. She had to admit, it looked exactly like something Nell would have created—warm, cozy and inviting. She turned to tell her that and caught her grandfather holding Nell's hand. He winked at her.

"So, what do you think, Moira? Is Chesapeake Shores the way we described it for you?" Nell asked.

"It's wonderful," she admitted. "And your house is like something from a storybook. I think I've fallen in love with it straight off. You've a great talent for gardening as well."

Nell regarded her with real pleasure. "Thank you. I hope you'll see it in summer when everything's in full bloom. And I truly hope you and your grandfather will be comfortable here."

"Of course we will," her grandfather said at once. "And we thank you for having us."

"It was very generous of you to include me," Moira told her.

Mick made quick work of getting their things inside. Though Nell offered her tea, Moira declined. "Mick said he'd show me the way to the beach, if that's all right."

"Of course it is," Nell said. "While you're here, you're to go and come as you like. I have a feeling I'll be seeing little enough of you after tonight's party."

Moira gave her a quizzical look, but didn't respond. Had her grandfather told Nell that she was here because of Luke? She sighed. Of course he had. Or Nell had put two and two together for herself. With them there was little point in denying her reasons for making this trip.

What remained in question was how Luke would react when he discovered that she'd invaded his turf. For one fleeting second, panic made her wish she was back in Dublin, serving pints of ale at McDonough's or launching that photography career at full throttle.

But then she thought of Luke, of the way he'd looked at her, the way he'd touched her and held her, and her heart raced with anticipation. Tonight's party couldn't begin soon enough.

5

Luke was late. He'd gotten totally absorbed in completing the painting of the wall that would be behind the bar, twice changing his mind about the color. The foreman Uncle Mick had put on the job had finally lost patience with it and told him to work it out in his head, then do it himself or leave it till morning. He could hardly blame the man. He suspected that Mick himself would have said far worse.

In the end, he'd raced home, showered and changed and was now walking up the driveway at Gram's over an hour after most of the others had arrived. In fact, several of his cousins who had small children were already leaving.

"Someone's in trouble!" Connor called out in a singsong taunt as he and Luke crossed paths.

"Stop it!" Heather told her husband. "Don't be spoiling the surprise."

"Heather's right," Shanna said just as Kevin looked as if he was going to add his own comment. "Quiet, both of you!"

Luke looked from one man to the other. Weren't

cousins, especially guys, supposed to stick together? "What am I missing?" he asked them.

"The party," Shanna said firmly, scowling first at Kevin, then at Connor, apparently to ensure their silence. "But you already know that, so you'd better hurry."

Connor grinned at the direct order, but Kevin merely shrugged as if he had zero control over his wife.

"Sorry, man," he muttered as he passed Luke.

As Luke got closer to the house, he heard noise coming from the backyard, so rather than going inside, he walked around the side of the house.

"There you are!" Mick boomed in a way that was far more welcoming than usual. "It's about time."

Luke frowned. "Why is everyone making such a fuss because I'm a little late?" he asked just as the crowd seemed to magically part, leaving him with a clear view of his grandmother, Dillon and, at Dillon's side, Moira. Luke's heart seemed to come to a complete stop in his chest as she met his gaze, her expression a familiar mix of defiance and fear. He knew that look all too well. She was scared to death about his reaction, but trying hard to pretend otherwise.

Luke crossed the lawn, unable to take his eyes off her. "You," he said softly. "You're here!"

"So I am," she said, her gaze searching his face. "Are you pleased?"

"Stunned, as a matter of fact." Her eyes clouded at his words, so he quickly added, "In a good way, Moira. In a very good way."

In fact, it was just about the best surprise he could ever recall…and that flat-out terrified him.

Her lips slowly curved into a smile at his words.

"Well, I suppose that's a warmer welcome than I gave you on the night we met in Dublin."

Luke laughed. "There was no welcome," he reminded her. "You'd have been pleased if I'd turned right around and left for the hotel. In fact, you did your best to see that not only I, but all of us, did just that."

"My manners and my disposition have improved since then," she told him. "Though I have a few things to say to you about yours."

Luke winced. "I know I've been neglecting you."

"And me," Dillon said, interceding. "It's good to see you again, Luke."

Luke shook the older man's hand. "I'm glad you're here, sir. Gram's been looking forward to the visit ever since we got back." He turned to his grandmother. "And you," he chided. "I assume you knew about the surprise."

"Of course I did. Dillon and I worked it all out and kept it to ourselves. I must admit I could hardly wait to see your reaction." She smiled at him. "It told me quite a lot."

"Gram," he warned, only to have her wave him off.

"Moira, why don't you go with Luke to fill a plate? I'm sure he's starving." She gave him a chiding look. "Though there's little guarantee that there will be much left to choose from at this hour."

"I'm sorry I was late," he apologized.

"And even sorrier now that you know who awaited you, I imagine," she teased. "Go on now and enjoy yourself."

Food was the last thing on his mind, but he took the time to choose a few things from the buffet, poured himself a glass of iced tea, refilled Moira's glass, then led the way to a pair of weathered Adirondack chairs facing the bay. At twilight the view was amazing with shades of purple descending to meet the last shimmering reflections of gold on the water as the sun set behind them to the west.

He set his plate on the arm of the chair, then took a step forward and reached for Moira, studying her face, remembering the way she felt, the way she tasted.

"I've missed you like crazy," he said right before he sealed his mouth over hers. "And this," he murmured eventually. "I've missed this."

She held his gaze as he slowly released her. "I was so afraid you hadn't," she admitted in a rare display of vulnerability.

"Why didn't you tell me you were coming?"

"It was only a couple of weeks ago when grandfather suggested it. You'd been saying less and less in your emails, and while I understood it was because you were busy, a part of me worried it was more than that. I even wondered if you'd tell me not to come."

"Why would I do such a thing?" he asked, genuinely shocked that she could even imagine it. "I'm glad you're here."

"Even now, when you've so much on your mind?" she asked, searching his expression for the truth.

"Especially now," he admitted, realizing it was true. Gram had tried to tell him that Moira belonged here, that she was a part of this pub dream of his, but he hadn't accepted it until he'd set eyes on her tonight. She'd been by his side as he'd worked out his ideas, listening to him, encouraging him, challenging him when she thought he'd got it wrong. "You'll be here for the opening, right? You're staying the whole time your grandfather's here?"

"Unless you try to chase me away," she said, then grinned. "And then I'll only go far enough to annoy you, but not so far that you can forget me."

Though he wasn't quite ready to let her go, he was aware that they had an audience of interested O'Brien onlookers not that far away. He nudged her toward a chair. "Sit before I'm tempted to do something that will shock my family."

She looked intrigued by that. "Really? Such as?"

"I want nothing more than to drag you down onto the ground and have my way with you," he said candidly, enjoying the quick rise of heat in her eyes.

Still, she only laughed. "You've some more apologizing to do before that's in the cards, Luke. Women don't appreciate being ignored, no matter what the circumstances. At least, I don't."

"You know it was only because of how busy I've been, right? It had nothing at all to do with my feelings for you. Nothing's changed about those. I swear it."

"Pretty words," she commented. "You've a way with them. We'll see if you can back them up with actions."

He smiled. "Is that a challenge?"

"Of course it is. Isn't that one of the things you said you liked best about me? I didn't fall easily into your bed in Ireland. I see no reason for that to change here."

Luke laughed. "I look forward to persuading you, then."

There was pure mischief in her eyes then. "And I look forward to being persuaded."

"I think it's going well," Dillon observed, casting yet another glance toward his granddaughter and Luke, who'd been keeping to themselves since the moment Luke had made his belated entrance at the party.

Nell gave him a wry look. "I suspect it would be going better if there weren't an audience over here who can't seem to keep their gazes to themselves."

Dillon chuckled. "Point taken. And the truth is, now that the rest of your family has left, I wouldn't mind having you to myself away from prying eyes as well. Since the seats by the water are occupied, would you like to go inside and snuggle with me on your sofa?"

"And risk scandalizing the young people when they come inside?"

"I don't think there's any danger of that," Dillon said. "Those two could easily be out here till sunup. They've a lot of catching up to do."

"Aren't you tired from your trip?" Nell asked, studying him with concern.

"I was, but that nap earlier refreshed me. I don't want to waste another minute of my first day here with you. It's been a very long time coming." He studied her and wondered if maybe the problem was with her, not him. "What about you, though, Nell? Have you worn yourself out getting ready for company? Would you rather call it a night?"

"I *am* a bit tired," she admitted with obvious reluctance. "All the excitement has taken more of a toll than I realized. Maybe we should call it an early night, so we'll be fresh for all the things I want to do with you tomorrow." She smiled at him. "There are so many places I want to take you, Dillon, so much I want to share with you. A month will never be long enough."

Now it was his turn to worry. She'd never expressed any interest in being the first to bed over the holidays in

Dublin. She'd had more energy than some of the women half her age.

He tucked a finger under her chin and studied her intently. "What's going on, Nell?"

"Just too much excitement," she insisted, her expression stubbornly defiant. "I'll be fit as a fiddle in the morning. I can't wait to show you the town."

He had no choice but to take her at her word, but he didn't like what he was seeing or hearing. It wasn't his usual nature to ask questions behind her back, but if he didn't find that this had passed with a good night's rest, he'd speak to Mick. He had no intention of losing Nell after having just gotten her back into his life.

"I've never seen anything more beautiful," Moira said, gazing at the moon rising over the Chesapeake Bay.

"Neither have I," Luke said, though his gaze was on her, not the water.

She smiled at him. "There's that pretty way with words again."

"Come over here and sit with me," he encouraged. "Everyone's gone inside now. We're out here on our own. I just want to hold you."

Moira hesitated, but the temptation was too much to resist. And why should she? Wasn't this what she'd come for, to discover if being with Luke was the same now as it had been a few months ago?

She crossed the few steps to his chair, then settled in his lap, her head resting on his shoulder. She sighed softly at how right it felt to be there. Even here, in a new land, it felt like coming home.

"You smell lovely," she commented, drawing a chuckle.

"Then it's a good thing I took the time to shower before coming over here tonight," he said. "After a long day at work, especially covered with paint as I was a few hours ago, you might not have felt the same way."

"Tell me about the progress on the pub," she said eagerly. "Will I be able to see it tomorrow?"

"You'll be almost the first I've let through the doors," he admitted. "I've been keeping most of the family at bay. I want them to see it first when I hold the grand opening. Matthew, my father and my uncle have seen it, of course, since they're doing the work, but no one else has stepped inside."

"Would you rather I stayed away, too?"

His silence sent a strange chill through her. Finally, he said, "No."

"There wasn't much sincerity behind that," she said accusingly. "If you don't want me there, just say so."

"Don't go getting prickly on me now," Luke chided. "I was just debating the value of having your opinion now versus seeing the look on your face when it's all completed."

She relaxed then. "And the verdict, then?"

"I want you to see it now. You more than anyone deserve to get an early glimpse. You were there while I was working it all out in my head. You know the effect I was hoping to achieve. You may be able to spot whether I've gone off course."

"And you'd want me to tell you that?" she asked.

He gave her a wry look. "Could I keep you from it? One of the many traits I love about you is your commit-

ment to saying what's on your mind and never holding back."

"I may not have much practice, but I could be sensitive and subtle if I put my mind to it," she offered.

"Absolutely not. I don't want censored remarks. I
want the truth."

She heard the faint hint of vulnerability in his voice
and knew she'd find the right words. She had to. She
touched his cheek. "It's going to be wonderful, Luke. I
know it is. Have you found music for the opening?"

"I have a stack of demo CDs in my office and no
time to listen to them. I have to do that soon, or I'll be
doing Irish karaoke on opening night."

"I could give a listen, if you like, and recommend a
few. Then you could make the final choice from those."

"That would be a godsend," he told her.

"It would make me feel a part of it," she said.

They sat there in companionable silence for a while
as the moon turned the bay to silver.

"Tell me about you," Luke said eventually. "You
mentioned taking photographs that Peter framed and
hung on the walls at McDonough's. How did that come
about?"

Moira sat up straighter in his lap and filled him in.
"Never in a million years did I expect such a reaction
when he glimpsed the picture I'd taken of you. I thought
he was just being kind, but people have been asking
about me, wondering if I'd be available to shoot photos
of their weddings or of their babies. Can you imagine?" she asked, unable to keep the excitement from her
voice. "I have actual jobs lined up for my return. Isn't
that incredible? In fact, I did a photo shoot of a baby
before leaving, and the mum and dad were absolutely

gaga over the photos, or so they said. They ordered a lot, so it must have been true."

Luke seemed to go very still as she talked. Though he said all the right words, he didn't seem to share her excitement. She frowned.

"I thought you'd be happier," she admitted. "I've finally found my niche, just as you have."

"But it means you'll be going back to Dublin," he said, sounding vaguely disgruntled by that.

"It's where I live," she said. "I'll be going back. Did you think I came all this way intending to take up residency? I would never be so presumptuous, Luke. This is a surprise visit—nothing more."

"Of course it is," he said. "And it's a wonderful surprise. Don't mind me. I don't know why I reacted like that."

Ironically, Moira thought she knew. And for the first time since Luke had set eyes on her earlier in the evening, she felt a real glimmer of hope that this visit and what it might suggest about their future mattered to him as much as it did to her.

Though it had been well after midnight when Luke had finally managed to tear himself away from Moira after the party, he was back by seven in the morning to share breakfast with her. But when he arrived at the cottage, it was only his grandmother he found awake and stirring. She was making oatmeal and checking on the cranberry-orange scones she had in the oven. He leaned down to kiss her cheek.

"Shouldn't you be sleeping in this morning?" he asked, studying her worriedly for signs of exhaustion.

"Have you ever known me to sleep past six?" she asked.

He looked around and listened for any hint that others were out of bed. There was nothing. "I thought Dillon and Moira would be up by now with the time difference and all."

"Oh, believe me, they were up before dawn. I found a pot of tea brewed when I got up and a note that said they'd gone for a walk on the beach."

"Then they're not here?" he asked, not even trying to hide his disappointment.

She smiled at his reaction. "Not to worry. They'll be back any minute," she assured him. "Or you could go out to meet them."

"No, I'll wait here and help you get breakfast on the table." He went to work setting four places at the large kitchen table, then asked, "Should I scramble some eggs? Perhaps fry some bacon? They might be hungry for more than oatmeal or scones after their walk."

"Meaning you're the one who's truly hoping for a heartier meal," Gram said with a grin.

He shrugged. "I've a long day of hard work ahead."

"And you hate oatmeal," she countered. "Even when I filled it with raisins and brown sugar, then topped it with cream, you always turned up your nose."

"Nasty stuff," he said, then grinned back at her. "No offense."

She shook her head, her expression one of amused tolerance. "Get the eggs and bacon from the fridge."

He'd just set a large platter of eggs and bacon on the table when the back door opened and Dillon and Moira came in. Moira's cheeks were flushed from the early-morning chill in the air and her hair was tousled by the wind off the water. Her blue eyes were sparkling with delight, either from the walk or the sight of him. He couldn't help hoping it was the latter. Since spotting her the night before, his emotions had been in turmoil, a mix of pure happiness and panic that her presence meant so much.

"This is a surprise," she said.

"I thought you could come with me to the pub after breakfast," he said, then greeted Dillon, who was watching the two of them with amusement.

"Ah, he's finally noticed I'm in the room," Dillon commented.

"And I faded into the background when the door opened as well," his grandmother said.

"If the two of you are going to give me grief, I'll lure Moira away to Sally's for a peaceful breakfast," Luke threatened.

"Not after you've insisted on cooking all these eggs," Gram retorted. "Sit, everyone. Dillon and Moira, you have your choice of eggs and bacon, oatmeal or scones, or all of it."

"I've worked up an appetite," Dillon said. "I'll start with oatmeal and go from there."

"Eggs for me," Moira said. "And then a scone. They smell delicious, Mrs. O'Brien."

"It's Nell, please. I thought we'd established that in Ireland." She turned to Luke. "What do the two of you have planned for the day?"

"I'm going to show Moira the pub," Luke said. "And she's going to help me sort through all the potential musicians for the opening night and make a list of those I should book for later."

"And will I be sneaking a peek at this pub of yours today?" Dillon asked.

Nell reached over and rested a hand on his. "Since I've been prevented from stepping foot inside until the opening, I'm afraid you'll have to wait as well. I'm not about to stand on the sidewalk feeling left out."

Luke heard the teasing note in her voice, but he also sensed that his grandmother had a real yearning to be among the first to see the pub. Since her financial support by signing over his trust to him had made the pub possible, he relented.

"You should all come. You, too, Gram. After all, if it weren't for you, I could still be struggling to put the financing into place."

Dillon gave him a sharp look at that. "Nell's given you the backing for the pub?"

Luke sensed his disapproval. "I would never take her money," he said, regarding the older man with a steady gaze.

"It was a trust his grandfather had set aside for him," Nell explained. "It was Luke's money. He didn't even know about it. Nor did he ask for it. He was prepared to do this on his own, Dillon."

"I see," Dillon said, though he still didn't look entirely happy about what he'd heard.

Moira suddenly stood up. "Luke, perhaps we should be going. I know you have a lot you need to accomplish today." She turned to her grandfather. "And perhaps you could listen more closely to what Nell has said."

Luke smiled at the implied rebuke. "You needn't rush to my defense, you know."

But before the words were out of his mouth, she had grabbed her coat and was gone. By the time he'd kissed his grandmother goodbye and shrugged into his own jacket, she was already out of the yard and marching determinedly toward town.

When he caught up with her, she finally slowed her pace.

"Mind telling me what that was about?" he asked. "I don't think it had anything to do with me or the financial arrangements I made with Gram."

She glanced at him, then sighed. "I didn't like him jumping to conclusions and making judgments about you."

"If I'd done what he suspected, the judgment would have been fair enough," Luke said.

"But you didn't," she said heatedly. "You're not that kind of man. You'd never take advantage of your grandmother in the way he was thinking."

Luke frowned. "Tell me the truth, Moira. Are you worried that your grandfather won't approve of me?"

"I've never given two figs about anyone's opinion but my own," she said.

He smiled at her fierce tone. "I don't actually believe that, if you don't mind my saying so. I think you care a little too much. And I think what he said to me may have reminded you of things either he or your mother have said to you. It cut a little too close, didn't it?"

She scowled, then sighed. "How do you know me so bloody well after so little time?"

He reached out a hand and halted her, then turned her to face him. It took a full minute, but she finally lifted her gaze to meet his. "Because," he said gently, "when you're not being all prickly and defensive, you've let me see into your heart."

"I'm not sure how I feel about that," she said, catching him by surprise. "I wonder if it wouldn't be better if I'd remained a mystery."

Luke laughed at the plaintive note in her voice. "Too late," he told her, leaning down to cover her mouth with his and cut off any further words. Eventually she relaxed into the kiss, clinging to his shoulders, letting the heat build and swirl between them.

When he finally released her, her gaze was a bit dazed, but there was a smile on her lips. "It *is* too late, isn't it?"

He nodded. "I'm afraid you're stuck with me knowing you inside out."

She grinned at his smug certainty. "Well, I suppose we'll have to see about that. I imagine I can still come up with a few surprises, Luke O'Brien."

He laughed then. "I'll look forward to them."

And, heaven knows, he would. Perhaps more than he should.

6

Moira and Luke had almost reached Shore Road when the first of the O'Briens popped up in their path. Moira recognized Heather, who was obviously on her way to open her quilt shop. A mischievous grin spread across Heather's face when she spotted them.

"How did you enjoy your surprise?" she teased Luke. "Aren't you glad my husband didn't give it away?"

Moira regarded her curiously. "That would be Connor, right?" she asked, trying to get all of them straight again in her head.

"Connor, the blabbermouth," Heather confirmed just as the man in question left a parked car and headed in their direction. "We met Luke just outside of Nell's last night. Connor used the opportunity to taunt him about being late and almost gave away the big secret that you were waiting out back."

"Nobody told me it was supposed to be a big secret," Connor protested as he joined them. "Everyone's known about Dillon coming for weeks."

"But not about Moira," Heather reminded him, then

faced Moira. "Was it too overwhelming being surrounded by O'Briens last night?"

"I had a taste of it in Dublin," Moira reminded her. "It's getting easier."

"Well, they still scare the daylights out of me," Heather confided. "We should have coffee and I could give you all my tips for survival. If you're free now, I have time before I have to open my shop."

"She's coming with me to see the pub," Luke said.

Connor and Heather both looked stunned. "She's allowed to cross the threshold?" Connor asked indignantly. "Why not us, then?"

"Because she's special," Luke said. "While you two are nothing but nuisances. Go away, and don't try sneaking a look when I open the door."

Connor laughed. "Don't you know we go by every night and peer in the window to see what's been accomplished? Dad's crew has performed miracles in record time, it seems to me. It already looks nothing like the French bistro that was there before."

Moira chuckled at Luke's stunned reaction. "You didn't think to cover the window from all the prying eyes? Even *I* would have known to do that."

"I asked them to stay away and I trusted them to do it," Luke said, scowling fiercely at Connor and his wife. "Believe me, I'll correct that the minute we get inside. In fact, I'm going to Ethel's this minute to see if she has some rolls of brown paper I can use."

Heather beamed. "Good, then that will give Moira time to come to Sally's with me. You can join us there, or I'll walk her over to the pub when we're through." She winked at Moira. "Okay with you? I think Luke needs time to come to grips with more evidence of his family's sneakiness."

"I would love coffee," Moira admitted, though what she wanted even more was to get to know another woman who'd had to learn to cope with the tight-knit O'Briens.

"I'll join you," Connor said at once.

"No, you won't," Heather said. "Not that I wouldn't love another few minutes with you, but you're due in court in half an hour. Weren't you already grumbling about how late we were when we dropped little Mick off at day care?"

Connor glanced at his watch, muttered a curse, then dropped a kiss on his wife's cheek. "Love you. See you later."

Connor took off and, after casting a suspicious look at Heather, Luke left them at the door of Ethel's Emporium. "If you don't have her at the pub in a half hour, I'm coming to look for you," he warned.

Heather grinned at him. "Don't you think I'm perfectly capable of running through all your secrets in half an hour? I can probably do the condensed version in fifteen minutes and scare her off forever."

Luke sighed. "Please don't."

Heather patted his cheek. "Okay, since you asked so nicely."

It was only a few steps to reach Sally's, but by then they'd passed both Shanna's bookstore and Bree's flower shop and caught their attention. The next thing Moira knew, they were tagging along, so there were four of them tucked into a booth at the small café, coffee and croissants in front of them. The three O'Brien women wore expectant expressions.

"Am I supposed to entertain you now?" Moira asked dryly.

"It must seem that way," Bree said, laughing. "Sorry. Having been born into this family, I never thought how intimidating it must be to be an outsider."

"Trust me, it's terrifying," Shanna said.

"Amen to that," Heather added. "But once you've been accepted, Moira, it's like being in some kind of giant coed secret society. For someone like me, who was an only child, it's been pretty amazing."

"All you need to know," Bree told her, "is that while O'Briens in general stick together against the outside world, the women stick together against the men. I was the quiet one in my family, and with a father like Mick, I can't tell you what it meant to me to have Abby and Jess as backup."

Moira looked from one woman to another and wondered if they could be friends. They were so different from the girls she'd known back home. These were confident, successful women in their own right. They'd not only found, but established, careers they loved, while she was still terrified to hope that she might have found her own sense of direction with just a handful of praised photos on a pub wall and a few jobs lined up for her return to Dublin.

"How did you all turn out this way?" she blurted without thinking how it might sound.

Heather regarded her curiously. "What way?"

"Strong. Sure of yourselves. Oh, I can hold my own in an argument. Some have even called me a pain in the butt or worse." She gave them a knowing grin, perfectly aware of the terrible first impression she'd made on them in Ireland. Without waiting for them to fumble around trying to deny it, she added, "But that's not the same as knowing who you are and what you're meant to be."

All three of them startled her by laughing.

"Oh, Moira, is that how we seem to you?" Bree asked. "You should have been around when I came home from Chicago with my tail between my legs, having failed at being a playwright, which was, I thought, my dream. I opened Flowers on Main because flowers were absolutely the only other thing I knew anything about, thanks to Gram and her gardening."

"But you have a theater of your own here in town now," Moira recalled.

Bree nodded. "I got my legs back under me, in part thanks to Jake believing in me even more than I believed in myself."

"And the bookstore wasn't my first career," Shanna said. "Only after I'd failed abysmally at my first marriage did I leave both a boring job and my old life and come here to do this. I met Kevin before I even got the doors open. Talk about the ultimate unexpected bonus!"

Heather glanced from Bree to Shanna. "I'd forgotten how much we all have in common. I was teaching and hated it. When I got pregnant with little Mick, I quit and was living with Connor. I left him when it seemed unlikely he'd ever want to get married, but his mother encouraged me to come to Chesapeake Shores and settle here. It was even her idea that I open the quilt shop after she saw some quilts I'd made. It was the smartest decision I ever made. The family and the town welcomed me, even before Connor came around and concluded that marriage wasn't quite as dismal a prospect as he'd always thought."

Moira was stunned by the admissions. "Then it's not so terrible that I'm just now figuring out what I want to do?"

"When I was twenty-two, I was definitely still floundering," Heather said.

"And though I thought I knew what I wanted, I wasn't a success at it," Bree added.

"And I was busy making the worst mistake of my life by marrying the wrong man," Shanna said. "The only blessing that came from that is my stepson, Henry. Kevin and I have adopted him now. And *that's* a long story for another day."

Moira felt her mouth curve into a smile. "You have no idea what it's meant to me to have you tell me all this."

Heather glanced at her watch, then sighed. "And it's given us no time at all left to grill you about your relationship with Luke. Very clever," she said, giving Moira an approving look. "You'll do well with this family of meddlers."

"We'll have to do this again," Bree said. "Anytime you're with Luke at the pub and want a break, come by the shop. I'm usually there in the morning. Sometimes I have to head to the theater in the afternoon if we have a play in preproduction, which we do right now."

"But I'm always around," Shanna said. "And I have coffee at the bookstore."

"But I'm the closest," Heather said triumphantly. "I may not have coffee, but I'm less of a blabbermouth."

The comment drew hoots of laughter from her sisters-in-law.

"I'm serious," Heather protested. "It's Connor you're thinking of, who can't keep a secret."

"And who tells things to Connor?" Bree teased.

On the sidewalk outside, they parted, Bree to step into her shop next door to Sally's, then Shanna into hers a few feet down the block. Heather walked the rest of the way with Moira.

"Have we helped or only terrified you more?"

"You've truly helped," Moira said, thinking of her relief at the discovery that in a family of so many over-achievers, she wasn't so far behind the pace, after all. She wondered if Luke had seen the same thing about himself. Maybe when things settled down a bit, she could reassure him about that. Because after this morning, she was pretty sure it was true that the only person putting pressure on him to succeed was himself.

Luke had just taped the last piece of protective brown paper over the windows when he spotted Moira and Heather on the sidewalk outside. He stepped out to join them, looking anxiously toward Moira to see if she looked dazed. To his surprise, she looked happier than usual.

"What on earth was on the menu at Sally's that has you looking so cheerful?" he asked after Heather had gone.

"Serious girl talk," she confided.

"About me?"

"No, about them. It was a revelation. I'll tell you all about it sometime, but right now, I want to go inside and see this pub of yours."

Luke hesitated. "You understand that it's not finished, right? The bar we picked out isn't in place yet, and the tables and chairs haven't been delivered. Nor have the china and glassware. It's still pretty much a work in progress. I've only a battered table and chair in what will be my office."

She touched his lips to silence him. "Would you honestly rather I wait to see it?"

He drew in a deep breath, then shook his head. "No, now is good."

"Then why do you sound so terrified that I'll judge it and find it lacking?"

He didn't want to mention Kristen's dismissive attitude. It would imply that her opinion carried weight with him. Somehow, though, Moira saw through his silence.

"Has someone seen it and criticized?" she asked.

Since he didn't want to start off with a lie that could eventually come back to bite him in the butt, he nodded.

"Let me guess. It was that woman, the one who came to Ireland. Though I'd only a glimpse of her once, she struck me as the type to prefer a sophisticated martini bar to a congenial pub."

Luke regarded her with astonishment. "How on earth did you figure that out, after only seeing her once? I don't think I caught on that quickly."

"Because you were thinking with something other than your brain, I imagine," she said dryly. "I'm not Kristen. Let's establish that now and let me inside, okay?"

Luke smiled at her display of attitude. Maybe it covered a bit of insecurity, maybe not, but he decided to go with his gut. He held open the door. "After you. Stop just inside and let me find you a hard hat. The crew's at work, and there's no telling what kind of debris could be flying around."

As soon as they were inside with the door locked securely behind them, Luke started to step away to grab a couple of hard hats, but Moira reached for his hand and kept him in place.

"Luke, it's amazing," she whispered, awe in her voice.

He tried to see it as she saw it, but all he noted was the unpainted drywall only now being taped, the bare lighting awaiting the brass fixtures he'd chosen and a wooden floor covered by layers of sawdust and cluttered with construction tools.

"You're just saying that because you think it's what I need to hear," he chided.

"Nonsense! Look at it. The bar's going across the back, right? Remember, I've seen it. It'll be amazing there with that huge old mirror catching glimpses of the sea on a sunny day. Can you show me pictures of the tables you've chosen? And what about the china? I want to see that, too. Is the kitchen finished?"

He laughed at the flurry of questions, the genuine excitement in her voice. "The kitchen is about the only thing we didn't have to touch, so, yes, it's finished." He led the way.

She stepped inside and clapped with delight. "The stove is huge. And all this stainless steel looks brand-new."

"There was only the one tenant before me, and they didn't last long. It was considered in turnkey condition for a restaurant."

She touched the gas stove with near reverence. "I would love to cook a meal on this. The one at Peter's is a much older version."

Luke regarded her with surprise. "That's right, it is. You've cooked on it?"

"When we've been in a bind, yes. Waiting tables is my forte, but I have experience with a few dishes. Most of the pubs where I worked didn't have the luxury of a huge staff, so we all knew a little of everything. Grandfather actually thinks my cooking is better than the regular cook's." She shrugged. "Of course, he's bound to be biased."

Luke nodded slowly. "Good to know."

"Now show me the rest," she said. "Pictures of the tables and chairs, everything. And I'll want to see the paint color, too. Have you chosen it?"

"To be honest, that's why I was late last night. I was painting test strips on the back wall to pick the final color, but after a while they all started to looked the same."

"Show me," she commanded, her eyes alight with interest.

He led her to the wall where it looked as if a mad artist had been testing every color from palest turquoise to darkest green with all the shades of blue and green in between.

Moira went straight to a shade of azure. "This one," she said at once.

Luke immediately knew that she was right. He could already envision it on the walls, drawing the sea inside. "You're right," he said with amazement. "But why that one? What did you see that I missed last night?"

"For one thing, it was probably dim in here last night, so none of the colors looked the way they do right now. This one…" She tapped her finger against the chosen test stripe. "It's the color of the sky and sea on a sunny day. With white trim, it will be bright and cheerful."

"Most pubs tend to have a dark decor," he reminded her.

"Reflecting the too-often dreary Irish weather, if you ask me," Moira said. "People respond to cheerful, warm and welcoming. It's the difference between a seaside town here and one in Dublin, just as the rest of Chesapeake Shores is. I felt it the minute Mick drove us into town. I told him exactly that." She grinned. "I think he was pleased that I'd noticed."

"I'm sure he was," Luke said, equally pleased to have her impression of his hometown be so obviously positive.

She stepped closer and held his gaze. "Luke, it truly is going to be amazing," she told him, then stepped back before he could steal the kiss he was suddenly longing for. "Now, put me to work. Let me look at the things you've chosen to get a sense of your style, and then I'll get started sorting through those musicians. Do you have a CD player in your office?"

He nodded. "Are you sure you want to sit inside, rather than going out to explore the town?"

"I'm sure I'll see everything there is to see eventually. For now, I'm exactly where I want to be, as long as you'll promise to take a break for lunch. I believe I'd like to have it where we've a view of the water. Although your weather's nothing like Ireland's, I've been conditioned to take advantage of the sun whenever it appears."

Luke smiled at the simplicity of her request. "Then that's exactly what we'll we do."

He wrote down the websites from which he'd ordered furniture and supplies for the pub and gave her model numbers. He stacked the CDs beside her and showed her how to work the player, then he left her to it, marveling as he went back into the main room to work that she'd fit in so readily. Who on earth would have guessed that the impossible woman he'd met just a few months ago would turn out to be both undemanding and soothing to have around?

Nell drove Dillon into town just before lunchtime. She could hardly wait to show off both the community and the way O'Briens were so much a part of it. She found a parking spot on Main Street right in front of Flowers on Main. Bree had her usual colorful assortment of bouquets lined up in buckets on the sidewalk and a window display of more formal arrangements. It delighted Nell that her granddaughter had learned the art of flower arranging from her and made a success of it.

"This is Bree's shop," Dillon said as they exited the car.

She regarded him with surprise. "You remembered!"

He laughed. "It was just yesterday when Mick was bragging about it as we drove into town."

"Ah, yes. I'd forgotten that. I probably shouldn't say this, because it's surely bragging, but Bree learned everything she knows about flowers from me," Nell confided. "Of course, I must admit the student has surpassed the master now. Her arrangements are quite dramatic compared to the simple ones I do at home."

"Don't be selling yourself short," Dillon scolded. "The bright flowers in your cottage are a welcoming touch. Better yet, I can see that they've come from your own garden." He studied her. "Is that something you enjoy doing, Nell?"

She nodded. "My knees are getting a little creaky, so getting up and down is trickier these days, but I can't imagine a time when I can't care for my garden."

"You can always hire help and supervise."

"It's not the same," she said sadly. "Not at all. Jake would come and do whatever I ask, but I like the feel of the earth between my fingers and knowing that I've coaxed something from seed to blossom."

"Or you could boss me around a bit," he offered. "I've some experience in the landscaping business, you know." He winked at her. "You might enjoy telling me what to do."

She laughed then. "I might at that. Shall we go inside and say hello to Bree?"

"Of course," he said at once. "I want to tell her how impressed I am."

Once they'd spent a few minutes with Bree, Nell led the way to Shanna's bookstore next door. She had to admit that she was relieved to take a seat in the café area and accept the cup of Earl Grey tea that Shanna brought her while Dillon explored the shelves for a supply of books about the region.

"I have most of those at home," Nell told him when he showed her his selections. "Thomas sees to it that I read everything on this area. He's always turning up with the latest book he feels supports his cause to save the bay."

"But I want to give Shanna the sale, and these can be shipped over to Dublin, so I'll have them on my own shelves."

His words sent a cold chill through her. "Are you already so anxious to get back home?"

He looked stunned by the question. "Good heavens, no. Why would you ask such a thing?"

She hesitated, then said, "The truth is that I've been hoping to convince you to stay longer. I didn't want to broach it just yet, but there it is." She met his gaze. "Will you at least consider it?"

Dillon reached across the table and covered her hand with his. "I thought we agreed—"

She cut him off. "I know what we agreed," she said impatiently, "but sometimes things change. People change."

Worry carved deeper lines in his forehead. "Nell, this isn't the first time I've sensed that something's wrong. Will you tell me what it is? Please. I'm worried. Are you ill?"

She sighed at having been caught so easily. "It's nothing, really. Nothing specific, anyway. When I came home, for the first time ever, my blood pressure was high. The doctor put me on medication and insisted I monitor myself. I know, in the overall scheme of things, something like that shouldn't be a shock at my age, but it was to me. After years of avoiding most medications, I'm now taking something that leaves me light-headed and tired. All of a sudden, I feel every one of my years. It's shaken me a little—far more than it should, given what a simple remedy there is for it."

"Has the medicine worked?"

She nodded. "The doctor's pleased. Other than the annoying side effects, I should be as well. Still, I know how these things go. First it's blood pressure medicine, then something for cholesterol. The next thing I know, I'll have an array of bottles on my kitchen table and one of those little daily pill containers so someone reliable can sort them all out and be sure I take them on schedule."

Dillon looked surprisingly relieved by her admission. He reached in his pocket and pulled out exactly the sort of pill container she'd just described.

"You mean one like this?" he asked. "I've had it for years. No one's filling it for me just yet, and I don't imagine that'll be necessary for a good many years to come as long as I keep my wits about me. I imagine you'll be in full control for a very long time as well, given that stubborn streak you O'Briens are known for."

She looked from the rectangular plastic container to his bright and sparkling eyes. "Mountain out of a molehill?" she asked.

He nodded. "That's the way I see it."

"I'm afraid I was seeing it as the first step on a slippery slope."

"Ah, Nell, don't give in so easily. There are far too many of us who need you right here and you're not the type to abandon ship."

"I never thought I was," she admitted. "I'll take what you've said to heart." She met his gaze. "But I still wouldn't mind it if you'd consider staying longer, as long as you'd like, in fact."

"Now that," he said readily, "would be my pleasure."

For the first time since the doctor had completely disconcerted her with that prescription and his dire warnings about ignoring her hypertension, she felt hopeful again. In fact, she was suddenly as optimistic about the future as she'd been when she'd first reconnected with Dillon in Dublin.

And, she thought wryly, she'd have to tell Luke

and his mother, they could stop hovering. The pair of them weren't nearly as subtle as they clearly thought they were.

7

Luke picked up sandwiches, sweet-potato fries and drinks from Panini Bistro, then led Moira to a bench across the street so they would be near the water while they ate. On a weekday in early spring, the narrow strip of sand was mostly deserted, and the only people out for a stroll were the locals. They had the view mostly to themselves.

"Would you have preferred eating in a restaurant?" he asked her. "I could have taken you to Brady's. It's on the water."

"No, this is exactly what I wanted," she said, unwrapping her sandwich and taking a bite. "Perfect. The jalapeños were a nice touch."

He chuckled. "I remembered how you love spicy things. That Indian curry we had just about took the top of my head off."

"As it was meant to do," she teased. "And there's a lesson in there as well. Spicy food encourages people to order more drinks."

"Pub food isn't known for its kick," he pointed out.

"That doesn't mean you couldn't make a few adjustments to liven up the menu."

"And give Gram heart failure?" he asked, feigning a scandalized tone.

"I'm sure she'd approve of a change here and there to make the menu more modern, as long as you don't alter the traditional dishes too much. Why don't I run the idea past her when she and my grandfather show up for their inspection of the place?"

"Sure," Luke said readily, oddly pleased that she wanted to take the initiative. "I wonder what's kept them. I expected them to be nosing around long before now."

"I imagine they've stopped to visit with the entire family en route. She'll want to show off all the O'Brien businesses. It's impressive how intertwined your family is with this town. They're an important part of the business community as well. Taken together, it goes far beyond your uncle creating Chesapeake Shores."

"True on all counts," he said. "And no one in my family is short-winded, either. It could be late afternoon when they finally get around to me."

"Or just now," she said, nodding in the direction of the pub.

Luke spotted his grandmother and Dillon on the sidewalk. She was giving the door a frustrated jiggle. Luke stood up.

"Over here, Gram! We'll be right there."

"No need," Dillon called back. "We'll join you. I'd like a closer look at the bay from here."

He guided Nell across the busy road, then patted the remaining spot on the bench. "You sit. I'll just wander closer to the water."

"Why don't I walk with you?" Moira suggested. "I wouldn't mind sticking a toe in to see if it's as freezing cold as the sea is back home."

As they went off, Luke glanced at his grandmother. "Have you been giving him the high-priced, all-inclusive O'Brien tour? It must seem to an outsider as if we own the whole town. Moira was just saying something very much like that."

She laughed. "So far, we've only been to Bree's and Shanna's. Dillon made all the appropriate noises of approval at the flower shop, then bought out half of Shanna's supply of books about this region. Thomas will be over the moon to have another convert to his cause."

"Does Dillon seem to like it here so far?" he asked, then saw the sparks of delight in Gram's eyes. "Or do I even need to ask? Has he already agreed to stay longer?"

"He has," she said. "It wasn't even a discussion. I just suggested it, and he agreed at once. We'll have to work out the details at some point, especially with Moira's schedule." She met his gaze. "I don't suppose you've been wise enough to try to persuade her to stay, have you?"

Luke shook his head. "Don't push. I'm just growing used to the fact that she's here at all."

She frowned. "You're not happy about it?"

"I'm delighted about it," he said. "But I don't know what will happen next. I don't even have time to stop and think much beyond tomorrow or the pub opening at the end of the month."

"Have you thought about what you'd like to happen?"

"Maybe, in a pie-in-the-sky kind of way," he admitted. "But it's not so simple."

She reached over and clasped his hand. "Yes," she said solemnly. "It is exactly that simple. It's only when your head gets in the way of what your heart wants that things get complicated. If you take no other advice from me, Luke, take this. Listen to your heart."

He smiled at her obvious conviction. "I would if I could hear it," he said. "Right now all the noise in my head is drowning it out. I have lists of my lists these days. Once I'm past this opening and that part of my life is on an even keel, I'll be able to hear more clearly."

"As long as there's not another excuse then, and another after that."

"No," he promised. "There won't be. I spent a lot of my life just drifting along, but now the path before me is straight and I can just about see to the end of it."

"Is it Moira who's waiting there?" she asked.

He smiled. "Could be. I'll know for sure when I get there, won't I?"

"Okay, then," she said with satisfaction. "I see our guests are heading this way. Let's go over and take a look at this pub of yours. I have to admit that I'm beyond curious."

Luke took her elbow and led the way. "I hope you won't be disappointed."

"As if I could ever be disappointed at anything you've poured your heart and soul into. What did Moira think?"

"She thinks it's amazing, of course," he said with a grin. "And since she's never hesitated to speak her mind, I'm taking it on faith that she meant every word."

As soon as Moira and Dillon had joined them, Luke

unlocked the door and stepped aside. Since the crew wasn't back yet, he let them enter without worrying about hard hats. It hardly mattered, though, because just as Moira had done earlier, his grandmother took one step, then halted.

"Oh, Luke, it's going to be fabulous," she said enthusiastically.

"You can tell that from here, just inside the door?"

She laughed. "I could tell it the instant I saw that color on the back wall. Did you not notice it's the one I have in one of the guest rooms at the cottage? I chose it because it brings the sea inside."

He turned to Moira. "Your room?"

She shook her head.

"Mine," Dillon said. "And Nell's exactly right. It's the perfect color."

"I told you," Moira said delightedly. "Now you'll have to accept that my taste is impeccable."

Luke slipped an arm around her waist and kissed her cheek. "Never doubted it. Why do you think it's already on the wall?"

"But I know you have at least two gallons in other shades sitting in the back, just in case you change your mind," she teased.

"They'll be gone before the day is out," he promised. "Now, come in the rest of the way, Gram. Maybe you'd like to hear some of the demo CDs that Moira has chosen for possible music for opening night?"

"I'd love it," Nell said.

"I'll turn the speakers up while you and Grandfather look around," Moira said.

Within half an hour, not only did Luke have their enthusiastic approval, but he had a final selection for the singer and band for the opening. The choice had been unanimous. It was one more thing to tick off on that endless to-do list of his. At this rate, he might actually get this place open on schedule.

He glanced at Moira, who had her head together with Nell's as they debated his choice of china, and smiled. Apparently the design he'd chosen had been dismissed as boring and the order canceled. He'd decided it was a small price to pay to have them so happily involved.

Thinking of his grandmother's earlier advice, he thought it was entirely possible that once he had O'Briens up and running successfully, he'd put his mind to the rest of his future and whether this was, in fact, the woman he increasingly wanted to share it with. In just the past twenty-four hours he'd become aware that the decision might be far easier than he'd ever imagined such a momentous one could be.

Mick dropped by the family's real estate management company office on Main Street, hoping to catch up with his brother. As usual, he found Susie at her desk, but no sign of Jeff.

"Where's your father gone now?" he grumbled.

Susie gave him an amused look. "He's left just to annoy you."

Mick tried to control his smile, but couldn't. "That sassy mouth of yours is going to get you into trouble one of these days, young lady."

Susie laughed. "But I live for those moments," she responded. "Is there something I can do for you?"

"Not really. I just thought your father and I should have a chat about Luke and Moira."

"No, you shouldn't," she said very firmly. "You

should leave them alone, stay miles and miles away from them, keep your mouths firmly shut." She gave him a penetrating look. "Am I getting through to you?"

"You're making your opinion plain, if that's what you mean," he said. "Do you honestly believe it will make a difference?"

She sighed. "Sadly, no."

He studied his niece intently. "You feeling okay?"

"I'm feeling great," she said. "All clear of cancer on my last follow-up."

"That's great news, darlin'. You and Mack given any more thought to adopting children?"

She gave him a resigned look. "There are absolutely no topics that are off-limits to you, are there, Uncle Mick?"

"Not when it comes to family," he said easily. "And I know you're perfectly capable of telling me to butt out, if you don't want me to know something."

"Butt out," she said.

"Is that because there's something to tell?" he asked. "Or because there isn't? Is Mack balking? I know he had his doubts about being a good father, but we all know better. I could convince him that he'll be a fine one."

Susie shook her head. "Mack's on board. I'm the holdout. And that is all I intend to say. This is between me and my husband. It's not a group decision."

Mick relented. "Fair enough. When is Jeff due back?"

"Sadly, he's just parking the car out front, which means he won't be able to avoid you," she said.

Mick leaned down and kissed her cheek. "Always a pleasure to see you."

Susie chuckled. "Maybe from your perspective," she said, just as Jeff came in.

"You here to see me?" he asked Mick.

"I am, but I've been catching up with your daughter in the meantime."

"Be careful, Dad. He's on a mission," Susie warned as she grabbed her purse and headed for the door. "I'm going to Sally's to grab a sandwich. Call me on my cell phone if he gets to be too much for you to handle."

"I've been dealing with Mick since birth. I know all his tricks," Jeff responded. In his office, he gave Mick a knowing look. "I'm guessing this is about Luke and Moira."

Mick regarded him with amazement. "How'd you figure that out? It didn't surprise me that Susie did, but you're usually less intuitive."

"Because everything's running smoothly at the real estate company. There are no family crises that I'm aware of. That leaves my son's social life for you to fret over."

"Tell me you're happy about the way things are," Mick said. "Is Moira the woman you'd have chosen for him?"

"She beats out Kristen Lewis by a country mile," Jeff retorted, then sighed. "But no, probably not. She was a hard woman to warm up to when we were in Dublin."

"She was at that," Mick agreed. "She seemed different when I picked up Dillon and her at the airport yesterday. She was a bit more mellow."

"She was the same at Ma's last night," Jeff added. "And Luke was obviously delighted to see her. Maybe, just this once, the rest of us could stay out of it and let them work through things on their own."

Mick lifted a brow at the suggestion. "That's the difference between you and me. You're content to sit on the sidelines. I like to take charge and be sure things work out for the best."

"That's the problem," Jeff said. "You don't always know what's best, any more than I do." He gave Mick a knowing look. "This is really about Ma, isn't it? She's told you to steer clear of her relationship with Dillon, so that's left only Luke and Moira for you to focus on."

Mick sighed with frustration. "When did you get to be so smart? Yes, it's driving me crazy the way those two seem to be getting closer every minute. Did you see the way Ma was looking at Dillon last night? She looked like a young girl with her cheeks all pink and her eyes filled with sparks."

Jeff chuckled. "I think we're meant to be glad about that. We want her to be happy, don't we?"

"Yes, of course," Mick said, disgruntled just the same.

"Mick, I don't think she's going to pack up and move to Ireland," Jeff consoled him. "If anything, I think this visit is the first step toward Dillon spending more time here."

Mick wasn't entirely reassured. "You don't think she wants to marry him, do you?"

"Would that be so awful?"

Mick thought it might be, especially if it meant she walked out on the family to live in Ireland. He thought Jeff was wrong in ruling out that possibility. She'd been happier there over Christmas than he'd seen her in years. How much of that had to do with Dillon and how much with being back in the country where she'd spent so many happy summers with her grandparents? Sometimes people reached a certain age and grew nostalgic about the past. Nell could be all caught up in those old memories and wind up making choices she'd regret.

"You know Ma is going to do whatever she wants to do," Jeff said quietly.

"I know," Mick said grimly. "But I don't have to like it."

"Maybe not, but you do have to respect it."

Mick sighed. "I know that, too."

Jeff studied him, then asked, "Feeling better?"

Mick put aside his worries for now and forced a grin. "Busting your chops always improves my mood," he told his brother.

Jeff laughed. "Glad to be of service."

"I suppose I'll wander around and check on the progress at Luke's now," he said, already heading for the door.

"No meddling," Jeff called after him.

"Yeah, yeah, I hear you," Mick responded, chuckling. Next to building great little communities, meddling was what he lived for. Thank goodness for a large family that gave him so many opportunities. If he was careful, it usually meant there was only one person at a time annoyed with him.

Jet lag had caught up with Moira. She'd left Luke's to get out from underfoot and crossed the street to sit by the bay, but the warmth of the sun had her seriously close to nodding off right out there in public. Rather than giving in, she went back to the pub to let Luke know she intended to walk back to Nell's cottage.

He frowned when she told him. "Of course you're exhausted," he said. "What was I thinking to keep you down here all day? I should have sent you home with Dillon and Gram."

"I wasn't ready then," she said. "But just now across the street, I could barely keep my eyes open."

"And by the time you've walked to Gram's, you'll be wide-awake, when what you really need is a nap." He took her arm. "Come on. Let's go."

"You don't have time to walk me there and then come back," she protested.

"No, but I do have time to walk you around the corner to my place and see you settled in my bed."

Despite her exhaustion, she felt a little frisson of excitement at his words. "Really?" she said suggestively. "Now?"

He laughed. "There'll be none of that this afternoon, Moira. You need to rest. I need to work. This is a perfectly innocent offer."

"More's the pity," she teased.

"You told me I was going to have to work to get you back into my bed again," he reminded her. "Have you changed your mind already? If so, I suppose I could spare some time this afternoon if the right offer came along."

There was an undeniable gleam in his eyes that told her he was more than eager to do just that. She decided that as attractive as the broad hint was, it was wise to pass on it for now.

"I think I'll hold out for the time when there's more

opportunity for real romance," she said. "But I won't say no to a nap at your place if it's close by."

"Just around the corner," he told her. "It's above the real estate office. It was Susie's apartment before she and Mack married. I took it over from her. It's tiny and not very fancy, but you'll be comfortable, I think."

He led her into an alley behind the shops, then up the stairs to an apartment that overlooked the town green. It had an open living room, dining room and kitchen, and a single bedroom and bath, but it was just right for a bachelor, she thought. Some of the touches were feminine, a dried-flower arrangement here, a collection of photos there, along with some plump, fluffy pillows and a soft throw tossed on the sofa.

"Were these left behind by Susie? Or has someone helped you decorate?"

Luke held her gaze, clearly aware of what she was really asking. "Kristen was never here," he told her. "She has her own place. We spent our time together there."

"Your choice or hers?" she asked before she could stop herself.

"Mine, if you must know. I knew we were never meant to last, and I didn't want this apartment crowded with memories of her wherever I looked. You're the only woman I've had up here, Moira, and that's the truth."

She wanted desperately to believe him, to revel in being the first to share this space with him, even briefly. She walked to the window and looked out. There were mums strolling on the green with their children. A few kids were kicking around a soccer ball. It reminded her so much of home that she couldn't help smiling. Luke, standing behind her, obviously noticed her reflection in the glass.

"What?" he asked. "Are you pleased by what I said or is it something else?"

"I was just thinking how our worlds aren't all that different. Somehow I thought they would be, but looking out there at the green, I could just as easily be looking at the neighborhood park in my hometown outside of Dublin."

"Then you already feel at home here?" he asked.

She turned to face him, so close she could almost feel his breath on her cheek, the heat from his body pulling her. "At this moment, I do," she said. "But that's because of you, Luke, not the scenery."

It was the most daring admission she'd ever made to anyone, letting someone see into her heart.

He smiled at her words. "I'm glad about that."

Filled with reluctance, she said, "You should probably go back to work. You've still got a lot to accomplish this afternoon."

"Or I could stay here with you," he offered yet again. "That appeals to me more."

"And the work? I don't want to be a distraction, Luke."

"You were a distraction before you ever arrived," he admitted.

She regarded him with delight. "How so?"

"I couldn't get you out of my head," he admitted with a shrug. "Maybe it will be easier now that you're here. I won't be wondering all the time where you are and who you're with."

"Surely you weren't jealous?" she said, genuinely shocked.

"Not jealous exactly," he corrected. "Just missing you and arguing with myself about it."

She laughed. "I was doing the same thing. I'd vowed not to, but I couldn't help it. It was pitiful, actually. Even my grandfather felt sorry for me. I think that's why he invited me along."

"Or perhaps, like Mick and Gram, he enjoys a bit of matchmaking."

Moira thought about that, then laughed. "You know, I think he might. I was never around him much before, so I wouldn't have seen that side of him, but I can see it now. Do you know he's even been trying to stir up interest between Peter and my mum."

"Kiera and Peter?" Luke asked, clearly startled. "No way!"

Moira nodded. "I was as shocked as you are, but I saw signs of his success with my own eyes the night before we left Dublin. I think Peter's been on board for years, if Grandfather is to be believed. My mum is less eager. I doubt she'll give in easily, but she may finally be more open to it."

"I'd never in a million years have seen it," Luke said. "I think the whole matchmaking gene skipped right over me. Even Susie and Mack, who were dancing around each other for years, could have kept at it for a dozen more before I caught on that they just needed a nudge to get over the hurdle."

"Maybe you'll be better at it now," Moira suggested.

"Why?"

"Because of us," she said. "It's as if I needed the experience of falling wildly in love before I saw the possibilities all around me."

"Wildly in love?" Luke said.

Though he didn't sound terrified by her choice of words, Moira blushed furiously. "Sorry, I shouldn't have put it that way."

"Was it the truth?" he asked.

She nodded, her breath caught in her throat.

"Then it wasn't a mistake to say it," he said, pulling her into his arms and sealing his mouth over hers.

Instantly, Moira was wide-awake, her blood humming through her veins. When he pulled away and studied her with a questioning look, she swore under her breath. "I promised myself it was too soon for this," she murmured.

He smiled. "Is it a promise you're thinking of breaking?"

She nodded slowly. "It's a promise I've already forgotten," she told him as she wrapped her legs around his waist and let him take her into his bedroom.

As they fell into his bed together, she thought that this might not be the reason she'd come all the way across the ocean to Chesapeake Shores, but it was definitely at the top of the list of reasons that could keep her here.

8

Luke had been wrong. Having Moira here was going to be an even bigger distraction than he could possibly have imagined. Now that she was back in his bed, responding to his every touch, he was remembering just what it felt like to make love to her. He didn't want to stop—not this afternoon, not ever!

Though he knew it was an inappropriate guy thing to make comparisons, he couldn't helping thinking how different it was to be with her than it had been with Kristen. Kristen might have been more knowledgeable, more cleverly inventive and less inhibited, but there was something so practiced about it all.

With Moira each time felt like an adventure of new discoveries. She was delighted with every sensation he aroused, curious about what effect she might have on him with this touch or that. She could drive him over the edge with her innocent explorations. He knew he wasn't her first, and yet he felt as if he were.

Still trying to catch his breath, he fell back on the bed, pulling her on top of him. "Do you have any idea how amazing you are?" he asked when he could finally speak.

"Me?" she asked, looking genuinely surprised and pleased.

"Yes, you. I don't know what it is, but you completely take my breath away."

She beamed at his compliment. "Then isn't it lovely that you do the same for me? I never expected to feel like this about anyone, Luke. Never." Her expression turned serious. "I think it's because I was far too successful at keeping most people at arm's length with that nasty temper of mine."

He smiled at the understatement. She'd been a tyrant, no question about it. "I can see how that might happen," he said. "It's a wonder I looked beyond it myself."

"It's what drew you to me," she corrected. "You'd never had such a challenge before. You said so yourself." A cloud passed over her face. "Am I too easy now, do you suppose?"

"Absolutely not," he said, drawing her face down so he could kiss her thoroughly. "I wish I could stay right here with you," he murmured with regret.

"But you have work to do and miles to go before you sleep," she said.

He regarded her with surprise. "Robert Frost?"

She laughed at his amazement. "I'm not entirely uneducated, you know."

"Of course not. I just wasn't sure your Irish schools would be teaching American poets."

"Have you studied Shakespeare?" she inquired tartly.

"To my everlasting regret, yes."

She smiled. "Well, there you go. Literature travels, Luke."

"For better or worse," he mumbled as he climbed from the bed.

"Oh, I don't know. Another look at *The Taming of the Shrew* might serve you well," she teased. "Some say it could have been written about me."

He laughed, but then thought he detected a hint of worry beneath the taunting words. He went back to the bed. "You won't be too much for me, Moira, mood swings and all."

She smiled slowly. "Good to know, since turning into a saint overnight could be beyond me."

He showered and dressed, then took a lingering look at her, still tangled in his sheets, several delectable curves bare. "Will you be here when I get back?"

She hesitated, then shook her head. "I'll need to get back to your grandmother's. I don't want to be rude by staying out all night on my second night here."

"I could call and let her know you have plans," he suggested. "That you're with me. Believe me, she'll understand." He was struck by a thought. "Or is it Dillon you're worried about?"

"No, I imagine he'd understand as well. It's me, to be honest. It's different being with you here, Luke."

He frowned at that. "How so?"

"More serious, somehow. In Ireland, we were mostly on neutral turf as we traveled. This is your world. I'm scared to discover if I'll truly fit in or if you'll even want me to, especially now."

"Why now?"

"Because there are jobs waiting for me back home, photography assignments that could actually lead to a real career. It's my first chance to be successful at something entirely on my own." She held his gaze.

"You of all people know how much that matters, how much dedication is required."

Despite his own sense that the timing for them was off, he was taken aback by her unexpected eagerness to get home to Dublin. And yet how could he not understand the draw of a newly discovered passion?

He sat beside her on the edge of the bed. "I don't know what the future holds for us, Moira. I do know you're important to me." He studied her. "Can that be enough for now? Can we figure this out as we go? What I do know is that when the time comes for you to go— as you planned—I know I'll regret it."

"But will you want me to stay?"

"Can you honestly tell me you'd want to?" he replied. "Weren't you the one just saying how much awaits you back home?"

His attempt to turn the tables on her clearly backfired, because she turned away and began gathering her clothes.

She finally turned to face him. "That doesn't mean I don't want you to fight to keep me here," she said in a contrary tone.

He might have laughed, but it was obvious she couldn't see the humor in the standoff. She was staring hard at him, her frustration plain.

"It's easy enough to say how much you care when you've just climbed from this bed," she grumbled. "But even I know it doesn't guarantee a future. We obviously need time to figure things out."

"We only have a month," he said, his own frustration mounting. "Let's not waste it being at odds over things we can't control."

"We had only a few weeks in Ireland," she reminded

him. "A month seems like an eternity stretching out ahead of us."

"Not to me," he admitted. Though he wasn't yet ready to admit it to her or even to himself, he was beginning to wonder if even forever might not be enough. He also knew he needed to figure it out, because right at this moment, his mixed signals could easily drive her straight back to that fledgling career awaiting her in Dublin. After that, it could well be too late.

When he got back to the pub, Luke found both his brother and his uncle there waiting for him, and looking unhappy.

"Where the devil have you been?" Matthew demanded. "I thought this was meant to be a rush job, but if you can't even stick around, why should Mick's crew be putting in overtime?"

Luke winced. "Was there a problem? Everything seemed to be under control when I left. It's not as if I'm doing the construction myself or even know that much about it. The two of you are in charge of that."

"You still should have been here," Matthew grumbled stubbornly.

Luke turned to his uncle. "I suppose you share my brother's opinion that I've been lax by taking a couple of hours off."

Mick chuckled. "Actually, I'm more curious about what was so important that it took you away from here. I'm guessing it was Moira."

Matthew looked startled for a moment, then stared hard at Luke. "Was that it? Did you go off with impossible Moira?"

"Stop calling her that!" Luke told him heatedly.

"How many times have you called her that very thing yourself?" Matthew asked.

"It's not the same when I say it," Luke said, even though he knew he probably sounded ridiculous. What else could he add—that he said it with love? Not likely. "Now, has there been a crisis here while I was gone or not?"

"Oh, don't mind your brother," Mick said. "Now that he's happily married to Laila, he's forgotten what it's like to court a woman. And, as I learned way too late, it doesn't hurt to keep your priorities in order and pay proper attention to someone you care about."

Luke gave his brother a closer look. "Have you forgotten what it's like to be in love so soon, Matthew, or is there trouble in paradise?" he speculated. "Is that it? Are you and Laila fighting over something? Shouldn't you still be in the honeymoon phase?"

"Even in the honeymoon phase, people have things to work out," Matthew said tightly. "And I do not intend to discuss my relationship with my wife with the two of you."

Luke exchanged a look with his uncle, but wisely kept silent.

It was Mick whose teasing quickly turned to visible concern. "If not us, who else should you turn to? We love both of you."

"Not talking about this," Matthew said. "I just came by to see if the bar had been delivered and if it fit into the snug space we'd left for it. I thought that was a priority."

Stunned by the reminder, Luke whirled around and looked behind him. How the devil could he have forgotten about the bar being delivered? Well, he knew how:

Moira. He looked at the huge mahogany bar with its
shiny brass trim, polished wood and detailed carving
and couldn't seem to stop the smile that spread across
his face.

"My God, it's perfect!" he murmured. "Suddenly I
have a genuine Irish pub."

"You do, indeed," Mick said, his approval plain.

"And it's the perfect size," Luke added. "See, Matthew, all your worrying was for nothing."

"Not for nothing," Matthew retorted. "I had to shave
off the doorjamb to the office and the molding on the
floor to slide it in there. Don't ever get any ideas about
moving it."

"Why would I? It's in the perfect spot." Luke moved
closer to inspect it. "And not a mark on it. It's none the
worse for the trip. Even the mirror survived without the
faintest crack. What do you really think, Matthew? Put
aside your annoyance with me and tell the truth."

"It looks as if it's always been meant to be there," his
brother admitted grudgingly. "Mick's right. It's turned
it into a genuine pub. Whatever else you do in here will
only complement that."

Luke could hardly wait to show it off. It made him
even more anxious for opening night. He faced his
uncle. "Are we on schedule?"

"The electrician will be here tomorrow. The final
touches on the molding and painting will be done by
the weekend, and then it'll be all yours to finish up."

"That quickly?" Luke asked, barely able to contain
his excitement…and his nerves.

"We've a deadline to meet, don't we?" Mick said.
"Word's already out that you're opening to the public
three weeks from Friday. It's a shame we didn't start all

this in time for a St. Patrick's Day launch, but having it ready before Memorial Day weekend will do. It'll get a buzz going among the locals before all the summer people and tourists descend. Have you thought of creating discount coupons for the guests at Jess's inn? She mentioned the idea to me earlier today."

"A great idea," Luke enthused. "I'll see if Trace can design something. He was asking if I wanted him to do ads for me for Mack's paper, so he can work on those at the same time."

"And having the whole family involved is another smart plan," Mick said approvingly. "O'Briens are never happier than when we have a chance to help out one of our own."

"To say nothing of the fact that even if we're the only ones to show up for the private grand opening for family and community leaders on that Thursday night, you'll have quite a mob," Matthew said.

The offhand comment set off panic. "Why would you be the only ones to show up? What did you mean by that?"

His brother clapped him on the back. "Sorry. I couldn't resist. It was just a comment to serve you right after you snuck out of here in the middle of the day."

"Well, it wasn't funny," Luke said. "I'm nervous enough about this as it is." So much depended on the pub's success, not just the self-respect he craved, but the approval of his family, which sometimes mattered even more.

"Chalk it up to my overall mood," Matthew said. He sighed. "Now I'd better head on home and face the music."

"What music would that be?" Mick inquired, always quick to seize on an opening.

Matthew actually laughed at the not-unexpected question. "Do you never tire of meddling?"

"Not once," Mick said without apology. "In this family, it's called caring."

"Trust me, more of us call it annoying," Matthew said, and walked out before the discussion could be prolonged.

Luke glanced at his uncle and saw that there was genuine concern on Mick's face.

"Whatever it is, he and Laila will work it out," Luke told Mick. "Let it be."

Mick sighed. "I suppose you're right. He warned me away emphatically enough. Even I can take a hint." He gave Luke's shoulder a squeeze. "Stop worrying. You're going to have a hit with this place. I'm proud of you."

"Thanks, Uncle Mick."

But as his uncle left, Luke couldn't help wishing that those words had come from his father.

Moira straightened up Luke's bed and the apartment before heading back to Nell's cottage after her nap. The walk revived her, but she knew it was being with Luke that had put the color in her cheeks and the spring in her step. Since she wasn't entirely sure how she herself felt about the afternoon's events, she hoped neither Nell nor her grandfather were good at seeing through the sedate demeanor she intended to project.

"And what have you been doing this afternoon?" Nell inquired when she walked into the kitchen.

Moira immediately felt the quick rise of heat to

her face and knew Nell had seen it as well, since she promptly chuckled.

"Perhaps I shouldn't have asked," Nell said. "I hope you're hungry. I've made chicken and dumplings. It's Luke's favorite. I spoke to him earlier. He'll be over as soon as he can get away from the pub." She gave Moira an expectant look. "Would you like me to teach you the recipe?"

Moira saw Nell's strategy. She was trying to guess whether Moira would have a need for knowing Luke's favorite foods.

"I'm always eager to learn a new recipe. I can try it out on the customers at McDonough's when I get back home."

Nell frowned at that. "Or you could try it out on the customers at O'Briens right here in Chesapeake Shores," she suggested.

Moira immediately shook her head. "This is Luke's business venture. I'm not a real part of it."

"That's not how it seemed to me earlier today. He was taking your advice on the music to heart, and he listened to you when you told him he should serve on different dishes."

"That suggestion came from you as well," Moira said. "And we all agreed on the best band."

Obviously sensing that Moira was vaguely out of sorts, Nell pointed to the table. "Sit."

"I was thinking of a shower before dinner," Moira protested.

"And you'll have time for it. First, I want to understand what's made you feel as if you're an outsider. Did you and Luke argue this afternoon? I had the impression when you came in that quite the opposite was the case."

Filled with reluctance, Moira sat as she'd been told to do. She knew her grandfather would consider it rude to do otherwise, even though she truly didn't want to have this conversation with Luke's grandmother.

Nell poured her a cup of tea, then offered Moira cookies. "Conversation goes best with something sweet, I think," she said.

Moira accepted an oatmeal raisin cookie, then proceeded to reduce it to crumbs on the napkin in front of her. Nell gave her an amused look.

"It works better if you actually eat it," she commented.

Moira glanced at the pile of crumbs, winced and then tried to force a smile. "Sorry."

"What did Luke do or say that upset you?"

Moira regarded her with surprise. "You think he's at fault?"

"My grandson is a wonderful young man. He has many fine qualities. Sensitivity is not always among them. He can be careless with feelings, though it's always unintentional. He cares for you, Moira. I know he does."

"I know it as well," she admitted. "I'm just not sure it's enough."

"Enough for what? A future?"

Moira nodded. "He was very clear earlier that he's already anticipating the end of my visit."

Nell looked dubious. "Really? Or was he only being realistic about the fact that you came for a monthlong vacation and hold a return ticket home? That's not quite the same thing, is it?"

Moira thought about the distinction, then nodded slowly. "The latter probably." She sighed. "I never realized how hard it would be to figure out how to blend two lives when the people come from places that are far apart. Who gets to decide?"

"The decision has to be mutual," Nell said at once. "Did you have some idea that Luke would move to Dublin?"

"No. I've known from the beginning that his heart is here. And, to be honest, I had no real ties there myself, but then, right before I left, this opportunity came along. The part of me that's never had any real sense of what I might accomplish wants to go back and see how things turn out."

"That's fair enough," Nell said. "You're talking about your photography, of course. Dillon's told me about it. I'd love to see some of the pictures you've taken. I assume you brought your camera along for this trip."

Moira nodded, thinking of it packed away in her room. She'd been half-afraid to take it out. What if she took photos here and they were terrible? What if they were proof that those back home had been flukes? She'd be embarrassed in front of people she wanted desperately to impress.

Nell regarded her with understanding, almost as if she'd been inside Moira's head. "Have you taken any pictures here yet?"

"No."

"Is there a reason for that?" Nell prodded.

Moira thought about it some more before answering. Had she been afraid that here, among all these successful people, her photos would seem amateurish, that the O'Briens would look on her picture-taking as a hobby and nothing more? The idea was ridiculous, really. The O'Briens might be boisterous and outspoken, but they were never cruel. Just look at how they were encouraging Luke in his new venture!

"I think I didn't want my confidence shaken," she admitted eventually. "This idea is still new to me."

"Do I understand correctly that you want to take pictures of weddings, baby showers and things like that?" Nell asked.

Moira nodded.

"Then you'll need to get used to people's reactions, won't you? Art—and it is art you'll be doing—is subjective." She patted Moira's hand. "Get your camera out of your bag and start taking pictures whenever you've the chance. I think you should plan to be the official photographer for the pub's opening as well."

Though she loved the idea of capturing that night's festivities for Luke, Moira wondered if it was wise. Wouldn't it be yet another reminder that she had a life back home to return to? How were they supposed to figure out a future for themselves, if it seemed as if it had already been decided that they'd live apart?

Nell studied her with an understanding expression. "Do you know what I've told my sons and now my grandchildren? If there's something in their life they're passionate about, and someone in their life who truly matters, they need to find a way to balance the two. You and Luke will find a way to do that. I believe that with all my heart."

"But is it selfish to want something so much, when I haven't even taken a serious try at it? What if I go back to Dublin and Luke forgets all about me, and it turns out I'm a failure as a photographer?"

Nell smiled. "Then you'll learn from the experiences," she said. "At your age, few have taken a serious try at anything. That doesn't mean they don't know it's what they're meant to do. The secret to finding balance once two people are involved is compromise."

"I don't think I'd be very good at it," Moira admitted, thinking of how often she argued just for the sake of winning, even when the point of it had gotten lost.

"Few of us are," Nell replied, clearly amused. "Especially in my family. But I'm here to tell you that not only is compromise necessary, the results are worth it."

Just then Moira's grandfather wandered in, looking refreshed from another walk on the beach. "The two of you look entirely too serious," he commented as he snatched a cookie from the plate with a wink at Nell. "Everything okay?"

"Just explaining to Moira the importance of compromise," Nell told him.

Her grandfather chuckled. "I've worked a lifetime to get the knack of that," he said. "Did Nell tell you it doesn't come naturally?"

"She did," Moira said. "Do you think I've the personality for it?"

"A few months ago I would have laughed myself silly at the thought of it," he admitted, then gave her an approving look that warmed her. "Now I think you've the wisdom to give it a try, especially if the end result is to be something that truly matters to you. Is that the case?"

Moira thought of Luke and the future that might be possible if they could only find their way to it together. "It's worth everything," she said quietly.

"Well, then, there's your answer."

She bounced up and gave both of them hugs. "I'll have that shower now, and then come back to learn your chicken and dumplings recipe, if that's okay, Nell?"

"I'll be right here waiting," Nell promised.

As Moira headed to her guest room, she thought about what had just happened. She'd had a mature conversation with two so-called authority figures without losing her cool. She'd felt accepted rather than judged, persuaded rather than lectured. It was a revelation that had her laughing.

Who would have thought it would take a trip to America to make her see that not all authority figures, whether parents or even grandparents, were the enemy? Sometimes they actually had opinions to offer and experience that made complete sense of things. She wondered if she and her mum would ever reach the same level of understanding. For the first time, she saw that she had her own role to play in assuring that they did.

9

Luke was on edge all through dinner at Gram's. Even though the chicken and light-as-air dumplings were his favorite, he could barely taste the food. He was all too aware of Moira and the remnants of the tension that had been stirred up between them earlier in the day. As soon as the meal was over, he stood.

"Gram, would you mind if Moira and I took a walk? Leave the dishes. I'll clean up the kitchen when I get back."

"I'll help with cleanup," Dillon offered. "You two run along and enjoy yourselves."

Moira hadn't budged from her seat during the exchange, but she frowned at Luke. "We should stay and put the kitchen back in order," she said. "Your grandmother cooked the meal. She and my grandfather should relax."

"But we have her blessing to go," Luke countered, "as well as your grandfather's. Do you really want to fight over doing dishes?"

"Maybe we're not fighting over that at all," she said.

Luke stared at her, unable to comprehend the ridiculousness of the argument. "That's it," he said with a shake of his head. He scooped her into his arms and headed for the door.

"Put me down, you idiot," she ordered.

"Not just yet," he muttered, shoving open the screen door with his elbow and crossing the porch in two strides. Only when he'd reached the Adirondack chairs did he pause to set her back on her feet. She punched him in the arm.

"Have you lost your bloody mind?" she demanded.

"No, but I'm beginning to think that perhaps you have. What on earth happened after I went back to work earlier? I thought things were fine between us."

"Of course you did. You're a man, aren't you?"

He couldn't help the smile that tugged at his lips. "I actually thought that was a part of the attraction."

She looked as if she was about to launch into another attack, but then his words sank in. Her lips twitched. "You did not just say that. You think being a man makes you something special?"

He fought an even broader grin. "I was just saying I thought it was helpful, given the circumstances. You and me, as a couple. One of us had better be a man." He held up his hands. "Lucky me!"

This time his words drew a full-fledged smile. "Why on earth did I fall for the likes of you?"

"I'm irresistible," he ventured.

"As if," she retorted.

"Charming," he said then. "Come on, Moira. You have to admit that I'm charming."

"Not so much right at the moment," she replied stubbornly.

"Then it has to be my sexiness and good looks," he concluded.

She gave him a wry look. "Do you have nothing more to offer than that?"

Turning suddenly serious, he held her gaze. "You tell me. Do I?"

She gave him an oddly bewildered look. "It's not so much one thing but the package," she said eventually. "You've patience and persistence, and that charm you mentioned. On occasion you've even shown a sensitive side. And there's your family, of course. I'm half in love with your family."

"They love me," he said, offering it up as proof of his worthiness.

"It's the one thing that makes me question their judgment," she teased, stepping at last into his arms and resting her head against his chest. "I'm sorry for lapsing into impossible Moira mode."

He gave a startled gasp that had her chuckling. "You didn't think you were the first to call me that, did you? Mum dubbed me with the name before I was ten, along with a few other disparaging phrases. I've done my best to live up to all of them."

"It's been a while since I've seen that side of you," he said.

"It comes out mostly when I'm scared and unsure of myself," she admitted.

"Are you feeling that way right now?" he asked.

She shook her head. "No, I'm suddenly feeling safe."

Luke held her close, feeling her slowly relax, feeling the steadiness of her heart as it beat next to his. She was a complicated woman, more than likely destined to drive him a little crazy, but he wouldn't have wanted it any other way. That was both the challenge and the joy of her.

"Mind telling me why we were arguing over the dishes back there?" he asked when he thought it was safe to bring up the topic.

She glanced up at him. "Do you honestly think I have an answer for that, at least one that makes sense?"

"I was hoping," he admitted. "If I'm not to stir up your ire over such things again, it would be best if I understand. Was it over walking out on the cleanup?"

"No."

"Was it over my presumption that you'd want to leave with me?"

He could feel her smile against his chest.

"That was annoying, but no," she said.

"Then I'm at a loss."

She sighed. "So am I, to be perfectly honest. I think I've been juggling a lot of emotions since I got here. This afternoon, being in your bed, made me start to want things that aren't necessarily in the cards. I had a perfectly lovely conversation with your grandmother when I got back here and thought I'd figured things out, but tonight the panic crept over me again. I can't seem to stop it from coming on when I least expect it. I should be over the moon every minute to be here with you, for however long it is. I should be living entirely in the moment, but there's this tiny part of me that keeps looking ahead to what might happen once I'm home. I hadn't expected that. I'm not sure I'm happy about it."

He held her away from him so he could look into her eyes. "Are you worrying again about a future for us, Moira? Who says it's not in the cards?"

"You're just launching something new and exciting

here. I have an opportunity to accomplish something back in Ireland. How is that going to work?"

"I have no idea," Luke admitted candidly. "But it will if we want it to. We just have to be honest with each other and try out all the alternatives until one fits our circumstances."

She looked surprised by his assessment. "Then you subscribe to the theory of compromise that your grandmother believes in?"

"I do. I've seen the disastrous results that can happen when it isn't tried and how well things can work out when it is."

"Tell me," she urged.

He settled into one of the chairs with her on his lap. "You know that my uncle Mick and Megan were divorced for many years. I was only a baby when they split up, but I've gathered it was because he was always gone for work and she felt as if she'd been left alone to raise five children. His priorities were all out of whack, but for some reason she hesitated to make that plain to him. Instead, she kept silent, hoping he'd figure things out on his own, until finally she lost patience."

"Jess mentioned something along those lines to me," Moira confessed.

"Well, before they reconciled a little over a year ago, they finally figured out how to get what they each wanted," Luke continued. "He cut back on his schedule. She learned to speak up about the things that she needed from him. That's just one example."

"Tell me another," she urged, clearly anxious for reassurance that there was hope.

"Trace and Abby. She was terrified that he'd be like

her first husband and insist that she quit work if they had a baby."

"Don't they have twins already?" Moira asked.

"They're Abby's from her first marriage. She divorced her husband because he wanted her to give up her Wall Street career to care for the girls. She was afraid that Trace would insist on the same thing." He smiled. "Now she's pregnant with a baby due any second, because she finally had faith that Trace meant what he said about wanting her to have a career and a home, too. He works at home and picks up all the slack with raising the kids. It works for them."

"But she's no longer on Wall Street," Moira said.

"No, she's with the same firm, running the Baltimore brokerage office. That's her side of the compromise."

Moira nodded, as if finally seeing it. "And Bree's content with her theater here, because Jake's here. She has her dream, just not in New York or Chicago."

"Exactly. I don't know what's in store for us, Moira. I only know I want the time to find out. And if we decide we want to be together forever, we'll figure out a way to make it work."

"I want to believe that," she admitted. "I really do, but we're in such different places, Luke, and I'm not speaking geographically. You figured out your dream in Ireland. You put all the ideas down on paper. You did your homework. And now it's all about to come true. In a few weeks, you'll have a gigantic success on your hands. You'll be at the start of your life's work. And where will I be?"

"You have your photography," he reminded her.

"But it's at a different stage. I have no idea if I'm

really capable of achieving any sort of success with it. A couple of jobs have given me a small taste of success, but that's not proof of anything. When it comes down to a real competition for a job, I could fall flat on my face."

"Has anyone who's seen it suggested such a thing?"

"No, but it's only friends and the McDonough's customers who've seen it, really. They're inclined to be kind."

"Is being a photographer something you really want, Moira? Is it something you believe you were meant to do?"

She shrugged, clearly uncertain. "For too many years I never allowed myself to dream of anything. I was like your cousin Jess—not good in school, not happy with anything I tried. I took pictures for my own amusement. I never considered that it could be something more, because it never occurred to me that I could be a success at anything. Mum disapproved of everything I did and Grandfather has only recently been in my life. I just saw disappointment when I looked into his eyes and frustration and weariness when I looked into my mum's."

"I can't speak for Kiera, but that's certainly not what I see when Dillon talks about you," Luke assured her. "He couldn't be more pleased about what you seem destined to accomplish. He's done nothing but brag about the pictures on the walls at McDonough's."

"But that's the thing. I haven't accomplished anything. I've only an inkling that's yet to be tested." She faced him. "I'm half terrified to admit that I really want it."

"Then you'll test it," he said. "And then decide."

She frowned at his words. "Is it so easy, then, for you to think of letting me go?"

He smiled at her evident frustration. "When I fell for you in Dublin all those months ago, easy was never part of it. I want you to find your path, Moira. And when you've done that, I'll be right here, ready to make it work for both of us. If need be, we'll pile up the frequent flier miles going back and forth between here and Dublin or wherever your work takes you."

He thought his words would ease her mind, but instead, her frown only deepened. "And if we can't handle the distance or find a proper compromise?"

"Then it wasn't meant to be, was it?" He touched her cheek, felt her skin heat, felt the surprising dampness as a tear spilled over. "What's this?"

"Sorry. You're being understanding and supportive again, and I'm being a pain."

"You're not being a pain. We're in the same place more than you realize, Moira. We both have a lot of things about our lives to figure out. It won't be done tonight or even tomorrow. We'll do it one day at a time."

"I've not much patience," she admitted.

He laughed. "I've noticed."

She sighed and settled against his chest again. For now, for this moment at least, they were in complete harmony. Maybe that was enough.

Mindful of his brother's criticism the day before, Luke was at the pub early, prepared to handle any crisis that crept up. Finding Matthew there ahead of him, looking glum, hadn't been the one he'd expected.

"I'm surprised to see you here at this hour," Luke

said carefully. "I'd have brought an extra cup of coffee if I'd known you were hanging around."

"That's okay. I'm on my third cup as it is. Sally offered to just give me the pot the last time I went in."

Luke regarded him with concern. "Is there a problem I don't know about?"

"With the pub? No. Everything's on schedule. Mick's got it handled."

"Okay, then," Luke said, at a loss as to why Matthew was here when he had a perfectly good office of his own across town. Then it dawned on him. This was about Laila. Matthew had hinted at it yesterday, but Mick's presence had obviously kept him silent. Apparently, he was back looking for moral support of some kind.

Now there was a minefield Luke would prefer to avoid, but why else would his brother be hanging around looking as if he'd just lost his best friend?

"Anything you want to talk about?" he inquired, treading tentatively into the danger zone.

Matthew shook his head, then contradicted the gesture by blurting out, "Laila's pregnant!"

"That's fantastic!" Luke said at once, then noted the lack of enthusiasm in Matthew's eyes. "It *is* great news, isn't it?"

"I thought so," his brother admitted, sounding weary and confused. "The timing makes sense. She's older, so it wouldn't be smart to wait around. She's doing accounting work for the inn and only a few other clients now, so it's not exactly the career she was dreaming of. I thought she'd be thrilled."

"But she isn't," Luke concluded.

"To be honest, she's furious, as if I did this all by myself to totally ruin her life."

"Okay, I'm taking a stab in the dark here, but you two hadn't planned on this? You hadn't discussed it?"

"Only in the most general way, as something we both wanted down the road a bit." He shrugged. "Best-laid plans and all that."

"But *you're* happy about it?" Luke persisted.

"Ecstatic," Matthew said, his eyes lighting up for the first time. "I can't wait to be a dad, and Laila is going to be the most amazing mother ever."

"I'm sure you're right on both counts. This has probably just come as a shock to her. She'll be on board as soon as the news sinks in," Luke said confidently. "Laila's one of the most unflappable, levelheaded women I know."

"A description she abhors, by the way," Matthew said. "She loves me because I see her as spontaneous and unpredictable. I don't think she was quite ready to be *this* spontaneous, though."

"Does anyone else know?"

"God, no," Matthew said. "Can you imagine the fuss this news will stir up? O'Briens go nuts over baby announcements. Laila is so not ready for that."

"She will be," Luke said again. "How long have you known?"

"Two days. The at-home test confirmed it a week ago, but she refused to believe that, so it was only the day before yesterday that she got undeniable proof from her doctor. She's been ranting and raving ever since."

"Don't women's hormones go a little crazy when they're pregnant?" Luke asked.

"I mentioned that and nearly got my eye poked out by a flying plate," Matthew said.

Luke started to laugh, but managed to choke it back at Matthew's expression of pure misery.

"You could send flowers," Luke suggested.

"As an apology?" Matthew asked incredulously. "I am *not* sorry about this."

"Just as a token gesture," Luke said. "Or candy? How about that? Women love chocolate." He was struck by a sudden inspiration. "No, wait, I've got it. Go out and buy some teeny-tiny little baby romper thing."

"That could be rubbing salt in the wound at the moment," Matthew argued.

"No, it won't. Don't you remember how Bree and Abby and all the other women in the family got all teary-eyed and sentimental when they saw all those itty-bitty clothes? It'll make it real for her. She'll start thinking about this wonderful little human being you've created together and forget all about it being the wrong time, or whatever it is she's thinking."

Matthew nodded slowly. "I suppose it's possible."

"If it doesn't work out, you can always sleep on my couch for a couple of nights till she calms down."

His brother scowled at the suggestion. "We won't work this out by my hiding out at your place."

"And yet here you are right now," Luke commented.

"I needed neutral territory to get my thoughts in order before the next round," Matthew said. "Is it so wrong to want to be excited about this in front of her and have her share that feeling?"

"Of course it's not wrong, and eventually she will," Luke said yet again. "Give her a little time to get used to the idea. Tell her whatever she needs to hear to believe this isn't the end of life as she knows it."

"But it is," Matthew said seriously. "It'll be a whole new world from here on out. We won't just be a rather unorthodox couple no one expected to hook up. We'll be a family. I think that scares Laila to death. I have a feeling that she thought as long as it was just the two of us, if things didn't work out, it would be no big deal. Now, with a baby, we're in this forever."

"Weren't you always?"

"*I* was. And on most levels I think she was, too, but the conservative part of her brain needed an out just in case she was right about us being a terrible match."

Luke smiled, thinking of how difficult it was to read between the lines with women. "If you've figured that much out, you're halfway to solving the problem."

For the first time, he managed to coax a smile from his brother.

"You know," Matthew said. "If all your advice is this good, bartending may be the best decision you ever made. And Will's likely to try to convince you to get a degree and join his practice, after all."

"Not a chance of that," Luke said. "I'm perfectly content being a sounding board. The advice is a bonus just because you're family."

"Thanks," Matthew said. "I'd better get to work."

He was almost to the door when Luke called out to him. Matthew turned back.

"Congratulations!" Luke said, grinning. At least his brother had one person in the family who could share his excitement. It wouldn't make up for Laila's reservations, but Luke was confident she'd come around before long, too.

* * *

Taking Nell's advice first thing in the morning, Moira grabbed her camera and left to go exploring. Though she usually preferred taking pictures of people to taking shots of scenery, she wanted to have her images of Chesapeake Shores captured in a way that would allow her to glance through the reminders once she was home.

After placing a note on the kitchen table for Nell and her grandfather, she left the house before the sun was fully up. Two hours later, she found herself in front of The Inn at Eagle Point, Jess's pride and joy. Sitting on a cliff overlooking the bay, she thought it was stunning.

And, she remembered with delight, it had a kitchen. She was starving.

Inside she found a young man behind the reception desk, his nose buried in a book. "Is Jess O'Brien around?" she asked, startling him so badly he nearly fell off his stool. He promptly winced at having been caught.

"She's in her office," he said. "Please don't tell her I was half-asleep on the job."

She laughed. "I never tattle," she promised. "Shall I find her office, or will you tell her I'm here?"

"I'll call her," he said.

"I'm Moira," she told him.

He grinning. "Oh, I know. There are few secrets in this town, and we've all been hearing about the visiting Dubliners. I'm Ronnie Foster. I'm training to be a chef so I can work in the kitchen here full time, but for now, I help out taking reservations and carrying bags." He shrugged. "At least that's what I'm supposed to be doing."

He called Jess, who apparently told him she'd be right down. "Take a look around while you wait," Ronnie suggested.

Moira nodded, already intrigued by the coziness Jess had achieved with the inn. The old wood floors gleamed. The carpets added warm splashes of color and there were flowers on the tables and in many of the upholstery patterns. With huge windows letting in light, it was a sunny, welcoming place. No wonder it had become a success.

Jess eventually found her in the main parlor looking out at the spectacular view of green lawn, flowers and the bay beyond.

"You're out early," Jess said. "I'm so glad you've come by to see the inn for yourself. Did my bragging do it justice?"

"It's fabulous," Moira told her honestly. "I thought it was impressive from the outside, but inside it's absolutely lovely. If Nell weren't such a gracious hostess and her cottage so charming, I'd want to stay here."

Jess beamed. "Considering how all of us treasure Nell's cottage, I'll take that as a huge compliment."

"It's meant to be," Moira said. "Now, do I have it right that you serve breakfast? I've been wandering around taking pictures for a couple of hours, and have suddenly realized I'm famished. I was hoping you could join me."

"I'd love it," Jess said at once. "I have to tell you, though, that I had a panicky call from Laila a few minutes ago, and she's on her way over. Since she's usually not in the office here today, I got the sense that she needed to talk. If so, I might have to abandon you when she gets here."

"Not a problem," Moira said, then smiled. "I still think about how romantic her wedding was in Ireland. I'm so glad that Mum and I were able to have a small part in making it happen. I've never seen two people look happier than she and Matthew did that day."

Jess laughed. "I think we all felt that way, as if it were magical. I was flat-out envious that my cousin Matthew, one of the greatest rogues of all time, pulled off such a coup."

She led the way into a dining room, which, like the rest of the inn, had towering windows letting in the morning light. "Have a seat, and I'll grab a couple of menus," she said, then came back with coffee as well. "Would you prefer tea? We have a selection of that, too."

"It would be sacrilegious to admit this in Ireland, but I love my coffee, especially first thing in the morning," Moira confided.

Jess laughed as she poured, then set the pot on a trivet on the table. Moira noticed that she didn't pour any for herself.

"No caffeine?" she asked.

"It doesn't go well with my attention deficit disorder," Jess admitted. "I'm scattered enough without it, so I try to avoid it. Gail will bring me some decaf in a minute. She's our chef."

"And Ronnie?"

"Ah, that's right, you met him just now. He's going to be an outstanding chef himself one of these days, according to Gail." She leaned closer. "He sucks on desk duty, but he's been trying harder in return for the inn picking up some of his tuition expenses at culinary school. He'll graduate in a few months and then he'll be our official sous-chef. I think it will be a relief for all of us."

Just then Laila strode into the dining room. However, the tall, elegant, starry-eyed woman Moira remembered from her wedding day looked frazzled and out of sorts this morning. She stopped short at the sight of Moira.

"I didn't know you'd be here," she said, already backpedaling.

"What a lovely welcome," Jess chided, causing Laila to turn pink with embarrassment.

"I'm so sorry," she apologized to Moira. "I just came barreling in here with my own agenda. I never meant to be rude."

"It's okay," Moira said, sensing that something was definitely amiss. As much as she'd like getting to know the woman who might one day be related to her if things worked out with Luke, she had a feeling that she was intruding now. "Jess explained that you were coming by. I'm the unexpected interloper. If you'd prefer to see her in private, I totally understand."

For what seemed like an eternity, Laila looked torn. "Oh, what the hell," she muttered and pulled out a chair. "The news will be all over sooner or later."

Jess's eyes immediately lit up. "News?"

"Coffee first," Laila said, then sighed and put the pot back. "Never mind. I'll have decaf."

Jess's mouth immediately dropped open. "You're pregnant," she guessed, looking stunned.

Laila stared at her in astonishment. "Am I wearing a sign on my forehead or something? I can't possibly have a baby bump yet."

"You turned down caffeine," Jess explained. "You *never* turn down caffeine."

"Congratulations," Moira ventured, though it was dismay, rather than excitement, that seemed to be radiating from Laila in waves.

"Thanks, I guess," Laila said without enthusiasm.

Jess regarded her with genuine concern. "Why aren't you over the moon about this? I'll bet Matthew is."

"Oh, Matthew is ready to shout the news from the rooftops," Laila confirmed. "You'd think he single-handedly invented pregnancy."

Moira chuckled, then hid her face. It didn't seem like the time to let her amusement show.

"Oh, go ahead and laugh," Laila told her. "The whole family's going to be laughing their fool heads off when they find out about this."

"Why on earth would anyone laugh?" Moira asked.

"Because, like my sister-in-law Abby, I was supposed to be the ultimate career woman. I was supposed to be running the family bank by now. Instead, I'm keeping the books for a few businesses around town, and if Matthew has his way, I'll be staying at home, barefoot and pregnant."

This time it was Jess who couldn't contain her laughter. "Matthew? Really? He loves you, Laila. He wants you to be happy and fulfilled doing whatever you want to do."

"How am I supposed to do that now? I'll be home with a baby."

"Abby's not home with the twins, and I guarantee she'll be back at work after the new baby arrives within weeks, if not days," Jess countered. "Bree stayed home barely a minute. She just takes Emily Rose with her to work. And when Will and I are ready, I certainly won't be a full-time, stay-at-home mom. Why should you be any different? Remember that great big office upstairs? There's plenty of room for a portable crib in there."

"It just seems as if staying home and having babies is what Matthew's going to expect."

"Has he even hinted at such a thing?" Jess asked.

"And would it be so bad to stay home and be a mother?" Moira dared to ask. It was something she'd wished for desperately as a child—that her mother had been at home, rather than working one and sometimes two jobs to make ends meet because she'd flatly refused to ask Moira's grandfather for help.

Laila whirled on her with a narrowed gaze. "You'd want that? To stay home? I thought you were about to launch a big career as a photographer. Won't that be demanding?"

Moira shrugged. "It remains to be seen if I'll be any good at that or not. I'm excited about the possibility. It would be nice to accomplish something, but I think it would be just as rewarding to make a wonderful home for my husband and children, not because he expects it, but because I'd feel fulfilled doing it."

"Seriously?" Laila asked, her expression bemused.

"I think so, yes. I might feel differently if I'd already made my mark. I might not want to give up the success of it, and I can understand your wanting something different. I'm just saying there's value in being a good wife and mum."

"Gram would applaud that," Jess said to Moira. "Does Luke know you feel this way?"

"It's not come up," Moira admitted.

"You do know it could make things easier," Jess suggested. "If you're not driven to have a big career, then it would make it simpler for him to ask you to stay."

"My going or staying isn't under discussion at the moment," Moira told her firmly, then glanced at Laila. "I'm sorry for turning the focus onto me. You have to decide what's best for you."

"I thought I had," Laila said wearily. "But now there's a baby to consider. I wasn't quite ready to take another person into account. And it's not as if my career plans have turned out the way I'd expected."

Jess grinned at her. "But a baby, Laila! A human being that you and Matthew have created together. He or she is going to be absolutely amazing. And you know you'll be wonderful parents."

"What if the baby already knows I have all these doubts?" Laila asked, looking chagrined. "I've probably already scarred it for life."

Moira smiled. "I believe at this stage, it's little bigger than a peanut. I don't think it's quite sensitive to your moods just yet."

Laila sighed, her hand resting protectively on her stomach. Moira smiled again at the instinctive gesture.

"How about some of Gail's stuffed French toast to celebrate?" Jess suggested. "I don't know about you two, but I'm starving. And you were hungry when you arrived, weren't you, Moira? Laila, how about you?"

A slow grin worked its way across Laila's face. "Well, if I'm going to be eating for two, I might as well enjoy it. Normally, I can't even look at the French toast without gaining five pounds. When I turn into a nice plump blimp, I'll blame it all on Matthew."

"Don't you think you should probably let him off the hook now?" Jess asked gently. "He didn't get you pregnant all by himself."

"But he's been so cute trying to calm me down,"

Laila said. "He brought home baby clothes this morning. He said they were Luke's idea. Of course, I went ballistic at first, because it seems that's what I do when he goes all gaga over the baby, but after he'd gone, I picked them up and really looked at them. I have to say that I still can't quite imagine that I'm carrying a baby that will eventually fit into them."

She looked a little dazed by the thought.

"Do you want to go on torturing him awhile longer?" Jess asked. "If it will make you feel better, I suppose it wouldn't hurt."

"Just until he's painted and furnished the entire nursery," Laila said with a grin. "Then I'll relent."

Moira stared at her incredulously. "You'd actually let him choose the decor for the nursery all on his own?"

Laila hesitated, then shook her head. "You have a point. I suppose sooner is better than later." She sighed. "I wouldn't mind chocolates, though. He offered to order my favorites. They seem to take the edge off my annoyance."

"If you tell Matthew that, he'll buy you the whole factory," Jess told her. "Give the guy a break."

Laila laughed. "Okay, okay. I knew when I came over here you'd take his side."

"Truthfully, I love both of you equally," Jess replied diplomatically. "But it's this innocent little baby you're carrying I love most of all."

As soon as Jess had placed their order with Gail, she came back to the table with a pad of paper and a pen. "Let's plan a baby shower."

"Oh, yes, let's," Moira said excitedly. "Can I take the pictures? Free of charge, of course."

Jess and Laila exchanged a look.

"Will you still be here?" Jess asked.

Deflated, Moira sighed. "I never thought of that."

"Whenever it is, you'll come back for it," Laila said at once.

Moira nodded, but she couldn't shake the feeling that in just a few weeks she'd be walking away from a world filled with people who'd come to matter to her.

And then what? Would it simply go on without her? Out of sight, out of mind—wasn't that what they said? Was that a risk she wanted to take? Or did she even have a choice in the matter?

10

After she left the inn, Moira walked back to Nell's cottage but found it deserted. There was a note from her grandfather that Mick had driven them into Baltimore to see someplace called the Inner Harbor. He'd tried to reach her on her cell phone to see if she wanted to come along, but had gotten no answer. She realized then that she'd left the cell phone in her room.

It was probably just as well. The time she'd spent with Jess and Laila had been a revelation. It had helped her gain a different perspective on what she did and didn't want for the future. As excited as she was by this opportunity back in Dublin, she knew now that she'd never view photography as more important than family. She wanted the accomplishment of it, perhaps even needed the boost to her self-esteem, but what she wanted most of all was a family of her own, people who loved her and counted on her.

It wasn't, however, a discovery she was particularly anxious to share. She'd seen the shock on Laila's face and even on Jess's when she'd mentioned her feelings. In this family of overachievers, such an admission wouldn't necessarily be applauded. Not that it should matter, if she was being true to herself, she thought.

Well, it was all a bit of a pipe dream, for now, anyway. Neither the big-time photography career nor the family were a given at the moment.

At loose ends, she took her camera and wandered into town, hoping Luke would have some free time or, at the very least, some tasks she could take over for him. But when she arrived at the pub, she was told he'd gone off to Mack's newspaper office to place ads for staff and for the opening.

"Do you know where that is?" one of the construction crew asked. "It's just a few blocks, if you'd like to meet him there. Here, I'll write it down for you."

"Thanks," she said, accepting the map he'd quickly sketched for her.

She was halfway down Main Street when she was distracted by the children playing on the town green. She stopped to take a few pictures and before long she was lost in the images that captured the carefree laughter and, on occasion, the tears when the concept of sharing didn't go over well or a helter-skelter run ended with a fall.

She'd finished taking her shots, the children were gone, but she was still absorbed in looking at the pictures on her digital camera when Luke found her.

"I heard you were looking for me," he said, grinning at her. "But then you obviously forgot all about me. I'm not quite sure how to feel about your losing interest so easily."

"Never that," she responded. "I just got caught up in taking a few pictures."

"Want to show me over lunch? We can go to Sally's, unless you'd rather have another picnic by the water."

"Outside by the water is definitely better," she said. "But I don't want much in the way of food. Jess's chef made stuffed French toast for us this morning, and I'm still regretting how much of it I ate."

"How'd you rate the fancy food?" he complained. "The best she's ever offered me was scrambled eggs and bacon."

"I think it was for Laila's benefit," Moira told him. "She was having a rough morning."

Luke frowned. "You saw Laila, too? Did she say what was going on?"

Moira sensed that he'd heard the other side of the story. "You know, don't you?" He must have if he'd been encouraging Matthew to buy baby clothes. Still, she didn't want to take chances with someone else's private squabble.

"Know what?" he hedged.

"You go first," she insisted. "I don't want to be the one spilling secrets."

"The baby," he said.

She nodded, smiling. "Isn't it wonderful?"

"Matthew certainly thinks so, and so do I," Luke said. "But I was under the impression that Laila has reservations."

"Oh, she does," Moira admitted. "But a little girl talk and a lot of food seemed to calm her down."

"Then she's not going to chop off any of Matthew's important parts while he sleeps?"

Moira laughed. "It didn't come up in conversation. I think he's safe enough." She gave him a thoughtful look. "I hear you recommended that he bring home baby clothes."

"I did," Luke confessed. "Did it work?"

"She saw it for the ploy that it was, but the last time I saw her, she was heading home to take another look at them. I think she's still coming to grips with the idea that in a few months' time, she'll be giving birth to someone who'll actually fit into them."

"I envy them," Luke admitted.

Moira regarded him with surprise. "You do? Really?"

He nodded. "I've never been serious enough about anyone to think ahead to having children, but when Matthew told me, it hit me that I want that, too. It seems to be the O'Brien curse that we all want what the others have." He gave her a wry look. "Whether I'm ready for the responsibility is a different story. First—"

She cut him off. "First you have a business to launch," she finished for him. "Do all men approach life in such a single-minded, orderly progression?" she asked. "First this, then that, never veering from the path for the unexpected surprise."

"Not all men," Luke responded. "Matthew, for one, seems to thrive on surprises. The effect Laila had on him caught him completely off guard. And now this baby. I've never seen him happier, even though neither were on his agenda when he first left college. He was the ultimate playboy, or at least that's what we all thought."

"I thought that was your role," Moira teased. "The one you relished above all others."

"It was," he admitted. "And then one day, out of the blue, I wanted something different. I wanted what the other men in my family had found. I wanted to be more than an aimless wanderer. I wanted to be settled in a career."

"With a family?" she asked.

"You already know the answer to that," he said.

"When the time comes," she said, knowing the words by heart by now.

She thought of the calendar ticking away the days of her visit, one by one. They would fly by and, once they were gone, what if the time for that family Luke was thinking about hadn't yet come? What then? Even with all their talks, not a one had dispelled the uncertainty. Panic, never far away, stirred once more.

Luke had seen a shadow cross Moira's face as they talked about Matthew and Laila expecting a baby. He realized as they sat across from the bay having lunch, though, that she'd never really said how she would feel about having a family. Did she not want one, or had his own responses daunted her?

Since any thoughts of a family were definitely down the road, he pushed aside his questions in favor of asking about the photographs she'd shot.

"Will you show them to me?" he asked her, pointing toward the camera. "Or are you one of those sensitive, creative types who doesn't want anyone to see anything except the finished product?"

"I'm so new at this, I haven't developed any idiosyncrasies quite yet," she said. "I'll let you look, but it might be better for you to see them on your computer, if it's equipped for photos."

"It is," he said. "We'll take a look as soon as we've finished lunch."

She sighed and leaned back. "I was finished before I'd begun," she said. "How can Jess be around such food all the time and still be so thin? I'd be the size of a house."

"Although I've heard a lot of talk about Gail's decadent chocolate cake being eaten late at night, it's been Will who's grumbling about gaining weight. I think he may be the only one in their household who indulges regularly in Gail's more caloric offerings. And Jess has always had energy to spare. She burns off everything she eats."

"Lucky woman," Moira said. "I doubt I'd have the willpower to resist anything, and everything I eat settles straight on my hips."

Luke grinned. "You have excellent hips. In fact, all your curves are just perfect."

She gave him a wry look. "Seriously, though, how is your kitchen at the pub going to compete with Gail's gourmet fare?"

"By not trying to," Luke said at once. "We'll have far simpler food, as you well know, having listed at least a dozen menu alternatives with Gram's help the other day."

Moira's expression immediately brightened. "You've gone over them? What did you think?"

"It looked excellent to me. The only hitch is that I can prepare only about half of them so far."

"I'll pitch in, if you like," she said eagerly.

"That would be great for the opening and a day or two beyond," he said. "But then what, Moira? You'll be heading back to Dublin. I'll have to manage on my own. I can't rely on Gram, either, not at her age. It wouldn't be fair. I'm thinking it will be necessary to hire a full-time cook, after all."

She looked as if she might argue, though Luke couldn't imagine what she could possibly contradict. Everything he'd said was true. Eventually, she sighed. "I suppose you're right, which means you'll need to hire that person right away, someone who can master all the recipes right along with you. I'll help Nell give you both lessons."

Luke chuckled for some reason. "I'm not quite sure how I feel about your bossing me around within range of sharp knives," he teased.

"I've seen no evidence that I intimidate you on any level," she replied. "What is the expression? Don't be a wuss."

Luke sputtered indignantly, but he couldn't help laughing in the end. He draped an arm over her shoulders and drew her close enough to peer into her eyes. "You do scare the daylights out of me, you know. You make me feel things that throw me completely off-kilter."

"Really?" she said, looking pleased.

He nodded. "For instance, right this second, I can't help thinking about the fact that my apartment is only a hundred yards or so away from here."

She smiled at the reminder. "And you'd like to play hooky from work to head over there with me?"

"I would," he said, still holding her gaze. "How about you?"

"There's nothing I'd like more," she said quietly, standing up. Then she kicked his hope aside by grinning. "But we're going back to the pub instead. I'll not be the one who throws off your timetable, Luke

O'Brien. I'd never hear the end of it from your family, and you'd only resent me on top of it."

"Aren't you the one who's been complaining bitterly about my strict attention to my priorities?" he grumbled as he followed her across the street.

"True, but when you have me in your bed, I want all of your attention on me, not half of it on the work you should be doing."

"Oh, I think I could promise that," he assured her.

She laughed at his last-ditch attempt to lure her in. "Then I'd be the one doing the worrying." She winked. "Maybe at the end of the day, then. What would you think of that?"

He nodded reluctantly. "A decent compromise," he conceded.

"I'm working on learning the art of it."

Just his luck she'd picked now to give it her first try.

Inside the pub, Moira tried to ignore the deafening noise of the construction crew as they cut and installed the last of the chair-rail molding that Luke had requested. The electricians had ladders scattered about as they finished with the lighting fixtures.

While Luke dealt with various minor crises that had crept up while he'd been out placing his ads and having lunch, she retreated to his office and loaded her photos onto his laptop. As she sorted through them, deleting a few and saving others to a file she labeled "Chesapeake Shores," she completely lost herself in what she was doing. Though it sounded ridiculous, it almost seemed as if she were seeing them for the first time, as if they'd been shot by someone else. She was able to look at them completely objectively, picking and choosing only those she thought were a notch above all the others, those that told a story in a single image.

The pictures she'd taken on the town green were the best. While those of the scenery were beautiful, these were full of life. She couldn't help smiling as she looked at them.

Suddenly she was aware of Luke standing behind her. Immediately feeling shy, she glanced up at him. "Well?"

"Moira, they're truly remarkable," he said. "Would you mind if I asked someone over to look at them?"

She frowned at the idea of a stranger viewing these, which, in her mind, were little more than vacation pictures. "Who?"

"Megan," he told her.

She frowned. "Why would you want your aunt to see them?"

"Because she owns an art gallery just down the block," he reminded her. "She'll want to see your work, I think. At the very least, you'll have some candid feedback from someone who knows about these things."

"Luke, I don't know," she said, uncertainty creeping in. Her photography was still so new. Was she ready to hear an expert's opinion?

"You said you didn't trust the comments you'd had so far because they were from friends and family. Megan's an authority."

She knew he was right, that it was an opportunity she shouldn't pass up, but the truth was that she was terrified. What if Megan said her pictures didn't measure up? What then? She could hardly ignore the opinion of someone who actually understood something about the world of art and photography. What if her dreams were dashed before they'd even begun?

Then reason kicked in. Would that be so terrible? In a way it would take the decision about the future out of her hands. If she wasn't meant to be any sort of photographer, she could focus on having the family she'd always felt was her destiny.

She drew in a deep breath, then nodded. "Call her."

Rather than listening while Luke spoke to his aunt, she concentrated on sorting through the pictures she'd selected as being better than average. Were they good enough, though? Suddenly she'd lost her earlier ability to be objective. She questioned each and every one of them. Was this one too dark? That one a bit fuzzy because of the child's sudden movement?

Fortunately, she didn't have to suffer all the uncertainty for long, because Megan arrived within minutes. Moira gave her a weak smile.

"I hope you'll not be sorry that Luke called you and wasted your time," she said to the stylish woman, who offered her an understanding look in return.

"No need to panic or make excuses, Moira," Megan said, giving her shoulder a squeeze. "I'm not here to rip your heart out. I'm just a friend who happens to have some experience in this field. I have a photography show hanging in my gallery right now, as a matter of fact. You should come back with me when we're finished here and take a look. I'd love to hear what you think."

Moira regarded her with amazement. "You'd want *my* opinion?"

Megan nodded. "Why wouldn't I? Luke wouldn't have called me if he didn't believe you have an eye for this." She nudged Moira aside to take her place in front of the computer, then met her gaze. "Seriously, do you mind if I have a look? If Luke bullied you into it, I can wait."

Moira shook her head and stepped away, unable to watch. Luke came up beside her and, as if sensing her panic, took her hand in his and gave it a squeeze. "It's going to be fine," he said. "You'll see."

Moira prayed he was right. It didn't help that Megan was silent as she went through the photos in the file. She lingered over each one for what seemed like an eternity. Occasionally, a smile touched her lips, but that was her only visible reaction.

Eventually she turned to Moira. "You took these this morning?"

"I was walking by the green and saw the children. I couldn't stop myself from taking their pictures."

"A couple of them are my grandchildren," Megan said. "Didn't you recognize them?"

Moira was dumbstruck. "I should have, shouldn't I? I was so focused on the shots, I wasn't really looking for O'Briens."

"I'm going to want prints of them for myself and for their parents," Megan told her. "More important, I'd like you to consider building a portfolio while you're here. If you do that, perhaps we can talk about a showing at my gallery sometime down the road."

Moira's mouth gaped. "You can't be serious!"

"Of course I'm serious," Megan said. "I'm thinking it could be called *The Faces of Chesapeake Shores* or something like that. The locals will go crazy for it and collectors will snap them up. I don't know what you were told in Ireland, but you capture the heart of people. I know because I see little Mick's exuberance and Davy's energy. And the little girl who's in tears as another child walks away dragging a pull toy is priceless. You have a gift for finding a defining moment and getting it on film."

"And the scenery?" Moira asked, wondering if Megan would feel as she did about that.

"It's beautiful, but it doesn't have the heart of the others, Moira." She studied her intently. "I hope that doesn't disappoint you."

Moira shook her head, suddenly feeling the knot inside her ease. "No, that's exactly what I thought as well. My talent, if I have any, is to take pictures of people."

"Exactly," Megan confirmed.

Impulsively, Moira gave her a hug. "Thank you. I can't tell you what it means to me to have you take the time to look at these."

Megan's warm expression sobered. "I mean it about putting together a show, Moira. It will take time to assemble enough of a portfolio to choose from, but I have confidence you can do it. And if the pictures are as good as I anticipate, I think I can get you noticed in the right places."

The excitement Moira had felt just a couple of weeks ago when Peter had sung her praises multiplied a hundred times as she basked in Megan's words.

"Honestly?" she said, hardly daring to believe it. The scale balancing one future against another immediately tipped in favor of a career again.

"I'm always serious when it comes to business," Megan said. "I came to this career late, but I've worked hard to make a success of it. I wouldn't jeopardize my reputation just to please you or Luke."

She glanced at her watch. "I need to get back to the gallery. It's time for my assistant to leave. You can come back with me now, if you like, or stop by whenever you have time to spare to take a look at the current exhibit."

"Could I do that tomorrow?" Moira asked. She wanted to stay here for the moment and absorb everything Megan had said to her.

"Of course," Megan agreed. "Why don't we plan to get together again one day next week as well, and you can show me any pictures you've shot to add to these. I know there's a time crunch given the length of your stay, but take your time, Moira. It's more important that you do your best work."

"I totally understand," Moira agreed at once. "And thank you. You can't possibly know what this means to me."

As soon as Megan had gone, Moira whirled around and threw herself into Luke's arms. "Thank you, thank you, thank you!"

He laughed. "I gather you're happy about the way it turned out."

"I'm over the moon," she said. "I can't believe that a real expert thinks I have talent."

"She means it about the show, too," Luke reminded her. "She wouldn't offer something like that lightly."

"But I'll only be here a few more weeks," Moira said. "How can I possibly take enough pictures?"

He grinned. "You took these in just a morning," he said. "I think you have enough time. If not, you can always extend your stay or come back."

She studied his face as he said that so casually. "Would it bother you if that happened?"

"You mean if you stayed longer or came back?"

She nodded.

"Of course not. I can't imagine anything better."

"Really?"

He frowned. "Why do you doubt me?"

"Because it's seemed from the time I arrived that you were viewing my stay as finite. It's one thing for me to be here on vacation for a month, and quite another to think of me here longer. I thought it might rattle you or change things if you thought I could be here indefinitely."

He cupped his hands around her arms and held her still. "Moira, I am happy you came. I would be even happier if your stay were extended for any reason, but especially for something like this. It means I'd be able to be right here to share in your success, just as you'll be here to be a part of mine. We can prop each other up when the doubts creep in as well. You were my biggest booster when I floated the idea for the pub. Now I'd like to be your biggest supporter."

"You've already done that by inviting Megan over here this afternoon," she said. "I would never have dreamed of such a thing. I wouldn't have wanted to be presumptuous."

"That's why we make an excellent team," he told her. "O'Briens are taught at an early age to be there for one another. It was one of Gram's biggest lessons. When my dad, Mick and Thomas had a falling-out during the development of Chesapeake Shores, it devastated her. She's spent years trying to make peace between them and reminding them that family's more important than any of their squabbles."

"There was none of that in my family," Moira admitted. "My brothers and I barely speak, and Mum's far too busy to worry about it. The truth is, she doesn't get along that well with any of us. It was only just before I left that she and I started to see eye-to-eye on anything. As for her and Grandfather, I think they're still a very long way from doing much more than spending a few hours at a time together without fighting."

"But it's so obvious to me how much your grandfather wants all of you to be a family," Luke said. "At Christmas, I could see how hard he was trying, and it wasn't just to impress Gram. It matters to him."

Moira nodded. "I saw that, too. It was a real revelation to me."

"Families are a work in progress," Luke said. "The dynamics are always changing."

"Do you think that's true for us as well?" Moira asked.

Luke smiled at her wistful question. "We're human, aren't we? I imagine there are a good many twists and turns ahead for the two of us. I, for one, am looking forward to them. How about you?"

She allowed herself a smile. "Truthfully? I can't wait."

For the first time, she wasn't terrified about the future. She found herself actually looking forward to it. Some of that, of course, was due to Megan's feedback. Most of it, though, was because of Luke. Right at this moment, she actually felt optimistic about all of it. The sensation was as wonderful as it was rare.

11

The speed of the O'Brien grapevine was astounding, even on a slow day. Once Mick got involved, it apparently worked at warp speed, at least as far as Moira could tell.

Mick came bursting into the pub within an hour of Megan's departure, followed by Shanna and Kevin as well as Heather and Connor. Megan trailed along behind, her expression sheepish.

"When Mick came in from his trip to Baltimore with your grandfather and Nell, I mentioned that you had taken pictures of Davy and little Mick earlier today," Megan said apologetically. "Naturally, my husband promptly told their parents. Moira, would you mind terribly showing them the photos?"

Moira chuckled, despite a lingering hint of embarrassment over all the hoopla. She supposed if Megan was right about her potential, she'd have to get used to this sort of thing. It was good that her first critics on American soil were basically friendly.

She turned on the computer and opened up the files,

then left the small group to scroll through the shots she'd taken, hovering in the background as they looked.

"I want that one on the wall in the quilt store," Heather said when she saw the picture of little Mick. "Trace has all sorts of enlargement capabilities. Do you suppose he could make a blowup for me?" She turned to Moira. "Would you mind? I absolutely love it. It's the best picture I've ever seen of our son."

"And this one of Davy is priceless," Shanna said. "He looks as if he's about to race right off the screen. Could I hire you, Moira, to come by sometime to take pictures of him, Henry and the baby? Not stiff, formal shots, but candids like these?"

"You don't have to hire me. I'd love to do it," Moira said at once. "I need more shots for my portfolio, anyway, according to Megan. You'd be doing me the favor."

She caught Megan rolling her eyes. "Young lady, you do not just give away your work."

Moira regarded her steadily, her chin up. "I do for people who've been kind to me. Now if the neighbors start lining up, I'll have to reconsider."

Megan chuckled. "Well, I can see that you have a stubborn streak to match any O'Brien's, so I won't argue."

Shanna beamed at the resolution of the argument. "Would tomorrow afternoon work? It's Henry's birthday and I'm throwing a party. He wasn't used to much commotion when he first came to live with me and Kevin full time, so last year's celebration was just a family affair. This year, though, I've gone all out. We're having not only family, but also his friends from school.

I'm even taking a rare Saturday off from the store to try to manage the chaos."

Kevin grinned. "Which means since you're in charge, I'll get to leave, right?"

"Not on your life, pal," Shanna said to him firmly. "You can have the morning to yourself, but from noon on you're mine. And if the thought of a couple of dozen little kids scares you, maybe Connor will come along to protect you."

Connor's expression immediately brightened. "Will there be cake? If there's cake, count me in. Is Gram baking it?"

"I asked Gail to do it at the inn," Shanna admitted. "There are way too many people coming to the party. Your grandmother could never have baked a cake big enough for this crowd." Her expression turned worried. "I think Nell was okay with that."

"Don't count on it," Connor said direly, then brightened. "But Gail's cake is pretty darn good, too. I suppose that could get me there to help out."

Heather grinned at her husband's reaction. "You are such a kid. Did no one ever throw you a party when you were Henry's age?"

"Of course we did," Megan said, then frowned. Before Connor could say a word, she amended, "At least we did before I left. I can't imagine that Nell broke tradition while I was away."

Connor regarded her evenly. "It's okay, Mom. I'm past thinking about what changed when you left. You're here now. That's what matters. And I had my share of birthday parties, even when I misbehaved and Gram threatened to cancel them."

"Still, I can't help thinking about how much I

missed, especially with you and Jess," Megan lamented. "You two were the youngest. I should have made sure you had magical celebrations every single birthday."

Connor circled an arm around her shoulders. "How about this? You can plan little Mick's party every year and deal with all the kids to make up for it. Heather and I will go out and have our own private, quiet celebration of the day our son was born."

"As if," Heather protested. "Our boy is not having a party without his mommy and daddy."

Connor shrugged. "Oh, well. It was a thought. I don't have nearly enough excuses to have you all to myself."

Moira listened to the exchange with a sense of wonder. The dynamics in this family were a constant source of amazement to her. People bickered and fought. They struggled to overcome the fallout from Megan's apparently ugly divorce from Mick all those years ago. And yet they were united by unquestioning, unwavering love. She couldn't help wondering how they'd managed that when she and her mum still struggled to be civil, as did her mum and her grandfather.

The O'Briens were still bickering as they left after getting Moira's agreement to take pictures at tomorrow's party. She turned to Luke.

"How do they do that?" she asked.

He regarded her blankly. "What?"

Clearly, it was something he took for granted, she thought, marveling at that as well. "The balance between speaking their minds, arguing and managing not to inflict hurt feelings."

"Oh, believe me, people get their feelings hurt from time to time," Luke said. "Sometimes words cut a little too close and leave wounds."

"Wounds, maybe, but not rifts," she said. "In my family we wind up not speaking for weeks. Sometimes longer."

"It's Gram," he said. "She doesn't allow the wounds to fester. For a little thing, she has a mighty power to force any one of us to shape up, and she doesn't hesitate to intervene." His expression suddenly turned sad. "I don't know what will happen once she's gone."

Moira regarded him with dismay. "There was something in your voice when you said that, Luke. She's not ill, is she? Grandfather hasn't mentioned it."

He hesitated a little too long before responding. "She's in her eighties. Things are bound to start going wrong," he said in a way that was revealing for its evasiveness. "I've been trying to keep a close eye on her. So has my mother. But Gram gets annoyed if she thinks any of us are hovering."

"Then don't hover," Moira said. "If Nell needs your help, she seems to me like someone who'll ask for it. Until then, treat her with the respect she's earned."

"There's no lack of respect in worrying," Luke argued.

"There is if it makes her start thinking of herself differently, as if she's an object of pity or suddenly turned frail, rather than the same vital woman she's always been."

He nodded thoughtfully. "I see what you mean. And I recall how put out she was when people thought she should stop taking charge of Sunday dinners. Since she's seemed better since you and your grandfather arrived, I'll try to heed your advice and quit hovering. Mum's much more subtle about it than I am, anyway. She'll alert the troops if she thinks there's a need."

Moira wound her arms around his neck. "You can hover over me instead," she suggested. "The clock says it wouldn't be amiss to go home now."

A grin spread across his face at the suggestion. "My home?"

"It's the closest and the least crowded," she told him. "I'm thinking a bit of privacy could be in order."

"And I'm thinking you're a genius," he said. "Grab your jacket and let's go."

"I'll only need a jacket if you're not up for the job of keeping me warm," she challenged.

He laughed. "I'll do my best, and you can rate me on it later."

"I'm thinking there could be an A-plus in your future," she teased.

In fact, she was counting on it.

After walking around the Inner Harbor in Baltimore most of the day, Nell was more than ready for a quiet evening at home with Dillon. The message from Moira that she'd be spending the night at Luke's couldn't have been more welcome.

"This is nice," Dillon said as they finished eating. "Just you and me at home for a meal. We missed out on a lot of years like this, Nell. I don't regret the life I had, but I do regret that."

"We can't go back and change anything," she scolded. "We need to be grateful that we've been given a second chance to have quiet nights together like this. We should count our blessings, not our regrets. Isn't that the mark of a life well lived—to have more of the one than the other?"

"You've always seen the glass as half-full, haven't

you?" Dillon said. "Your ability to be optimistic is one of the things I admire about you."

She smiled at him. "If I needed to bask in your approval, I'd insist on your listing a few of the others," she teased. "But I'm content with just the one for now. Would you like a glass of wine or a cup of tea? I think it's warm enough that we could sit on the porch and enjoy the sunset."

"Nothing to drink," he told her. "Just you and that lovely view you have of the water. Rather than the porch, let's sit in those chairs you have on the lawn. It's been a long time since I've been able to look up in the sky and see so many stars as they make their debut at night."

"Thank goodness we don't have as many bright lights as the city," she told him as they walked outside. "Sometimes I'm awake before daybreak, and I come out here and look up. It seems as if the sky's a field of diamonds. Being able to pick out a constellation here and there takes me back to the nights we used to lie on a blanket in that field near my grandfather's house in the country."

Dillon chuckled. "That's not what I remember most about those nights. I remember only that you occasionally let me steal a kiss. They were all the sweeter because we risked getting caught."

Nell smiled at the memory and reached for his hand. "There's no one around to catch us tonight, if you wanted to do the same thing," she said.

"Now, how could I pass up an invitation like that?" he asked, and pulled her into his arms.

The touch of his lips against hers had the pull of nostalgia, the tenderness of who they were now. Nell was just starting to enjoy it when a voice cut through the still night air.

"What's this?" Mick demanded, sounding irritated.

Nell would have moved away, but Dillon refused to let her go. He turned a level gaze on Mick.

"What does it look like?" Dillon inquired mildly. "A sensitive man wouldn't need to ask. Nor would he want to embarrass his mother."

Nell had to contain a laugh at Mick's chagrined expression. He looked as guilty as he might have at seventeen after being scolded by a parent in front of company.

"It's my duty to look out for Ma," Mick replied stiffly.

"And I can respect you for that," Dillon said. "But your mother needs no protection from me."

Nell decided it was time to step in before these two strong-willed men started some ridiculous turf war. "Enough, both of you. Mick, if I want to kiss someone, it's my choice. I'm not a foolish teenager. Nor am I your child. I'm your mother. Allow me a little dignity."

Mick stared at her in dismay. "I'm not trying to rob you of your dignity. Nor did I come by to embarrass you."

"Then why are you here?" she asked.

When he had no ready answer, she gave him an amused look. "Since you're silent, I'll answer it for you. You came over to check up on me."

"I did no such thing," he blustered, then sighed. "At least I didn't mean for it to seem that way. I've just gotten into the habit of dropping by."

"Then I'm part of your usual route? Don't think I

don't see how you make stops at everyone's home or business during the course of your day."

She stepped away from Dillon and touched her son's cheek. "I love how you care for me, Mick, for this whole family. But just as you had to do with your children, you have to let me go."

Her words seemed to alarm him. "Let you go? What does that mean? Are you planning to go back to Ireland, after all?"

"No. I'm just planning to live what's left of my life in the way that seems right to me. While your opinion will always matter, it's not what counts the most."

Mick looked oddly thrown by her determined reply, but he nodded slowly. "Fair enough. I guess I'll be going then."

"Unless you'd like to stay and join us for a bit," Dillon said, holding out an olive branch. "We can always retrieve another chair from the porch."

"And be a third wheel? No, thank you," Mick said, visibly shuddering. "But I do appreciate the offer. I'll see both of you tomorrow. If you'd like, Dillon, Kevin has said if we can go early, he'll take us out on the foundation's research boat for a closer look at the bay."

"I'd like that," Dillon said at once. "Assuming you've no intention of tossing me overboard."

Mick laughed. "Not a chance, especially with Ma and my son along as witnesses."

"Then we'll see you bright and early," Dillon said eagerly. "I'll ask Moira if she'd care to come along, if that's all right."

"It would be fine," Mick told him. "She agreed earlier to take pictures at Henry's birthday party, so she may need to make preparations for that. But since

Kevin will want to be back in time for the party as well, I imagine she could do both. It's up to her."

"I'll give her the option, then," Dillon said.

Nell watched her son walk away and shook her head. "For a few minutes there, I felt like a teenager again."

"He sounded a lot like your very protective grandfather, didn't he?" Dillon agreed. He looked into her eyes. "Now, where were we?"

Nell stepped back into his arms. "About here, as I recall."

"Ah, yes," he said, then once more touched his lips to hers.

Moira stood at the rail of the boat Kevin had commandeered for the day from Thomas's foundation. Originally having intended it as a charter fishing boat, Kevin had instead given it to the foundation and joined his uncle in the work there. Moira gathered that his decision had caused some friction with Mick, who'd felt his son was going over to the enemy—his brother Thomas.

Now, though, here was Mick, right alongside his son, so apparently this particular O'Brien rift had healed. It was yet another example of the family dynamics for her to ponder.

As she watched the passing scenery, her grandfather joined her at the rail.

"You've some color in your cheeks this morning and a sparkle in your eye. May I assume things are going well with you and Luke?"

She smiled at the diplomatic phrasing. "Quite well, as a matter of fact." She grinned at him. "I'm assuming you'd rather not have details."

He laughed at that. "No, the details are definitely none of my business."

She turned to study him. "You seem especially cheerful and content this morning as well. May I assume that you and Nell are having a wonderful time?"

"We are," he said. "In fact, I've been meaning to talk to you about that."

Moira stilled. Was he about to announce that they were marrying? She wouldn't be that surprised to hear it, but what would it mean in terms of him staying on?

"About what?" she asked hesitantly.

"Nell's asked me to stay on longer and I've agreed. I've left my businesses in capable hands, so there's no need for me to rush back to Ireland. I can arrange for the extension, so I've decided to do it."

"I see," she said softly, not sure how she felt about the news. It meant she would be returning to Dublin alone.

He tucked a finger under her chin. "Don't look so gloomy. You'll be able to continue to live at my house in Dublin, if you like. That won't change." He held her gaze. "Or you could consider staying on here as well."

As tempted as she was by the suggestion, Moira shook her head. "Not unless Luke were to suggest it," she said insistently. "I came for a visit. That was the understanding."

"I don't think he'd object to your visit being longer."

"Perhaps not, but he hasn't asked me, as Nell asked you. Besides, there's my work to think of. Peter has a few photography assignments lined up for me. I can hardly turn my back on those commitments. It wouldn't be the best way to start a business, would it?"

"I suppose not," he conceded.

In a way his agreement was a disappointment. A part of her wanted to stay—no question about it. Her real hesitation had far less to do with any work commitments than it did with worry about what Luke's reaction might be. Ironically, she could justify staying here for work just as easily as she could going home, thanks to Megan's interest in her photographs. No, the real issue was Luke.

Thankfully, though, her grandfather backed off. "The offer is on the table, if you change your mind," he said. "Nell's more than willing to have you as a houseguest for as long as you like. We've already discussed it."

She smiled. "Do I sense a bit of matchmaking at work in that?" she asked. She wouldn't put it past either of them.

"Nothing more than a gracious invitation," her grandfather insisted, his expression all innocence.

Moira laughed. "You're not fooling me!"

"I just want to see you happy, darling girl. That's all."

He headed off to find Nell, and Moira once more turned her attention to the beautiful scenery. She could fall in love with this place, she realized. It was a good thing, since she was already madly in love with one of its residents.

Luke stood off by himself at Henry's birthday party, smiling at his young cousin's delight at all the attention. A year ago, Henry would definitely have been too shy to enjoy it, but now he was as much an instigator of trouble and noise as anyone else.

Luke's real focus, though, was Moira. Watching her

work was a revelation. She insinuated herself right into the middle of all the kids, teasing them, her demeanor as carefree as theirs. It was extraordinary to see, as he'd not yet forgotten their uneasy introduction when she'd barely spoken a word to anyone. No wonder she excelled at taking photos of people. She transformed herself, especially around children. He realized for the first time what a wonderful mother she'd be.

To be honest, he'd had his doubts about that. Her moodiness, which was merely challenging to him, would be daunting for a child. Just thinking about it had given him pause every time he'd had a fleeting thought about taking another step in their relationship. Seeing her like this, though, reassured him.

Not that he was ready to take another step, not toward marriage, much less toward parenthood. As the pub's opening crept closer and closer, his nerves were increasingly frayed. Every day was a battle between him and his endless lists of details. Truthfully, he had no idea if he even had all the necessary details on his lists. He just added things as he thought of them, crossed them off when they were done.

He should probably be at the pub right now, attacking a few more chores, but he hadn't been able to pass up the chance to stop by Henry's party. Like Connor, he was a sucker for cake. And, to be honest, he hadn't wanted to miss the chance to glimpse Moira in her element.

She broke free, laughing, and headed his way. Sunlight caught in her hair, and her face was alight in a way he'd too rarely seen it.

"Having fun?" he asked as she neared.

"The best time ever," she admitted. "I've never been

around a more rambunctious group of kids. The best part is seeing Henry at the heart of it. He was already coming out of his shell when I met him at Christmas, but clearly he's taken even more strides since then."

Luke chuckled. "You should have been here when he first came to live with Shanna, before she and Kevin married. He practically faded into the woodwork because of the circumstances at home."

"I heard his father—Shanna's ex-husband—is an alcoholic. Is that right?"

"And has several serious related health issues. Henry was left to tiptoe around trying not to disturb his father. He had only a nanny to look out for him once Shanna divorced his father. It was his father's parents who realized he'd be far better off with Shanna and negotiated the arrangements so she and Kevin could adopt him. Shanna sees that he still has frequent visits with his father and his grandparents, but they're carefully controlled so that his dad is having his best possible days while Henry's there. It's worked out well all around."

He smiled. "When he first arrived here, they actually thought quiet, studious Henry would be a good influence on Davy, but it's turned out to work the other way. Davy's given Henry back his childhood. And with a new baby in the house, I imagine there will be even more changes ahead."

Moira glanced back toward the impromptu soccer game going on across the lawn. "It's wonderful to see, isn't it?"

"It is," Luke said, but his gaze was fixed on her. "Are you happy with the pictures you've been taking?"

"I won't know till I've a chance to look at them

later," she said with a shrug. "But there are bound to be one or two special ones."

He regarded her with surprise. "But you must have taken hundreds."

"At least," she agreed, then grinned. "Special's rare."

"You're already thinking like a professional," he said. "Megan would be impressed."

She drew in a deep breath, as if she were contemplating returning to a battle of some sort. "I suppose I should get back out there," she said.

"Don't you want time out for cake, at least?" he asked. "I could grab a slice for you. It came from Jess's chef and it's excellent, even if Gram has been muttering all afternoon about being relieved of cake duty."

"Grab me a piece and save it for later," she said. "I don't want to miss any potentially great shots. Will you be around till the end?"

He shook his head. "I'm about to go back to work." He looked into her eyes. "Meet me there when you're finished?"

"It's a plan," she said at once, then pressed a quick, unsatisfying kiss to his cheek.

She was about to dart away when Luke snagged her hand. "Not so fast," he said.

"What?"

He lowered his head and settled his mouth over hers, then lingered there until he heard her breath hitch and felt his own pulse scramble. When he stepped away, he smiled. "There now," he said with satisfaction. "That's a proper goodbye."

"It is, indeed," she agreed, her eyes sparkling. "Now I can hardly wait for hello."

Neither could Luke.

12

Moira picked up pizza on her way to Luke's pub. It was the quickest, easiest meal she could think of, one he'd surely have enough time to eat. Truthfully, she was eager for a chance to put her memory card into his computer and see the results of her work at Henry's party. She was almost as excited about that as she was about the prospect of spending time with Luke. And since he was increasingly distracted by his to-do list, she assumed she'd have plenty of time tonight for her own work.

As she'd anticipated, she found him in the office grumbling to himself about something. She set the pizza on the lone table in the main room, then headed off to get Luke.

Rather than talking to himself, though, he was on the phone complaining to a supplier.

"The linens were to be here yesterday," he said. "I don't care what the shipping report shows, they're not here. And no, I don't want to be on hold while you investigate. Don't put me on hold." A shocked expression crossed his face just before he glanced up and noticed her presence.

"She put me on hold," he said, looking dumbstruck.

Moira bit back a chuckle. "I'm not surprised. I doubt I'd want to deal with you right now, either." She gestured toward the phone. "When she comes back, no matter what she says, thank her politely and hang up. Monday's soon enough to resolve this. Nothing's going to be shipped today, anyway. And the opening isn't tonight or even tomorrow. Your precious timetable's just fine."

"But it was already supposed to be en route," he grumbled. "I wanted to check it off my list."

"And you will get to do that on Monday. If they say it's on a truck, it probably is. I'm sure there's a tracking number somewhere that will tell them exactly where your tablecloths and napkins are hiding out."

He frowned at her reasonable tone. She knew the role reversal must be astounding to him. He was supposed to be the calm, unflappable one, she the shrew.

"Yes, hello," he said into the phone. "The package is at the substation in Baltimore? You're absolutely sure? And it will be here Monday morning? Okay, then. Thank you. Sorry for biting your head off before."

He put down the phone and heaved a sigh of relief. "Another crisis averted."

She smiled. "It wouldn't have been a true crisis unless it were the night before the opening," she suggested. "Now, come into the other room. I've brought pizza."

"But I was going to take you out," he protested.

"Do you honestly want to be away from your lists for an evening? Not that I don't think it would be good for you to have a break, but you seem to be increasingly obsessed with them."

He laughed, his expression sheepish. "I am, aren't I?" He studied her. "You honestly don't mind spending the evening here?"

She gestured toward the window, still covered with brown paper. "I'd be happier with a view, but otherwise, as long as I can be here with you, I'm exactly where I want to be." She grinned and admitted, "Besides, I'm itching to get on that computer of yours to look at the pictures I took this afternoon."

"So this wasn't an entirely noble sacrifice?" he teased.

"Not entirely," she admitted.

"Did you get pepperoni?"

"Of course."

"And sausage?"

"Yes, my dear meat-lover, your side is covered with all those artery-clogging things you love."

"And yours?"

"Green peppers, onions and mushrooms."

He made a face. "Too healthy."

"It just means I'll outlive you," she teased. "Something you might want to consider."

He opened the box, drew in a deep breath and sighed happily. "Nope. I'm good."

He snagged a couple of beers from the refrigerator in the kitchen, then sat down across from her. Once he'd grabbed his first slice of pizza, Moira dared to bring up something that had been on her mind all day.

"Grandfather mentioned something to me this morning while we were out on Kevin's boat," she began.

Luke nodded. "How was that, by the way? Did you have fun?"

"It was great. I loved seeing all the little towns along the water, though, if you ask me, some of the homes are way too big."

"The McMansions," Luke said. "I hate them, too, and you should hear Uncle Mick and Uncle Thomas get going on them. It's a rare moment of unity between them, especially with those owners who let their contractors clear-cut all the trees before building. They paid huge fines for doing it if they got caught, and I think Thomas made it his business to catch as many of them as possible."

"As well he should," Moira said. "What a terrible destruction of natural beauty." She hesitated, then said, "My grandfather mentioned to me that he's planning to stay on here for a while. Did you know about that?"

Luke nodded. "Gram told me right after you all arrived."

Moira frowned. "So the decision was made that quickly?"

"Sure. I know Gram wanted it resolved as soon as possible and intended to ask Dillon the minute you got settled. She said he agreed immediately."

"I see," Moira said. "Then she'd talked to you about it ahead of time?"

"She mentioned it." He studied her curiously. "What's wrong? Aren't you happy that he's staying?"

"That's fine, I suppose. It's up to him, really."

Luke watched her with a frown knitting his brow. "You're saying all the right words, but you're still not sounding happy. Is it the thought of flying home alone? Being in his house in Dublin on your own? What?"

"Both of those, I guess," she said, because she wasn't about to admit that she was perhaps irrationally hurt because it hadn't once crossed Luke's mind to suggest that she stay on longer. She told herself that wouldn't have mattered had everyone stuck to the original plan. Nell's invitation to her grandfather had changed things, though, and Luke had known about it. Yet he'd not felt at all compelled to suggest that she do the same thing. She knew she was being unreasonable, but her feelings were her feelings. She couldn't always control them, and sometimes acting rationally was beyond her.

She put aside her pizza and stood up. "I think I'll look at those pictures now, if you're not planning to be on the computer."

"That's fine," he said, though he continued to regard her with confusion. "Moira, what am I missing?"

"Nothing," she said softly. "Not a bloody thing!"

Even as the words left her mouth, she knew only someone very dense would believe them. Luke wasn't dense. Distracted, maybe, but never obtuse. Feeling foolish for giving away her distress, she left the room before he could ask whatever questions might occur to him and start a conversation it was probably far better for them to avoid. Letting him see that she was hurt was embarrassing enough. Letting him dig any deeper would be humiliating.

Luke stared after Moira as she hurried into the office. He'd obviously screwed up in some way, but it was beyond him how. They'd been talking about her grandfather and Gram. That's when the temperature had cooled below freezing, but what did that have to do with the two of them?

It had been his experience that it was always best to resolve a situation like this immediately, but he'd had to learn with Moira to bide his time. Her temper needed to settle a bit before she'd open up with the truth. Otherwise, they'd wind up yelling to no avail.

Fortunately, he was able to give her plenty of space. Earlier he'd downloaded and printed a couple of dozen applications from potential employees. He'd scheduled the interviews for Monday, and now was the perfect opportunity to sort through the résumés and make a few notes for himself so he'd be able to see if experience on paper matched up with initial impressions in person.

He'd even found three people with a decent amount of kitchen experience who might be able to take over the cooking. All three had agreed to do a test run with a few of Gram's recipes, so Luke wanted to narrow down those options to see which would provide the greatest challenge. This afternoon Gram had agreed to come in to taste the results and help him make his final choice. If Dillon and Moira joined them, they could make a party of it, he thought, turning the project into something he could actually look forward to.

He was completely absorbed in his work when he sensed that Moira was standing next to him. He hadn't even heard her leave his office.

"Hey!" he said, blinking up at her. "What time is it?"

"Getting on toward eleven," she said. "I think I'll head back to your grandmother's."

He frowned at that. Obviously, the thaw hadn't set in yet. "Is that what you want to do?"

She sighed and shook her head. "I just think it's best."

"Mind telling me why? Is this about whatever upset you earlier?"

She sighed and sat down beside him, then leaned forward, her expression earnest. "Luke, I'm trying really, really hard to understand your need to compartmentalize your life and proceed along at an orderly pace, but it's hard. These circumstances make it hard."

Though he didn't yet understand, he nodded. "I'm listening," he said, hoping to encourage her to go on.

Instead, she gave him an impatient look. "You should be able to figure it out. I've given you enough hints."

He laughed, though he saw at once that that only irritated her more. "Sorry, but I've never professed to be a mind reader, Moira. And, to be honest, I've never been so involved with anyone that I've needed to practice being one."

"And is that the case with me? That we're not so involved that you have to waste any energy trying to figure out what's upsetting me?"

He knew it was a trick question, one likely to land him in even hotter water, but he opted for honesty. "Frankly, one of the things I've liked the best about you is that from the beginning you've always spoken your mind. I always knew exactly where I stood. Even now, I know you're thoroughly annoyed with me. I just keep waiting for you to tell me why."

"I shouldn't have to," she said in frustration.

"But isn't it easier to just say it than to try to prod me into guessing?" he replied, equally frustrated.

He held her gaze as he asked it, and eventually he saw the faint tug of a smile at the corners of her mouth.

"So I've reverted to being impossible Moira?" she suggested.

"Maybe just a little," he said. "Don't you know you can be straightforward with me by now? I'm trainable, Moira. I swear it."

Now she did laugh and the tension broke.

"I think people have had it all wrong," she told him. "*You're* the impossible one. How am I supposed to stay mad at you?"

"Honestly, I wish you wouldn't," he replied. He reached for her hands. "Talk to me."

"Okay, here it is. When grandfather told me he was staying on and then you said you'd known about it, it hurt my feelings that you hadn't thought to ask the same of me."

Luke regarded her with astonishment. "The one thing has nothing to do with the other," he said. "We're talking about your grandfather and Gram. They're at an entirely different stage of their lives. They have the leisure to do whatever they like. You have this wonderful opportunity waiting for you in Dublin. I thought you were excited to be testing your wings at that. And I have this place to launch and manage and figure out how to make a success of it. I assumed you wanted to go home and that it would be selfish of me to suggest that you change your plans."

"Which leaves us precisely where?" she asked. "Is there some sort of timetable in that logical, orderly head of yours?"

"Not really," he admitted.

"So, what? If I happen to cross your mind, you'll give me a call or send an email? If you've a free moment, you might fly over for a visit someday? Or if I have a sudden urge, I can do the same thing? Is it all that casual to you, then?"

"Yes," he said, then immediately saw the mistake of his quick response in the darkening of her eyes. "I mean, no, not the way you're taking it."

"I don't think there are that many different interpretations," she said. She stood up. "I need to get to Nell's."

"No," he argued. "You need to stay here so we can finish this conversation."

She gave him a sad look. "I think we just did."

And then, before he could react, she'd grabbed her jacket and purse and was gone.

The man was an idiot, pure and simple, Moira thought as she plodded her way back toward Nell's cottage. There wasn't a question in her mind that she'd be safe enough walking home at this late hour, but she did shiver as a breeze blew in off the bay. There was a storm brewing. She could feel it in the air. Anyone from Ireland would have recognized the signs.

The chilly rain started to fall just as she started up the road to Nell's. She still had at least a half-mile walk ahead of her. She heard the car before the headlights appeared as it came around a bend in the road. It pulled to a stop beside her.

"Get in," Luke said.

"I'm almost there. I can walk," she said, still moving forward.

"Do not make me stop this car to drag you in here," he said, clearly beyond annoyed.

"Go home, Luke. I'll be fine."

"And I thought my family was stubborn," he groused, cutting the engine and climbing out of the car.

She turned to warn him off. "I'm not getting into that

car with you and if you try to drag me in, I'll scream my head off."

He shook his head. "I'm sure you will, so I'll just walk along with you, and we'll both risk pneumonia. It doesn't make a lot of sense to me, but I can't allow you to walk home at this hour alone."

"It's perfectly safe. Besides, I'm almost there."

"And if you walk in looking like a drowned rat and you're all by yourself, I'll never hear the end of it," he said, shoving his hands in his pockets and falling into an easy stride next to her.

She could tell there was absolutely no way she was going to shake him. Still, she tried again. "Luke, no one will be up. I won't tell a soul that I walked home by myself in the pouring rain. Your honor will be perfectly intact come morning."

"Not taking the chance," he said, matching her stubbornness.

She uttered a sigh of resignation. "Whatever made me think we were a good match?"

He actually had the audacity to chuckle at that. "I could show you, if you'd like to pause for a moment."

"We're out here in the pouring rain, and you're thinking of sex?" she asked incredulously.

"You always make me think of sex," he responded.

She rounded on him then, not sure whether to be appalled or pleased by the remark. "Seriously?"

"Always," he reiterated.

"Even now, when I'm mad at you and being difficult and arbitrary and stubborn?"

"A few of your more alluring traits," he insisted.

"Now you're just hoping to get lucky, after all," she said.

They walked in silence a little farther before he slanted a look in her direction. "Did it work? Am I going to get lucky?"

"Not in your grandmother's house, that's for sure," she retorted.

"That wasn't exactly a no," he said hopefully. "Was it?"

"Alas, no," she said, regretting how easily he managed to ease past her defenses and defuse her temper. "I suppose we should make a U-turn and head back to your car."

She thought she glimpsed a smile on his lips just then. "Are you smiling?" she asked. "Please tell me that is not a smug smile I just saw on your face."

"No smile," he said at once.

She elbowed him lightly in the side. "Yes, it was. It's absolutely pitiful how easy I am."

"Easy?" he echoed, sounding incredulous.

She laughed. "You know what I mean. It's impossible to stay mad at you even half as long as you deserve."

"I'm glad," he told her.

"Yes, you would be, wouldn't you? It works out quite nicely for you."

Just before he opened the car door for her, he looked into her eyes. "I'll do my best to make sure it works out nicely for you as well."

And she knew he would. That, perhaps, was the reason it was going to be all but impossible for her to ever walk away and make it stick.

Sunday dinner at Mick and Megan's was yet another of those O'Brien family gatherings that made Moira yearn to be a part of this family. Even more so than little Henry's birthday party, it was the kind of occasion that showcased the family ties at their best. There were debates among the brothers—Mick, Thomas and Jeff, as well as laughter among the women preparing the meal in the kitchen. Children were underfoot everywhere Moira turned, admonished only rarely for making too much noise or running too fast in the house.

"God, I love this," she murmured to herself, unaware that Luke's mother was close enough to overhear.

"It's the O'Briens at their best," Jo said, startling her. "It can also be a little intimidating. It took me a long time to feel a real part of it. I'm not as quick to jump into an argument as most of them are."

"But I'll bet you've learned to stand your ground," Moira said.

Jo nodded. "I've had to. Fortunately, though, Jeff isn't the kind of man who needs to battle over everything. We can actually hold a perfectly rational conversation and reach a mutually satisfying agreement. We're amazingly civilized compared to the rest of the family."

"That must drive his brothers mad," Moira guessed. "Mick and Thomas seem to enjoy the sheer challenge of the debate."

"They do," Jo confirmed. She regarded Moira intently. "Are you enjoying your visit to Chesapeake Shores?"

"I am. It's been wonderful. And I can't wait for the opening of Luke's pub."

"Neither can I," Jo said. "I'm actually jealous that he's let you get a glimpse inside, while the rest of us have been banished until opening night."

"He wants the *wow* factor of that first impression,"

Moira said. "Of course, a few people have been sneaking in the past few days for a variety of reasons. I think once the furnishings have been delivered, though, he'll have it on total lockdown."

"You've been a huge help to him," Jo said.

Moira was surprised by her assessment. "I haven't done much. This was all his idea. I was just along for the research."

"But you've been exactly what he needed, a knowledgeable sounding board. You've been around pubs your whole life. You've worked in several. I'm sure you know the pitfalls and can point out what makes one successful."

"I'm not sure there's a magic formula," Moira said. "But the best ones create a sense of community. I think Luke will have no problem doing that here. He has the personality for it, don't you think?"

Jo nodded. "In a family of gregarious people, he's always been a notch above. He can be a peacemaker, too, if need be. That's the role he played for his sister when he feared her marriage might be in danger. He saw it, I think, before any of the rest of us did, and just stepped in."

"You're referring to Kristen, the woman who had some sort of past history with Susie's husband," Moira guessed.

"She's the one," Jo said in a way that made it absolutely clear how she felt about the woman. "And though I didn't approve of Luke's means, I'm eternally grateful that he stepped in before the situation deteriorated any further."

"He says that's all there was to it," Moira said, curious to know Jo's perception of the situation.

"I think it was," Jo said. "At least on Luke's part. With a woman like Kristen, it's hard to say. She doesn't seem like the kind to let go easily, which is what started the problem in the first place. She wanted Mack back and didn't care if Susie was hurt in the process. That would have been offensive enough under any circumstances, but Susie was battling cancer at the time. It struck me as heartless. I'll never forgive Kristen for being so callous. Thank goodness she's no longer in Luke's life, either. She'd never have been welcomed in this family."

She waved a hand in the air. "Enough of that. Luke's moved on, and from what I can see, he's happier than he's ever been. That's due in great measure to you, so thank you for that."

Moira regarded her with surprise. No one had ever suggested that her presence in someone's life might actually be a blessing. Her own father had thought she was the last straw and hadn't even wanted to know her. Her mother tolerated her. Her grandfather was the one person in her family who had shown her true kindness. It was only since Luke that she'd begun to view herself as more than a nuisance.

"I'm the one who's grateful," she told Jo candidly. "Luke's looked at me as no one else ever has, as if I'm more than an impossible problem to be dealt with."

Jo frowned at her words. "Surely not. I know that's not how Dillon views you at all."

"But Grandfather's only recently come into my life. It's because of him and Luke that I'm starting to see myself in a different way."

Jo regarded her with sympathy. "Self-esteem can be a fragile thing," she said. "I teach physical education and spend a lot of time with young women. They all struggle with self-esteem and body image, often confusing the two. It makes me wonder what sort of homes they've come from, what sort of parents let them harbor even the tiniest doubts about their worth."

"Careless ones, I think," Moira said, thinking of her own mother. "My mum wasn't cruel or even thoughtless. She was just too busy trying to keep us afloat financially to see what my brothers and I really needed, which was a stronger sense of family and belonging."

"Well, you've found that here with us," Jo said, giving her an impulsive hug. "Now I see my son on his way over here, probably in a panic that I'm telling you tales about his misdeeds as a boy."

"And have you?" Luke asked her as he joined them.

"Not a one," Jo told him. "We've both been singing your praises."

He gave Moira a curious look. "Even you?"

She laughed at his skeptical expression. "Even me. You've done nothing yet today to annoy me."

"Then I'll do my best to make sure it stays that way," he promised.

When Jo had left them, he looked into her eyes. "Did she scare you off?"

"Far from it," Moira admitted. "I'm more convinced than ever that you're quite a knight in shining armor."

The bigger question, still unanswered, though, was whether he was hers.

13

Even though she'd put her cards on the table with Luke
a couple of nights ago, by Monday Moira was back to
wondering how she fit into Luke's life. It was the draw-
back of a life spent questioning her own judgment and
decisions.

It was true that spending nights in his bed was amazing, but in reality that told her nothing about the future.
And she knew from prior conversations that nothing
was likely to change for some time to come. It left her
feeling disgruntled and alone. Add in Luke's increasing distraction and she was having one of those days
when she wondered if it was even wise to stick around
for the scheduled month.

Today there'd been a steady parade of potential employees through the pub. Luke hadn't suggested that
she sit in on the interviews, and she hadn't offered. She
knew that made sense, since it wasn't her business, but,
as hard as she'd tried not to, she'd felt left out.

She'd spent most of the day closeted in his office,
going through the pictures she'd taken on Saturday and
making prints for Kevin and Shanna and the rest of

the family, then putting certain ones into the file for her portfolio to show to Megan. While seeing so many laughing images made her smile, ironically they left her feeling more like an outsider than ever. This wasn't her family, no matter how she might wish it were. And at the rate things were progressing, it might never be. The date of her departure loomed ahead, unmistakable in its possible finality for the relationship.

By midday she was restless and out of sorts. Since the sun was shining, she slipped past Luke and his applicants and headed for the beach. Perhaps a walk by the water would clear her head. It sometimes worked in ways nothing else did.

But at the end of an hour, she was still trying to analyze her mood. She could hardly complain about the sex, because that was as magical as it had ever been. There was plenty of laughter and teasing and quiet conversation as well. So what was missing? Eventually she realized that, for the first time ever, she wanted something more from a relationship, something she didn't dare ask for. She wanted forever. And Luke, she knew all too well, did not. At least not now.

Should she decide totally on her own to stay and fight for what she really wanted, or should she accept that Luke might never be ready and cut her losses by going home now? Losing him would hurt whenever it happened, but now might be for the best, when she at least had the prospect of an exciting career to explore when she returned to Dublin. A call from Peter had promised a half-dozen assignments on her return, all of them for more money than she'd ever dreamed of making from her photography.

She wasted most of the afternoon waging an internal war with herself. By the time she returned to the pub, she'd reached no conclusion, which left her feeling more out of sorts than ever. She should have gone straight back to Nell's till the clouds over her dispersed, but she didn't. Maybe she was itching for a confrontation, after all.

Seeing that Luke was on the phone in his office when she returned, she sat at a table by the window he'd been using earlier and peeked out at the bay through a sliver of an opening between the sheets of protective brown paper. She thought she'd never tire of that view, especially on a sunny day like this one.

When he finished his call, Luke joined her, dropping a distracted kiss on her cheek, then pausing to take another look.

"Are you unhappy about something, Moira?"

"Just feeling a bit at loose ends," she admitted, dancing toward the topic, but not yet ready to bring it up.

"You spent the whole morning working on your photographs," he reminded her, looking puzzled. "Were you unhappy with them?"

"No, some are quite good, in fact. And I have prints to give to Shanna and Kevin and some of the others. I've made several for Nell as well. I hope to find frames and give them to her as a thank-you for welcoming me into her home."

"She'll love that," he said. "So what is going on in that complicated mind of yours?"

She met his gaze and risked expressing just a bit of what she'd been thinking on her walk. "I'm not entirely sure I'm cut out to be a career woman."

"But you've barely even begun," he protested. "How

could you possibly know? I thought the idea of being a photographer was exciting to you."

"It was," she said. "In a theoretical way. It's the first time I've ever had people tell me I'm not just good at something, but possibly even extraordinary. It took my breath away, to be quite honest. And Peter has jobs waiting, so the pressure's already on to treat this as something more than a hobby."

He was obviously floundering, but she had to give him credit. He kept trying to figure out what she was saying.

"You don't want to be a photographer?" he asked. "You've figured that out after only a few days at it? How can that be?"

She sighed. How could she tell him that what she wanted was something much simpler, to be a part of his life, to be a wife and mother and partner? That was so politically incorrect it made her feel as if she must be slightly crazy for wanting it. She couldn't help recalling how Laila and Jess had looked at her when she'd admitted as much to them.

"Having the whole photography thing dangled in front of me, first by Peter back home and then by Megan, it was exciting. I know I should be ecstatic to have gotten such reactions from the two of them, and I am. But a whole lifetime of it? I don't know that I have the drive for it, Luke. And that's what it will take to be a success, isn't it? It's not something to be done by half measures."

Luke shook his head, clearly bemused by her change of heart. "No one is saying you have to pursue it, if it's not what you want," he told her. "But shouldn't you at least give it more of a chance?"

"Oh, I will," she said. "I'm not foolish enough to turn my back on something I might actually be good at, not after never excelling at anything before. And Peter's committed me to doing these jobs. I certainly won't let him down."

She met his gaze. "You know what's ironic? For years I had no direction for my life back home. When Grandfather suggested this trip, I thought I'd find what I needed here. Amazingly, all the signs here point in exactly the same direction—toward photography. And yet I still feel unsettled and at loose ends, like it's all a bad fit."

Luke frowned at her words. "How were you hoping to fit in here?"

"I don't know exactly," she responded evasively, though it wasn't true. She'd wanted more here. She'd wanted *him,* not in the way she had him, but with a future all tied up in a pretty bow. It had been a girl's daydream, really.

"Is this about me?" he asked, his expression wary. "Is it about me not being ready to take the next step in our relationship?"

Usually she appreciated his directness, but right this second she found it annoying and egotistical, especially with that look on his face like a cornered animal. "Not everything is about you, Luke."

"I'm well aware of that," he said patiently. "But I'm asking if you made this trip hoping for something more to happen between us. You've been hinting at that for days now, and I thought I'd explained where things stood."

She regarded him with a touch of defiance that eventually faltered. "Oh, you have. Don't worry, I know the way of things, Luke. We had a bit of a fling in Ireland. It's continuing quite nicely here, but that's all it is."

He actually looked shocked by her assessment. It had him unexpectedly backpedaling. "And if I were to say it's not that casual? Would that make you happier?"

She frowned at the question. "What do you mean?"

"What if it's more than a fling to me? What if I truly care about you?"

"Do you?" she pressed, fighting to keep her hopes from spinning wildly out of control. It wouldn't do to leap to conclusions, not about something like this.

He smiled, taking her hands in his, but then his expression turned serious. "Here's the truth, Moira," he said. "My feelings for you were strong from the moment we met, but, like you, I've had little sense of direction in my life. This place is my chance to prove myself, not just to my family, but also to myself. I want to have something to offer you when the time comes. Until I have that, I've been trying not to rush into any-thing else."

She found his earnest tone oddly endearing. "One thing at a time, then? How many ways do you have to repeat that to me before I can accept it? I must be making you crazy, coming back to the same thing time after time. You'll make a wild success of this place and then decide whether I fit in. That's the bottom line."

"Not *if* you fit in," he corrected. "There's no ques-tion of that. It'll be more a matter of whether you want to. You could move forward with your photography and discover that you're truly passionate about it. I think right now you're all nerves, wondering if it's real. I think you'd rather not try than risk failing."

"It's not about being afraid to fail," she said fiercely.

"I've failed at plenty in my life. I'm used to it." What she'd never reached for before was love, and she *was* terrified of failing at that. She looked him in the eye. "Since we're being honest, do you really want to hear what I want now?"

"Sure."

"I want to help you make a success of this place," she said with total candor. "And that's not entirely so I can work side by side with you and sneak kisses every chance we get." At least that was a partial truth, if not the whole truth.

He grinned at that. "Then why else would you want to do it?"

"Because it's something I love," she said simply. "I left school because nothing there seemed to excite me. I was wasting my time and theirs. The only time I've felt at home was working in places just like this, chatting up the customers, making someone lonely smile just a bit. Mum and my granddad would never have approved of such a thing as a career. They would have seen it as wasting my life." She shrugged. "But even more than photography, it feels right to me."

Luke regarded her with amazement. "Moira, if you wanted to stay and work here, why didn't you say so from the beginning? If we can work out all the proper visas or whatever it takes, nothing would please me more. I'm sure Connor could make the arrangements."

Finally, an invitation to stay! But coming only after she'd all but dragged it out of him, his response irked her. "Was this a job interview, then?"

He frowned at the question. "I suppose it was, in a weird way."

"Then, no thank you," she told him, politely but firmly.

He regarded her in stunned silence, then muttered, "No? Didn't you just give an entire speech about why you wanted to work here?"

"You apparently heard only the part you wanted to hear," she corrected. "I will not be just some little bit of Irish fluff meant to lend this place authenticity."

"I never said that," he protested.

"Didn't you? That's what I heard. I want more than that from you, Luke O'Brien."

"We've yet to talk about money," he said, obviously frustrated and clearly operating on some entirely different wavelength from the one she'd been on.

She stood up at that, and barely resisted the urge to use the nearby rolls of architectural plans to hit him. "Now you're just being obtuse," she said, stalking off.

Apparently, even in America, men of Irish extraction were doomed to be dumber than dirt when it came to women!

"I don't get it," Luke complained later that evening to his brother and Laila. "I offered her a job so she could stay here. I said we'd work out the legalities. I'm sure Connor could have figured out something."

"And that's when she stormed off?" Laila asked, her eyes twinkling. "Imagine that!"

Luke frowned at her sarcasm. "You're taking her side?"

"I wasn't aware there were sides," Laila replied. "But if there are, then, yes, I'm on hers."

"You're going to have to explain that to me," Luke said.

Laila rolled her eyes. "Obviously. Matthew, what about you? Do you get it?"

There was a definite challenge in the question. Luke saw his brother squirm uncomfortably.

"If I had to take a stab at this," Matthew said, "and apparently I do, Moira was actually angling for a partnership, and not of the business variety."

Laila patted his cheek. "Is it any wonder I gave in and married you? You're so evolved. You actually get these things."

Luke laughed. These two were a never-ending source of amusement for everyone in the family. Laila was more than ten years older than Matthew. She'd been considered by everyone, including herself, to be boring and stuffy and rigid. Matthew had been an irrepressible scoundrel. They shouldn't have worked as a couple, but they did. Fantastically well, as a matter of fact. Luke was envious, especially now that they seemed to have resolved their differences over her pregnancy.

He met his sister-in-law's gaze, wondering if she could possibly be right. "Moira wants a commitment? Immediately? I told her I have to focus completely on getting this business going right now. I didn't close any doors, just explained the reality."

"How incredibly romantic of you," Laila said. "I'm sure her heart went pitter-pat at such a lovely declaration. I'm surprised she didn't put you in traction before she walked out on you."

Luke winced, then glanced at his brother. "It was really bad, wasn't it?"

Matthew nodded. "I'd say yes," he agreed, glancing at his wife for confirmation.

"Really bad," Laila said emphatically. "Do you love her or not, Luke? Isn't that the real issue here?"

"But the timing—"

"Maybe it sucks or maybe it's just the way it is," she said. "I wasn't exactly ready to jump into this relationship with Matthew, you know, but there he was, all sexy and cute and persistent, and look where we are now."

"Please God, don't start seducing each other right here in front of me," Luke pleaded, seeing the way Matthew's eyes darkened at Laila's words. He shook his head. "Never mind. I'll be on my way now. Thanks for the advice."

But even as he practically ran for the door, he realized they were no longer listening to a word he said.

Nell had detected Moira's unhappiness when she came back from spending her day with Luke at the pub. The girl hardly made a secret of it when she was having a bad day. Her dark and gloomy expression told the story.

"Where's my grandfather?" Moira asked.

"Resting," Nell told her. "He helped me work in the garden this morning, getting it ready to plant. It took a bit out of him."

Alarm immediately crossed Moira's face. "I don't understand. Grandfather never tires. Are you sure he's okay? Maybe I should check on him."

Nell held up a hand. "Let him rest. When you're our age, it takes a lot longer to completely recover from jet lag than it does at yours. At the end of a week, we're just beginning to get our feet back under us." She smiled at her. "It's nice to see you so concerned about him."

"Well, of course I am!" Moira said with a hint of indignation.

Nell's smile widened. "It's not a side of you I saw in Ireland," she said.

Moira flushed. "You're right, and I'm sorry. I was in a terrible mood over the holidays, and intent on taking it out on everyone else. I'm afraid that became a habit of mine over the years. I'll go to my room now, so you don't get sideswiped by my temper as well."

"Oh, I'm sure I'm tough enough to take it," Nell commented. "Why don't we have a cup of tea and you can tell my why you looked so unhappy just now when you got back from Luke's?"

Moira looked as if she'd prefer to get into the garden and dig for snails to eat, but she clearly couldn't come up with an excuse that wouldn't be considered impolite. "Sure," she said reluctantly, following Nell into the kitchen.

Nell always had a teakettle on the stove ready to be heated. While the water came to a boil, she put loose tea into one of her china pots, then poured the steaming water over it.

While it steeped, she put two of the traditional currant scones she'd baked earlier onto plates and set one in front of Moira, along with a pot of jam and some Devonshire cream that Jess ordered for her from one of the suppliers for her inn.

"I love this room," Moira said quietly as Nell finally joined her. "There's so much light in here, and the view is spectacular. It soothes me just to sit here and look out the window."

Nell nodded. "It does the same for me. Add in a cup

of tea, and there's virtually no problem that I can't tackle right here at this table if I put my mind to it."

"I wish I had a place like that," Moira blurted, then looked embarrassed at having revealed so much about her state of mind.

Nell took the comment in stride. "We all need a place like that. Why are you troubled today? Are you feeling homesick?"

Moira shook her head. "In an odd way, it's because I *don't* feel homesick that I'm in this mood." She regarded Nell earnestly. "I don't have a life there—not really. I've worked jobs, if you know what I mean. I don't have a career or a calling, at least not in the way that Mum and Grandfather would want for me to have. And the promise of a career in photography, despite the potential of it, doesn't excite me the way I know it should."

"But your future is your choice, not theirs," Nell said, beginning to detect the problem. Moira, for all her rebellious ways, wanted to please her family, just as most young people did, whether they admitted it or not.

Moira seemed surprised by her comment. "Do you truly believe that?"

"Of course. Look at the paths my grandchildren have chosen. Abby seemed to know straightaway what she wanted. She has a gift for the financial world and has made her mark there almost from her first job on Wall Street. Bree had great ambitions about becoming a playwright, but her heart was here with Jake. She's found a way to balance both, and added a wonderful flower shop as well. And Jess…" Her voice trailed off as she thought about Mick's youngest.

"She has a successful inn," Moira filled in for her. "She found her passion."

"That she did," Nell agreed, "but she tried any number of jobs before that. Not a one of them suited her, and not a one of them lasted."

"She has attention deficit disorder, though," Moira said. "Isn't that why it was hard for her to find her way?"

"That was one of the reasons, certainly," Nell agreed. "But the real key was for her to find the one thing she was passionate about, just as you said. You need to do the same thing. Some people gravitate directly to it. Others have to try a variety of things until they find the one that fits. Maybe photography is it, maybe not. You've won some accolades from Megan, who knows the field, so it's surely worth considering."

Moira nodded, her expression intrigued. "If I confide something to you, can you keep it to yourself?"

Nell smiled. "With all these grandchildren, I've learned to keep a secret or two."

"I've never said all this to another soul, aside from hinting at it to Laila and Jess, who looked horrified, but what I want more than anything is to have a family— the kind I didn't have when I was growing up. I want to be the mum who bakes cookies and walks my children to school, who volunteers for classroom outings and has dinner on the table when everyone gets home at the end of the day."

Nell regarded her with amusement. "Why would you need to keep such a goal to yourself? It's a good path. It's the one I chose."

Moira shrugged. "When there's not a man in the immediate future, it's a hard thing to admit."

"I thought there *was* a man in your future—my grandson."

Moira sighed. "He made it quite clear to me today that he's a long way from wanting a future with me. His entire focus is on his new pub." She met Nell's gaze. "Which is as it should be. I understand how important this is to him, how badly he wants to make a success of it." She shrugged. "I suppose I was just hoping I could be by his side to help."

Nell frowned. "Did he turn away your offer of help?"

"Oh, no," Moira said, a trace of bitterness in her voice. "He told me if I wanted a job, I could have one." Her expression turned indignant. "Which wasn't the point at all."

Nell laughed. "Perhaps you were too subtle," she said, though she couldn't imagine such a thing. Moira struck her as pretty forthright.

Moira gave her a wry look. "Have you ever once known me to be subtle?"

Nell chuckled. "But it's much harder to say what's really in your heart when you're not sure of the reception it will get."

"That's exactly it," Moira said, looking surprised. "I got all bumbly and far too careful with my words, especially when I sensed that Luke was on an entirely different wavelength." She regarded Nell hesitantly. "Is he the kind of man who will only appreciate me if I have some high-powered career?"

"Why would you ask that?"

"It's just that it's sometimes seen as politically incorrect for women today to choose family over work. When I talk about this with some of my girlfriends, they tend to think I'm daft. Laila and Jess certainly did."

"Raising a family is never a bad choice, in my opinion," Nell said. "There's nothing more important that a woman can do. That said, I completely support any woman who is excited about her career and wants that balance in her life. How could I not, in a family like mine?"

Just then Dillon walked into the kitchen, took in the sight of them together at the kitchen table and smiled. "It's nice to see two of the most important women in my life getting along so well," he said, dropping a kiss on each of their foreheads.

"We've been having a wonderful chat," Nell said.

"We have," Moira confirmed. "Thank you for giving me a fresh perspective on things, Nell."

"I always have a pot of tea and a friendly ear for family," Nell said, winking at her.

"I think I'll go for another walk on the beach," Moira said. "You've given me a lot to think about. Perhaps this time things will fall into place."

After she'd gone, Dillon regarded Nell with a lift of his brow. "I never expected to see the day when you and my granddaughter would be chatting away like magpies. What were you talking about?"

"This and that," Nell said, chuckling at his obvious frustration. "I like her, Dillon. When she lets down that guard of hers, she's lovely. She's young and struggling to find her way, but I think she's determined to make sense of her life and choose a future that will fulfill her."

"You are speaking of Moira, is that right?" he asked, clearly not quite believing her unexpected praise.

Nell nodded. "I think I understand where that rebellion of hers comes from. She's at a crossroads in her life, wanting things and not sure she's making the choices that will please you and her mother."

"All I want is to see her settled and happy," Dillon said. "Isn't that all any of us want for our children and grandchildren?"

"We know that," Nell concurred. "But sometimes we don't convey it all that well to them. We push and prod them to achieve various goals, be it in education or in their choice of a career. Sometimes we just need to let them be to find their own way."

"And you honestly think Moira has found hers?"

"I think she's getting there," Nell confirmed.

"And would you like to share anything about this path she's chosen? Is Luke in the middle of it?"

"That's for them to decide now, isn't it?" Nell said. "You and I need to spend this time forging our own path."

But even as she said the words, she regretted that she had no idea what lay at the end of it. Even with Dillon's promise to stay on for a time, there was far too much uncertainty about things at their age.

14

Moira steered clear of Luke's the day after their argument. She still had plenty of thinking to do. She was weighing her various options, which in some ways was a ridiculous waste of time. If her mental pro/con list came down on the side of a relationship with Luke and a family, it wasn't as if she could snap her fingers and make it happen.

Her lack of control over her own destiny annoyed her as much as his intransigent attitude did. Was the man incapable of bending, of seizing an opportunity that was here now rather than pushing it off to a more convenient time? It was ironic, because the Luke she'd first met in Ireland had been charmingly spontaneous.

She'd spent most of the day alone on the beach, arguing with herself and getting nowhere, when she saw Laila approaching.

"Mind if I tag along?" Laila asked.

"Of course not, but why are you here, if you don't mind my asking?"

"Do you want my trumped-up excuse?" Laila inquired with a grin. "I'm supposed to get more exercise, according to my obstetrician."

Moira regarded her curiously. "But that's not the real reason?"

Laila shook her head. "I heard about the fight between you and Luke. I decided that you and I have something in common."

"We're both involved with impossible O'Brien men?" Moira asked. "Though after yesterday, it seems as if I'm much less so than you are. You, at least, have a ring on your finger."

Laila smiled. "That's the thing," she said. "Relationships aren't entirely about whether there's a ring on your finger."

"Where I grew up, that was supposed to be the goal," Moira said. "Even my mum, who's been bitterly divorced for a very long time, preached that every chance she got."

"I suspect what she really wants for you is to find a man who'll love you with his whole heart, not just put a ring on your finger."

Moira thought about that, then slowly nodded. "I do think that's how my grandfather feels, so perhaps my mum does as well."

"Not that you asked for my opinion, but personally I think that's how Luke feels about you," Laila said. "I can't read his heart, but his actions certainly seem to indicate that his feelings are very strong. I've known him most of his life. No woman has ever kept his attention for so long. And I was there that night at Nell's when he saw that you'd come with Dillon. The expression on his face was one of undisguised joy."

Moira gave her a wry look, suddenly understanding what this visit was really about. Laila had come as a fence-mender. "Did he come blathering to you about offering me a job, then?" she asked her.

Laila laughed. "Yes, I believe we're all agreed now that it was a boneheaded move on his part. Even Luke saw the error of his ways. He realized that he hadn't read between the lines at all."

Moira wasn't convinced of that, but she didn't argue. He hadn't called last night or even this morning to beg her forgiveness or even to explain himself. She'd kept her cell phone with her for that very possibility, but it had remained stubbornly silent. She'd even checked the battery and the bars for reception to see if the phone was at fault. It wasn't. It was Luke himself who'd remained silent.

"If not the O'Brien men," she said to Laila, "what is it you think that you and I have in common?"

"We're both at loose ends," Laila said readily.

Moira listened in amazement as Laila described the way she'd quit the family bank after a feud with her father over her relationship with Matthew.

"So, here I am, having spent my entire life in banking, and now I'm running this little one-woman accounting office that's so dull it bores me to tears. Even with the inn as a client, I have barely enough work to fill the hours of a couple of days a week. I'd done this before and it hadn't seemed nearly so awful, but after having a taste of working at the bank for a short time in a challenging capacity, it feels as if my life is moving backward."

"But your father came to the wedding," Moira recalled. "Haven't you made peace? Couldn't you consider going back to work for him?"

Laila shook her head emphatically. "We've reconciled, but I can't go back to the bank. I've accepted that my father will never really believe I belong there. Maybe it's sexist, maybe it's just an inability to see the extent of my competence." She shrugged. "In the meantime, though, I'm floundering a bit, trying to find my way, to come up with a new direction, the same as you are."

"It's a bloody awful feeling, isn't it?" Moira said, delighted to have found someone with whom she could honestly commiserate without feeling like a failure.

"Bloody awful," Laila agreed. "But here's the thing— I know one thing for sure. It's not up to Matthew to fill that void for me or to point me in the new direction. Our relationship is separate."

Moira regarded her with sudden understanding. She could see exactly how she'd managed to twist it all together. "So you're saying that if I want this job at the bar, if I think it would fulfill me in some way, that should be entirely separate from Luke, even though it might bring us into daily contact?"

"Exactly," Laila said. "Take the job, if you want it, and the legalities for you to stay here can be worked out. At the same time, if you and Luke build a relationship, if the love between you continues to grow, well, that will just be a further blessing, won't it?"

Moira gave her a considering look. "Perhaps you're the one who should be joining Luke behind the bar. You seem to have a real knack for giving out practical advice that makes total sense. Until this minute, I'd just worked myself into a frenzy expecting him to give me a package deal that would guarantee personal and professional happiness until the end of time."

Laila laughed. "Who knows, though? Something tells me you could get both. If Luke's anything like his brother, he's an excellent multitasker. And despite Mick's ridiculous split with Megan for a number of years, it's evident that the men in this family tend to mate for life." She grinned. "Once they get around to it, anyway."

Her assessment made Moira smile. "What about you, though?" she asked Laila. "Do you have any idea about what you want to fill the void in your life?"

Laila rested a hand on her stomach, though it was far too soon for any evidence of a baby bump. "I think perhaps fate has stepped in," she admitted, though she still didn't sound entirely happy about it.

Moira frowned, wishing in some ways they could trade places. "A baby is a blessing, especially when the parents love each other, as you and Matthew do."

"I know that, and we wanted children from the beginning, but I wanted to be settled as *me* first, if you know what I mean. I wanted a professional identity— the same as Abby and Bree and Jess. I spent most of my life envisioning myself as president of the Chesapeake Shores Bank. With that dream over, I need a new one."

Moira thought she detected something in her voice that Laila might not even be aware she was conveying. "Is that because you really wanted to be president of the bank, or because you thought you should? Was it more about impressing your father, pleasing him? Or perhaps trying to prove something to your friends? Believe me, I can understand how spending time with such high achievers like the O'Briens can influence a person. People have seized on my sudden display of photography talent and taken off like a runaway train, thinking it's the answer to my prayers."

Laila looked surprised. "And it's not? Truly?"

"Maybe it is," Moira said. "But, to be honest, I don't think it's where my heart is. It's just been a pleasant change to think I have such a grand option and to see something other than disappointment in my grandfather's eyes." She shrugged. "I suppose I'll know with more certainty once I'm back in Dublin and have worked all those jobs Peter's lined up for me. Then I'll know if photography is truly satisfying to me or if I was only relieved to finally have a goal of some kind."

"And you think the bank was something I'd built up in my mind, maybe even because I knew my father wanted Trace to take over, not me?"

Moira glanced over at her. "Is that possible? Sibling rivalry can be a powerful thing, especially if you felt you were competing for the approval of a parent."

Laila looked genuinely surprised by the suggestion. "I've never looked at it that way before. And the truth is, I always chafed at the kind of person I felt I had to be—rigid, controlled, predictable—in order to hold that position. I've been much happier since Matthew lured me into breaking free of the way I saw myself and lived my life."

"So maybe you haven't lost as much as you thought you had," Moira suggested.

Laila's startled expression turned to relief. "Oh, my God, you could be exactly right, Moira!" she said excitedly. "I have the perfect chance to completely reinvent myself, don't I?"

"Seems that way to me," Moira said. "And what would you choose to be?"

The question seemed to dim Laila's excitement. "Now that," she said, "is the million-dollar question."

Moira couldn't help chuckling at her suddenly woe-begone expression. "You've just officially joined the club I've been in all my life," she said. "If it's any con-solation, I'm beginning to believe that there may be hope just around the corner for both of us."

"Really?" Laila said doubtfully.

"Weren't you the one who said just moments ago that it's up to us to seize what we want and not to look to anyone else to hand it to us?"

"I did."

"Well, then, that seems like a fine bit of information to have. It's certainly given me a new perspective."

"Do you have a next step in mind already?" Laila asked curiously.

"I'm going to see Connor about getting a work visa," Moira said decisively.

Maybe staying on was a risk. Maybe it would give her and Luke the time they needed. There was no way to tell how things would turn out. The only thing she knew for sure was that if she went back to Ireland as scheduled, she might never know what could have been. As for those jobs she'd already accepted, she could fly home long enough to honor the commitments and then race right back here to follow her heart.

Luke had been dismayed, but not surprised, when Moira didn't turn up at the pub the morning after their argument. After his conversation with Laila and Mat-thew, he knew he had some serious apologizing to do. Today just wasn't going to be the day for it.

Not only were the dishes, silverware and glassware

to be delivered, but so were the tables and chairs. That meant he had to get the construction crew and its debris out of here by midmorning. After that he had to be on the scene for all the deliveries. He couldn't leave that to anyone else.

In the meantime, though, he did call Bree at Flowers on Main. "It has been reported to me on more than one occasion by the other men in this family that you're great at creating the apology special," he told her.

She laughed. "You need to be apologizing to Moira? I never saw that coming. She seems like the one more likely to say or do something requiring penance."

"That's family bias speaking," he scolded her. "I'm no saint, and on occasion I can be a real dunderhead."

"Really? What did you do?" she asked eagerly.

"Nothing I care to discuss with you," he told his obviously fascinated cousin. "Can you come up with flowers for Moira or not?"

"Of course I can," she said at once. "But she won't be impressed."

"Why not?"

"Too little effort on your part to call on me to help you make amends," she told him. "Now if you want to do this right, you'll go to Gram's, risk life and limb by sneaking into the garden, and cut a proper bouquet."

"You just want Gram to catch me and chase me with a broom, don't you?" he accused.

"I was hoping maybe she still had one of Granddad's old shotguns," Bree admitted. "She used to threaten me with it enough when I yanked out flowers rather than weeds."

"I think that was just meant to terrorize you," Luke said, but he wasn't entirely certain of that. "So, you really think fresh flowers I've picked myself are my only option?"

"It would be a sweet gesture," she told him. "Few women could resist it."

"The only problem is I'm stuck at the pub all day waiting for deliveries. This probably shouldn't wait."

"Boy, you really are in some kind of trouble, aren't you?" Bree teased.

"You have no idea." He paused, then said, "I suppose I could call Gram, throw myself on her mercy."

"Not the same," Bree said emphatically. "Your apology, your bouquet. Trust me. I'm a woman. I understand these things."

"I believe you're also the one who tried to convince me if I tied a blanket over my shoulders I could fly off the porch roof," he said.

He heard a guffaw she obviously tried to hide.

"That was a bit of a miscalculation on my part," she admitted. "You were annoying me."

"And, of course, no one in the family believed you'd been behind it and the resulting broken wrist, because you were the quiet, solitary one who hid out in her room with her books," he recalled.

"It was one of the rare times when that worked in my favor," she said proudly.

"Does Jake have any idea what a devious woman you're capable of being?"

"Absolutely not," she said. "That also works in my favor."

Luke laughed. "Yes, I imagine it does. Okay, Bree, thanks for the advice. I'll figure something out."

"One more suggestion?"

"Sure."

"There's a patch of shamrocks in the far back corner of the garden," she revealed. "A few of those tucked into your bouquet might be a nice touch."

"Now I really do owe you," he said. "See you."

"Good luck."

"Thanks," he said, hanging up. At least he had a plan, even if his timetable for executing it was a little shaky. Hopefully, if he showed up by nightfall, Moira would be in a receptive mood. Trying to find the perfect spot on the pendulum of her mood swings—somewhere between furious and listening to reason—was probably one of those life skills he was going to need a lot.

Moira's meeting with Connor had been productive. He'd helped her complete all the necessary paperwork for getting a short-term work visa and promised to do his best to hurry it through the process. He'd encouraged her, though, to use Megan's offer of a gallery showing as her reason for staying, not a waitressing job at Luke's pub.

"They'll be far more likely to grant it when it's for something unique that only you can do," he advised.

"But I'm not sure if I'll pursue that," she argued.

"It would be crazy not to," Connor countered. "Mom would never have suggested this if she didn't believe in you. She'll vouch for you. It'll be better than trying to convince them you're uniquely suited to working in a pub."

"Well, I am, aren't I? Who in Chesapeake Shores has more experience working in genuine Irish pubs? You could call me a consultant. That would be closer to the truth than relying on the photography approach."

In the end, she'd managed to convince Connor to stick more closely to the reality of her plans.

"Luke will need to verify that you have the job," Connor said. "Does he know?"

Moira grinned. "It's a surprise," she admitted. "I suppose if he thinks it's a terrible one, I could still catch my original flight home and all of this would be for nothing."

"You're quite the risk taker, aren't you?"

"Not until recently," she said. "I've finally discovered that there are some risks worth taking."

"Okay, then. I'll be in touch as soon as I know anything," Connor said. "Meantime, you need to get Luke on board."

"That's my next stop," she assured him.

On the short walk from Connor's law office to Shore Road, Moira mentally worked on what she was going to say to Luke to convince him that hiring her would be the smartest thing he'd ever done.

She arrived at the pub just as all the deliveries seemed to show up at once. It was chaos, with boxes being shoved into corners and furniture left wherever there was room. Luke was standing with a clipboard and his checklists trying to keep up with the pace of it all. Moira shook her head.

"You," she said, stopping the UPS deliveryman, who was carrying in yet more boxes of china and glassware. She gave him her sunniest smile. "Do you think it might be possible to put those in the kitchen where they'll be out of harm's way and will be nearest to where they belong?"

He looked as if he might argue, but she grinned. "I think I can persuade Mr. O'Brien to give you one of our discount coupons for a free drink and a discounted meal during the first week we're open."

The man relented. "Show me the way. I'll get those other boxes from the corner and get them out of the way as well."

"And I'll get your coupon," she said, relieved that Trace had delivered them a few days ago so most could go to the inn for Jess's guests. They'd kept a few on hand for situations just like this one. There was nothing like the promise of something free or discounted to gain cooperation.

While the breakables were all moved out of harm's way, the tables and chairs were shoved to one side of the room to await final placement after the hardwood floors had been given one last polish. She presented coupons to those deliverymen as well.

"Tell your friends there will be lively music when we open," she told them as they left.

Luke regarded her with appreciation when they were finally alone. "You appeared in the nick of time. Why didn't I think not only to bribe them, but to point out that we'd welcome them coming back for a meal and a pint?"

"Because you were busy checking things off on that clipboard of yours," she said, tapping a finger on it. "That's why we make a good team."

He blinked at that. "A team?"

"In the professional sense," she verified.

He seemed to be struggling to catch up. "Have you reconsidered working here, then? After all the fuss the other day, I thought you weren't interested."

She shrugged. "I've changed my mind. I've already spoken to Connor and he's at work on the visa." She gave him a saucy grin. "I'm to be your consultant, brought all the way from Ireland to see that this place is authentic."

"So you're not longer concerned about being—what was it you said—a bit of Irish fluff?"

"Not with a fancy title like consultant," she said, as if that were what made the difference.

He set down his clipboard and took a step in her direction, his expression hopeful. "Are we done fighting, then?"

"Oh, I'm quite sure we'll fight again and again," she said. "It's the nature of who I am." She held his gaze. "Are you up for the challenge of it?"

His lips quirked. "You know I am."

She stepped closer, meeting him halfway. "I'm sorry about trying to force a commitment from you before you were ready, then getting insulted when you wouldn't go along with it."

"And I'm sorry for offending you by not understanding what you really wanted." He pulled her close and rested his chin atop her head. "You've saved me by coming here, you know."

"How's that?"

"I had every intention of sneaking into Gram's garden to cut a fancy bouquet for you by way of an apology."

Moira regarded him with dismay. If she understood little else, she knew what that brilliant summer garden meant to Nell. "She'd have killed you," she said, shocked.

"A risk I was willing to take," he assured her.

"You wanted to make amends that badly?"

He nodded. "Moira, I'm not really ready to make

a lot of promises, but I will make you this one. I will try not to be obtuse or careless with your feelings ever again."

"And I will try not losing my temper when I don't immediately get my way," she said.

He studied her with a little too much amusement. "Can you do that?"

She laughed at his skepticism. "I can try."

"That'll be progress, then, for both of us, won't it?"

"And peace will reign over all the land," she declared.

Now it was his turn to laugh. "Now there's an unexpected bit of optimism it's a pleasure to hear." He reached up to stroke a finger along the curve of her cheek. "I've missed you."

"We've barely been apart. It's not like it was with you here and me in Ireland."

"Somehow it felt as if there was even more distance between us," he said. "Let's not let that happen again."

"Never again," she said, then tilted her face up for his kiss.

She understood, then, the power of a kiss. Not only could it stir the sort of intense passion that carried people away. It could heal. And that's exactly what this one did.

15

Jeff had been steering clear of the pub for a couple of weeks now. He knew that he tended to ask too many questions, express too many doubts. Jo had been all over him tonight, trying to make him see that he needed to offer their youngest unconditional support.

"That's what Luke needs from you now," she said, pressing her point yet again. "You've expressed all your concerns, and if I know you, you've done it repeatedly. Either he's heard you or he hasn't, but it's time to move on and let him know you'll be proud of him, no matter how this turns out."

He'd frowned at her choice of words. "That sounds as if you have doubts, too."

"Not doubts, concerns," she corrected. "I know how important this is to Luke. He wants so badly to accomplish something of his own. There's a lot of pressure in this family to succeed. It can be daunting. Thankfully, Susie was always immune to it, at least in the sense of establishing some high-flying career, but look at Matthew. He risked your wrath to follow in Mick's footsteps. And the way I hear it, everyone thinks the student will surpass the teacher. Have you told him how proud of him you are, or does it still stick in your craw that he's an architect, rather than a Realtor like you?"

"Of course I've told Matthew I'm proud of him," Jeff said, indignant that she could think he'd put his own feelings ahead of what was best for their son. Sure, he and Mick had their issues, but he'd vowed not to let them spill over into Matthew's relationship with Mick. "I saw those plans for that community he designed in Florida. They're truly astonishing, Jo. How could I not be proud of that?"

She smiled. "Glad to hear it. Now, rise above your concerns—whatever they are—and be there for Luke. I'm sure he has enough fears of his own without your doubts weighing him down. You see, the thing about all the kids in the entire O'Brien clan is that they're determined to succeed on their own, but they also desperately need the approval of everyone else—parents, aunts, uncles, siblings, cousins and, of course, Nell."

"I only want the best for all three of our kids," he said. "I want them to follow whatever path will make them happy. I'm not setting the standard. They are."

"I believe you mean that," Jo said with absolute confidence. "They may not. For a family as outspoken as ours, sometimes we fail to say the words that will be the most meaningful."

Jeff knew she was right. Jo was always right about things like this. She understood their kids in ways he never had. She understood *him,* too. Often lost in the shadow of his outspoken, dynamic, powerful older brothers, he'd sometimes felt left behind. She'd seen a value in the quieter traits *he* possessed and made him see it as well.

"You're very smart," he told her.

She grinned. "Isn't that why you married me?"

"Nope. I married you because you were the only kid in high school who could outrun me. You were a challenge." He hesitated, suddenly struck by another insight. "Is that the attraction between Luke and Moira? She's a challenge?"

"I think that's certainly part of it," Jo said. "I also think there's a streak of vulnerability that hides beneath that rebellious, tough facade of hers. Luke, like all the O'Brien men, has a soft spot for a vulnerable woman. All of you like to be our knights in shining armor."

"I wasn't much of one when Susie was sick," he reminded her. "I was scared out of my wits that we were going to lose our daughter."

"We all were, and you handled it just fine. You were right there whenever she needed you."

"But you were the rock," he said candidly. "No question about it."

"It's teamwork, love. Don't you know that by now? I'll always have your back, and I know with every fiber of my being that you have mine."

"I do," he promised. "Always."

"And you'll see Luke first thing in the morning so he knows you have his back as well?"

"I will if you'll put down that book you were reading and come to bed with me."

She grinned at the invitation, responding as she always had with an eagerness that made him feel as if he was the luckiest man on earth. Just as Susie had with her Mack, Jo had needed to slow down a bit to let Jeff catch her, but from that moment on, the balance of power between them had been perfectly even, dipping and swaying from one to the other depending on who needed the other the most, but always coming back into perfect alignment. It was the kind of harmony a lot of marriages never achieved.

As they headed upstairs, hand in hand, he smiled. Mick might have more in dollars and cents. He might have a larger, more exuberant family. But Jeff had found everything he'd ever needed in this woman and their children. He *was* the luckiest man alive.

The floor in the main part of the pub had just been polished for a final time. Luke had been advised to avoid dragging the furniture across it and, if possible, not even to walk on it for the next few hours. That meant he was confined to his office for the time being with nothing but his lists for company.

He'd just settled down to make phone calls to the people he'd decided to hire for his waitstaff when someone started banging on the front door. Then he heard a key turn in the lock.

"Wait!" he shouted. "Dad, is that you?" His father was the only one with a key likely to turn up without an invitation. Even Mick and Matthew had agreed to stay away between now and the official opening—on Thursday for the family, on Friday for everyone else. And his sister, though she had access to the keys, was unlikely to barge right in.

"I just stopped by to check on you," his father responded, as he opened the door.

"Dad, come around to the back," he pleaded, trying to halt him. "The floor's just been finished."

One foot in midair, his father glanced down at the gleaming wood, then stepped back. "Sorry."

"It's okay. You had no way of knowing. I'll open the back door for you."

A couple of minutes later, Jeff came in bearing coffee and, if the aroma coming from the bag was telling, some of Sally's raspberry croissants fresh from the oven.

"What's this?" Luke asked, diving eagerly into the bag. "Ah, just the treat I needed."

His father shook his head. "The whole family has an addiction to those things, but I think yours is the worst. Will I get so much as a sniff?"

Luke sighed heavily and held out the bag. "I suppose I can share."

"And done so graciously, too," Jeff said, laughing.

"What brings you by, Dad?" Luke asked, unable to hide his wariness.

"I just wanted to check with you and see how things are progressing. The opening's getting close."

"Thursday night for the family and the town bigwigs," Luke confirmed.

"You're ready for it? You have everything you need?"

"I'll have my staff hired by the end of the day. Moira's going to train them. Gram's working with a cook to make sure the food's up to her standards. I think she gladly gave up on turning me into a chef. I could see the despair in her eyes every time I tried something and failed to meet her expectations."

"She is a perfectionist," Jeff agreed. "But isn't that what you needed?"

"Absolutely," Luke said. "She's been a godsend, as has Moira."

"That's the second time you've mentioned Moira in just a few minutes. How does she fit in exactly?"

Luke grinned. "She's declared herself my consultant. Connor's making it legal. Hopefully, she'll have her paperwork in place by the opening."

Jeff looked surprised. "I thought Megan was all set to turn her into a photography star. Is she willing to settle for working here with you?"

"To my astonishment, she doesn't seem to consider it settling. And there will be time for her to take pictures, if that's what she wants to do. I won't stand in her way."

"And beyond that? Have you made plans?"

Luke shook his head. "The pub's my focus now. Once it's proven itself, then I can think about the rest of my life."

His father frowned at his response. "Moira strikes me as impatient. Is she willing to sit on the sidelines while you think?"

"I've really given her no choice," Luke admitted, well aware by now of just how risky his posture was. "I'm assuming because she decided to stay on that she's giving me at least a few months to figure out where we go from here."

Jeff regarded him with amusement. "You sound very analytical, not at all like the impetuous son I recall who plunged headfirst into a relationship with Kristen Lewis in a gesture meant to save his sister's marriage."

Luke shrugged. "What can I say? I'm growing up. There are some, including you, who think I haven't done that fast enough."

His father gestured toward the front. "I can have no

complaints about that now, can I? I'm proud of you for having the vision to create a place like this."

"Seriously? All you've done since I first mentioned it is tell me the drawbacks."

Jeff gave him a chagrined look. "Yes, your mother pointed out to me that I have a bad habit of focusing on the negative. I only meant to give you things to consider, not to imply that I thought you weren't capable of figuring out whatever needed to be done. In fact, I think it's going to be a roaring success. I imagine I'll find myself here most nights for a pint of ale at the end of the day."

"Just to do your part to make it a success?" Luke asked with a frown. He could imagine all the O'Briens assigning each other time slots to ensure that there were customers in the place and money flowing in.

"Absolutely not," his father said. "I'll be here because it will remind me of Ireland, because I can expect friends and family to be stopping in and because I'll get a taste of Ma's food on a few days other than Sunday. Jo will be here because it will keep her out of the kitchen."

Luke relaxed at the response. "I hope everyone views it that way," he said. "Not just the O'Briens."

"Oh, I think you can count on it. And the Irish music you're planning will be a huge draw for the community and the surrounding area. If St. Patrick's Day is any indication, the world is populated with people who are either Irish or wish they were. They'll be your regular customers."

Luke smiled at him. "I know Mum put you up to it, but thank you for coming over here and saying all this. It's just the boost I needed to calm my nerves."

"Would you like me to repeat it on opening day?" Jeff offered.

Laughing, Luke shook his head. "Now that's a day I think it will take more than kind words to calm me down. I can't wait, though. I still have a long to-do list, but Moira swears we'll be ready. I'm trusting her judgment on that."

His father gave him an awkward hug. "You need anything at all, give me a call. The same with the rest of the family. We can pitch in on anything, large or small, okay?"

"I know that, Dad. It's the best part of being an O'Brien."

Moira had heard Jeff's voice when she arrived at the pub in the morning, so she went around the corner to Sally's for a cup of coffee to give Luke some privacy with his father. She knew things were often contentious between them. She also understood from living with her grandfather that the best way to solve that was through spending time together.

She'd been seated for barely a minute when Bree appeared and slid into the booth opposite her.

"Did Luke apologize?" she asked Moira at once.

Moira stared at her. "How did you know about Luke needing to apologize? Was it the infamous O'Brien grapevine?"

"No, I got this straight from the horse's mouth," Bree said with a grin. "Luke called asking for my help with flowers."

Understanding dawned. "And you're the one who told him to sneak into Nell's garden?"

"I did," Bree said proudly. "I thought it was inspired. Did it work?"

"Actually, I forgave him before he had to risk Nell's wrath."

Bree immediately looked disappointed. "Now what fun is that?"

Moira regarded her with amazement. "You *wanted* him to get caught?"

"Well, sure," Bree said unrepentantly. "When we were kids, all the others were constantly getting into mischief. I was usually hidden away in my room reading or daydreaming. I made a great target for their pranks. Now it's my turn to get even, because I know Jake won't let them hurt me."

Moira laughed. "This family is just a little nuts."

"More than likely," Bree agreed. "So you and Luke are okay now?"

"I hear she's going on the payroll as his Irish consultant," Heather said, joining them with an amused expression.

"I know where you heard that," Moira said. "Isn't Connor supposed to keep his clients' business to himself?"

"Oh, he was quiet as a church mouse when I tried to find out why you were at his office yesterday. It was my mother-in-law who filled me in."

Moira winced. "Megan already knows about this?"

"And before you ask," Heather said, "I have no idea who spilled the beans to her, but she is married to Mick, who finds out everything."

"Is she upset because I'm going to be working at the pub, rather than taking pictures for my portfolio?" Moira asked.

"You can ask her that yourself," Heather said, already slipping out of the booth as Megan came into the café. "Come on, Bree. We need to go to work."

"But all the excitement is going to be here," Bree protested.

"Come on," Heather insisted, pausing to give Megan a hug before dragging her sister-in-law away.

"I'm sorry," Moira said at once. "I wanted you to hear about all this from me."

"You mean the fact that you're giving up the opportunity of a lifetime to be a waitress?" Megan asked quietly as she signaled Sally for a cup of coffee.

"Not a waitress," Moira objected. "A consultant."

Megan lifted a brow. "Seriously?"

"Okay, yes, I'll be waiting on tables and cooking from time to time, but it's what I want," she told her, her jaw set stubbornly.

"If it truly is, then you have my blessing," Megan said. "But if this is because of Luke, you're making a terrible mistake. Are you afraid he can't handle you becoming a huge success?"

"Absolutely not," Moira said, then frowned. Megan sounded so sure that what she was doing was something she'd come to regret. "Do you think he'll never want me the way I want him? Is that why you think I'm making a mistake?"

"No. What I fear is that you're walking away from a career that could give you fame and creative satisfaction, to say nothing of great financial rewards."

"Do I have to choose?" Moira asked wistfully. "I mean, right at the moment? I know you're an expert and I respect your opinion, but there's no certainty that I could be a success at photography, is there? I know it's a world that can be capricious, especially at the artistic end of it, as you're proposing."

"So you're scared of failing?" Megan asked, looking disappointed.

Moira shook her head indignantly. "Not at all," she insisted. "Luke asked the same thing, but it's not that. I swear it isn't."

"Then explain it to me, because I honestly don't understand," Megan said.

"It would mean giving up a certainty, something I know and love, for what could be no more than a pipe dream," Moira told her earnestly. "It's as if I'm at this fork in the road and I'm choosing the one that feels right, familiar to me."

"But it's only when we take the other fork that we grow," Megan said. "I'm sure you've heard the story of me walking out on Mick all those years ago. If I'd listened solely to my heart, I'd have stayed right here with my family, even though I was terribly unhappy. By choosing to take the risk of losing, look at all I gained. I have a career that truly fulfills me."

"But you came close to losing your children in the bargain," Moira reminded her. "Was it worth that sacrifice?"

Megan's face clouded over and, for a minute, Moira thought she might have gone too far, broaching a subject that was way too personal. But Megan, after all, was the one who'd brought it up to make her own point.

"I'm sorry," Moira apologized. "I shouldn't have said that."

"Of course you should have," Megan replied. "And it was a terrible sacrifice. I'm still making up for it. The hurt I caused might not have been intentional, but it's taken me years to make amends to my children."

"Knowing all that you know now, would you do it again?" Moira asked.

Megan's lips curved slightly. "I like to think that I'm far wiser now, that I would fight harder for what I wanted in the first place, rather than walking away in frustration and anger. In the end, though, if the circumstances were precisely the same, I would probably do it over again. I hope, though, that I wouldn't allow my children to stay behind. That was the real mistake I made. I let Mick convince me that they should stay here in their own home, surrounded by friends and family. I could see the blessing in that, but I know now that they lost something as well. They lost me. Worse, they didn't understand why." She shrugged. "So, while they might have hated moving with me to New York, they wouldn't have felt abandoned. The scar that left will never be entirely healed."

"I suppose there can be unplanned repercussions to any decision, even those that are the most carefully thought out," Moira said.

"No question about it." Megan smiled. "And have you carefully thought about yours? Or did you make the decision on impulse?"

"A mix of the two, I imagine," Moira admitted. "I gave it thought, of course, but there hasn't been a lot of time to weigh the pros and cons."

"Could we make a deal, then?" Megan suggested. "Will you promise me not to give up entirely on photography? Will you continue to build your portfolio and work with me to mount a show here? There's little risk in that, and you'll be right here with Luke while you try. It seems to me it could be a win-win. If the show's the success I envision, you'll have a real choice to make then, not one that's based on fear or what-ifs."

Under the circumstances, it was the fairest offer imaginable. Moira knew she'd be an idiot to reject it. "I can promise that much," she said.

And if it turned out that the path she thought she wanted—one that led to a home with Luke and a family—was her destiny, she'd have chosen it fair and square, rather than by default.

"You've a great talent for negotiating," she told Megan.

Megan winked at her. "In my business, it's why I make the big bucks for my clients. I'm convinced that you're going to be one of them, Moira. Perhaps one of the best."

When Moira was about to speak, Megan held up her hand. "Before you argue that I shouldn't count on that, that you could decide photography is not what you want, keep in mind that there's a third option. Some people manage to blend a family and a career without sacrificing either one of them. It doesn't have to be an either/or decision. You could have the best of both worlds. The only certainty, Moira, is that you'll never know if you could be one of them unless you try."

Moira was still sitting where Megan had left her, sipping her fourth cup of coffee, when Nell and her grandfather came in.

"Here you are," Dillon said, looking delighted. "Everyone's been wondering where you were."

She smiled at that. "It's not as if the town much cares about my comings and goings," she said.

"Luke does," Nell responded. "And he's been watching the door at the pub all morning. You're supposed to be there to begin training the waitstaff soon."

Moira had a moment of panic, then drew in a breath. "Not today," she said. "Luke's only hiring them today. Training's due to begin tomorrow."

"When we were there just now, he was grumbling that he wanted your input on his final choices," Nell said.

Moira brightened at once. "Really? I thought he'd made the decisions."

"I gather it dawned on him that he should run them by his consultant," her grandfather said, a mischievous twinkle in his eyes. "How exactly did you get hired on in that capacity?"

She grinned at him. "I was very clever about it. You would have been proud. I suppose for the exorbitant salary I intend to talk him into, I'd best get over there." She met Nell's gaze. "You'll be training the new cook starting tomorrow?"

Nell nodded. "I hope to goodness he comes to us with more experience than my grandson. Not that I would ever say this to Luke, but he was the closest I've ever seen to hopeless. I thought for sure I was going to wind up with a full-time job at my age."

Moira chuckled because Nell almost looked as if she regretted that it wasn't going to turn out exactly that way. "Well, he'll obviously need the both of us, if he's to make a success of his place."

"And though Thursday's a test run for family and a party, I've promised to help with the cash register for the official Friday opening, since we expect the place to be mobbed," Dillon said, looking pleased to have been asked. That had been Moira's suggestion, after explaining to Luke that he'd need to be spending his time with the customers, not counting out change as he might on a regular night.

"It's all coming together quite nicely," Nell said. "I predict that O'Brien's will be a huge success."

"From your mouth to God's ear," Moira said.

Because if anything went wrong, she couldn't imagine how Luke would cope with it. He was counting on the pub to measure his worth. She could have told him there were other, far more important measures, but he'd never take her word for it. He needed this success in ways she was just beginning to fully understand as she faced the decisions that would ultimately determine her own destiny.

16

Luke had been over his pages of lists at least a dozen times by late afternoon on Thursday. Every item had been checked off and rechecked. The aromas in the kitchen reminded him of Gram's, and he knew for a fact that the dishes tasted just the way they were supposed to. The bar was stocked. The tables and chairs were where they were meant to be. The waitstaff had all been here early, listening intently to Moira's suggestions. It should have put his mind at ease, but so far he felt only a terrible churning in his stomach.

"What can I do to help?" Moira asked, standing behind his chair to massage his shoulders, which were knotted with tension.

"Nothing," he said, wanting only to get through his momentary panic on his own. This was *his* pub, *his* success or failure. He'd never had so much at stake before in his life.

"Everyone's ready," she said, obviously trying to soothe him. "You've hired an excellent waitstaff. They're all reasonably experienced and more than eager for this place to do well. They'll provide just the right combination of energy and solicitous service."

"I know that," he said. "I don't need a pep talk, Moira."

She frowned at his impatient words. "I'm just trying to help, Luke."

Regretting that he'd snapped at her, he touched her hand. "I know that, but all I need is for the doors to open and for this night to get started. I'll calm down then." Another stab of panic knifed through him. "Did the band get here? They were lost on some country road an hour ago when they called for directions."

She smiled and motioned for him to listen. "Can't you hear them tuning up?"

"And the setup is okay for them? I should go out there. Make sure everything's the way they want it."

Pressure on his shoulders kept him in place. "I've already checked," Moira reassured him. "They have everything they need. The sound check has gone off without a hitch. I promise you, Luke, it's all good. Would you like me to bring you a drink? It might steady your nerves."

He shook his head. Taking a drink now would send him off on a dangerous path. He'd never been especially tempted by alcohol, but he didn't want to chance turning to drink to get through a bad case of nerves. It was far too easy to go from an occasional excuse to a nasty habit. He'd seen too much of it at college, had lost a friend to it after a party had gotten wildly out of hand and the friend had tried to drive home drunk. He'd hit a tree and died at the scene. Luke had found his twisted car just moments after the accident. He still shuddered when he thought of it. Now, as the owner of a pub, he'd vowed that no one would leave here with car keys in hand if they'd had too much to drink. Not ever. Law or not, he took it as a personal responsibility.

He forced himself to shake off the memory from that long-ago tragedy, which was easier when he heard Moira's next attempt to quiet his worries.

"We could run to your place for a quick tumble in your bed," she suggested, at least half-seriously judging from the glint in her eyes. "There's time enough."

He laughed at last. "Since when has a few minutes ever been enough for us?" he asked. "But thanks for the incredibly tempting offer. If anything could distract me right now, that could."

She smiled, though he sensed that she was trying to mask a hint of disappointment.

"There's nothing I can do, then?" she inquired plaintively.

"Nothing except to run for your life, so I don't wind up snapping your head off when I don't mean to."

She nodded. "Okay, then. I'll be out front if you think of anything I can do to help."

After she'd left his office with unmistakable reluctance, he felt awful for banishing her, but he knew he needed to face tonight alone. This was his life on the line, his future.

How could Moira possibly understand what it meant to him to prove himself? Only one other O'Brien had ever failed spectacularly, and that was Bree. She'd more than made up for it now, both with her business and her theater, but it had taken her a long time to get past feeling like a failure when she'd come back from Chicago after a play of hers had bombed with the critics. And she was a woman. It was, he thought, worse for a man, though he could think of a few O'Brien women who'd chop off his most valued parts for suggesting such a thing.

He drew in a deep breath, then set his clipboard down on his desk. That wasn't going to save him now. Murmuring a little prayer under his breath, he opened the door and went out to face whatever the night would bring. At least, he told himself, he'd be surrounded to-night by a horde of friendly O'Briens.

Even though this was Luke's big night, Moira was a nervous wreck on her own behalf as well. Not only was she going to be taking photos and trying to pitch in with the waitstaff or wherever else she might be needed, but she would be on display as Luke's girlfriend. It was one thing to have his family's approval, but now she had to impress the elite in this tight-knit community. Having Luke reject her earlier attempts to bolster his spirits hadn't helped with her sudden flood of insecurities.

It was Jess who found her hovering in a dark corner of the pub before the doors opened, doing her best to stay out of Luke's way. He'd spent the day stressed and irritable and she'd been his handy target. Since her usual style would be to fight back, it was smarter to steer clear until his nerves settled. She was proud of the fact that she'd gotten out of his office as requested, rather than staying to remind him that they were sup-posed to be a team.

"Why are you hiding over here?" Jess asked. "You and Luke haven't had a fight, have you?"

"No, but he's looking after a million-and-one de-tails. Rather than letting me help, I seem to annoy him by asking what I can do." She shrugged. "So I've done whatever I've noticed that needs to be done and now I'm biding my time till the doors officially open."

Jess laughed. "Pay no attention to Luke. That's the O'Brien independent streak talking. Don't take it personally. We all get a little crazed when we have something major on the line. You should have seen me the night the inn opened. I was a nervous wreck. I would have alienated a saint. He'll calm down once the rest of the family gets here and the invited guests begin to pour in, proving that this pub was a brilliant idea."

Moira met her gaze. "It really is going to be a huge success, isn't it?"

"I certainly think so. And I heard the band you chose tuning up. They're perfect for an opening night. It will set the tone and lure people into coming back anytime music's on the schedule. No one will be able to resist such a lively atmosphere. I'm so glad he hired them for tomorrow night's official opening, too." She looked at Moira. "Your idea, I assume. I imagine he was worried about the expense."

Moira grinned. "Yes, I managed to convince him that it would be shortsighted not to let the general public get its own glimpse of the atmosphere we'll be promoting, from food and drink to music."

"Well, they sound fantastic," Jess said.

"That's what Nell and I thought," Moira said, relieved to have their vision supported.

"Why don't we sneak over to the bar and get something to drink?" Jess suggested. "Luke's standing over there, and despite whatever he said earlier, I think a glimpse of you might calm him about now. He's looking a little frantic."

"It might make more sense to open the doors and let

the rest of the family pour in. They'll calm him more than I will."

Jess smiled. "You've honestly no idea of the power you have over my cousin, do you? He adores you. I have to admit that at first none of us could see it, but now that I've gotten to know you, I do."

Moira chuckled at the candid comment. "You're referring to my charming behavior when you came to my grandfather's at Christmas. I'm surprised you didn't have me put on a watch list to keep me out of your country."

"And risk Luke's hating all of us?" Jess asked. "No, we gave him credit for seeing something in you we'd missed and gave you the benefit of the doubt."

They were almost to the bar when the door opened and a tall, willowy, blond beauty walked in as if she belonged there.

"No way!" Jess said, momentarily frozen in place.

Moira stilled beside her. "Who is it?" she asked, though if memory served her correctly, she thought she already knew.

"Kristen Lewis. And trust me when I say she does not belong here. She can't possibly have been on the guest list."

Jess was obviously about to bolt in her direction, but Luke got there first. To Moira's relief, he didn't look any happier about Kristen's arrival than Jess had. Putting a soothing hand on Jess's arm, she said, "Maybe we should join them, but only if you can keep your temper in check. Let's not start out the night with a scene, if one can be avoided."

"I wouldn't count on that," Jess muttered. "But we are definitely going to join them, if only long enough to kick her sorry butt right back out the door. She needs to be gone before Susie and Mack get here."

To be honest, Moira was less concerned about Susie's reaction than she was about whatever hold this woman might still have on Luke. She was gorgeous and clearly predatory. Moira had recognized the type instantly. She'd met her share of them over the years, clinging possessively to men in the pubs where she worked. Often they were staking a claim to perfect strangers, men they'd stumbled into and were determined to hold, if only for the night.

As she and Jess neared, Moira heard Luke quietly trying to reason with her and Kristen just as stubbornly resisting his suggestion that she leave.

Suddenly feeling fiercely protective of her own turf, Moira slipped her arm through Luke's and beamed at Kristen. "I don't believe we've met. I'm Moira."

"Ah, the Irish holy terror," Kristen said, her expression smug.

After all her advice to Jess about behaving civilly, Moira found she was barely able to hold on to her own temper, even as Luke stepped in with a sharp warning.

"Enough, Kristen!" he commanded. "Please don't make this any more awkward. There was a reason you weren't on tonight's guest list, and I'm certain you know exactly what it was."

Kristen gave him a defiant look. "Is this really about poor Susie?" she inquired, then turned her arch gaze on Moira. "Or don't you want your little friend here to know just how close we are?"

Even before Moira or Luke could reply to that, Jess inserted herself into the middle of the fray. She latched onto Kristen's arm with a white-knuckled grip that was likely to leave bruises. "Say good-night, Kristen," she ordered in a low tone. When Luke opened his mouth to intercede, Jess gave him a hard look. "I've got this. Do some fence-mending. Now!" she added emphatically.

She steered Kristen toward the door at a pace that had her stumbling in her very high heels.

"Lovely woman," Moira commented lightly.

Luke turned to her with an apologetic look. "I'm sorry. She was deliberately taunting you. It's what she does. She's angry with me and she enjoys stirring up trouble. It's an ugly combination."

"She can only cause real trouble if there's some truth to what she says." She leveled a look into his eyes. "Is there, Luke? Is something still going on between the two of you? Have I somehow missed the signs that it's not entirely over? It would certainly explain why you don't seem willing to take the next step with me."

"Absolutely not," he swore. "I've broken it off."

"When?" she asked. "In Ireland, before she left after that new year's visit? Before we got together?"

His hesitation was all she needed to figure out the truth. "More recently, then," she concluded wearily. "Was it going on until the day I arrived, then? Did my unexpected appearance put a crimp in the romance?"

"No, absolutely not," he repeated. "And it was over in Ireland, I swear it. I just didn't tell her point-blank until I got back here."

"After sleeping with her how many times?"

The question clearly rattled him. "Could we hold off on this discussion until later?" he pleaded. "People are starting to arrive. We shouldn't be fighting."

"Yes, that would make this an inconvenient time, wouldn't it?" she said quietly. "Later, then."

She turned and walked away.

"Moira, wait."

Fortunately for her, people were indeed surging into the pub. The band began playing. Guinness was being poured at a record clip and the noise level was almost enough to drown out all the voices in her head telling her that on the biggest night of Luke's life, she'd lost the one thing that truly mattered to her...her faith in what they were building together.

There was no question that the night had been a rousing success. Luke knew that from the laughter and conversation that flowed easily around the room, from the people who came and stayed on rather than leaving after offering a few polite comments. Positive remarks were directed his way not just from his own family, but from all the invited guests who'd dropped by to wish him well and lingered for the party atmosphere.

The band was a huge hit as well. As his father had suggested, the locals must have considered themselves in some part Irish, because they seemed familiar with most of the lyrics and sang along lustily to all the traditional songs.

Over the course of the evening he'd caught barely more than a glimpse of Moira. He knew Kristen's comments had hurt her, just as they'd been designed to do. His inability to defend himself against what she'd implied had made it worse. After weeks of looking forward to this opening, now he only wanted for it to be over so he could find Moira and mend fences with her. They should be celebrating together, but it seemed they were further apart than ever.

It was nearing closing time and the crowd had yet

to thin out. He was mentally wishing them away when his parents came up to him.

"You must be so proud," his mother said. "Just look at what you've accomplished, and in record time, too."

"It's only the grand opening party," he cautioned. "It'll take time before I know if this enthusiasm will hold once people have to pay for their food and drink."

"It will," his father said. "Things went like clockwork. I've been to other openings when the kitchen was overwhelmed or the waitstaff inexperienced and clumsy. That never happened here."

"I can thank Moira and Gram for that," Luke said candidly. "I don't think Gram left the kitchen for more than a minute all evening. She seemed to thrive on supervising. And Moira was at work behind the scenes to make sure things ran smoothly."

"Where is she now?" Jo asked. "I'd like to thank her and say good-night."

"I'm not sure," Luke said. "The kitchen maybe. Or perhaps she's taking a well-deserved break in the office."

"I'll take a look," Jo said.

That left Luke alone with his father. "Do you really think it has staying power? Tell me honestly."

"I do," Jeff said. "You've done not just yourself, but the entire family, proud."

"I concur," Mick said, joining them. "Your Irish ancestors are looking on tonight with delight. Any one of them would be comfortable in a place like this. It's everything a place called O'Brien's ought to be.

"I'll second that," his uncle Thomas added. He circled an arm around his wife's expanding waist. "I'd stay for another set of that fine music, but if I don't get this mama-to-be home soon, she'll be asleep on her feet."

"I'm afraid I'm exhausted all the time," Connie added. "But I wouldn't have missed this for the world, Luke. And I can tell our little one here that he or she was here for the grand opening of Chesapeake Shores' hottest nightspot. That's what you'll be soon, you know."

Luke was embarrassed by all the accolades. "You don't have to keep cheerleading for me," he told them all, feeling chagrined by their apparent need to keep re-assuring him. "I'm feeling okay about the chances for this place after tonight."

"It's not cheerleading," Mick said. "We just want you to know how proud we are." He glanced toward his brother. "In case your father here can't find the words."

"I found plenty of words," Jeff grumbled. "You just insist on having the last one."

"He's got you there, Mick," Thomas said. "That is your habit."

"Well, tonight I'll leave it to Jeff to have the last one." He winked at Luke. "It's only fair."

Luke recalled the plea he'd made to Mick weeks ago to let him be the one to fill Jeff in on his plans. "Yes, it's only fair," he confirmed. "Good night, everyone. Thanks so much for being here."

Once again he was left alone with his father, but only for a moment, because his mother returned just then, her expression perplexed. "I couldn't find Moira any-where," she said. "Nell said she thought maybe she'd already left." She gave Luke a sharp look. "Why would she leave early on a night like tonight? She should be here so the two of you can sit quietly and share a toast to the pub's success."

"I don't know," Luke said evasively, but, of course, he knew precisely why she'd left. What he didn't know was how he was going to fix things.

On the walk back to Nell's, Moira told herself a thousand times that she should have stayed at the pub till the final customer had gone. Leaving had been cowardly, and she had never in her life been a coward.

Her convenient excuse was that she hadn't wanted to ruin Luke's exhilaration by forcing the fight that had been brewing since Kristen's untimely appearance.

Grateful to have Nell's house to herself, she took a shower, wrapped herself in a thick terry-cloth robe and made herself a cup of tea. With the tea in hand, she settled into one of the Adirondack chairs in the yard, hoping her grandfather and Nell wouldn't even notice her out here when they eventually returned home. With the soft sound of the waves breaking on the shore and a gentle breeze in the air, she finally managed to relax and think about what had happened earlier tonight.

Luke clearly hadn't been expecting Kristen. As Luke had reminded Moira, Kristen hadn't been on the official guest list, which said a lot about her character. She'd intruded for the sole purpose of making Moira uncomfortable and stirring up trouble between her and Luke. Should she really blame Luke for that? Probably not.

But she did blame him for not calling it quits sooner, for coming back to Chesapeake Shores and spending even a moment in that woman's company, much less in her bed. Had he thought that was okay because he hadn't yet made a commitment to Moira, in fact, hadn't even expected to see her again soon? Well, it wasn't okay! And if he didn't get that, then she intended to make it plain to him.

Satisfied that she would face the issue head-on, she allowed herself to relax at last and enjoy the night air and the pub's amazing success. She even let herself bask in satisfaction over her tiny part in it. She heard Nell's car in the driveway, the slam of a door, a murmuring of voices, but no one came around the side of the house. Lights came on in various rooms, then went out again, filling her with relief.

Curled up and comfortable, she might have fallen happily asleep if it hadn't been for the sound of another car, another door and then the sound of pebbles against glass. She knew at once it was Luke trying less than subtly to get her attention. She could ignore him, hoping that the new moon wasn't casting enough light to give away her presence, or just bite the bullet and deal with the issues between them now.

In the end, she opted for the latter. Padding across the lawn in her bare feet, she said, "Stop that before you wake up the whole house!"

He whirled in her direction, obviously startled. "You're out here," he said, stating the obvious.

Despite her mood, she smiled. "So I am. I was having a lovely quiet time of it until a few minutes ago. Could I persuade you to leave me to it?"

His jaw set stubbornly. "Do you really want me to go?"

She debated her reply, then sighed. "I suppose not," she said, and returned to her chair and her now-cold cup of tea.

Luke followed her over and sat down next to her. "It was quite a night," he said, clearly testing the waters.

She smiled. "A glorious success from all the comments I heard."

"You and Gram played a huge part in that," he said. "I'll never be able to tell you how much that meant to me."

"It meant a lot to me to share the occasion with you," she said.

He drew in a deep breath, then said, "I'm sorry if Kristen spoiled it for you. You do know she wasn't invited, right? I wasn't just saying that for your benefit."

"I'd seen the list," she said. "I knew. Obviously, though, crashing a party is nothing new to her."

"No, she definitely goes wherever she wishes, welcome or not."

"I don't understand how anyone can do such a thing," Moira admitted. "It's one thing for her to want to get a closer look at me or make me uncomfortable, but surely she has to know that everyone there hates what she tried to do to Susie."

"Oh, believe me, she knows that, but she believes time will eventually make everyone forget. I have to admit that I might have been partially responsible for giving her that impression."

Moira frowned. "How?"

"Right when things were at their trickiest a few months ago, I took her with me to Mick's for Sunday dinner."

Moira didn't even try to hide her astonishment at his insensitivity or Kristen's audacity in accepting the invitation. "Why on earth would you do such a thing?"

"I was in peacemaker mode," Luke admitted, his

expression rueful. "Kristen was here to stay. She was working for Mack. She was with me, not him. I thought we should all forgive and forget." He gave a bitter laugh. "Except nobody had forgiven or forgotten. It was the most miserable Sunday I'd ever spent, especially with Gram looking at me as if I'd killed someone's prized pet."

He gave her a hopeful look. "To my credit, I didn't try to inflict her on everyone in Ireland. She only came after the others had left, and even that was a mistake, because by then there was you."

She finally dared to face him. "If I mattered so much, why did you go right back to her when you got back home?"

"I didn't go back, exactly," he said. "She came after me. That I allowed that, even for a few weeks, doesn't speak well of me."

"No, it doesn't," she said, refusing to let him off the hook. "Talk about mixed messages, Luke."

"I get it," he said.

"Do you really? Because you're still sending them out, only now it's to me."

"I did not invite Kristen tonight," he repeated.

"I'm not talking about Kristen now. I'm talking about your taking me into your bed, letting me share in your business, but refusing to commit to anything more and, worse, admitting that there's been someone else all too recently."

"But I've said all along I'm not ready for more," he complained. "There's nothing mixed about that message. Haven't I been clear?"

"Your words have been," she conceded. "But your actions have kept me close, given me hope."

"As they were meant to," he said. "I care about you, Moira. There's no doubt in my mind about that. It's the future that seems too far away to predict."

"The future is only tomorrow, Luke, or just an hour from now. We don't even know how much of one there will be. We can never know. It's only this moment that we can be certain of."

"And in this moment," he responded quietly, looking at her until she met his gaze, "I'm exactly where I want to be, Moira. I'm with the person I want to be with. Can't that be enough for now?"

She understood that it was all he could offer. She even thought she understood what was holding him back—that bloody timetable of his. But was it enough? She sighed. She couldn't force him into taking the leap of faith that she had taken by getting on a plane and coming to Chesapeake Shores.

And she'd already decided that she needed to stay and fight for what she wanted. Was she now ready to give up at the first big bump in the road?

"For now," she said. "But not for long, Luke. Not for long. I've too much pride to cling to something that might never be."

He nodded then. "Could I persuade you to come back to my place, so we can celebrate tonight's success properly? I want to be with you."

She saw the need in his eyes, felt the pull of an attraction that was always there and slowly stood up. "Let's go," she said quietly. "I'll grab my things and meet you at the car." She gave him a challenging look. "Do you suppose anyone will be scandalized if I arrive at your place in my robe, wearing nothing underneath?"

He looked as if he were about to swallow his tongue. "Nothing?" he echoed.

"Not a thing," she confirmed with a grin.

He moaned. "I think you were put on this earth just to torment me."

"I believe so," she agreed readily, smiling. "And I plan to do a very fine job of it."

17

Despite a very short night with very little sleep, Luke was at the pub soon after dawn to meet the cleaning crew he'd hired to deal with the opening night debris. After this he and his employees would handle the cleanup, but Moira had persuaded him to bring in the extra help just this once. And, yet again, she'd been right. He was increasingly awed by her understanding of how to manage the place, to say nothing of the way she seemed to know him inside out.

Though he'd suggested that she stay in bed at his place, she'd insisted on coming with him, stopping off only to pick up coffee and breakfast for them at Sally's. He expected her to be coming through the door any minute, which was why it was all the more distressing to see Kristen entering instead. If the dark smudges under her eyes were indicative, she hadn't had a good night after leaving the pub where she'd been so unwelcome. Under other circumstances, he might have felt a smidgen of pity at the humiliation she'd experienced, a humiliation of her own making.

"Back for another round?" he asked, his tone unfriendly.

She winced at his question. "Truthfully, I came to apologize," she said. "I knew I wasn't on the guest list last night, but I came, anyway. I have no idea why."

"I could explain it to you, if you like," Luke offered. "I think I have a pretty good idea. You wanted to stake a public claim on me that you knew would hurt Moira, a woman you don't even know."

She looked even more chagrined by his obviously accurate assessment. "I've turned into such a bitch since I moved here," she admitted. "First, I kept trying to rekindle things with Mack, and now I can't seem to walk away from you. What the hell is wrong with me? I was never needy like this before. I keep humiliating myself over and over again. I should have taken Mack up on it when he offered to let me out of my contract and help me find another job."

"You probably should have," Luke agreed bluntly. "Chesapeake Shores is never going to be a good fit for you, Kristen. You need bright lights and a man who'll truly appreciate you, preferably one who's not already taken."

"*You* weren't taken when we started going out," she reminded him. "In fact, you pursued me."

"I did," he conceded. "But things have changed."

"You're with the little Irish milkmaid now."

He scowled at the disparaging comment. "Why do you have to do that? Do you have to cut Moira down to feel better about yourself?"

"I suspect that's exactly it," Moira said from the doorway, startling them both. "Good morning, Kristen. Were we expecting you?"

"I came to apologize," Kristen said, though her expression was anything but contrite as she faced Moira.

"To Luke, not me, I imagine," Moira said. "Have you finished?"

Kristen looked startled that Moira had not only stood her ground, but actually dismissed her. She held Moira's gaze for a moment, but, to Luke's surprise, Kristen was the first to blink.

"I should go," she murmured to Luke, looking as if she still hoped he might beg her to stay.

"Probably a good a idea," he confirmed.

Then in one last attempt to reclaim her dignity or her superiority, Kristen gave him a long, impudent survey, then said, "I'll see you soon, Luke."

He watched her walk away, shoulders straight, head held high, and wondered if she was really half as tough as she wanted everyone to believe. He'd seen another side of her at one time, or at least thought he had. Even now, he'd heard a hint of vulnerability behind her apology, a hint quickly undercut by her deliberate jab at Moira.

"Are you feeling sorry for her?" Moira demanded, her expression indignant.

"Just a little," he admitted, smiling. "You did a fine and well-deserved job of putting her in her place."

"It shouldn't be up to me," she said.

"In other words, I should have kicked her back out the door the second she turned up here," he guessed.

"Seems that way to me," she replied.

"She came to apologize. I let her. It would have been rude not to."

Moira shook her head, as if she found him too pitiful for words. "Is that really what you think, that she was here to make amends?"

"It's what she said," he argued.

"She was here to test the waters, to see if she'd accomplished her goal last night of causing a rift between us. I'm sure she would have happily consoled you if you said I'd gone running home to Ireland."

"But she hasn't caused a rift, and now she knows that."

"Because I walked in," Moira countered. "Would she have known it if I hadn't? Would you have told her, Luke?"

"I did tell her," he said in frustration. "Or I tried to."

Moira finally smiled at that. "Imagine that, a stubborn, hardheaded woman. Who else would an O'Brien man be attracted to?"

He laughed. "Pot calling the kettle black," he pointed out.

She smiled and the visible tension in her shoulders eased, as she settled onto his lap. "That it is," she said. "And if I've a need to stay right here in your arms whenever there's anyone else about, I'll do it just to show the world that you're taken."

"Then you're not giving up on me?" he inquired, relieved by that.

"Not just yet," she confirmed. "Weren't you the one who assured me you were trainable? I'm counting on that."

"Since when do you claim to have more relationship experience than I do?" he inquired.

"It's not experience that counts in these circumstances," she told him with a saucy grin. "It's determination, and I have that in great supply."

And thank God for it, he thought, just before he kissed her, until Kristen Lewis was the last thing on either of their minds.

Though it had been a late night with plenty of excitement, Dillon had been up early and gone for his morning walk on the beach before he heard Nell stirring. When he returned, the house was still quiet. Too quiet, perhaps.

He tapped on her bedroom door, his heart in his throat. "Nell? Are you awake? Is everything okay?"

He heard what sounded like a moan, and panic clawed its way up his throat. "Nell, dear, I hope you're decent, because I'm coming in."

When he opened the door, he spotted her at once on the floor beside the bed, lying in a crumpled heap. He rushed to her side.

Her eyes were open, thank God, and her breathing was shallow, but steady enough.

"Are you hurt?" he asked.

She shook her head. "Just my pride," she said. "I stood up too quickly and had a bit of a dizzy spell. I'd just fallen when you knocked. It took the wind out of me for just a minute, so I couldn't answer."

"Here, my darling, sit up slowly," he said, easing an arm behind her shoulders. "Not too fast." He watched the color return slowly to her too-pale cheeks. "Better?"

She nodded. "I feel like such an old fool."

"We've all taken a spill from time to time," he said. "It's nothing to fret about, as long as you're sure you're not hurt. Your hips feel okay? Your legs? Do you think you can stand?"

"If you'll help me till I'm steady on my feet, I'll be

fine," she insisted. "It's just this blood pressure medicine. I think it's too strong, but the doctor says it's working and I need to adjust to the side effects."

Dillon frowned at that. "That doesn't sound right to me. Maybe you should get a second opinion."

"If I go racing off to another doctor, Mick and the others are bound to find out. They'll make much more of it than they should. You know how they are."

"I know they'd be concerned about you," Dillon said. "And rightfully so."

"Well, I don't want the commotion. The next thing I know, Mick will move me out of here and into his house."

Dillon held her gaze. "Not as long as I'm around," he reassured her. "I promise you that."

He helped her up, then encouraged her to get back into bed. "Rest for a little while. I'll make tea and bring you breakfast in bed. You deserve to be pampered after the long night you had helping out at Luke's opening."

"But you're my guest," she protested.

"Not if I intend to stick around," he argued. "Then we're partners, and I'll do my share to help out." He regarded her with amusement. "You do know I've been on my own for a while now. I'm capable of scrambling an egg and making toast and tea. Let me impress you. You had a long day yesterday. A little extra time off your feet is probably in order."

Though she looked as if she were about to argue, she finally nodded. "I believe I'll give in graciously just this once."

That she did told Dillon just how shaken she was by the fall. The outcome this time had been fine, but at their age who knew what might happen if she fell again? It was something they all feared, a broken leg or hip that would be the beginning of the end of mobility, if not life as they knew it.

When he returned with a tray laden with eggs, toast, jam and tea, she was propped up against the pillows, looking more like herself.

"I don't believe I've ever felt so pampered," she said. "This will be just what I need before we go over to the pub today."

"You're not going anywhere," he said. "You're going to spend the day taking it easy."

Her blue eyes flashed at his order. "You don't make those kind of decisions for me, Dillon O'Malley. Luke needs me to supervise in the kitchen."

"Luke needs to run his own business," he replied with equal firmness in his voice.

"And he will," she said. "But for now, he needs my help and I intend to give it to him."

He heard the intractable note in her voice and smiled. She was definitely back to her feisty self. "How about a compromise? We both go over to check on things. You can spend an hour with the cook, tasting today's specials, and then we come back here, so you can take a nap. Will that work? If you feel rested enough, we'll go back over this evening for another check."

She smiled at him over the rim of her teacup. "A compromise? I imagine I can live with that."

"You know if we're going to make a go of this, Nell, we'll have to do a lot of compromising along the way. We're both two old people who are set in our ways."

"Speak for yourself," she teased. "I'm the most flexible person you'll ever meet."

"I'll believe that when you've shown me evidence of it," he taunted right back.

She reached for his hand then and held on tight. "I'm so very glad you're here and not just because you rescued me this morning."

He smiled at her. "I'm glad I'm here, too."

It was a late-in-life blessing he'd never anticipated. And, God willing, they'd both have a long time yet to enjoy it.

Though Moira spent the morning trying to put both incidents with Kristen out of her mind, she simply wasn't able to forget easily, much less forgive. She couldn't help wondering how Susie had tolerated it when Mack had been on the receiving end of Kristen's predatory wiles.

Maybe this was the perfect chance to get to know Luke's sister a little better. Since Luke was on the phone placing orders or bossing around the cleaning crew, she paused long enough to give him a quick kiss, told him she was taking a break, then headed around the corner to the real estate office.

When she walked in, Susie looked up from her computer with a surprised expression.

"Moira, how are you? Have you and Luke been celebrating all night? Last night's party was absolutely amazing. I felt as if I were back in Dublin. Mack and I can't wait to come back."

"That's exactly the effect your brother was going for," Moira said, pleased that they'd accomplished it. "I was wondering if you had a little time so we could talk? Maybe over lunch at Sally's or somewhere else, if you'd prefer. My treat."

Though Susie looked startled by the invitation, she didn't seem dismayed. Moira figured that was a good sign. She still wasn't one-hundred percent certain of her welcome with any of the family members, even though none of them had tried to keep her at arm's length.

"I can get away, sure," Susie said. "Would you rather take a ride over to my house? I'd love for you to see it."

Moira nodded eagerly. "That would be wonderful," she said at once. "I've been dying to get a look at your place. I've heard so much about it and about your fabulous view. Should we pick up lunch before we go?"

"No need. If a salad's okay, I have everything we'll need."

"A salad works for me," Moira told her.

Susie locked up the office, then led the way to her car. "I'm really glad you came by," she said as they drove out of downtown. "We haven't spent much time together. Since you're obviously special to my brother, I want to get to know you better."

Moira smiled. "I know everyone in the family was a bit taken aback that Luke and I hit it off," she admitted. "I hope I'm making a better impression this time around."

"Much better," Susie confirmed. "Mom is one of your biggest fans. So is Gram."

"They're wonderful women," Moira said. "I wish I were as close to my own mum as you all are to yours."

"If you want it, you'll get there," Susie assured her. "Mom and I were always close, but it's not always that way between mothers and daughters. Sometimes you have to work at building a good relationship. Just look at the struggles Abby, Bree and Jess had making peace with Megan, and now they're getting closer all the time."

"I think time is exactly what it will take for my mum and me," Moira said. "There's a lot of past baggage to overcome."

When they'd turned onto Beach Lane, Moira spotted two amazing homes nestled in the woods along the cliff overlooking the bay. They looked as if they'd always been there, a part of the scenery, rather than an intrusion on it.

"Oh, my," she murmured, her eyes wide. "And Matthew designed these?"

Susie nodded, her pride unmistakable. "Mine first, then the one just up the road for him and Laila. He'll design Luke's next, when the time comes." She shook her head. "Luke considered selling his lot, but thank goodness Gram was able to talk him out of it."

"Why would he have sold such a beautiful piece of property?" Moira asked, stunned.

"For the money to open the pub," Susie said. "But he found the financing another way. I think it's made him even more determined, though, to make a success of the place, to prove that Gram wasn't misguided in giving him his trust money early."

"I'd forgotten about that," Moira admitted. It reminded her of why Luke was so obsessed with the pub's success. It went beyond his own need to prove himself. He wanted to justify Nell's faith in him. She couldn't fault him for that.

The inside of Susie and Mack's home was as spectacular as the outside. The rooms were warm and filled with sunlight, the decor cozy and inviting.

"I just love it," Moira said, spinning slowly around to

take in the open downstairs floor plan. "I think Nell's is more my style because it's so cozy and intimate, like an Irish country cottage, but this is amazing, Susie."

"We've been happy here," Susie said, leading the way to the kitchen with its granite countertops and cherry custom cabinets. "When we built it, I was so sick. I wasn't sure I'd ever have the chance to live here with Mack, so I'm grateful every day, not only for my health, but to be here with him."

"Your cancer was that serious?" Moira asked.

Susie nodded, then waved off the topic. "But enough about that. I'm in remission for now, and that's what counts." She gestured toward a table by the window. "Have a seat there. I'll have our lunch ready in a jiffy."

"Let me help," Moira said.

"It's a salad," Susie protested. "I'll dump a few greens in a couple of bowls, add a few things and we're done."

"At least let me fix the drinks."

"Okay, then. Iced tea for me. It's in the refrigerator. There are sodas in there as well, along with a pitcher of water. I used to drink bottled water by the caseload till Uncle Thomas convinced me I was single-handedly ruining the environment. Now I've taken to filtering plain old tap water."

Within a few minutes, they were both seated at a round antique oak table by a floor-to-ceiling window with a spectacular view of the shimmering blue bay.

"I'll never get enough of this view," Susie said. "I'm so glad Dad had the foresight to buy this land and hang on to it for us." She turned to Moira. "So, you didn't come by just to get to know me better, did you? It's about Kristen. I heard about her little scene before the party started last night."

Moira shook her head, astonished once more by how word traveled. "Jess told you?"

She nodded. "She was furious. She tried not to say anything, but I could tell she was upset, so I pried it out of her."

"Would it be out of place for me to ask how you coped with knowing Kristen was after your husband?"

Susie smiled. "I can probably tell you now without wanting to race out of here and rip her hair out. There was a time there when just the mention of her name was enough to make me nuts."

"How did you get to this point?" Moira asked. "I'm still fairly eager to have a go at her hair."

Susie grinned. "I'd still be willing to help without requiring a lot of persuasion."

"Maybe I'll take you up on it," Moira said. "I know I shouldn't let her intimidate me, and I make a great show of being tough in front of Luke, but inside I'm quaking. She's so polished and sophisticated—not at all like me."

Susie nodded in obvious understanding. "That was me, probably magnified a thousand times. You know she came after Mack when I was sick?"

"I heard that," Moira confirmed. "How could she? What sort of woman does that?"

"I'm convinced now that for all her brilliance at business, she has no compassion or sensitivity. Women with no heart take whatever they want, or at least try to."

"Did you take her on?"

"I was too weak to take on a kitten," Susie admitted. "I think I would have otherwise, or at least I like to think so. Fortunately, Mack made it clear to her that she was out of line." She smiled. "And then there was my baby brother, my hero."

"Luke," Moira said.

Susie nodded. "He swooped in and became her fall-back guy. I have to say I was furious when I figured out what he was up to, but Luke knew how to take care of himself and he was determined that she would not hurt me, not when I couldn't fight back."

"Was it ever serious to him, do you think?" Moira asked hesitantly, not sure she wanted to know the answer.

Susie's hesitation was slight before she asked, "What does he say?"

"He says it wasn't," Moira admitted. "But then why didn't he break it off at once when he got involved with me?"

Susie's expression turned thoughtful. "Okay, I'm only guessing here, because he hasn't said a word to me," she said eventually, "but you were still in Ireland. Unless I'm wrong, you hadn't made plans for the future, hadn't even scheduled a visit. Kristen was here and handy."

"Is that all that's necessary for a man?" Moira asked in frustration.

Susie smiled. "Sometimes I forget how much younger you and my brother are. Yes, that's all it takes. It doesn't make it right. It doesn't speak well of my brother, so I can't defend him, but I do think that's all it was—a convenience or maybe just a habit. And you've seen for yourself—Kristen doesn't give up on getting what she wants. I'm sure she threw herself straight into his arms every chance she got."

"If he really cared about me, I mean even a little, shouldn't he have resisted?" Moira asked, unconvinced that the responsibility could all be laid on Kristen.

"Of course," Susie said readily. "But Luke's a guy. I think once he makes a commitment to you or anyone else, he'll be as honorable as they come about keeping it. In the meantime, though, I suppose he figured there was nothing to prevent him from taking advantage of what she offered. He has cut it off now, right?"

"So it seems."

"Then focus on that," Susie advised.

"I suppose the fact that he has to deal with her determination to rub their connection in my face every chance she gets is just punishment for what he did," Moira said.

"It's bound to make his skin crawl when he sees her coming his way for that very reason," Susie agreed. "I know one thing about Luke. However little he cared for Kristen, he probably feels bad that he's broken it off. Even more, though, he would give anything not to have you hurt by her. It's quite a balancing act for a mere man to tackle."

Moira smiled at the assessment. "Will she give up, do you think?"

"She gave up on Mack," Susie said. "She'll eventually give up on Luke. Her pride won't let this drag on for too long."

"Should I wait her out or try to make things clear to her?"

"Which will make you feel stronger and more in control?"

"Telling her off," Moira said at once.

"Then that's what you should do."

"And Luke won't freak out if I stake my claim?"

"Do you honestly care?"

Moira thought about that, then smiled. "No, this is my battle. I'll wage it however I like."

Susie laughed then. "Good for you. Mind if I tag along whenever you go after her? It'll do my heart good." She shrugged. "And it probably wouldn't hurt to have backup if things get out of hand."

Moira chuckled with her. "I'll give that some thought and get back to you. I'm not sure a witness is a good idea, especially if things take a turn for the worse and I go for her throat."

"Aw, come on," Susie pleaded. "How can you expect me to miss that?"

"You've a devilishly wicked streak, haven't you?" she said approvingly. "I think we're going to be great friends."

"I hope we're going to be more than that," Susie replied. "I think sisters-in-law would be fantastic."

Moira regarded her with surprise. "Then I've your blessing as far as Luke's concerned?"

"You do," Susie said quietly. "But don't expect him to rush into anything, Moira. He has a lot he wants to accomplish before he'll be ready for the next step."

"So he's mentioned," Moira said wryly. "More than once."

"If you can respect that, I think the day you're hoping for will come sooner than you think."

Moira wished she shared Susie's faith in that, but she intended to hang in there just in case Susie had pegged it right. After all, with her heart already on the line, what choice did she have?

_18_

To Luke's astonishment, Friday and Saturday nights were even busier than the party had been. Word had apparently spread through the region about both the atmosphere and the music. It helped, too, that it was a gorgeous spring weekend, which had drawn the summer tourists to their cottages by the bay. The slow opening he'd envisioned before next weekend's traditional Memorial Day onslaught hadn't happened. None of the O'Briens had even an instant to catch their breath.

Each night, he and Moira had fallen into bed exhausted but exhilarated. As tired as they were, they were awake late, talking about how things had gone, what needed improvement, what was drawing raves. He hadn't realized how wonderful it would be to have someone by his side who understood how a pub operated, whose praise—or criticism—came from knowledge rather than bias.

"It's a good thing I decided to be closed on Mondays at first," Luke said with Moira wrapped in his arms. "I think by this time tomorrow, I'll barely be able to keep my eyes open."

"Perhaps if we went to sleep, instead of all this fooling around we're doing," she teased, "you'd be more rested."

He laughed. "Fooling around, is it? I thought we were making love."

She regarded him with surprise. "I thought just using the phrase might scare you."

He knew the comment had been made in jest, but he hesitated, thinking about it. "I think it might have as recently as a few days ago," he said, "but not now."

"What's changed?" she asked, looking deep into his eyes.

It seemed to him that she was all but holding her breath as she awaited his response. He knew he had to get it right. "You," he said, then shook his head. "No, it's more about me when I'm with you. It all feels right. Yes, it was about the challenge when we first met and you brushed me off. And then it was about you fascinating me. Now it's about all of that plus being comfortable with you."

"Like an old shoe?" she inquired, eyes sparkling with mirth.

"No, sexier than that by far."

He waited for her to press for more, which is what she would have done just a couple of weeks ago, but she merely smiled, apparently satisfied with his response.

"That's good, then," she said quietly, and snuggled closer. "Now, go to sleep or we'll both be dragging through the day tomorrow."

He grinned. "We don't open until noon, which gives us an entire morning to sleep."

Her expression brightened. "Well, in that case, then," she said, moving into his kiss.

The weekend had been so frantic that it wasn't until Monday that Moira had a chance to load the pictures she'd taken at the opening onto Luke's computer and begin sorting through them. Once again, she was surprised by the way certain personalities had been captured in a single shot. She always hoped for that, of course, but until she saw the proof in front of her eyes she was never certain she'd managed it. More often than she liked, she hadn't.

But today, here was Mick with his head thrown back in full-throated laughter. She'd caught Nell bending over a pot of Irish stew in the kitchen for a final sniff of the aroma, eyes closed, a smile on her lips. And Luke's uncle Thomas with an arm around Connie's shoulder, his hand resting on her enormous belly and a look of utter satisfaction and joy on his face.

Though there were dozens of photos she loved and at least half of those that she thought might be good enough for the walls of the pub or to share with the family, only a few were special enough for the portfolio she was putting together for Megan's approval. She printed those out in snapshot size, then headed down the block to Megan's gallery. Though it, too, was closed on Monday, like so many other tourist-oriented businesses in town, Moira knew Megan would be in back catching up on paperwork.

At her knock, Megan came out of her office and smiled when she recognized her.

"Please tell me you've come to show me pictures

from the opening," she said as soon as she'd unlocked the door.

"Right here," Moira told her, still clinging to the envelope she'd brought along. "Just a few."

"Judging from the size of it, that must be a mere sampling," Megan said, clearly disappointed. "You could always let me look at all of them and be an impartial judge."

Moira shook her head. "I want you to see only the best, and then choose from those the ones you think are really extraordinary." She shrugged. "If any of them are."

"Don't be so modest," Megan said. "We both know you have the talent for extraordinary."

"You may believe that, but I'm still struggling with it," Moira said. "Every time I load a new batch of pictures into the computer, I'm filled with doubts."

Megan wiggled her fingers. "Hand 'em over. Let's see what you have."

Moira gave Megan the small test prints, then left her alone while she walked through the gallery. She'd been meaning to come by for a while to see the photography exhibit, but this was her first chance.

As she studied the shots, admiring the use of light and shadow in the photographs, she remained attuned to Megan on the other side of the room behind her desk. Each time she heard a small gasp, her heart leaped.

"Moira," Megan said eventually.

She turned back, noted the neutral expression on Megan's usually transparent face and felt her heart dip. Filled with anxiety, she crossed the room. "Well? Is there anything there that will meet your high standards?"

A wide, reassuring smile broke across Megan's face. "I know I'm biased because these are people I know and love, but just as you did with the children in the park, you've brought them alive. I can hear Mick's laughter and feel Thomas's joy at the prospect of being a father. As for Nell, showing her in the kitchen, where she's most at home, was a perfect choice. They're truly remarkable, Moira. If you ever try to tell me again that you want no part of this, I'll fight you. Moreover, I'll have the entire family gang up on you. You have no idea how persuasive we can be when we're all dedicated to the same cause."

"You're not just saying that?" Moira asked nervously. "Are you trying to be kind to me because of Luke?"

Megan shook her head at once, clearly impatient with the question. "This is business, Moira. Luke is completely separate. And, before we put that topic aside, let me say that I was impressed with how well you worked together at the opening. You do make a terrific team."

Moira allowed herself a momentary hint of triumph. "Really? I mean about the photographs," she asked, not quite daring to believe her.

"Really," Megan reiterated. "You'll need many more before we can put a show together, but since you'll be in Chesapeake Shores for a while now, you'll have plenty of opportunities to take pictures at various town events. I'd like you to take some in the businesses as well. Once we have a full complement, we'll have a better idea of what to call the show. I'm still leaning toward *The Faces of Chesapeake Shores,* but *The Heart of a Town* might work nicely as well. It would travel better, perhaps, if the show were to be mounted in other cities."

Moira felt the first faint stirring of real excitement.

She hadn't permitted herself to believe anything about this opportunity. Having her own show had seemed far too grand for someone like her. Taking pictures at weddings or baby showers had seemed attainable, but this? Viewing her pictures as art? It was completely unbelievable. What would Peter think when she told him?

"It doesn't change what I really want," she warned Megan. "This is exciting and more amazing than anything I ever imagined, but it's still a family that I truly want."

"You'll have both, if it's what you want," Megan assured her.

Of course, Moira thought yet again, the family side of her dream—the biggest part of the future she wanted—wasn't entirely hers to decide, at least not if she wanted all that with Luke. He still had a say, and though she thought they'd made some progress, he was far from ready to dive in now.

Perhaps while he continued to sort out his feelings, it wouldn't hurt to grab on to this amazing opportunity and see just how far it could carry her.

Megan sat back, studying her. "So, Moira, what did you think of the current exhibit?"

"It's interesting," she said carefully, hesitant to express her reservations to the woman who'd obviously had faith in the photographer who'd taken the pictures. "It's very different from what I do."

Megan smiled. "Very different," she concurred. "Mike's pictures strip down the beauty of something to its bare essentials. A twig covered with snow, the dew on a flower. I think that's often best achieved in black and white."

"They're still," Moira said, choosing her words carefully. "Quiet, if you know what I mean."

"And yours radiate life and energy," Megan assessed. "Thus the difference. I'm glad you understand it. You may be very new to looking at your work analytically, but you have a basic understanding of why it's so special. That tells me you'll always recognize the most magical moments in your shots."

"I'm actually afraid to think about them too much," Moira said. "If I get too much in my head, won't I lose something of the spontaneity?"

Megan grinned. "I think so. Good for you for understanding that. I think we're going to work well together, Moira. And if this show goes as well as I think it will, you'll have more attention and more opportunities than you ever imagined."

"Please, don't get too carried away beyond this one show," Moira pleaded. "The thought of more terrifies me. And I do have commitments back in Dublin. I'm thinking I'll still fly back to do those jobs. It's only fair."

"I suppose I can live with that," Megan told her. "Though I'm anxious to get moving, I'm impressed by your loyalty to the man who inspired you back home."

Moira regarded her with real gratitude. "Thank you again for giving me this chance to prove myself. I'd have been content to take the occasional pictures at weddings, I think."

"They would have been very lucky brides," Megan told her. "Now I'm going to be the lucky one, because I get to launch your work to a much larger world."

"I still can't get used to the idea that you see it that

way," Moira admitted. "I mean it when I say that just thinking about it scares me to death."

"Heavens, that's the last thing I want to do," Megan said. "Run along quickly before you decide never to touch a camera again."

Moira smiled. "I won't do anything that drastic," she promised. "But I will run along. Luke's probably wondering where I've gone, if he's even looked up from his paperwork to notice that I'm not where he left me in his office."

"He must be thrilled by how well this weekend went," Megan said. "Mick and I popped in for just a minute again on Saturday night and it was so mobbed we couldn't find anyplace to sit."

Moira was chagrined. "You should have looked for Luke or me. We'd have found chairs for you. There will always be room for family, even if we have to boot another customer to squeeze you in."

Megan laughed. "Now that's a sure way to destroy your business, showing preference for certain customers. Don't worry. You know we'll be back again. I'll come by if only to make sure you're taking all the photos you should be. I can be a bit tyrannical when it comes to business. Fair warning."

"Oddly enough, *that* doesn't scare me," Moira said. "Though it probably should."

"I'll see you soon, then."

Moira took her time walking back to the pub, absorbing every word of Megan's praise, replaying their entire conversation. She was so lost in thought, she stumbled when she nearly ran down Luke as he stepped outside the pub and directly into her path.

"There you are!" he said as he reached out to steady her. "Where did you run off to?"

"Megan's," she said.

He searched her face, then smiled. "It went well, didn't it? She loved the pictures you showed her?"

Moira nodded. "She really, really loved them. Or at least she said she did." Barely able to contain her excitement, she said, "Luke, it was truly the most remarkable thing that's ever happened to me. And to think it might never have happened if I hadn't come here. I mean there was work to be had in Ireland, but this… It's beyond my wildest dreams."

Luke swooped her up in his arms and spun her in a circle.

"Put me down, you idiot. You're making me dizzy."

"I thought I always made your head spin," he teased as he put her back on her feet.

"Not in the same way."

"Let's have lunch and you can tell me every word she said," he suggested. "We'll go to Sally's and sit at a real table and celebrate by letting her wait on us."

"Add in one of those banana split things I've seen her serving and I'm in," Moira said at once.

"Do you want your own or will you share?" he asked.

"I imagine I can let you have a bite or two," she said. "But if you get any greedier, you'll have to order your own."

He smiled. "I love seeing you like this."

"Like what?"

"Truly happy and excited."

"I'm happy when I'm with you," she argued.

"Most of the time," he agreed. "But it's not the same.

There's a sense of accomplishment that comes from a career success that can't be matched. I've just gotten a taste of that with the pub's opening, and now it's your turn. I want you to have it all, Moira, to be everything you can possibly be."

Though he'd obviously meant the words to be positive, she felt oddly deflated, as if he valued the professional over the personal. And, if that was the case, she despaired of them ever reaching common ground.

Luke had no idea what he'd said or done, but a light had died in Moira's eyes while they were on the way to Sally's. She went through the motions of eating her lunch but left most of her sandwich on her plate and, when the time came for dessert, she turned down the banana split she'd claimed to want.

Though he thought he was used to her mood swings, this one felt different. While he waited for Sally to bring their check, he tried to get Moira to meet his gaze.

"Mind telling me where you've gone off to in that head of yours?" he asked. "One minute we were celebrating and then you turned quiet. You've hardly said two words during lunch."

She responded with a smile that was obviously forced. "Sorry. I suppose the pressure of everything that happened sank in."

"What sort of pressure? Has Megan put you on a timetable? You can always tell her to back off if it's too much."

"No, it's just all these expectations. I thought it was awful when nobody thought I was ever going to accomplish anything. Now that someone thinks I have this previously undiscovered talent, I feel as if I have to start taking myself seriously."

"I'm confused," Luke admitted. "Don't you want to succeed?"

"Doesn't everyone?" she said, though there was an oddly bitter note in her voice.

"Apparently not you, if your tone is anything to judge by," he said, completely at a loss about her change in attitude from just a half hour ago. "You sound as if it's this huge burden that's been placed on you, when you should be dancing with sheer joy. You were, just a short time ago."

"And then reality set in, I suppose. I know it makes no sense to you. The pub is your dream."

"It wasn't always," Luke said. "I had no sense of direction not that long ago."

"And neither did I," she said. "But you seem to have latched onto the dream and are intent on riding it full throttle. I think maybe I'm just used to a slower pace. The speed of this has me reeling."

"I'm sure it does," he said, because that was a feeling he could understand. He'd watched members of his family get swept up in things, so he'd been prepared for the wave of exhilaration that had come with the pub's opening weekend success. Moira was clearly more used to failures, had even come to accept that failing was all she deserved.

"Are you feeling as if you don't deserve this?" he asked, still trying to understand. "Because obviously, based on Megan's reaction to your talent, you do."

She sighed. "I honestly don't know what I'm feeling right now. Would you mind terribly if I left and went for a walk? That usually clears my head."

Though he wanted her to stay so he could get to the bottom of this, he gestured toward the door. "Go, if that's what you need."

"There's nothing you need me for at the pub?"

"Nothing that won't wait," he assured her. "Will you come back after your walk?"

She hesitated. "Maybe we should take a break, just for tonight."

Luke frowned at the suggestion. "Okay, though I'm suddenly getting the feeling here that your mood has as much to do with me as it does with your future in photography."

She sighed. "It probably does," she admitted.

"If that's the case, then you need to stay right here and spell it out for me, Moira. Let's deal with it head-on."

She gave him what might have been the saddest smile he'd ever seen. "I don't think this is something that can be fixed, Luke. I really don't. Certainly not with a chat or a snap of the fingers."

"Just tell me and let me decide if it can or can't be," he said in frustration.

"Okay," she said. "You've once again made the assumption that a career is the only thing that matters, is the only thing that measures the worth of a person. I don't think like that at all."

"I never said it was the only thing that matters," Luke protested. "It's important. There's no denying that, maybe more so for a man than a woman."

She frowned. "I imagine there are a few in your own family who'd take exception to that statement."

"Probably so," he agreed readily. "More important, though, is whether you're one of them. How do you feel about this? Do you not understand why I want to succeed with the pub?"

"Of course I understand. You feel you owe Nell for her faith in you, for one thing. For another, you're holding yourself up to the O'Brien gold standard of accomplishment. Success is what matters, no matter what the personal cost."

Luke regarded her with shock. "I've never said such a thing. Nor do I think that way. Don't you suppose I can recall what thinking like that cost Uncle Mick? He lost Megan and made things difficult for all my cousins by being so committed to his career above all else. He thought he was working so hard for his family, but it was really all about feeding his own ego, I think. I'm not doing that."

"Perhaps not, but what you have said is that until you've attained whatever constitutes success by your standards, everything else remains on hold."

"By everything, you mean a wife and family," he guessed, finally making sense of where this whole afternoon had gone off course.

She nodded. "And that's the very difference between us, Luke, because for me the *only* thing that really matters is family."

She regarded him thoughtfully. "Maybe it's different for you because you've always had this storybook family, while I grew up with one that barely spoke. We didn't have the big holiday celebrations or even the conversations over dinner. Family is a reality for you—one you take for granted—but for me it's a fantasy. It's all I've ever really wanted. For me this chance at a career is just the icing on a cake. It's not the cake."

"And you think I'm withholding the cake," he said quietly.

She nodded. "And it scares me, not because you say you're not ready for anything more now—I could handle that—but because I'm terrified that you never will be."

Luke wanted to reassure her that wasn't the case, but how could he? Work *was* his priority for now. He didn't have an end date for that. He had no measure for when his feelings might change. Would it happen when the pub had been successful for six months? Or a year? How could he predict something like that? He simply knew he'd recognize the moment when it came, just as Matthew had known Laila was the woman for him and Susie had fallen in love with Mack and spent years waiting for him to return her feelings. Was that what he expected from Moira, that she'd wait quietly until he was ready? He knew better, or should.

Or, and this was the real rub, was his hesitation because he didn't trust his feelings for Moira, at least not enough to act on them? Gram had told him often enough to listen to his heart. He'd thought he was. But if he kept pushing Moira away, refusing to make promises, maybe that wasn't the case. All he knew for sure was that his indecision was hurting her, and that wasn't fair.

"I'm sorry," he said quietly. "I wish I could tell you what you want to hear. I can only say that there's no one else I'd rather have in my life right now. You matter to me, Moira, in so many ways, but if that's not enough for you, I'll understand."

She looked shocked that he'd put it so bluntly, offered her the chance to walk away. He held his breath, waiting to hear her verdict, because it was her decision to make. He prayed she'd have the same patience as Susie, but he also knew they were two different women. There was nothing patient about Moira.

A tear spilled down her cheek. "It's not enough," she said, her voice barely above a whisper. "It's not nearly enough, when we could have so much more."

And before he could blink or apologize or beg her to stay and reconsider, she was gone.

Luke sat in stunned silence, realizing immediately that without a doubt, he'd just made the worst mistake of his life. The only problem with seeing that was that he also had absolutely no idea what he could have done differently.

19

Moira couldn't believe what she'd just done! She'd taken Luke at his word and walked away. How had her fears overtaken her last shred of sense? That was the only thing that could explain what had just happened. She'd panicked, seen the future unfolding and herself being in this exact same position months, maybe even years, from now, waiting for Luke to be ready for a family.

Even as tears rolled down her cheeks and she walked faster and faster back toward Nell's until her breath was catching in her throat, she was still stunned that it had ended so easily. This was the man she loved, the man she wanted as a husband, as a father to her children, as the core of that family she claimed so desperately to want. And she'd just folded and walked away as if it were a foregone conclusion that she'd never have it.

But was it? In her view, Luke's priorities might be all screwed up, but he wouldn't have let her leave Sally's if even some tiny part of him had envisioned a future for the two of them. He obviously couldn't see it happening, so this was for the best.

Even though she kept telling herself the same thing for the entire twenty minutes it took her to reach Nell's cottage, it didn't feel as if it were for the best. It felt awful. It hurt deep inside, where an emptiness was opening up that she couldn't imagine ever being able to fill again.

She debated going down to the beach and walking and walking until the pain went away, but if she tried that, she knew she'd be down there for weeks. No, what Moira really wanted was to crawl into her bed under one of Nell's Irish quilts and never show her face in Chesapeake Shores again. If she thought she'd be able to slip out of town in the dark of night, she'd have planned to do just that.

But, she thought with a sigh, there was her ticket, which had already been canceled for the original return date. There was her grandfather, who might feel compelled to leave with her if he thought she was suffering from a broken heart.

And there was her pride, something she'd always had in spades. She wasn't going to let Luke drive her away from a place she was starting to love and an opportunity that might give her life a sense of direction and purpose, at least for now. The jobs Peter had lined up in Dublin might suit her, but what Megan was offering held hope of real success. It might not be the goal she'd envisioned, but it promised financial security, something she'd come to value thanks to her mum's struggles to make ends meet.

Maybe she'd even find someone else who had his priorities in order, marry and settle down right here just for the sheer joy of driving Luke nuts. She smiled at the thought.

She was almost to Nell's when she spotted her grandfather coming up from the beach. She tried to wipe any
trace of tears from her face, but he took one look at her
and asked, "What happened? Did you and Luke have a
fight?"

"Why does everyone always assume if a woman's
crying, it's over a man?" she grumbled.

He smiled at her. "Because it often is, especially at
your age. Am I wrong? Is this not about Luke?"

"Oh, it's about Luke," she admitted. "We've broken
up."

Her grandfather looked stunned. "But why?"

"Because it was in the cards already," she said. "I
just decided to take matters into my own hands and do
it on my timetable."

"*You* broke it off?" he asked, his astonishment plain.

She nodded, not even trying to hide her misery. "It
was for the best."

"Then you're not in love with him?"

"Of course I'm in love with him," she said impatiently. "I even think he's in love with me."

Dillon took her hand and drew her across the yard to
the Adirondack chairs in Nell's summer garden, where
she'd spent so many wonderful moments snuggled in
Luke's arms during this visit.

"Okay, now, you'll need to be explaining to me
what's really happened, because you're not making a
lot of sense," her grandfather urged quietly.

Though she hadn't intended to pour out her heart,
that's exactly what she did. Her grandfather, to his
credit, listened without comment, nodding occasionally, even smiling a time or two. Her gaze narrowed
at that.

"There's nothing to smile about in this," she told him.

"There is if you're familiar with the tendency of two mules to butt heads," he commented.

"You're saying I'm stubborn?" she asked indignantly.

He didn't even try to hide a smile at the question. "Would you even dare to deny it?"

That finally drew her own smile. "No, I suppose not."

"And Luke certainly comes by it naturally as well," he said.

She frowned. "You are not suggesting I was in the wrong to walk away, are you?"

"Not wrong exactly," he said. "I'm just thinking that your timing could have been better. It seems to me the decision was a wee bit premature and based on the emotion of the moment. Luke's head is caught up in his new business venture. He needs time to sort things out."

"Time? Should we wait till we're both old and too feeble to crawl out of these chairs?" she retorted.

"There's the sense of drama that got you into this fix," he chided. "No one is suggesting you wait that long, but Luke barely has the taste of the pub's success on his lips. He's had no time at all to bask in it or to feel certain it will continue, and now you've gone and issued your ultimatum."

"There was no ultimatum," she said.

"Really? That's not how I heard it. Maybe you didn't give him an either/or choice, but it was definitely implied that you'd lost patience. The proof of that is that he didn't offer exactly what you wanted, when you wanted it, and you walked away."

"I hadn't lost patience," she corrected. "It's hope I

lost, and there's a difference. If there was an ultimatum, it came from him. It was wait and wait, indefinitely as near as I could tell, or call it quits now."

"So your pride won out and you called it quits," he concluded. "That won't keep you warm tonight."

She understood the truth of that. "Then what was I supposed to do?"

"It's a little late to figure out how you could have handled it any differently. And if it helps at all, I imagine Luke is wondering the same thing now. It's a waste of time, looking back. Now you have to put your mind to what you intend to do next."

She bristled at the implication of that. "Apologize? Hell will freeze over first."

He chuckled. "I imagined you'd say something like that. Perhaps, though, rather than an apology, you could simply go to him and talk things through."

"To what end? It's not as if he'll have had an epiphany and declare his undying love. No," she said adamantly. "If there's talking to be done, he'll have to come to me."

"And if he's just as stubborn and refuses?"

"Then it wasn't meant to be, was it?"

Dillon shook his head. "An ending based on assumptions is never a test of what was meant to be," he said. "Fate's no competition for stubbornness."

Moira let his words sink in, then sighed. She feared he was exactly right about that, but she wasn't quite ready to act on his wisdom just yet.

"Were we ever that young and foolish?" Dillon asked Nell after describing what had happened between Moira and Luke earlier in the day.

Moira was locked in her room, and Nell and Dillon had gone outside to wait for the sun to set. Nell savored these moments she had alone with him, time to talk over their day, to share bits and pieces of memories. There'd been too few moments like this since Dillon's arrival, quiet times for reflection and simply being together. She'd spent too much of the time she'd hoped to devote to him helping out at Luke's pub instead.

"For whatever comfort it might be, Luke was in no better frame of mind when I popped into the pub this afternoon," she told Dillon. "I had no idea exactly what had happened, but Moira was missing and his mood was foul. It didn't take a genius to put two and two together."

"Do you think we should intervene?" Dillon asked. "In a way, I feel responsible for her misery, since I encouraged her to come here with me."

Nell thought about the question. She'd seen Mick's interference go awry often enough to know better than to try it herself. Sometimes matters needed time to settle on their own.

"You told Moira what she needs to do," she said thoughtfully. "And, though she can be impetuous, I think once she's mulled over your advice, she'll see the wisdom of it. Let's give it some time."

She turned her head and smiled at him. "These nights out here like this have been too few and far between. Let's leave the children to sort out their own problems for now and concentrate on us. I feel as if we have a lifetime to catch up on and, even with the extension of your stay, only limited time to do it."

"We do," Dillon said simply. "But do we really want to waste the time we have now thinking about the past?

Perhaps we should be looking ahead, making plans of our own."

Nell felt a quick stirring of anticipation. "What sort of plans?"

"Precisely how long I'm to stay, for starters," he said, then reached for her hand. "Nell, is an interlude all you want? Ironically, it's my granddaughter who's gotten me to thinking about this. I'm content to be with you under any circumstances, but, to be honest, you've owned a part of my heart for most of my life. I'd be honored if you'd agree to be my wife and claim the rest of my heart from now till eternity."

Nell had thought that if her heart ever began beating this hard at her age, it would be a terrible thing, but it wasn't at all like that now. She was suddenly filled with a profound joy she'd never expected to experience again. She held Dillon's gaze.

"Are you sure marriage is what you want?" she asked. "Perhaps it's foolish to consider taking such a step at our age. It's not as if we'd scandalize anyone by just living together."

"I've dreamed of the day I could put a ring on your finger," he admitted. "I dreamed of it sixty years ago, and now I've a chance to make that dream come true." He reached over and held her hand. "But, unlike Moira, if you say you're content with the way things are, I'll stay right here by your side. I just want you to understand the depth of my feelings for you."

Nell felt the surprising dampness of a tear trickling down her cheek. "Now you've gone and made me cry," she said.

He frowned. "Is that the good sort of crying or the bad?" he asked anxiously.

"The very best kind," she said, laughing through the tears she couldn't seem to stop. "I think I'm going to have to marry you, Dillon O'Malley. My heart will never forgive me if I don't, because I've loved you all these years as well."

Until just this moment, she hadn't realized how true that was. Though she'd loved her husband, though her life with him had been blessed in so many ways, including three fine sons and so many incredible grandchildren, Dillon had claimed a part of her heart years ago in Dublin. He still owned it.

"Then we're agreed?" Dillon asked, as if not daring to believe he'd heard correctly.

She squeezed his hand. "We're agreed. We'll need to break the news carefully, though."

"I'll go to Mick tomorrow," he said at once. "As the oldest, and the least likely to be receptive, I'll do whatever it takes to win his approval."

"Some might say a better strategy would be to win others over first," she suggested.

Dillon shook his head. "I owe Mick the courtesy."

She laughed at his old-fashioned belief in the order of things, but it touched her just the same. "Do I need to come along to protect you?"

"Mick doesn't scare me," Dillon said with confidence. "Because in the end, he and I both want only the best for you. I think we'll come to terms."

"As long as you don't throw a couple of cows or sheep into the bargain, I'll leave you to it, then."

Dillon's booming laugh carried on the surprisingly cool evening breeze, filling her heart with unexpected joy. And with her hand nestled in his, she was overcome with a contentment so pure it was unlike anything she'd ever experienced before. And at her age, that was saying quite a lot!

Luke was fairly certain he hadn't slept a wink all night. Just after dawn, he showered and headed for the pub to get ready for the noon opening. His eagerness to see how well the place would do on a day in mid-week was overshadowed by his realization that he was on his own. There would be no Moira at his side, looking out for details, backing him up, giving his hand a quick squeeze as she passed by.

Well, he thought, that was just the way it was. He could hardly blame her for walking away when he'd given her little reason to stay.

He spent the morning checking supplies, even though he'd gone through the same lists just the day before. He confirmed orders with suppliers, who responded that yes, the information they'd given him yesterday was correct, deliveries would be on schedule. In a few cases he could hear the amusement in the voices of the customer service representatives.

"You're newly opened," one woman said. "I can tell."

"Sorry. I'm still a little paranoid about things not going smoothly."

"Understandable," she said. "And the woman I spoke to earlier said the same."

Luke went absolutely silent for a moment as her words sank in. "A woman called? From O'Brien's? Are you sure?"

"As sure as I am that I spoke to you yesterday as well as just now," she confirmed. "She called not fifteen minutes ago. I keep a notation of all calls in the account record."

"I see," he said softly. "Thanks."

What on earth did it mean that Moira was conducting pub business as if nothing were awry?

He didn't have long to ponder that, because a key turned in the lock and she breezed in, barely sparing him a glance as she headed for the kitchen. Luke trailed along behind her.

"Moira, what are you doing here?" he asked, even as she walked into the freezer obviously intent on checking something.

When she emerged, she shrugged. "What does it look like? I'm doing my job."

He faltered at that, trying to decide if he should make an issue of this unexpected turn of events or let it pass. In the end, though, he had to understand.

"I thought you'd quit."

She leveled a defiant look straight into his eyes then. "It was you I quit, Luke. Walking out on this job would be irresponsible." Her expression dared him to challenge her.

Ah, he thought, fighting a smile. This was the salve to her pride, a way to come back into his life without letting him off the hook at all.

"Okay, then," he said, grateful for the tiny opening, however it had come about. "I'll be in the office, if you need me."

She picked up a pot then and dropped it on the floor, causing a clatter that stopped him in his tracks. "That's all you have to say?" she demanded.

"I'm at a loss," he admitted. "You're here to do a job, nothing else, isn't that what you said?"

She clearly wasn't pleased to have been taken at her word, but he wasn't quite ready to bend yet, either.

"That's what I said," she agreed tightly.

"Would it help at all if I said I was sorry about how things ended yesterday?" he asked carefully. "I had a miserable night because of it."

Her lips twitched at that. "Really? How miserable?"

"Lousy enough," he said. "You'd have been quite content, I'm sure, if you'd seen me tossing and turning and wondering how I mucked things up so badly."

"Do you need me to explain it to you?" she inquired, the faintest hint of a twinkle in her eyes at last.

"If it would make you feel better, go right ahead and tell me all the things I did wrong."

She hesitated, then shook her head. "No, I think you should probably ponder the situation a bit longer and figure out your own answers." She finally grinned. "I'll be in here helping Bryan with lunch once you've come up with any."

He risked a grin of his own. "Good to know."

Though things between them were far from settled and nowhere close to back on an even keel, he felt a faint stirring of hope that he hadn't blown any chance for them entirely out of the water.

To Luke's utter horror, given how precarious things already were with Moira, Kristen wandered in around one-thirty as the brisk lunch business was winding down.

"Since the official, invitation-only festivities are over and this place is open to the public, I thought I'd give it a try," she said, her expression daring him to dismiss her.

"Sure," he said reluctantly. "Have a seat and I'll send your waiter over."

"I thought maybe you'd have time to at least have a cup of coffee with me," she said.

"Why would you think that?" he asked in frustration. "You know I'm with Moira. I've explained that."

"The way I hear it, there was a fight of some kind yesterday at Sally's and she walked out on you," Kristen said, clearly gloating about the news.

Luke muttered a curse under his breath at the efficiency of the Chesapeake Shores grapevine. Who the devil had been in Sally's to spread the word? And why would they tell Kristen, of all people? Was there someone in town who wanted to screw with his life that badly?

Kristen laughed when he didn't respond. "I can just about hear those wheels in your head going round and round as you try to figure out who spilled the news to me."

"It did cross my mind to wonder," he admitted.

"No one in your family betrayed you," she said, "at least not intentionally. Sally was apparently worried about whatever she witnessed. She mentioned something to Susie, who dropped in to talk to Mack, wondering if she should try to intercede. She didn't realize I was around."

"And you couldn't resist eavesdropping," he concluded.

"Not once I'd heard your name, of course not," she said unrepentantly. "Newspaper reporters often get the hottest news by overhearing things meant to be kept secret." She held his gaze. "Is it true, Luke? Have you finally had the good sense to call it quits? She was all wrong for you, you know. Anyone could see what a terrible mismatch it was. She'd have made you miserable."

"Is that so?" Moira said, appearing suddenly beside them.

Luke couldn't be sure how she'd turned up so quietly, or how she'd even known Kristen was near the place. Was it some sort of female sixth sense or something?

"You're here," Kristen said, looking stunned.

"Right here," Moira confirmed. "And wondering why you are. Come to pick over the bones, Kristen? That's what predatory animals do, I'm told. Sadly for you, the news of the death of my relationship with Luke has been premature."

Kristen looked shocked by her words, but Luke had never been more proud. This was the Moira with whom he'd fallen in love, the one who spoke her mind without heed to the consequences. And if she was publicly claiming him, he could only hope that meant she'd forgiven him and not just that she wanted to stick a sword through Kristen's heart.

Kristen whirled on him. "Luke, are you going to allow her to say such things to me?"

He merely smiled. "You're on her turf. It's your battle, Kristen. You've always prided yourself on your ability to handle any situation. I have to admit that I'm fascinated to see how you'll handle this one. Susie let you off too easily, if only because she was so sick, but it seems to me you've met a worthy opponent this time."

"You're actually enjoying this," she said incredulously.

"I am," he admitted. "I've never had two women fight over me before."

She turned to Moira then. "And you're willing to feed into his display of ego?"

"Truthfully, Luke's less of a concern to me right now than you are. When will you get the message, Kristen? Luke's no longer interested in you. From all I've heard about you, you're not the sort of woman to keep humiliating herself by coming by to beg for a scrap of his attention. You did the same thing with Mack. Have you learned nothing from the shame of that terrible situation?"

Luke saw that Kristen's hand was shaking as she reached for her purse, and he knew it was time to intervene. Even for a woman with Kristen's arrogance and insensitivity, some words could strike a little too close and leave wounds.

For all his increasing impatience with her deplorable behavior, he'd once seen another side of her. And he'd drawn her into his orbit, albeit to save Susie's marriage, but he'd kept her in his life for longer than he should have. He had to accept some responsibility for this mess.

It was that sense of honor that had him saying quietly, "Kristen, why don't I walk you out?"

Though Moira looked as if she had quite a lot more she wanted to say, she nodded and walked away, clearly satisfied at having accomplished what she'd set out to do.

Outside, he touched Kristen's shoulder, realizing that this strong woman he'd assumed was indomitable was near tears. "I'm sorry," he said sincerely. "But you intentionally pushed her. All she did was push back."

"But you did nothing to stop her," she accused.

"How could I? Nothing I've said to you seemed to

sink in. I thought perhaps Moira would have better luck making things clear."

She drew in a deep breath and straightened her shoulders. "Well, they're clear enough now. I still think you're going to regret this, Luke, but I'm done."

"And I think when enough time has passed, you'll realize it was all for the best. I'm not the right one for you, Kristen. I never was."

"And you're the right one for her?" she asked disparagingly, fighting till the bitter end.

"We're still working that out," Luke told her candidly. "But I want the time to try."

She shook her head. "I honestly don't see it."

He laughed. "But you're not the one who has to, are you?"

"No, I suppose I'm not," she said, then turned and walked away.

Luke stared after her for a moment, then drew in a deep breath and headed back inside to try to figure out just exactly what that whole little scene had really meant. Much as he wished it might be otherwise, he had a sinking feeling that it had been played totally for Kristen's benefit and not because he'd been entirely forgiven for yesterday's debacle at Sally's.

20

The audacity of the woman, Moira thought as she paced the kitchen waiting for Luke to return. They'd been broken up for what, not even twenty-four hours, and Kristen Lewis had swooped in to stake her own claim. Did the woman have no shame? Apparently not.

"Do I need to lock up the knives?" Bryan inquired as she stalked around, muttering to herself.

"It might be wise," she said, then sighed. "Sorry, I am acting like a bit of a lunatic, aren't I?"

"Was that the other woman, then?" he asked.

She regarded him with surprise. "How did you know?"

He chuckled. "No one gets as worked up as you are over an innocent visit from a casual acquaintance. I got a glimpse of her as well. I recognized the type."

"Predatory, right?" Moira said, seeking confirmation for her own possibly jaded view.

"Oh, yeah," he said.

"Why doesn't Luke see that? After all, she was chasing his brother-in-law when they first met. Shouldn't that have given him a clue?"

Bryan looked stunned. "His brother-in-law?"

"Mack, who's married to his sister," Moira confirmed. "Luke swooped in to protect his sister's interests and got caught in Kristen's web, apparently."

A grin spread across Bryan's ruddy face. "God, I'm going to love working here. I've been in the city too long. Small towns are clearly far more fascinating."

Moira laughed. "It's been a revelation to me, too, though my town back in Ireland wasn't much bigger than this. Truly, the only excitement we ever heard about was when Mr. O'Meara came wobbling home after having a bit too much to drink and Mrs. O'Meara made him, quite literally, sleep in the doghouse. It was such a regular occurrence that, after a time, we didn't give it a second thought."

Just then Luke walked into the kitchen. "Do you have a minute?" he asked her in what sounded like much more of a command than a question. As she headed dutifully out the door, he turned to Bryan. "The lunch hour went great today. Everybody was raving about the fish and chips. My uncle Mick said they were the best he's had outside of Ireland."

"I'll accept the compliment in Nell's absence, but we owe it to her," Bryan told him. "She had the secret recipe for the batter that's made all the difference."

Luke nodded, then joined Moira as they walked to the privacy of his office. His silence was beginning to unnerve her a little. Was he mad at her for causing a scene? Well, if he was, that was just too bad. Even if the pub had been crawling with customers, which it hadn't been at that hour, she was never going to be polite to Kristen when she was only here to prey on the man in Moira's life.

Luke followed her into the office, then closed the door and turned to back her against it. With one arm braced on either side of her, he pinned her in place.

"I know this is probably exactly the wrong thing to say in these circumstances, but do you have any idea how hot you made me out there when you were putting Kristen in her place and staking your claim on me?" he asked.

She blinked at that. It was the last thing she'd expected him to say. "You thought that fight was hot?"

He nodded. "Oh, yeah."

"Why?" she asked, bemused. "Because it was all about you?"

"No, because it told me that you are not through with me, after all."

"Well, that was hardly in doubt, was it?" she asked, a hint of self-loathing in her voice. "I don't know about you, but my feelings don't turn on and off like a faucet, Luke. Just because I was ready to call it quits doesn't mean that I'd suddenly fallen out of love."

He smiled in a way that set her nerves on edge. It was the smug smile of a man who thought he'd won the battle, if not the war.

"You're still in love with me, then?" he asked, clearly intent on confirming the information, or just because he liked hearing her admit it.

"Yes, though right at this second, I'm wondering why. You'd test the patience of a saint, Luke O'Brien. You truly would."

"But I haven't run you off for good, is that right?"

She sighed heavily at the question. The answer was probably too obvious to be denied, whether she liked it or not.

"No, you haven't run me off for good."

He gave a nod, his expression filled with satisfaction as his gaze held hers. "Okay, then, fair warning."

"Warning?"

"I'm going to kiss you now. If you don't want me to, if I'm violating some principle you're hung up on at the moment, all you have to do is say the word and I'll back away."

Moira thought of all the reasons why she should stop him, why she shouldn't let herself be swayed by desire, not when there were so many bloody principles at stake.

Then she thought of the one reason that outweighed them all: she wanted to be kissed. By him. Right now.

She lifted her hands to rest on his shoulders, stood on tiptoe to angle her head just so and then waited as his breath feathered over her face, as his eyes glittered with passion. And when his mouth eventually covered hers, she sank into the kiss, letting it smooth away yesterday's heartache, letting the wonder of it dissolve all her doubts.

For now, for this one quiet moment, she was exactly where she wanted to be—in Luke's arms. How had she ever thought she could walk away from him so easily? The truth was, she knew with every fiber of her being that this was where she belonged. She supposed she was just going to have to be reasonable—a tricky business for a woman of her passionate nature—and give him a little more time to catch up.

Luke could have kicked himself for starting something there was no time to finish. There was no way he could drag Moira off to his apartment, as he desperately wanted to. There were too many things that needed to be done right here before the evening crowds descended.

And despite the promise of the way she'd melted in his arms, he knew well enough that they still had plenty to resolve. All those things that had sent her bolting from Sally's yesterday were still hanging in the air between them.

Ironically, he realized that he had Kristen to thank for the truce. Seeing her here had obviously sparked Moira's possessive streak in some way and sent her right back into his arms. He doubted, though, that sending Kristen a note of gratitude would be appropriate.

For now, he sighed against Moira's lips and reluctantly released her.

"That was nice," he said.

She smiled. "Better than nice." Her smile faded. "But we still have things to work out, Luke."

"I know that, and we will. If I'm sure of nothing else, I'm sure of that." He touched a finger to her chin and forced her to meet his gaze. "We will," he added firmly.

"Okay, then. Bryan's probably wondering if you've banished me for causing a scene. I should get back to check on things in the kitchen."

Luke nodded. "Before you go, though, is he working out okay?"

"He's wonderful," Moira said at once. "He's grasped everything Nell or I have told him and taken it a step beyond. If I didn't know better, I would have sworn his experience was in a Dublin pub and not a deli in Baltimore."

"That's my impression as well. And the waitstaff? Is everyone working out as we'd hoped? Everyone's pulling their weight?"

"Terry's a little slower than I'd like to see, but she's catching on, and the customers seem to love her just the same. Josh has an awful lot of Irish blarney for a kid who came from the Bronx. He'll do."

Luke was relieved by her assessment. The last thing he wanted was to have to shake up the staff this early on. He wanted a reliable team who'd be here for the long haul, though it was clear he was likely to have Josh only until he completed his computer courses at the community college and went off to launch some dot-com business that eventually sold for millions.

That, he reassured himself, could be a while, since Josh was working his way through school, taking only a class or two at a time as he could manage the expense. He'd come to Maryland chasing after a girl, then stayed on when the romance ended. That had been several years ago. He'd taken an instant liking to Moira, but then so had all the staff. If she so much as whispered a desire for something to be done, they all swarmed to do it.

"Luke, you can stop worrying. It's all running quite smoothly for a new place," Moira said, as if she were in his head. "I've seen my share of disasters, and this has none of the signs."

"Thanks for saying that," he told her.

"It's only the truth." She dropped an easy kiss on his forehead. "To wipe away that frown line," she said as she left.

Luke watched her go, a smile on his lips. What had ever made him think, even for a minute, that he could let her walk out of his life? He was pretty sure he could make a case for temporary insanity.

* * *

It was just after five. Uncle Mick and his father had claimed spots at the bar and were arguing over something. Luke smiled at the sight of them. Thank heaven he and Matthew didn't share the gene for sibling rivalry that those two had. He imagined Thomas would be in, too, as soon as he'd made the drive home from Annapolis and checked on Connie. Mick had suggested that Luke add a dart game to the pub, but Luke feared that the way those three could go at it, a dart would eventually wind up someplace it shouldn't.

In general, though, there was a nice buzz in the air as people came in to unwind at the end of the day. He stood behind the bar looking around, feeling an amazing sense of accomplishment steal over him. It was too soon to declare O'Brien's an unqualified success, but tonight, more than the weekend, reassured him that it was well on its way.

When the door opened, Susie and Mack came in. Susie looked happy enough, but Mack looked as if he was spoiling for a fight.

"Everything okay?" Luke asked as he seated them at a table by the window.

"I think everything is great," Susie said. "Mack's not so thrilled."

"About?" Luke asked tentatively, not particularly eager to be drawn into some spat the two of them were having.

"Kristen Lewis quit today," Mack said, turning an accusing gaze on him. "It's not that I haven't been anticipating it. I've even come close to firing her myself because of the circumstances, but I wasn't expecting it to happen today." He studied Luke with a narrowed gaze. "What does it have to do with you?"

Even Susie blinked at that. "You think Luke's responsible for this?" she asked. "Maybe she just finally came to her senses and realized no one wanted her here."

Mack scowled at the comment. "Something tells me Luke's opinion was the one that counted. What happened? I know she was here earlier."

Luke sighed. "She and Moira got into an argument," he admitted.

Susie's eyes brightened, which was probably less than diplomatic but entirely understandable. "A turf war over you?" she guessed, looking delighted. "What happened?"

"Moira won. I backed her up. Game over."

"And Kristen wasn't happy about the outcome," Susie concluded. "I'm sure she couldn't believe she'd come out second best with two men in this town."

"No, she couldn't," Luke said, then looked at Mack earnestly. "Look, I know she was a huge help to you at the newspaper, but there are other people out there you can hire who won't bring all this baggage to town with them. This is for the best."

Mack sighed. "I know that. I know it's best for everyone's peace of mind, but I wanted to get through the paper's first year at least with the best possible person in that position. Newspapers all over the country were taking note of what we were doing on the digital side of things. I don't want to lose the momentum."

"You won't," Susie said. "Everything's in place, and if I understand anything about Kristen, the organization of it all is written down somewhere in black and white, so someone else can readily step in."

"Sure, for the day-to-day stuff," Mack agreed. "I can probably take over that myself. It's the innovation that concerns me. She was way ahead of the curve on that. I want us to keep breaking new ground."

Luke drew in a deep breath. Something told him he was going to hate himself for this, but he glanced across the room and caught Josh's eye, then waved him over.

"Mack, you should talk to Josh Jackson. He's a computer geek from what I understand. Working here is just a sideline until he gets his degree. He might have some ideas for you or some contacts."

Mack's expression immediately brightened. "Do you know anything about newspapers? Are they even teaching anything related to the news business in college these days?"

"I haven't been a journalism student, so I don't know much about what classes they're teaching, but I do know something about newspapers—they're dying," Josh said. "My dad worked for one till he got a buyout. The internet's taking over."

"Not here in Chesapeake Shores," Mack told him.

Luke listened as Mack launched into a description of what he was trying to accomplish with the digital component of his local weekly. Josh nodded attentively, chiming in eagerly with comments and suggestions. To Luke's everlasting regret, it looked like a match made in heaven.

He slipped away from the table, only to have Susie follow him.

"Thank you," she said, giving him a fierce hug.

"What for? Sacrificing my waiter to soothe your husband's nerves?"

"No, for finally getting that awful woman out of town."

Luke touched her cheek. "I know you have every reason to despise Kristen, but she wasn't an awful person, Suze. She did some rotten things to you, but I saw another side of her, too."

"Then you're a better person than I am," she said. "I'll bet Moira would be on my side in this, too."

Luke laughed. "No question about it. Now, can I get you a drink? You might as well sit up here with Dad and Uncle Mick for a while, because it sounds to me as if Mack's going to be caught up in newspaper business for quite some time."

"I'll take a Guinness," she said at once. "And I'll give Mack another fifteen minutes before I go back to stake my claim. I have my ways of getting his full attention."

Luke clapped his hands over his ears. "Too much information, sis. I'm the baby brother, remember?"

She laughed. "From what I've seen, you're no slouch when it comes to charm and trickery in the romance department. I doubt I could say a single thing that would shock you."

"Let's not put that to the test, okay?"

He left her with their father and uncle, then went in search of Moira. "Something tells me we're going to have to find another waitperson."

She frowned. "Why?"

He filled her in on Mack's annoyance about Kristen and how he'd all but handed over Josh to make up for it.

"A small sacrifice to keep peace in the land," Moira

said at once. She regarded him skeptically. "Kristen's really leaving? Do you believe that?"

"That's the word on the street," he confirmed.

"Excuse me while I do a little victory dance," she said lightly.

Luke rolled his eyes. "You should join Susie out there. She's ready to set off fireworks."

"And you?" she inquired, studying him intently. "How do you feel?"

"It's for the best," he said at once. "I can't help feeling a little sorry for her, though. She made a lot of people here unhappy, but I think she made herself unhappiest of all."

Moira shook her head, regarding him with amazement. "You really do have a heart of gold, don't you?"

"Will it get you home with me, and into my bed, if I say yes?"

She grinned. "It just might."

He tapped his chest. "Twenty-four karat," he assured her.

"I'll have to think about whether that's to be a blessing or a curse," she said, giving him a peck on the cheek. "We'll discuss it later. If you've turned Josh over to Mack, I imagine someone needs to be out there paying attention to the customers. I'm all you have left on this shift."

"I knew there was a reason I hired you as my consultant. You keep a close eye on the big picture," he praised.

"While you fret over the details," she said.

"It makes us a good fit, doesn't it?"

"I like to think so, but last I heard the jury was still out."

Luke smiled at her response. He had a feeling that the jury warring in his head was closer to a verdict than he'd ever imagined. Those hours they'd been on the outs had scared him in ways he'd never imagined it possible for a woman to make him feel.

All too aware of Megan's expectant expression every time she and Moira crossed paths, Moira took to carrying her camera with her everywhere she went. Sometimes it worried her that she was sacrificing quality for quantity, hoping that if she took enough pictures, lightning would strike and at least a few of them would be good.

More than once, when she went to look at the shots on the computer, she wound up deleting all of them. She was beginning to panic that she'd never get another picture worthy of all the fuss Megan had made about her previous ones.

She was sitting in Luke's office going through the latest batch when Megan herself came in. "So, you are still taking pictures. I was beginning to worry since it's been a while since you last stopped in at the gallery."

"I've taken nothing worth showing to you," Moira replied in frustration.

"Move over and let me take a look," Megan said.

Moira stayed where she was, one finger ready to delete the entire file.

"Don't you dare!" Megan commanded. "Not till I've seen them for myself and can give you a professional evaluation."

Moira sighed and stood up, though she'd never been more reluctant to show her work to anyone.

Megan sat down and went through the couple of

dozen photos Moira had shot earlier in the day, then she went back and took a second look.

"They're terrible," Moira said, before Megan could say it.

"They're not your best work," Megan agreed candidly.

Her words sent Moira's confidence dipping even further. If she'd found even one to praise, it might not have hurt so badly.

"I don't understand what's happening," she admitted to Megan. "It's the same camera I'm working with. I've my same two eyes. Yet nothing is coming out quite right."

"How much time are you spending at this?" Megan asked.

"I go out on my breaks from here and try to take some pictures every day."

"An hour then? Less?"

Moira flushed at the implied criticism. "Probably that."

"And that's the problem," Megan said. "You're rushing. You're not taking the time to observe these people before you snap the shutter. You're too eager to get a few shots and then get back to what you think of as your *real* work."

Moira couldn't deny it. "That's true."

"It won't work," Megan said gently. "The value of your work is your understanding of the people whose pictures you're taking. In all the others I've seen, you've observed first, then captured them at the precise moment when they're showing a side of themselves that sums up their personality in the blink of an eye or, more precisely, the click of a shutter."

Moira felt a sudden burst of understanding and a renewed sense of purpose. "You're exactly right. I've been rushing through it, hoping for something magical but not doing my own part to see that I get it." She met Megan's gaze. "But how am I to do that with all my time tied up here?"

Megan held her gaze. "You're not going to like my answer to that."

Moira saw exactly where she was headed without Megan saying it directly. "You want me to quit," she said, her tone flat.

"Or at least to cut back your hours," Megan confirmed.

"But you said I could balance the two sides of my life," Moira protested, as if it were Megan's fault somehow that she obviously couldn't.

Rather than taking offense, Megan merely smiled. "And the day will come when you can do that easily, but you may not be there yet. Until the photography is second nature to you, you might have to work at it a bit harder, take the time to truly master it." She gave Moira a direct look. "Or you can choose to let it go."

Luke walked in at the end of the conversation. Apparently, he'd overheard just enough, because there was worry in his eyes.

Megan gave Moira's shoulder a squeeze. "Let me know how it's going, okay?"

Moira nodded as she left, then sank down into the chair with a heavy sigh.

"There's a bump in the road?" Luke asked.

She nodded. "She thinks the only way I'll be able to get enough incredible pictures for a show is to quit my job here with you or at least to cut back on my hours so

I can focus on my photography." She gave him a rueful look. "I guess I took it for granted that all I needed to do was snap the shutter to create something wonderful, but it's a job like any other, isn't it? It requires real dedication."

"Sounds that way to me," he said. "Have you decided how you want to handle Megan's suggestion?"

"I want to pretend she's wrong," Moira said, then sighed. "But she's not."

He sucked in a breath. "Then quitting is what you need to do," he said decisively. "A consultant's role was only meant to be temporary, right?"

"I never thought of it that way," she argued. "I love working with you."

"Is it forever that you'll have to focus a hundred percent on the photography?"

She shrugged. "Probably not, but it's impossible to say."

"Then it's only temporary."

"How can I walk out on you when this place has only just begun? And Josh will be leaving in a week or two as well to work with Mack. We've yet to hire and train a replacement."

"I can handle that," Luke said. "You have this place running like a well-oiled machine. I'm sure I can manage."

"Would it be so easy for you if I walked away?" she asked irritably.

"Not easy at all," he soothed. "Just a sacrifice worth making."

"I don't see it the same way. I see it as throwing away something I love, something I *know* I'm good at, for a risk."

"Megan doesn't think of it as a risk, does she? Shouldn't that at least give you the courage to try?"

"I'm not scared!" she retorted heatedly.

He merely lifted a brow at her display of temper.

"I'm not," she said, though with slightly less force. "Not of failure, as you're thinking, anyway."

"Of what, then?"

Could she admit her heart's deepest secret and risk total humiliation? Did she have a choice? Luke deserved honesty.

"I'm afraid you'll discover you don't need me at all."

His eyes widened in shock. "There's nothing that could be further from the truth," he said. "I need you in a hundred different ways, and only a handful of them have anything at all to do with your working here. I can bear to lose my consultant, but not my partner. You'll always have a role here, if you want it."

She took some solace from his words. "You're sure? You're not just saying that because you don't want to stand in the way of my big opportunity?"

He smiled. "I'm probably not that unselfish," he admitted. "What I'm saying is the truth. Cross my heart."

She nodded slowly, letting his certainty steal into her heart and calm her fears. "Then I suppose I could take a brief leave of absence, no more than a couple of weeks, to see if I can do this photography thing right. If I give it my full attention, maybe that's all it will take, and I'll be back here before you even have time to miss me."

"You're going to succeed magnificently," he predicted with confidence. "And I'm going to be standing in the background at Megan's gallery in a couple of months while people heap tons and tons of praise on you. Then I'll be the one worrying if you're going to be so wildly successful that you'll run off and leave me in your dust."

"Never," she said, standing up and moving into his embrace. "I will only go if you no longer want me."

His eyes lit with satisfaction at her words. "Then we have nothing to fear at all," he said, kissing her thoroughly to prove it.

21

Mick was about to leave his house and make the usual rounds of his family's businesses just to check in with everyone when he saw Dillon walking up the driveway. He took a seat in his favorite rocking chair on the porch and waited for him.

"It's a lovely morning," Dillon called out. "Were you about to go somewhere? I can come back another time."

"I usually take a walk around town this time of day to see how things are going with my children. You're doing them a favor by keeping me out of their hair. Being semiretired is a blessing in many ways, but I find that too often I have no idea what to do with myself. Doing this, I can at least claim I'm out walking for my health, though I doubt any of my children actually believed that. So, tell me, what brings you by?"

"I thought we should talk, man-to-man," Dillon said, his expression serious.

Mick's heart seemed to thud at Dillon's words. No good ever came out of a conversation that began like that.

"About?" he asked.

"Your mother and me."

"I thought we'd settled things between us over you and Ma," Mick said, really wishing he'd been ten minutes quicker about getting away from home this morning. An oddly meandering call from his mother had kept him here. He wondered now if that was a coincidence.

"Something's changed," Dillon said, looking him straight in the eye. "Since I've always thought the direct approach to be the best, I'll be blunt about it. I've asked her to marry me, Mick, and she's said yes. I've come here to tell you that I love her, that I've always cared for her and that I'll be good to her. There's no woman who's as special as Nell, but you know that." He kept his gaze steady. "So I've come to ask for your blessing."

Mick felt as if all the air had been sucked right out of him. He wanted to be the kind of son who put his mother's happiness first. He really did. But the thought of her marrying this man, perhaps moving to Ireland, yanked the heart right out of him, as it would from the entire family. How could they watch Nell leave and do nothing to stop it?

"I've left you speechless," Dillon said, a smile on his lips. "I should probably take some pride in that."

"Oh, I've quite a lot I want to say," Mick began, then tried to calm his temper. He had to do what he knew his mother would want him to do. He had to be a better man than perhaps he was.

"Congratulations!" he said eventually, proud that he hadn't stumbled over the word. He thought he'd even managed to put a reasonable amount of sincerity behind it.

Now it was Dillon's turn to look stunned. "That's it? We've your blessing, just like that?"

Mick smiled. "I know I've fought this far longer than reasonable and in ways I shouldn't have," he told Dillon. "But this is obviously what Ma wants, and I would never deny her anything that truly matters to her. More people should be as blessed as I've been to have someone like her as a mother. She was right by my side when Megan left. She looked after my children. I owe her, and goodness knows, she deserves all the happiness she can find."

He sighed, then admitted, "My worries are more for the rest of us than for her. I know you'll make her happy."

"I wouldn't be doing that if I tried to take her from here," Dillon said. "From the moment I arrived, I could see how important not just her family, but also this community, are to her."

Mick sat up straighter, feeling hopeful. "Are you saying that you'll live right here in Chesapeake Shores?"

Dillon nodded without hesitation or any hint of regret. "I believe that's what Nell wants and, like you, I can't deny her anything. When everything's settled, I'll speak to Connor about any legalities that need to be managed. Nell and I will travel to Ireland when and if we can, but I have a feeling at least some of my family will be right here, so it will be reason enough for the others to come."

"You're referring to Moira and Luke," Mick guessed. "That does seem to be progressing rather well."

Dillon smiled. "Especially given the rocky start of it and a few more recent bumps in the road. Despite all that, I'm hopeful." He regarded Mick curiously. "Has she won you over yet?"

Mick laughed. "I have to say that, surprisingly, she has. And Megan can't sing her praises enough. I don't know if Luke has worked his magic on that temper of hers or if she's mellowed, but she's a different woman now."

"Thank the heavens for that," Dillon said with obviously heartfelt emotion. His expression sobered. "Will you tell your mother you approve of us getting married? She'll want to hear it directly from you before we let anyone else know."

Mick nodded at once. "I'll walk back to her cottage with you now. There's no need to keep her in suspense. In fact, I'm a little surprised she's not out in the garden hiding amid the rosebushes trying to eavesdrop."

"She could be, for all I know," Dillon said with a chuckle, "though we did agree I'd do this on my own."

"You're a brave man."

"Not really. Your love for Nell shines through in everything you do, even when you were busy misjudging me and my intentions. How could I not admire and respect a son who has so much devotion to his mother?"

"Then let's go and set her mind at ease," Mick said, then grinned. "Or should we take our time and let her wonder if I've tossed you off the cliff?"

"I don't think unnecessary worry is called for," Dillon chided.

"I'll want to throw the two of you a proper engagement party," Mick said as they walked toward his mother's cottage. "The diplomatic question will be if it's to be at Jess's inn or Luke's pub."

"We could always have the engagement party at one

and the wedding reception at the other," Dillon suggested.

Mick smiled at the compromise. "No wonder you and Ma get on so well. You both have a tendency to be peacemakers. In this family, someone has to do it. I'm glad to know that Ma will finally have backup. She's had to handle the duty all on her own for too long. It hasn't always been easy."

"She'll have that and more from me," Dillon promised.

And for all his doubts and concerns, Mick finally felt reassured that this wedding truly would be a blessing.

As they continued on toward Nell's cottage, he slanted a look toward Dillon. "I'll not be calling you Dad, you know."

Dillon laughed. "And if you try welcoming my Kiera as a sister, who knows what she'd be likely to do. She's not the easiest woman, you know. If anything, she makes her own daughter, Moira, look like a positive saint."

"I remember," Mick said. "But they will be welcomed as family, just as you will be. Ma wouldn't have it any other way. She's taught us all to value family above all else, however someone comes to be a part of it."

"It's a lesson you've learned well, Mick."

Mick accepted the compliment graciously. "It's probably the best part of who I am," he said quietly.

The truth of that settled in his heart and gave him comfort, even as he reluctantly let go of his role as his mother's protector.

Luke hadn't realized how hard it would be to have Moira missing for most of the day. Though she popped into the pub from time to time for a chat, he'd gotten too used to her being within sight just when he needed a glimpse of her. He wondered if he hadn't pushed her away, just when he should have been keeping her close.

He knew better, though, because when he did see her now at the end of the day, her eyes were shining with excitement over her day's work. He'd insisted that she keep the laptop at his apartment and work there once she'd taken however many photographs she wanted to. He often came home late at night to find her asleep on the sofa, the computer on the table beside her, the pictures still on the screen. That's how he found her tonight.

Not for the first time, he was unable to resist stealing a look at the pictures before waking her and urging her to get ready for bed. Megan was right. Even to his untrained eye, he could see that she had an incredible talent. He'd done exactly the right thing by pushing her to take the time to do justice by it.

More than once, though, a nagging fear set in that in doing that, he'd pushed her into a different world, one where he wouldn't be able to follow. Not that he thought he couldn't cope with her success, with others feeling they had a right to a piece of her time and attention. That was the least of it. What worried him was that she'd no longer be content with the small-town owner of a local pub. Artistic triumph and success did strange things to people, and he had no idea how Moira would cope with it. After all her years of feeling like a failure, would she be one of those who got swept up in the glamour of it?

It was amazing to think that a woman who'd been as lost as she had been such a short time ago was now on the verge of finding herself in such a huge and public way. He wanted to be happy about that—he *was* happy about it—but it made him uneasy. He couldn't deny it.

She woke while he was pondering all that, rubbing her eyes and blinking at him. "How long have you been home? Why didn't you wake me?"

"I was enjoying the view," he teased.

"Of me, sleeping?"

"Actually, no. I was talking about the pictures you left on the screen of the computer. They're remarkable, Moira."

"I think they're better now that I'm taking the proper amount of time to get to know people," she confessed. "Megan was right about where I'd been going wrong. I spent all morning watching Ethel in front of her shop doling out penny candy to wide-eyed children before I saw exactly the shot that captured not just their delight, but hers."

"Then this break has worked out well?"

She nodded, then slid over to snuggle against him, her head resting on his shoulder. "But I miss you, Luke. I miss the pub. I thought I'd at least have more time to stop in for a visit, but the days seem to pass in a blur, and the next thing I know, you're here and waking me."

"I think it's probably good that you're so caught up in your work, don't you? That's what it takes to be successful in that field."

"But I don't want to sacrifice the other things that are important to me," she said. "I can see how that could happen. I don't know that I can give this my all and do the same with you. Eventually, you're bound to get tired of my being distracted or absent, and there will be someone who will have the time for you."

Luke smiled. "Are you already jealous of a woman who doesn't exist?"

"Oh, she exists," Moira said direly. "It's just that you may not have crossed paths yet."

"No one will be more fascinating to me than you," he promised. "And if I get only these late-night hours, well, then, having you in my bed is not exactly a punishment."

She searched his face, her expression uncertain. "It's enough?"

"For now," he said. "And for as long as it takes."

"If that changes, if you start to lose patience, you'll tell me?" she said.

"I will," he assured her, but he knew he wouldn't. He couldn't, not if he was going to be the kind of man who supported the woman in his life while she followed her dream, just as she'd supported him in following his.

Rather than the two weeks she'd planned, Moira had spent three focusing entirely on her photography. In the end she'd even called Peter and told him he'd have to find someone else to handle the assignments in Dublin. Thankfully, there'd been enough time left.

The results of her extra efforts were good, she thought. Maybe even spectacular. She held her breath as Megan looked through the photos she'd brought by the gallery as possible additions to the portfolio.

This time when Megan looked up, she was beaming. Relief flooded through Moira.

"They're better?" she asked.

"A thousand percent better," Megan confirmed. "It's going to be very hard to choose, which is an amazing dilemma to have. I think if you spend another couple of weeks at this, we'll have more than enough for an amazing show."

"You need more?" Moira said, her heart sinking. She'd been counting on getting back to the pub—and Luke—tomorrow.

"Yes," Megan said firmly. "And this is only the beginning of putting the show together, Moira. I'll be able to do most of it, but there will be mounting the pictures to be done. You'll want a say in that, and in how they're hung in the gallery. And I'm anticipating a lot of publicity, so you'll have to be available for interviews."

In the back of her mind, Moira had known all that, but it hadn't seemed real to her. Even on her most hopeful days, she hadn't envisioned things going so far, that expectations would be so demanding and time-consuming.

"It's part of the job," Megan said, when she was silent for too long. "An important part. You have to be willing to commit to all of it."

Moira nodded. "I know that. And I won't quit now. It's just given me a lot more to think about, that's all."

Megan smiled. "It's all going to be worth it," she promised. "Now get back out there and take more pictures. At our next meeting, we'll start to narrow them down and make the final selections." She reached over and touched Moira's hand. "And try to look a bit happier about this, okay? I'd hate to think I'm forcing you into something that's making you miserable."

Moira managed a tight smile. "I'm grateful," she said. "More than grateful."

"But you're still uncertain," Megan said. "I can understand that. You won't know if all the sacrifices have been worth it until the show actually opens. If it goes as I anticipate, that's when you'll have the really tough choices to make. I've already shown a few of the sample prints to my former boss in New York. He's very interested, and he'll be here for the show. I'm fairly certain he's going to want to do something at his gallery."

New York? It seemed inconceivable to Moira. And much too far away from Chesapeake Shores and Luke. If a show like that actually happened—and she had no reason to doubt Megan's optimism—Moira wasn't sure what she would do.

Luke looked up from his spot behind the bar and saw Moira coming in, her expression dejected. He knew she'd been planning to see Megan today, so he immediately worried that the meeting had gone badly.

"You okay?"

"Fine," she said, slipping onto a bar stool.

"Want something to drink?"

"A diet soda will do."

He poured the drink, then came around the bar and sat beside her, turning her to face him. "Didn't things go well with Megan? Wasn't she happy with the latest pictures?"

"She loved them," Moira responded gloomily, "but she wants more."

"And that's bad?" he asked carefully, trying to see it the way she obviously did.

"It means I won't be back here tomorrow or the day after that or the one after that," she said miserably. "I don't know when I'll be back, and you can't hold a place for me forever. You'll need to fill the position."

"I can hang on awhile longer," he reassured her. "This place should be the least of your concerns."

"But I miss you. I miss this," she said.

"You're here now, and I'm right here with you. We're together most nights."

"I know I sound like a whiny five-year-old who wants it all, and wants it now," she said. "I know I've accused you more than once of having your priorities all mixed up, but just look at mine. I thought I was so superior because I knew exactly what I wanted. And now, it turns out, I'm a total mess. I have no idea what I want from one minute to the next."

Luke risked a smile. "You *can* have it all, you know."

"That's what Megan says. I'm not sure I believe her. Just look how this show in a small town has taken over my life. And now she's talking about a show at a gallery in New York."

Luke's eyes widened. "She's talked to her old boss about you?"

Moira nodded. "She's even sent him a few prints."

"That's amazing. You can't walk away now."

"I'm not going to," Moira said irritably. "I'm no quitter. But I feel as if I've crawled onto this bloody treadmill that's going faster and faster and I've no way to get off. Or perhaps not the sense to, even if I could."

Luke put his hands on her arms and waited until she'd looked him in the eye. "What is it you really, really want? What is your heart telling you?"

She gave him a look filled with such sorrow it almost broke his heart.

"I can't hear it anymore," she said in a voice barely above a whisper. "Every time I think I know, someone tugs me in another direction."

"I have an idea," he said. "Gram and Dillon were in here earlier. They're thinking of taking a day or two and going sightseeing in New York. You'd have the cottage entirely to yourself. Maybe that's what you should do. Stay there in the peace and quiet until you can hear yourself think again."

"Away from you?" she said, sounding alarmed.

"Just for a few days, Moira. I think you need that time to get your bearings. I'm bound to be one of those who's been tugging you in one direction or another. So has Megan, and who knows who else has, given this family's tendency to meddle. I'll make sure no one bothers you there. It can be totally restful."

"I'm not sure I know how to do restful," she said. "I could go completely stir-crazy."

He laughed at that. "Then you'll come looking for me, won't you? What do you say? I think it makes sense. I think it's exactly what you need."

She nodded with obvious reluctance. "When are they going? Did they say?"

"Tomorrow. They're catching a morning train."

She looked relieved by the news. "Then we still have tonight," she said eagerly.

He nodded. "And we'll make the most of it. I promise."

Moira took her accumulation of things from Luke's back to Nell's cottage very early in the morning, hoping to spend a little time with her grandfather before he and Nell left on their trip. He greeted her at the door with a smile.

"It's about time you put in an appearance over here, young lady," he chided. "I'd begun to feel abandoned."

Moira laughed. "I doubt that. I hear you're about to go gallivanting off to New York with Nell this morning." She regarded him worriedly. "Are you sure you're up to it? I understand it's a hard city to manage in if you don't know your way around."

"Nell has it all planned out."

"Is there some reason you decided to go now?"

"Let's have a cup of tea and I'll explain," he said.

When they were settled at the kitchen table, he said, "I doubt this will come as any surprise to you, but Nell and I have decided to marry. This trip is a little celebration. When we get back, we'll tell the rest of her family, but I wanted you to know now. You and Mick are the only ones we've told."

Moira regarded him with astonishment. "You're getting married?"

He searched her face. "Are you shocked that two people our age want to get married?"

She took a second to think about it, then shook her head, a smile breaking across her face. "Quite the opposite. I'm thrilled for you, and it's given me hope that things always work out the way they're supposed to, even if it takes more time than you'd anticipated."

"I believe that with all my heart," Dillon said. "Will you be okay here in the house alone with Nell and me gone? Or will you be alone?"

"I will be," she said. She explained what she and Luke had decided. "It's not a breakup or anything like that. I'm just sorting through all these conflicting emotions about what I want." She shrugged. "It's probably foolish."

"Why would giving careful thought to such important matters ever be foolish?"

"Because the choice might not be mine in the end," she said.

"Decisions that affect your life can't be taken out of your hands," Dillon said.

Moira shook her head. "That's not entirely true now, is it? As soon as another person's involved, they get to make their own choices."

"Then, as it often is, it's Luke we're discussing," Dillon said wryly. "And you still don't feel confident that he feels the same way you do."

"In my heart, I believe he does, but I can't help wondering if he'll ever be ready to put his heart on the line. I'm afraid it will be one excuse and then another."

"If that's what happens, then you'll make your own decision about how long to wait," he told her. "See what I mean? In the end, you make your own choices, even if they're not the ones you'd envisioned needing to make."

Moira sighed heavily. "You're right, as always."

Her grandfather chuckled. "I'd like a recording of that to send your mum, if you wouldn't mind."

She laughed with him. "She'd never believe it, would she?"

"And never utter the same thing, that's for sure."

Moira couldn't help wondering how she and her mother could see this same wonderful, wise man so very, very differently.

Luke was wiping down the bar when Connor came in. He glanced at the clock on the wall, noted the lateness of the hour, then regarded his cousin with surprise.

"It's awfully late for a married man and father to be arriving in a bar," he teased Connor. When there was no answering smile, he felt a momentary stirring of worry. "Is something wrong?"

Connor nodded. "There have been some problems

with Moira's paperwork for her work visa," he said, his expression grim.

Luke threw down his rag and walked around the bar to take a seat. "Tell me about it."

"It seems that someone informed an investigator that she is no longer working here and suggested that her application should be voided."

Luke stared at him in shock and then with dawning anger. "Kristen!"

"That would be my guess," Connor admitted. "But I have no proof of it. And the point is that since it's widely known that she isn't consulting for you at the moment, we have to start from scratch, and they're going to be looking to see that every *i* is dotted and every *t* is properly crossed."

"Won't it be even better for her with Megan vouching for her and the show they're about to have at the gallery scheduled?" Luke asked hopefully.

"But that gives the investigator a time line," Connor pointed out. "When the show ends, so in all likelihood does the visa. Where is Moira now?"

"She's taken refuge at Gram's for a few days to catch her breath. Your mum's been putting a lot of pressure on her, and it's rattled her. With Gram and Dillon away, it seemed like the perfect hideaway."

Connor blinked. "Gram and Dillon have gone off somewhere together? And Dad hasn't had a coronary?"

Luke laughed. "I know. It's stunned me, too. He's been in here most nights, calm as can be, as if nothing's amiss."

"Maybe he doesn't know about the trip."

"Oh, he knows. In fact, he's the one who told me even before Dillon and Gram came by to share the news. Gram wanted to spend extra time with Bryan to make sure he has the menu under control. I think she takes our culinary success here very personally."

Connor smiled. "That's Gram, all right. But I don't get Dad's reaction," Connor said. "He was practically apoplectic over every second they spent together in Dublin."

"I know." Luke shrugged. "Go figure."

"Well, since Moira's not here, I'd better get back home. I'll stop by Gram's tomorrow and fill her in."

Luke shook his head. "I'll go by tonight and tell her myself. I'll make sure she comes by your office first thing in the morning."

"Okay, then. Make certain she does. We need to handle this as quickly as possible. Even though her tourist visa is still in effect, this paperwork needs to be approved before it does run out."

"I'll see to it," Luke promised.

After Connor had gone, he muttered a curse about Kristen's likely final act of pure spitefulness. Maybe Susie had been right about her all along and he was the one who'd been wearing blinders. What did that say about his judgment?

22

On her second night at Nell's, Moira had gone to bed, but she hadn't been able to fall asleep. She'd grown too comfortable falling asleep in Luke's arms. Being all alone again felt strange and desperately lonely. Rather than trying to force a sleep that wouldn't come, she got up and made herself a cup of tea, then settled on the sofa with a quilt and the TV remote.

She was trying to focus on some late-night comedian's jokes when there was a knock on the door. Rattled, she tiptoed over. "Who is it?"

"It's me. Luke."

She swung open the door at once, delighted by the interruption. "I thought you'd ruled out all visits," she said. "Believe me, though, when I tell you that I'm not complaining that you decided to break the rules."

It dawned on her then that he didn't look half as thrilled to be here as she was to see him. "You're not here to make up for lost time, are you?" she asked with a frown.

He did smile at that. "We've lost little more than

twenty-four hours," he told her. "Surely we're both strong enough to weather that."

She sighed. "I'm not so sure. Well, no matter why you've come, I'm glad, and I'm not afraid to admit it."

He wrapped his arms around her and pressed a kiss to the top of her head. "It's nice to be welcomed so warmly," he said as he came inside.

"I could make the welcome even hotter," she offered, grabbing his hand, prepared to take him to her room.

"Not so fast," he said with a shake of his head. "We need to talk."

Her heart stilled at his words and at the dire expression that went with them. "Is it grandfather? Or Nell? Has something happened to them?" She pulled away and began to pace. "I knew this trip was a terrible idea, that it would be too much for them. They're far too old to be traipsing around in a big, unfamiliar city, battling with crowds and such."

"They're fine," Luke said, catching hold of her and looking directly into her eyes. "They're absolutely fine, and having the time of their lives from all reports."

She wasn't entirely ready to believe him. "You've spoken to them?"

"No, but Mick has. Nell's called at least twice to keep him from chasing off to check on them himself."

She finally allowed herself a sigh of relief. If her grandfather and Nell were all right, then nothing else could possibly be so bad.

"If they're okay, why do you look so unhappy? And what does it have to do with me?"

"Connor stopped by the pub a little while ago," Luke said, then filled her in on the issues with her paperwork.

As Moira listened, her temper stirred. "Now who do you suppose would be so jealous of me they'd file a report like that?" she asked angrily.

"Stop," Luke commanded. "It would only be a guess, and it hardly matters now. The important thing is to fix this. You'll need to see Connor in the morning and get Megan to vouch for you and the upcoming show. I gather it would be helpful if the date were set."

Moira nodded. "Okay, that's not so bad, I guess. We can do that first thing tomorrow."

Luke held up a cautionary hand. "It's not quite as simple as all that."

She frowned. "There could be a problem even if Megan vouches for me?"

"Not with getting a temporary work visa, most likely, but it could mean you'd be expected to leave once the show is over," he explained. "The show sets a time frame for your visit. The consultancy didn't."

She blinked at the news, her heart thudding dully. "I'd have to leave, just like that?"

"Connor seems to think so. He could be wrong, of course, but he thought it best for you to be prepared for the possibility."

"But by then I'll be back to working with you."

"He seems to think that won't fly a second time."

Moira sank down on the sofa, stunned. "I'd have to go back to Dublin," she said, her voice flat as she considered the magnitude of that. She met his gaze. "But it's too soon. I'm not ready."

"I've been thinking about that ever since I spoke to Connor," Luke said, though he seemed to be avoiding her gaze. He sucked in a deep breath, then added,

"There may be another alternative. We'd have to run it past Connor and see if I'm right."

She studied him suspiciously. He didn't look over-joyed by this alternative, whatever it was. "What?"

He finally looked her directly in the eye. "We could get married."

Moira heard the words as if they'd come from very far away. They were the words she'd been dreaming of from the moment she'd arrived here. No, even before that. But not like this. Not just to play a game with im-migration rules. Tears welled up and spilled down her cheeks, even as she shook her head.

"Not like this, Luke," she whispered, heartbroken.

"But it's the perfect solution," he argued. "We'd have gotten to this point eventually. Why not now, when it can make a difference?"

She regarded him sorrowfully. "Because it sounds far too much like a timely business proposition. If and when you ever ask me to marry you for real, it has to be because you're in it heart and soul, not just as a matter of convenience."

He seemed stunned that she'd rejected the idea, but what else could she have done? Neither of them would have been happy with a bargain like this. He'd pro-claimed too often that marriage wasn't yet on that an-noyingly predictable timetable of his.

"I think you should go," she said quietly.

"I've made you angry, and I'm not sure why," he said, his expression charmingly perplexed. "I'm sorry. I thought I was doing the right thing."

"I know you did," she responded. "And I love you for making such a grand offer. But just because something might seem right for one reason doesn't mean it's for the best. Go, Luke, please. We'll talk tomorrow."

"Not just yet," he said stubbornly. "I thought marriage was what you wanted."

"It is," she assured him. "But not like this. Never like this."

That he didn't understand why she felt that way left her feeling empty and lost.

When Moira arrived at Connor's office in the morning, Megan was already there.

"Moira, I don't want you to worry. We're going to fix this," Connor said as soon as she walked in. "Mom and I already have a plan."

"That's right, and you're absolutely not to worry," Megan told her.

Moira wanted to feel reassured by their confidence, but she was still too hurt by last night's conversation with Luke.

"I'll leave it in your hands, Connor," Moira said. "Whatever you need to do. If I have to go back to Ireland right after the show, it's okay."

Both of them regarded her with surprise.

"You'd be okay with that?" Megan asked. "What about Luke?"

"I'm not talking about Luke right now. He's not part of this decision."

Even Connor looked flabbergasted by that statement. He exchanged a bewildered look with his mother.

"Connor, unless you need something more right now, I think Moira and I should be going," Megan said, already standing up and tucking her arm through Moira's.

"She'll be with me at the gallery if you need her to fill anything out or to sign anything."

Connor nodded, looking relieved to have his mother take charge, especially since there were things going on here that clearly mystified him.

En route to the gallery, they stopped to pick up large containers of coffee from Sally's.

"Raspberry croissants as well, I think," Megan told Sally. "Or would chocolate be better? This may be a chocolate occasion. What the heck. Give us both."

"I don't think I can eat," Moira argued, but Megan ignored the protest and ordered them, anyway.

Once they'd arrived at the gallery, Megan encouraged her to sit, but two seconds later, Moira was up and pacing.

"I know this is upsetting," Megan began.

"You have no idea," Moira told her miserably.

"You do understand that Connor will do everything in his power to fix it," Megan said.

"I know, but I'm beginning to think that going home to Ireland sooner, rather than later, would be for the best. I spoke to Peter this morning, and my old job will be waiting. Perhaps some of the photography assignments I'd declined will still be available, too."

Megan regarded her with dismay. "Your old job at the pub?" she asked incredulously.

Moira nodded. "Along with a few photography assignments. There were new bookings just yesterday for a wedding and two baby showers, if I want them. I told him I'd take them."

"But why?" Megan asked. "How can you do this sort of turnaround just when everything is falling into place here for a much more phenomenal future?"

"It won't matter without Luke," Moira said. "I'll be better off on my home turf, living far more simply. I won't give up on photography, not after this, but I don't need it to be on such a grand scale."

"What's Luke done?" Megan asked bluntly, looking as if she was one second away from heading back up the street to the pub to throttle him if she didn't like the answer.

"Why would you assume my decision has anything to do with him?"

Megan smiled at what she apparently considered to be a disingenuous question. "Because he's the reason you came here, and I can only assume he'd be the reason you're suddenly so eager to leave."

Moira paused in her pacing and sighed. "He asked me to marry him," she told Megan. Before her mentor could express her joy at the news, Moira added, "It's a legal maneuver, nothing more."

"I don't believe that, Moira. I truly don't. O'Brien men are more than capable of the magnificent gesture, believe me, but a marriage of convenience? No, I don't think so. If Luke asked you to marry him, it's because he wants to be married to you."

Moira shook her head. "He doesn't want me unceremoniously shipped off, that's all."

"Why are you so certain of that?"

"Because," she began, tears stinging her eyes, "he never—not even once—mentioned that he loved me. The proposal was all about the legalities."

Megan blinked, but remained depressingly silent. Obviously, no amount of optimism was enough for her to find a positive spin for that.

* * *

"Okay, what did you do when you saw Moira last night?" Connor demanded when he walked into the pub at midmorning.

Luke stared at him, his temper stirring. He'd been itching for a fight all night, and it seemed that his cousin might be on the verge of providing the perfect opportunity. "What makes you think I did anything wrong?"

"Because I expected Moira to come into my office today ready to go into battle to stay here indefinitely, and what I saw was a defeated woman who was all too eager to leave. Mum saw it, too. She's dragged her off for a heart-to-heart chat, and I'm here to try to figure out what the devil is going on."

Luke sighed. Unfortunately, there was nothing in Connor's comment to justify Luke's punching his fist through anything. He explained the entirety of the conversation he'd had with Moira the night before. "And then she threw me out," he summed up.

"Oh, boy," Connor murmured. "Been there, done that."

"What?" Luke asked in bewilderment.

"Made an untimely proposal that got tossed right back in my face. You were away at school when Heather was in that awful accident, but I had this huge epiphany that day and realized I didn't want to live my life without her. Unfortunately, after all the years I'd been protesting that marriage is nothing more than an unnecessary piece of paper, Heather didn't buy my sudden conversion."

"How'd you convince her you were ready to take that next step?" Luke asked, understanding at last what had gone so terribly wrong the night before. He'd changed his priorities on a dime and done it for all the wrong reasons, just as Moira had suggested before tossing him out of Gram's cottage.

"Time and actions," Connor said. "I waged a carefully calculated campaign to prove my sincerity to her. A few of those blew up in my face, too, like buying Driftwood Cottage for her."

"But I thought she'd fallen in love with that house," Luke said. "Wasn't that why you bought it?"

Connor nodded. "And she accused me of buying it out from under her when she'd intended to buy it for herself. She wanted no part of it. Dad finally convinced her that she might as well participate in the remodeling or she'd wind up living in a house I'd renovated and it would be nothing like she'd imagined."

Luke shook his head. "Women are a mysterious breed, aren't they?"

"In my experience, they certainly are," Connor said. "Did you at least declare your undying love when you were making this proposal last night?"

Luke winced. "Not exactly."

Connor grinned. "Yeah, I blew that part, too. Women don't seem to get that we mere mortal men sometimes have difficulty putting all the right words together. Personally, I think there ought to be a textbook available, or at least some kind of romance for dummies guidebook. I still blow things on a regular basis. Fortunately, Heather usually just rolls her eyes and patiently explains how I've gone so far off course. At least when she's not freezing me out and waiting for me to figure it out for myself."

Luke wasn't entirely reassured to know that communication didn't always improve just because two people had taken a walk down the aisle. Apparently, saying "I do" was the least of it. At least there was nothing unclear about those two words.

Connor gave him a commiserating look. "Do you really want to marry Moira?"

"I think so," Luke said, then cringed at the lack of enthusiasm in his voice.

"No wonder she didn't fall on her knees in gratitude if you sounded that enthusiastic last night," Connor said with a shake of his head. "Look, if you're not ready to get married, then you shouldn't do it. Period."

"I have this timetable," Luke said.

Connor stared at him incredulously. "How do you envision that working? Were you going for a head count of women? So many dollars in the bank? What exactly?"

"It sounds ridiculous when you put it that way," Luke said.

"Because it *is* ridiculous. Either you know in your heart that Moira is the one or you don't. Which is it?"

Luke didn't really have to think about it. "She's the one," he said with conviction. "I knew it the night we met."

"Then maybe you need to consider scrapping that timetable of yours and grabbing her before she gets away, because if her mood earlier was any indication, she *will* go away, Luke." He held Luke's gaze, then added, "And once she's gone, with all that physical *and* emotional distance between you, it'll be that much harder to win her back."

Luke sighed as Connor left him alone to ponder what a mess he'd made of everything.

He might have spent the entire afternoon in a funk if Dillon hadn't called just then to let him know that they'd just returned home and he was taking Nell straight to the hospital.

"The hospital? Why?"

"She's had a bit of a spell," Dillon said, sounding shaken. "She fainted at the train station. She came around right away and wanted to continue on home, but I persuaded her she needs at least a night in the hospital to be checked out. Mick's already alerting the others, but I need you to find Moira and let her know where I am."

"I'll tell her," Luke promised. "And we'll be there within the hour. Tell Gram I love her."

"Will do," Dillon promised.

"You're okay?" he asked worriedly. The stress of watching Nell pass out couldn't have been easy for Moira's granddad.

"I'll be a lot better once the doctors have confirmed that Nell is okay," Dillon said. "I'll see you soon."

Luke hung up the phone, told Bryan to take over for him and headed to the gallery in search of Moira. But when he arrived, Megan told him she wasn't there, and she wasn't a hundred percent certain where she'd gone.

"Back to Gram's?" he asked.

"Possibly." She studied him curiously. "Is this about making things right with her?"

"No, it's about Dillon and Gram. They're at the hospital. I thought for sure Mick would have called you by now. Gram's had a fainting spell."

Megan muttered a surprisingly vehement curse. "I knew she was trying to do too much, but she wouldn't let any of us pitch in. Okay, you go and try to track down Moira. I'll head for the hospital. I'll be in touch on your cell phone if there's any news."

"Thanks, Megan."

Luke had never felt a greater sense of panic as he headed for Gram's cottage. He had huge fences to mend with Moira, but right this second all he could think about was what the O'Briens would do if they lost Gram. It just couldn't happen. Not yet. Not like this.

Moira had walked and walked despite the surprising level of heat and humidity on the June day. She wasn't used to weather like this. It certainly didn't help to clear her head the way a chilly breeze might have.

She was almost back at Nell's when she spotted Luke coming toward her, his expression grim.

"We need to talk, Moira," he said when he was close enough for her to hear him.

She shook her head. "Not now. My head is already spinning from our last talk."

"This isn't about you and me or whether you go or stay. It's about Gram."

Alarm shot through her. "What's happened to Nell?"

"I'll tell you what I know on the way. We need to get to the hospital. Your grandfather's asking for you, and I need to be there for Gram."

They practically ran back to the house, where she paused only to grab her purse and put on a pair of shoes. Then they were driving to Baltimore.

She listened as Luke told her the little he knew. She could see the fear in his eyes, hear the distress in his voice. She reached across and rested a hand on his leg just long enough to give it a reassuring squeeze. "She's strong, Luke. She'll be fine. And didn't my grandfather say it was only a fainting spell?"

"People don't faint for no good reason," he argued.

"But sometimes it's nothing more than needing to eat or being overly tired. The trip to New York may have been too much for her."

"I told you, didn't I, that she almost passed out right in front of me once before? I put my mum on the case, but Gram managed to convince her, too, that there was nothing to worry about."

Moira fell silent then. After all, what could she say that could possibly boost his spirits when neither of them knew the truth about the situation?

At the hospital waiting room, they found most of the family already assembled. Abby had apparently gotten there first, coming straight from her Baltimore office. Thomas had been hard on her heels, coming from Annapolis. Mick and Jeff had arrived soon after, thanks to using back roads and speeds that likely defied the limits.

Moira went straight to her grandfather, who was sitting by himself, looking distraught and pale. She sat beside him and took his hands in hers. His were ice-cold.

"Are you okay?" she asked.

"I will be when they tell me Nell is fine," he said. "I'm glad Luke found you, though. It's good to see a friendly face."

She frowned at his words. "Don't tell me the family is blaming you for what happened?"

"Oh, they're not saying as much, but I'm sure they think Nell's been overdoing it during my visit and that this trip to New York was too much for her. How can I argue about that under the circumstances?"

"But she wanted to go," Moira protested. "It was her idea, wasn't it?"

He nodded. "But I should probably have thought better of it. I knew she'd had a couple of spells. She dismissed them as nothing, blamed it all on adjusting to a new medicine, and I let her get away with it. What was I thinking?" he asked miserably.

"You were thinking that Nell is a woman who knows her own mind and body and is perfectly capable of making decisions for herself," Moira told him firmly.

He smiled at her fierce words. "I'm not entirely sure if that defense was meant to be of me or of Nell, but I appreciate it either way."

"Well, I meant every word. This isn't your fault, and I'll take on anyone who says it was."

Just then Mick joined them. He'd apparently overheard at least some of their conversation, because he gave Dillon an apologetic look. "I had a feeling you might be thinking that we're all over there ganging up to cast blame on you. That's not the case, Dillon. I know Ma's stubbornness as well as anyone. This trip was something she wanted, and none of us would have been able to discourage her."

"But I should have tried," Dillon said.

"And wasted your breath?" Mick said. "Why? And none of this matters, anyway, because she's going to be up and running things back in Chesapeake Shores in no time."

Moira saw her grandfather draw in a relieved breath and in that moment she felt a surprising surge of gratitude toward Mick. "Thank you for saying that," she told him.

Mick nodded, his expression filled with understanding. "Let me go and rattle a few cages and see if I can get some information. We could all use a bit of good news, I think."

When he'd walked away, Moira turned to her grandfather. "You see, if Mick can be so understanding, then for sure no one else is blaming you."

He smiled tiredly. "Perhaps not, but if this doesn't end well, sweetheart, I'll blame myself."

23

Moira's grandfather had refused to leave the hospital, even after everyone had been reassured that Nell's dizzy spell had likely been caused by a combination of low blood pressure and low blood sugar. Her blood pressure medicine had apparently been working too well, according to the doctor. He'd recommended they all go home.

"You should all get a good night's rest," the doctor told them. "If she does well on the new blood pressure medication overnight, she'll be released in the morning."

"I intend to be right beside her when she wakes up," Dillon had responded stubbornly. "The rest of you should go."

With obvious reluctance, the family had taken him up on his offer to stay. And because Moira refused to leave her grandfather here alone, Luke had stayed with her.

It had been a long night. They'd already consumed more cups of god-awful coffee and stale vending machine junk food than he'd imagined was humanly possible. If they kept it up, they were likely to wind up hospitalized right next to Gram.

Each time Luke had tried to broach the subject of their own differences, Moira had shaken her head and silenced him.

"Not now," she said. "This isn't the time."

"When will be the time?" he'd asked in frustration. It had only earned him another shake of her head.

So he'd settled for sitting beside her, fetching coffee, checking occasionally on Dillon, who was at Gram's bedside, and letting Moira's head rest on his shoulder when she risked falling asleep for more than a heart-beat.

Morning light was streaming in the waiting room windows before they knew it. Luke looked up to see Dillon regarding them with a benevolent smile.

"You're a thoughtful man," he told Luke.

"I doubt Moira would concur at the moment. She's annoyed with me."

"Then perhaps a visit with Nell is just what the both of you need," Dillon suggested. "She's asking for you."

Luke frowned. "Both of us?"

"She insists on it," Dillon told him. "I'll tell her you'll be there in a minute."

Luke nodded, then gently tried to rouse Moira.

"What?" she murmured, snuggling closer.

"Time to wake up. Gram's awake and she wants to see us."

She blinked at that. "You and me? Why?"

"I've no idea, but your grandfather says she's deter-mined to have a word with us."

Moira nodded and stood, stretching in the slow, sinuous way that always captivated him in the morning…and made him want to crawl right back into bed with her.

"Okay, then," she said, then frowned at his expression. "What?" Apparently, she noticed a giveaway glint in his eyes, because she said incredulously, "Now? You're thinking about sex now?"

Luke grinned. "I always think about sex when we're together."

"Even here? In the hospital?"

He shrugged. "Can't help it."

She shook her head, but there was the tiniest hint of a smile on her lips as she walked away. They walked down the hospital corridor, which brought back way too many memories of the hours Luke had spent here when Susie had been so ill. He'd hated it then, but at least there had been a good outcome. He hoped this incident would turn out just as well.

To his relief, Gram was sitting up in bed, her cheeks filled with color, her eyes sparkling.

"Well, you certainly did stir things up yesterday," he teased her as he pressed a kiss to her forehead.

"Oh, you know how I enjoy being the center of attention," Nell responded. "I just wanted to see who'd show up if they thought I was on my deathbed."

Luke frowned. "That's not even close to being funny, Gram. You scared us." He leveled a look into her eyes. "And it's not the first time you've taken ten years off my life recently."

She reached for his hand. "I know, darling, and I am sorry," she apologized, then gave him a stern look. "Don't think I don't know that you're responsible for your mother suddenly hovering over me, either. It was thoughtful of you, but entirely unnecessary."

"Unnecessary?" Luke scoffed. "Look where you are."

"That's not important, except for the fact that it's giving me the perfect opening to say a few things that I think the two of you need to hear. Perhaps under these circumstances, you'll actually listen. Moira, come over here, please."

Luke risked casting a glance at Moira, who inched cautiously closer to the bed. She seemed stunned that she was about to be lectured by a pint-size woman in a hospital bed. He knew better than to try to silence Gram, even though he suspected the bulk of her words were likely to be directed at him.

"Okay, Gram, what's on your mind?" he prodded reluctantly.

She gestured for Moira to come even closer, then reached for her hand and held it tightly, probably anticipating the moment when Moira would decide to bolt from the room. But even as she clung to Moira, her gaze was directed at Luke.

"Timetables are a fine thing," she began, "especially for a young man who had no real sense of direction when he graduated from college. But a smart man recognizes when it's time to let them go, when they're no longer relevant."

"But—" Luke began, only to be cut off.

"Let me finish," she commanded. "You've had me as an example that life can be long, that it can be full and rich with love and wonderful memories. Now let me be the example that it can also be entirely too short. Dillon and I have just found each other again. We have a second chance at happiness, but these little episodes of mine are proof positive that we've no way to know whether that chance will be for days, months or, bless-edly, years. The same is true for you and Moira. You may be young, but life is uncertain. We're not put on this earth with a timetable," she said, obviously using the word deliberately.

"I know that," he said.

"Then act as if you understand the meaning of it," she scolded. "Seize what's important when it's there for the taking. Don't wait for the perfect moment. There will always be challenges that can be offered up as ex-cuses. What's important is to understand that love and family are the only things that matter. I know you've heard that from me so often that it washes over you like background music, but stop just this once and listen to my advice, Luke. Heed the meaning of those words."

She looked from Luke to Moira and then to Dillon, where her gaze lingered. "Love and family are the only things that matter in the end," she repeated qui-etly. "Jobs come and go. Careers come and go. Love is the one constant, the one thing that makes all the rest worthwhile."

Luke knew then just how stupid and mule-headed he'd been with his determination to stick to a plan. As Gram had just said, plans were all well and good. Risks and unexpected twists were what kept life interesting.

Gram gave them both a hard look. "Have I gotten my point across?"

"I heard you, Gram," Luke said.

"And it's nothing I've not said and thought myself," Moira confirmed, giving Luke a defiant look.

"Okay, then," Gram said, looking pleased. "It's time for the two of you to run along home. Mick will be back soon. I'm being discharged in an hour or two, and he can drive Dillon and me home. I'll see you both there later."

Luke nodded, then bent down to press another kiss to her forehead. "I'm glad to see you're back in fighting form," he said.

"And intend to stay that way," she retorted with conviction.

Moira gave her a hug as well, then followed him from the room.

"We should stop for breakfast somewhere and talk," Luke said as they left the hospital.

Moira shook her head. "I'd rather go straight home and straighten up the cottage," she said, avoiding his gaze.

Luke frowned. "Moira, what she said made perfect sense. I get it. There's a proposal still on the table. We need to discuss it."

"I've turned it down," she reminded him. "My reasons for that haven't changed. An immigration snafu and a lecture from Nell may have given you some kind of change of heart, but you've said nothing to me to change my mind."

"Which is why we need to talk," he repeated impatiently.

She regarded him with the same sorrowful expression she'd worn the other night when she'd kicked him out of Gram's cottage. "Not today, Luke. I'm exhausted. You must be, too."

"This is more important than catching up on a few hours of missed sleep," he argued.

She finally met his gaze. "Yes, it is, which is why you need to be giving it more than a few minutes' thought. Whatever you say could change the course of both our lives. It's too important to be tossed out impulsively, then regretted for years to come."

Luke understood what she was saying and, thinking of Heather's reaction to Connor's sudden epiphany, he grasped why she wanted to be cautious. What he didn't know was whether a few hours or even longer would give him enough time to come up with all the right words to prove that he was finally ready for the life she'd wanted all along.

Apparently, word had spread like wildfire along the O'Brien grapevine not only that Nell would be home by early afternoon, but that Moira had once more turned down Luke's attempt to persuade her to marry him. How they knew about the latter was anybody's guess. Luke himself might have sought commiseration from his cousins for all Moira knew.

What she did know was that first Laila and then Jess magically appeared at the cottage not fifteen minutes after her return from the hospital.

She'd barely settled Laila in the kitchen with a cup of tea when Jess arrived.

"Not that it's not a joy to see you both," she said, her tone wry, "but I'm wondering why exactly you're here. It will be a while before Nell's back."

"It's not Gram we've come to see," Jess said. "We've come to try to talk some sense into you."

"You turned down Luke's proposal," Laila said incredulously. "Not once, but twice. Who does that?"

Moira couldn't help it—she laughed at the question. "You, of all people, would ask me that? How many times did Matthew try to persuade you to marry him before you said yes? I've heard the stories, so please don't pretend otherwise."

Jess chuckled. "She has a point, Laila."

Moira whirled on her. "And you? It's my understanding that Will jumped through hoops for years before you even agreed to a date with him."

Laila flushed. "Unlike Jess, there were extenuating circumstances in my case," she insisted defensively.

"And in mine," Jess said, just as defensively.

Moira nodded. "There are quite a few in mine as well."

"But you don't have the luxury of waiting around," Jess said. "Not if you expect to stay in Chesapeake Shores. Connor was very clear about that."

"So Connor's the blabbermouth who filled you in?" Moira asked.

Jess shrugged. "One of them. Mum's worried about you, too."

"Lovely to know my future is a hot topic among the O'Briens."

"Your future and *Luke's,*" Jess emphasized. "He's one of us, so naturally we're concerned with how this turns out. This is what O'Briens do."

"Luke is the one who, up until a few days ago, wanted no part of marriage," Moira reminded them.

Laila leveled a solemn look directly into her eyes. "But he's always wanted *you!* That should count for something, don't you think? Men don't always know their own minds the way Matthew did with me or Will did with Jess."

"Oh, yeah," Jess confirmed. "They get all tangled up when marriage is mentioned, even when they're crazy in love. If you went through our family one by one, there would be a lot of different variations about what it took for the men to make a commitment, but the one thing never in doubt was that they loved the women."

She glanced to Laila, who nodded confirmation.

"Sometimes it took a gentle push to get them to say the words," Jess continued. "Sometimes it took a crisis, as it did for Connor and Heather. Sometimes it even took a divorce, as it did for my mum and dad, but in the end the love itself was a constant."

Moira appreciated Jess's attempt to give her a different perspective, but she wasn't quite ready to embrace it. "But—"

Jess cut her off. "Everything you want, or at least that you've indicated you want, is right there for the taking, Moira. Sometimes it's not about the pretty words. It's about the guy being right there when you need him most, proving his love with his actions. Isn't that what Luke, in his own misguided way, has been trying to do?"

Laila nodded. "He's made no secret about that time-table of his and his reasons for it. All of them valid, at least to him. But he's willing to toss that aside to step up for you, to keep you here because he doesn't want you to be forced to go and because he can't bear the thought of losing you."

Moira couldn't deny that they were giving her an entirely different take on Luke's actions. She'd been looking for the pretty words, just as they said, when what mattered far more was that he was willing to put his heart on the line, to do something he hadn't planned for now because the thought of her going wasn't acceptable to him. There was only one reason why that would be—because he loved her.

"Okay, you've made your point," she told them.

"Then you'll accept his proposal?" Jess prodded, a gleam in her eyes as she clearly jumped feetfirst into making plans. "We'll have the wedding at the inn. I think that's best, don't you? I can pull it together in no time."

Moira laughed at her enthusiasm. "Hold on. I haven't even spoken to Luke yet."

"Well, what on earth are you waiting for?" Laila asked. "Get over to the pub and straighten this out now."

"I'd planned to clean up the cottage before Nell gets home," Moira protested. "While I've been hiding away here the past few days, I've let dishes pile up in the sink. She can't come home to that."

"We'll take care of it," Jess promised. "The cottage will be spotless by the time Gram gets here. Just go."

Moira regarded them both with a mix of gratitude and dismay. "Is anyone ever able to get out of the way once the O'Brien bulldozer kicks into gear?"

The two women exchanged a look, then chuckled.

"I haven't met anyone yet," Laila said.

"Me, either," Jess added. "You'd be the first." She grinned. "But only if you're a lot more foolish than I think you are."

"Am I allowed time to shower and change?"

"I suppose that would be okay," Jess said. "But don't dawdle. We want to have an announcement ready when Gram gets home. The prospect of another O'Brien wedding will be the best medicine possible."

Moira smiled at that, but she didn't blow Nell's

news—that Nell had a wedding of her own in the works. Unlike the rest of this family, she at least knew how to keep a secret.

Luke was conducting job interviews when Moira walked into the pub. He'd decided he couldn't put off hiring extra waitstaff or a potential new manager. Though he'd scheduled these interviews before Moira had twice turned down his proposal, he saw the inevitability of needing the help as more critical than ever now. With the photography show on the horizon and then her likely departure, he had no choice.

Startled, he watched as Moira eyed the assembled women with a malevolent look that probably should have scared them off, but none of them appeared smart enough to notice. He'd grown weary of their stock replies to his standard questions. It would have been all too easy to dismiss the entire lot of them, especially with the prospect of settling things with Moira right here in front of him.

Instead, though, he went ahead and started to call for the next candidate. Moira held up a hand, then stepped in front of him.

"A moment, please," Moira said quietly.

"I'm in the middle of interviewing prospective employees," he told her, mostly to be obstinate.

"I can see that. This is more important."

He took heart at that. "Okay, then."

He excused himself and followed Moira outside, where presumably they'd have more privacy than they would in the pub in front of a suddenly attentive audience.

"I wasn't sure I'd see you again," he began. "You've seemed determined to put an end to things between us."

"And would it have mattered to you if you hadn't?" she asked, then waved off the question. "Don't answer that. I'm here professionally, not personally, right at the moment."

He frowned. That didn't seem to bode well. "What exactly does that mean?"

"It means you're wasting your time talking to all those women in there. The job is filled." She held his gaze. "Unless you intend to rescind your offer."

Luke's heart skipped several beats. "Which offer are we talking about?" he inquired hesitantly. She'd said she was here professionally, after all.

"It's a package deal," she told him. "You get a wife, a partner and a consultant, all rolled into one. It remains to be seen if you'll have some famous superstar photographer in the bargain, so you need to focus on the first three things. Those are the ones that matter."

As she spoke, she gave him a challenging look. He had to look closely to see the hint of uncertainty behind it.

"Are you sure?" he asked.

"I've been sure from the beginning," she said. "It's your certainty that's been in question. I don't want to stay if it's only to beat off immigration. I don't want to be in your life if it's only to please your grandmother."

Luke smiled at that. "Those were just the excuses I needed to do what I've longed to do since the night we met," he said. "That's when I fell in love with you, but the tiny shred of common sense that I was working so hard to nurture kept screaming that no one falls in love like that, not for keeps. When Connor broke the news the other day and I thought you might leave, that you might *have* to leave, I panicked. I know I didn't say it right, but I love you and I *want* to marry you, Moira. It's all I've wanted from the beginning."

Her expression turned hopeful. "Do you swear it? I don't want you to have regrets."

"My only regret would be letting you get away."

She nodded then, and stepped into his arms. "Then we'll figure out all the rest," she said softly.

"What about your photography, though? If you're spending all your time here, you won't have nearly enough time for it. I don't want you to squander that amazing talent to work in a pub."

"My choice," she reminded him. "Not yours. I love photography. I can't wait for this one show that Megan's planning." She held his gaze. "But I don't need fame or fortune, Luke. I need you. I'll be content with the photography as it began, taking pictures of people I know at weddings and other occasions that truly matter to them. And, since I'll have an in with the boss here, I imagine I can have a permanent collection right on the walls of this pub. If there's more and I've the time for it, well, we'll see how it goes."

"I'm sure you can manage it all," Luke said, taking the first deep breath he'd had in what seemed like days. He felt as if his world had finally righted itself as they stood on the sidewalk, oblivious to everything except each other. He never wanted to let her go, not even to go back inside and finish those ridiculous interviews.

"I should get back in there," he said eventually. "What kind of boss leaves a slew of potential employees waiting while he stops just sort of seducing a woman right out here in public?"

She smiled at that, then glanced inside. "Is there a one of them worth hiring? I may want a day off now and again."

He grinned at that. "Would you care to sit in on the interviews with me?"

"I could just take over, save you the trouble."

"The pub is O'Brien's," he reminded her dryly, but he couldn't help chuckling at her take-charge manner.

She glanced up at the sign over the door. "So it is." She winked at him. "Then, again, aren't we about to add me to that roster? In no time at all, I'll be an official O'Brien."

Luke laughed at her sudden embrace of the concept. "Then, by all means, get in there and take charge." Still, though, he held her in place. "But not before we clarify just how much I love you. I've said it before, but I think it bears repeating until you truly believe it. I've loved you since the first night I laid eyes on you when you were behaving at your absolute worst."

She smiled at that. "Now that's just plain crazy," she said. "Only a fool could have fallen in love with me then."

"It was Christmas," he reminded her. "In my family the season of miracles seems to work out pretty well." He studied her. "So, is it yes? Just to have it on the record, I'd like a formal acceptance."

She gave him an odd look. "Why are you so intent on solidifying my response?"

"Just answer me. Is it yes? Are we to be engaged for something like five minutes, and then married at the first opportunity?"

"We are," she said demurely, then leaped into his arms with an exuberance that had him staggering back.

It also drew applause and cheers from quite a crowd of people gathered on the sidewalk, openly listening in—most of them O'Briens. He'd seen them gathering as word apparently spread about what was happening in plain view on the sidewalk outside the pub. He'd wanted witnesses. He smiled, satisfied.

Now there'd be no turning back. Moira would never back out on a deal she'd made in front of the family she'd always envied and wanted so much to be a part of. He'd always taken it for granted, but it was new to her and he'd come to view its value through her eyes.

As she saw it, the things he'd considered a nuisance—the meddling, the intrusiveness—were the best things about this town and about this family. There was unconditional support to be found everywhere. Even when it was at its most exasperating, it was exactly the thing that made Chesapeake Shores the best possible place to build a life.

Add in this impossible, maddening, wonderful woman by his side and the future looked very bright indeed.

Epilogue

The white Victorian gazebo in Nell's backyard was decorated naturally with climbing yellow roses in full bloom. The groom stood by the steps in his tuxedo, his eyes filled with anticipation. A quartet usually more adept at traditional Irish tunes than the wedding march began to play. As it did, all eyes turned toward the house, where the bride emerged wearing a simple silk suit and holding a bouquet picked from her own summer garden.

Nell took Mick's arm and walked slowly toward the man she'd once fallen in love with as a very young girl, and now had the chance to love again in the twilight of her life.

A few steps behind her, another bride stepped out of the house and took the arm of her mother, who'd flown over from Ireland just days before.

Nell glanced back over her shoulder and smiled at them.

The July day couldn't have been more perfect. She and Moira had agreed to a double ceremony, since time was definitely a factor for both of them, though for entirely different reasons. Nell had been willing to wait for her own wedding, but Moira had taken one look at her grandfather and shaken her head.

"You've waited long enough," she'd told them. "Luke and I want to share this day with you, if you don't mind. And we'd like it to be simple, right here in your garden. I can't imagine a more perfect setting for the start of our marriage."

"If you're certain, then nothing would please us more," Nell had assured her.

Beside her now, Mick gave her arm a squeeze. "You sure about this, Ma? It's not too late to make a run for it."

"Stop that!" she scolded. "You know I want to marry Dillon."

Mick grinned. "Just checking. Sometimes women can be fickle."

"I've loved the man for more than sixty years," she said. "There's nothing fickle about that." She gave him a rueful look. "And that's meant as no disrespect to your father. He was a wonderful man, and he gave me three of the most amazing sons a woman could ever hope to have. I have no regrets on that score, either."

"I know," Mick said quietly. "And you deserve this, Ma. Dad would want it for you, too. I know he would. You deserve Dillon's love and the happiness it will bring to your life."

"I don't know if I deserve it, but I'm grateful for it. It's a blessing at my age to find this kind of joy. I feel like the girl I was when he and I first met."

"Would you two stop with the heart-to-heart chat en route to the priest?" Luke called out from his place beside Dillon. "I have a bride back there, too, you know."

The entire family laughed at his impatience. It had been a while coming, but there was no denying it now.

"Behave," Moira called back. "It's not too late for me to change my mind."

Beside Nell, Mick chuckled. "So much for a solemn, dignified ceremony."

"Oh, who needs that?" Nell said. "We're O'Briens. We do things our own way."

"So we do," Mick said quietly. He bent down and kissed her cheek before placing her hand in Dillon's. "God bless, Ma. I love you."

"I've always been able to count on that," she told him, misty-eyed even though she'd sworn that today was not a day for tears, even of the happy variety.

Then Moira was there, her hand in Luke's, and the priest began the service. He'd argued for holding the ceremony at the church in the traditional way, but Nell had been adamant.

"The Lord is everywhere," she'd insisted. "And this town, the beautiful bay, they're a part of who I am. I want to be surrounded by family and friends in God's setting."

He'd had no further argument for that.

As they said their vows, all four voices rang out strong and sure, the promises carried on the breeze.

"I will love you now, and always," Luke assured Moira.

"And I will love you with the very best part of who I am," she responded.

Dillon gave his granddaughter a wink before turning to Nell. "My love for you has been a constant for a very long time, through a lifetime apart and too little time together. For whatever time we are given, I will count you as my greatest blessing."

Once more, Nell felt her eyes sting with unexpected tears as she heard his heartfelt words. She glanced around at her family, took in the scenery and the garden that meant so much to her, then faced Dillon.

"All of this—the blessings I've had throughout a rich, fulfilled life—pale beside this chance to share the rest of my life with you. For the one thing I've always believed is that it is the people who live in our hearts who make us strong, who give us hope. There may be tears along the way, but in the end without those we love, there can be no true happiness. I've had great joy as an O'Brien all these years, and I will continue to take pride in the name and in this incredible family." She smiled at Dillon. "But I will embrace being an O'Malley for as long as we both shall live."

When the priest would have concluded the ceremony, Nell stopped him, drawing laughter when she said, "I'm not done just yet. I don't plan to do this again, so indulge me."

She turned to Luke and Moira. "Though my name may be changing today, the family is gaining another O'Brien who'll do the name proud. Moira, when the reviews of your show rolled in, no one could have been more thrilled than we were. You have an exceptional talent and, if you'll take one last bit of advice on this day of all days, it's to stay true to your heart. There are many paths open to you, and I have no doubt that you can succeed at whichever one you choose. All I ask is that you choose wisely." She grinned. "And I wouldn't mind a few more great-grandbabies."

The words had no sooner left her mouth than there

was a startled gasp from the front row. Nell turned to see Connie clutching her stomach.

"How about one more grandchild first?" Thomas asked, his complexion pale. "I think we can grant you that any minute now, if you can wrap this up so I can get my wife to the hospital."

The declaration that Dillon and Nell, and Moira and Luke, were wed was made in a rush and then the entire family piled into cars and headed for the hospital to await the arrival of Thomas's first child. Sean Michael O'Brien came into the world, screaming impatiently, barely an hour after they got there.

It was late evening before the wedding reception finally got back on track. Nell was already beyond eager for bed and a night's rest, but she couldn't help gazing around at everyone one last time. Dillon stood beside her as the sun set.

"It's been a memorable day, hasn't it?" he asked quietly.

She nodded, looking into his eyes. "One of the best yet," she said.

"I'm counting on many more, you know."

She touched a finger to his lips. "Hope for them, but treat each one as a miracle. That's what they'll be."

He smiled as he looked from her to his granddaughter and Luke across the yard, wrapped in each other's arms. "It seems we've been showered with miracles today, doesn't it? Our grandchildren settled. A new life to give us hope for the future."

He was right, she thought. And that he'd lived long enough to understand all that was reason enough to love him. But, she thought, her heart full, there were so many more reasons. Too many to count.

She hoped Luke and Moira would be wise enough and lucky enough to be able to say the same sixty or seventy years from now. Looking at them tonight with stars shining in their eyes, she felt confident that they would. At least she'd be around for a while to give them a gentle nudge from time to time if they got off track.

That, after all, was the reason she'd been put on this earth, to see her family happy and content. Thinking of Thomas and Connie so elated about their new son, then glancing around from Luke and Moira, to Mick and Megan, to Jeff and Jo, to Abby and Trace, Jake and Bree, Kevin and Shanna, Connor and Heather, Jess and Will, Susie and Mack, and finally to Matthew and Laila, she thought in all modesty that she'd done a darn fine job of it so far!

* * * * *

Look for Sherryl's next original
SWEET MAGNOLIAS *novel,*
MIDNIGHT PROMISES,
coming in July to your favorite retail outlet.

QUESTIONS FOR DISCUSSION

1. Before Moira Malone leaves Ireland for Chesapeake Shores, she worries that her holiday fling with Luke O'Brien might not have meant as much to him as it did to her. Have you ever taken a risk to see someone again after a casual encounter? What happened?

2. Luke is very single-minded about his goal of opening the pub and keeping romance on hold until he sees how it's likely to turn out. Have you known men like this, who like to approach life very methodically? If there's someone in your life like this, did you try to change them?

3. After a lifetime of feeling as if she's a disappointment to her family, Moira suddenly has a chance to grab possible fame and fortune through her photography. Do you think she should pursue that, no matter what, so she has a career and the recognitions she's long wanted? Or can you identify with her desire to focus on a family first?

4. Moira struggles with her realization that love and family will always matter more to her than a career. Have you ever felt that you had to choose between the two? What did you decide? If you've tried to balance both, how successfully do you think you've done it?

5. As the youngest in his family, Luke feels tremendous pressure to succeed with his new venture.

Have you ever felt pressured to achieve a goal because of the successes of people around you, whether family or friends? How have you handled that?

6. Mick struggles a lot with his mother getting involved with another man, especially someone she knew before she married his father. Have you ever had to cope with a parent remarrying after a divorce or the death of a spouse? Was it difficult for you? What did you do? How about your siblings? Did it cause problems for your family?

7. Nell views this as her second chance with Dillon O'Malley, the man she fell in love with years ago in Ireland. Do you think this in any way lessens the love she felt for her late husband, the father of her children? Or are the two relationships entirely separate?

8. O'Brien's is intended by Luke to be more than just a place to drink. He wants it to be a community gathering spot. Do you have a place in your neighborhood where you go to see friends, have a meal or a drink? How important is it to a community to have a place like that?

9. The O'Briens are well-known for their meddling. Mick, at least, views it as evidence of how much they care. Do you agree with him? When does meddling cross the line and become intrusive and

controlling? Have you ever told a parent, sibling or well-meaning friend to "butt out"? How did that person take it?

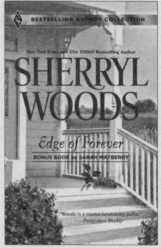

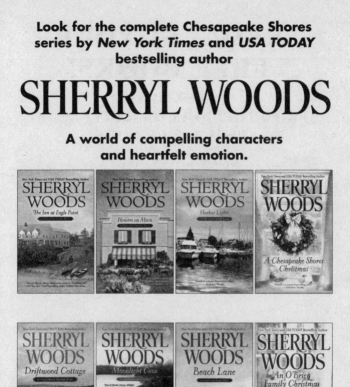

REQUEST YOUR
FREE BOOKS!

2 FREE NOVELS
FROM THE ROMANCE COLLECTION
PLUS 2 FREE GIFTS!

YES! Please send me 2 FREE novels from the Romance Collection and my 2 FREE gifts (gifts are worth about $10). After receiving them, if I don't wish to receive any more books, I can return the shipping statement marked "cancel." If I don't cancel, I will receive 4 brand-new novels every month and be billed just $5.99 per book in the U.S. or $6.49 per book in Canada. That's a saving of at least 25% off the cover price. It's quite a bargain! Shipping and handling is just 50¢ per book in the U.S. and 75¢ per book in Canada.* I understand that accepting the 2 free books and gifts places me under no obligation to buy anything. I can always return a shipment and cancel at any time. Even if I never buy another book, the two free books and gifts are mine to keep forever.

194/394 MDN FELQ

Name	(PLEASE PRINT)

Address	Apt. #

City	State/Prov.	Zip/Postal Code

Signature (if under 18, a parent or guardian must sign)

Mail to the **Reader Service:**
IN U.S.A.: P.O. Box 1867, Buffalo, NY 14240-1867
IN CANADA: P.O. Box 609, Fort Erie, Ontario L2A 5X3

Not valid for current subscribers to the Romance Collection
or the Romance/Suspense Collection.

Want to try two free books from another line?
Call 1-800-873-8635 or visit www.ReaderService.com.

* Terms and prices subject to change without notice. Prices do not include applicable taxes. Sales tax applicable in N.Y. Canadian residents will be charged applicable taxes. Offer not valid in Quebec. This offer is limited to one order per household. All orders subject to credit approval. Credit or debit balances in a customer's account(s) may be offset by any other outstanding balance owed by or to the customer. Please allow 4 to 6 weeks for delivery. Offer available while quantities last.

Your Privacy—The Reader Service is committed to protecting your privacy. Our Privacy Policy is available online at www.ReaderService.com or upon request from the Reader Service.

We make a portion of our mailing list available to reputable third parties that offer products we believe may interest you. If you prefer that we not exchange your name with third parties, or if you wish to clarify or modify your communication preferences, please visit us at www.ReaderService.com/consumerschoice or write to us at Reader Service Preference Service, P.O. Box 9062, Buffalo, NY 14269. Include your complete name and address.

SHERRYL WOODS

(limited quantities available)

TOTAL AMOUNT	$ _____
POSTAGE & HANDLING	$ _____
($1.00 for 1 book, 50¢ for each additional)	
APPLICABLE TAXES*	$ _____
TOTAL PAYABLE	$ _____

(check or money order—please do not send cash)

To order, complete this form and send it, along with a check or money order for the total above, payable to MIRA Books, to: **In the U.S.:** 3010 Walden Avenue, P.O. Box 9077, Buffalo, NY 14269-9077; **In Canada:** P.O. Box 636, Fort Erie, Ontario, L2A 5X3.

Name: _____
Address: _____ City: _____
State/Prov.: _____ Zip/Postal Code: _____
Account Number (if applicable): _____

075 CSAS

*New York residents remit applicable sales taxes.
*Canadian residents remit applicable GST and provincial taxes.

MIRA | **H**ARLEQUIN®
™ www.Harlequin.com

MSW0212BL